Praise for Elizabeth Bear

'Bear builds her future nightmare tale with style and conviction and a constant return to the twists of the human heart'
Richard Morgan, author of *Altered Carbon*

'A remarkable SF writer who's leaving many of her contemporaries in the dust'   *SFReviews*

'What Bear has done in *Hammered* is create a world that is all too plausible . . . an unnerving peek into a future humankind would be wise to avoid'   SciFi.com

'A tense, involving and character-driven read . . . A doozy of a ride'   *New York Review of Science Fiction*

'A rollercoaster of a good thriller'   SFCrowsnest.com

'[A] combination of toughness and humanity that makes Bear one of the most welcome writers to come over the horizon lately'   *Locus*

'Enjoyable, thought-provoking . . . like the best of speculative fiction'   *Washington Post*

Also by Elizabeth Bear from Gollancz

Pinion
Sanction
Cleave
Ancestral Night

CLEAVE

Elizabeth Bear

This edition first published in Great Britain
in 2019 by Gollancz, an imprint of The
Orion Publishing Group Ltd
Carmelite House, 50 Victoria Embankment
London EC4Y 0DZ

An Hachette UK Company

1 3 5 7 9 10 8 6 4 2

Copyright © Elizabeth Bear 2011

The moral right of Elizabeth Bear to be identified as
the author of this work has been asserted in accordance
with the Copyright, Designs and Patents Act of 1988.

A CIP catalogue record for this book is
available from the British Library.

ISBN 978 1 473 22942 6
ISBN (eBook) 978 1 473 21181 0

Printed and bound in Great Britain by
Clays Ltd, Elcograf S.p.A

MIX
Paper from
responsible sources
FSC® C104740

www.orionbooks.co.uk

This book is for Stella Evans,
Liz Bourke, and Maddie Glymour

And, behold, I am with thee, and will keep thee in all places whither thou goest, and will bring thee again into this land; for I will not leave thee, until I have done that which I have spoken to thee of.

And Jacob awaked out of his sleep, and he said, Surely the Lord is in this place; and I knew it not.

And he was afraid, and said, how dreadful is this place! this is none other but the house of God, and this is the gate of heaven.

—GENISIS 28: 15–18, *King James Bible*

As for ideology, the Hell with it. All of it.

—URSULA K. LE GUIN

God make thee good as thou art beautiful

—ALFRED, LORD TENNYSON, 'The Holy Grail'

1

when the world ended

In action how like an angel, in apprehension how like
a god! the beauty of the world, the paragon of animals—and yet, to me,
what is this quintessence of dust?
—WILLIAM SHAKESPEARE, *Hamlet*, Act II scene i

Danilaw Bakare was on a nightclub stage when the
world ended.

His third-day job was as a classical musician. He held
the lease on a baby blue electric fab bass, and two nights a
nonce he joined up with two guitarists and a drummer to
play the greats in a repro dive bar in Bad Landing, on the
east rim of Crater Lake. They did all the classics—Buddy
Holly, Buddy Guy, Gatemouth Brown, Page and Plant.
Thompson, Hendrix, Li, Morris, Mitchell, Kaderli, Kas-
paryan, Noks, Hynde.

It was one hell of a relief from the first-day job where he
spent five days out of nine, and it filled his arts requirement
in style. The first-day job was as City Administrator for
Bad Landing, which loaned the band a certain notoriety
and filled his admin and service logs. He completed the
nurturing requirement with volunteer work and babysit-
ting his sister's kids, half grateful that, given his other com-
mitments, it was a tertiary and half worried he was never
going to find the time himself to reproduce.

So he happened to be onstage before a crowd of about

one hundred and seventy-five, holding up Therese while she laid fire through "Johnny B. Goode," when the end began.

As poets had long suspected, it happened so subtly that Danilaw at first had no idea of the historic significance of events beyond a sensible level of unease. There was no drama. Just a brown-faced citizen in a suit and some discreet hardware, as out of place in mufti—and in the club crowd—as a dodecapus at a tea party. She slipped in through the kitchen, pausing behind the tables where the patrons were seated so only the musicians and staff would see her, planting herself at the end of the bar like she'd been carved there. When Danilaw caught her eye, across all those rapt faces, she frowned and nodded.

She had a round face, a straight nose, and a finely pointed chin. He imagined brown or amber eyes behind smoky lashes, and schooled himself to professional coolness.

Damn, he thought. *There goes the second set.*

His own security was out in the crowd, but he didn't know who most of them were and he wasn't supposed to try to find out. So the citizen must have come with a message too sensitive to transmit, even encrypted.

Thinking too much, he fluffed a chord change, but got it back before the progression fell apart on him. He turned over his shoulder and shot a signal to Chuck, the drummer, who threw in a special fill to let Therese know to end the set. She wrapped up the Chuck Berry in half the time it usually took—a minor tragedy. But as soon as she announced the break, he set his bass in the stand and jumped off the stage, landing between two tables surrounded by startled patrons.

"Sorry, Ciz." He had to turn sideways to slip between them; the aisles were narrow, and Danilaw both broad and tall. When he got closer to the watcher, he began to realize the true depth of the problem. In addition to her suit and chrome—headwire and earset—the citizen wore a Captain's crimson Free Legate jewel over her left eyebrow and a worried expression across the entirety of her face. When Danilaw came up, she didn't hesitate and she did not mince words.

"Premier, I'm sorry." Her voice was light and well modulated, but he would bet it could carry across a crowd if necessary. "I'm Amanda Friar. We haven't met. I've been sent to inform you that the homeward perimeter registers a blip."

Nothing was scheduled incoming for over four hundred days. And certainly nothing from Earth.

"Rogue ship?" he asked. *"Pirates?"*

There had been no reliable reports of piracy in Danilaw's lifetime. But there was history, and there was always a new first time.

Captain Amanda shook her head, giving Danilaw an increment of relief. "She's broadcasting an identity tag, one there would be no reason to fake."

That relief faded as he watched her nerve herself.

"An antique tag. On antique equipment. We had to break open the original code files."

He knew the answer. "The *Jacob's Ladder*."

He might as well have said the *Flying Dutchman*. But, incredibly, she nodded.

Danilaw rocked restlessly from foot to foot, controlling his body's desire to fidget by force of will. Floorboards of salvaged wood creaked under his weight, reprimanding him. "Wrack and waste, the Kleptocracy actually *did* it."

"And only a thousand years late." She took his elbow as she led him from the room, back the way she'd come. "Administrator Danilaw?"

"Captain Amanda?"

Her thin throat showed it when she swallowed. "Do you suppose anyone's alive on it, sir?"

He shook his head, but he didn't mean *no*. Something

more like awe and incredulity. "I hate to guess. And if they are, what sort of condition do you suppose they're in?"

Danilaw collected his open security detail, and Captain Amanda brought him topside. Much of Bad Landing was underground—a compact, low-impact settlement burrowed out of the already-shocked earth surrounding Crater Lake. Surface paths shaded by native vegetation and foul-weather awnings threaded between the gentle slopes of constructed hills. Dwellings, gathering places, and the scattering of rare commercial buildings clustered around meadows and diversity zones. Solar leaves laid flat for the night scaled the water-grooved roofs of earthed buildings and, across the lake, ranks of solar-skinned wind turbines followed the arc of an artificial reef habitat.

Three smeeps and a robin hopped or flapped a few steps as Danilaw and his entourage stepped out of the bio-mimetic berm housing the nightclub, encouraging him to smile. The seventeen-year smeeps hadn't been out much lately—it was coming up on one of their breeding and hibernation cycles—and he missed their dusty rose-violet plumage and trilling cries.

Tonight's open security detail were well-known to both Danilaw and each other. Karen took point; Banko and Keebler followed along behind, silent in their tuned awareness. Alert but not worried.

Rightminding was a cure for all sorts of things, but political violence wasn't *always* one of them. There were logical reasons, sometimes, for war—although in practice that had not happened in centuries. And even for assassinations. But in a community as small and tight-knit as Bad Landing, security had the advantage of already having a pretty good idea of who the crazies and the justifiably dissatisfied were, and Danilaw made sure there were always routes of complaint open to every citizen.

On such a pleasant night, the trails were busy under

their canopies. Solar-storing fairylights shimmered in the overarching branches of several varieties of violet-black xenotrees, and the nightbirds—robins, screamers, shutterlings—flitted among their branches. The drone of insects hung heavy in the evening cool, throbbing and slower now than it had been at the height of summer. Danilaw kept an eye peeled. A pack of native wild "dogs" had begun patrolling inside the boundaries of Bad Landing—a good sign that the settlement was integrating well, but a possible contributor to the sudden rarity of smeeps. He hoped to catch sight of one, but they were shy and fleeting, and he had yet to glimpse more than eyeshine and a silhouette.

Along the way, Captain Amanda briefed him on her capabilities and what she knew about the incoming vessel. Danilaw listened and observed, for the moment defaulting to learning mode, while the walkers and the wildlife carried on around them. A couple of joggers passed, running either for the fun of it or to fulfill their Obligation. As Danilaw, Captain Amanda, and the security stepped aside to let them by, something small, nocturnal, and fast-moving brachiated past overhead. It could have been any of half a dozen varieties of treeswinger. It was gone before Danilaw looked up, or maybe it hadn't gotten close enough to the directional lights for him to pick up more than a suggestion of how it moved.

The closest Administration Building access was within sight of Crater Lake, out from under the edge of the big xenos.

It was *called* a lake, and drainage meant the water was conspicuously less saline than seawater, but the impact scar from the eponymous bad landing communicated directly west to the Sunrise Sea. There was no sunrise over it now. Favor—dark, reflective oceans agleam behind argent bands of cloud—would already be setting as a waning crescent over the forests in the east. Danilaw couldn't see Fortune's poisonous sister-world through the trees, but the skies were spread with silver behind heavy boughs.

He sighed, and turned to enter the access. Danilaw stepped through on Captain Amanda's heels, all but one of his security peeling away now that he was within the safety of Admin. The access sensors identified his microchip and granted him access, an air cushion lowering the platform smoothly to the deepest level.

He stepped out of the shaft and tugged his clothes back into order. Captain Amanda walked forward, outlined against the observation blisters that bubbled into the water. Karen followed behind, professionally unobtrusive. Using the access had activated the lights, now glowing dimly around the rims of the windows. Danilaw scanned the port briefly for any sign of an inquisitive dodecapus, but no twisting arms or sucker-feet rewarded him.

The creatures, with their color-shift skins and multiple eyes, liked to gather around the windows when the Admin offices were occupied. Although they were gentle omnivores, their size and power were sufficient that they could kill any of Fortune's waterborne apex predators by suffocation, and they lived largely unmolested among the artificial reefs created by the wind farms.

Danilaw tended to think of them as watching over the human settlers; he was disappointed that none were in evidence. He and Captain Amanda walked the whole length of the observation hall and, before he let her chip-key open the meeting room door, he paused and stuck his head into the final blister.

It was cooler here, surrounded on three sides by the thermal mass of all that water. Danilaw peered into the blackness of the nighttime lake and frowned. What would it be like if that blackness were outer space? What would it be like if that were all you had ever known?

Captain Amanda didn't sigh, but he heard her shifting from foot to foot.

"Just collecting my thoughts." He turned back.

She smiled. "Collect mine, too, while you're in there?"

"If I see 'em," he said, liking her. You didn't need affection to work well with someone, but if it happened, it could necessitate fewer adjustments to the rightminding. And it was always easier to like funny people—if they could be funny without it being at anyone else's expense.

Danilaw thought it might be because humor was on some level an admission of weakness. *I'll show you my defense mechanisms if you show me yours.*

Danilaw tipped his head at the door to the conference room, just to the other side of the entrance to his tiny private office. Another weirdness engendered by his role as City Administrator—who worked in an *office* anymore? Who met face-to-face? Who *commuted*? But authority required trappings, and to some people archaicism still meant authority.

Danilaw did sigh now. "Come on. Let's go tell them the paradigm has shifted."

2

a child was not to blame

As the stars that shall be bright when we are dust,
Moving in marches upon the heavenly plain;
As the stars that are starry in the time of our darkness,
To the end, to the end, they remain.
—LAURENCE BINYON, "For the Fallen"

Perceval Conn glided through warm water, feeling the swirl and suck of eddying currents along her skin, over her scalp, through the tendrils of her unbound hair. The River flowed across open eyes and around the stumps of long-amputated wings. Her corneas adapted to the water's greater angle of refraction, so her vision lost no clarity.

She moved through a world of slanted light, warped and repaired River channels, and darting animals: a world brighter than she had seen in decades. As the *Jacob's Ladder* approached the destination star, more daylight flooded the world's arrays, collected and reflected and refracted through sweeping energy nets. Every watt and every joule no longer must be rationed, hoarded, and accounted for. The world could be bright again—and soon, Perceval knew, there would be direct daylight through the world's many windows. Then the problem would be keeping her cool instead of warm.

Perceval held her breath comfortably, her symbiont reporting excellent oxygen saturation and low levels of muscular fatigue. She let the River sweep her between thick feathering cables in their corrosion-resistant plating, and slanted columns of ceramic and light. There were fish here, silvery and rose, their backs dappled or freckled or banded or striped.

Once upon a time, Tristen and Benedick and Rien and Gavin had run along the banks of this River to Engine. In those days, the River had been a poisoned, radioactive coil. The River had been inhabited by the ghost of the world's broken reactors in the form of a djinn called Inkling, and the run had nearly killed three of the four who made it. That mission of mercy had been on Perceval's behalf, but Perceval had not been with them. She had been held prisoner by Dust, another fragment of the world's broken consciousness—the Library, more or less.

The Angel of Memory, as he styled himself. Perceval remembered him as more of a demon.

But now the River was clean enough for an Exalt to swim in—cleaner than it needed to be, for such purposes. And now Rien and Gavin were gone, consumed by other intelligences. Inkling and Dust had been assimilated too. They had been folded into Nova, a new Angel—the same being that Rien had given herself up to create. And now they were all three as inextricable from the final product as eggs and flour from cake.

Perceval had been slow in forgiving herself for her lost loved ones and enemies, and slower in forgiving the new Angel so forged for the exigencies of her birth. But there was only so long one could hold a grudge, and as the years passed, Perceval found it helped to think of Nova as the child, and of Rien and the others as her parents. Nova was not a shadow of them or something constructed of their remnants . . . but a new person derived from the old.

A child was not to blame for the death of a parent.

It helped, and the River helped too. Swimming its currents wasn't really like flying—no one who had ever had wings of her own would make that mistake, or use that metaphor. But the warm water *was* a comfort, and the River was a place where she could be alone—Perceval, just Perceval, and not the Captain. Not in command. This was a place where she could shut out the voices of her internalized ancestors, their wisdom and advice and the constant need to integrate herself while still maintaining connections to their memories.

She carried a council of elders in her head and in her hardware—with all their egos and all their expectations. And, sometimes, a girl just wanted a minute to herself.

She missed Rien so much. She had needed Rien so much—needed someone to whom she would always be herself, and not a commander or a tool. But she couldn't have that. Rien was gone, consumed by the ship's revenant Angel, and fighting to bring her back or to remake Nova into something more like Rien would lead to the kind of destruction that Perceval's aunt and enemy Ariane had caused, before Perceval consumed *her*. But here at least Perceval could have some of what she wanted—the silence inside her own mind, the peace to dwell there, and the smooth tug of water flowing over skin.

Even to wings, air never felt like something you could grasp and haul yourself up on. The viscosity was too low: it was slippery stuff, running away between your feathers just when you needed it most. But here, she was surrounded, immured, in a substance she could pretend was as solid and protective as the skin of the world.

Everyone knew to leave the Captain alone while she was swimming. Even the Angel.

So when Nova's voice broke through her reverie—not so much a sound carried by vibration as a tickle in Perceval's awareness, urgent with latent information—Perceval felt the sting of adrenaline through every vein.

The contact unfolded, expanding from a shimmering thread to a landscape of information. Perceval quit stroking forward, allowing the buoyancy of her body to carry her to the surface. She did not bob up as she once would have. Hollow bones served no purpose in a girl with no wings, and now she was stronger and heavier than ever she had been when she was a flyer.

As she broke the surface, her head came back, mouth open, lungs expanding her deep chest as she filled herself with air. Her body—flesh and symbiotic colony—took care of that automatically. Which was as well, because Perceval's awareness was half a hundred miles away, spun out through the fabric of motes, colonies, and electromagnetic webs that made up the ramscoop and nervous system of the *Jacob's Ladder*.

The world was braking sharply through the gravity well of the first stellar system she had encountered since leaving the shipwreck stars the better part of fifty years before. Perceval bestrode the vast construction-toy webwork of the world's frame—its spokes and wires and the baubles of habitats strung between them—and she watched the distant stars turn in the cold dark on every side.

Only one, the destination sun, was close enough to seem warm, and even it was but a brighter mote, alight on the Enemy's black bosom. Somewhere between here and there lay the potentially habitable world—with its massive satellite—that they had come to colonize.

Astrogator Damian Jsutien, who had plotted their course, relying on information gleaned from an alien prisoner, had taken to sardonically calling it Grail, and the name had stuck.

Perceval's crippled artificial world was limping to drink from a healing cup. The creature—Leviathan—that had given them the data on where to find this planet had also almost destroyed the *Jacob's Ladder*. And given what the *Jacob's Ladder*, in the person of Cynric, had done to Leviathan—enslaving it, creating symbiotic nanocolonies from the corpse of its mate—Perceval did not blame the monster for waging war on them.

Perceval found herself conflicted. This—the *Jacob's Ladder,* the world she had been trying to teach herself to think of as only a ship, only a temporary haven until they found some planet full of trees and rocks and oceans and solid, reliable gravity that nobody ever had to twiddle with—*this* was all she'd ever known. The *Jacob's Ladder* had brought Perceval and her people all this way, through the claws of the cold and cunning Enemy, even though she had been designed by the treacherous Builders to fail and kill them.

The *Jacob's Ladder* had borne Perceval and her family through coups, wars, and internal conflict. Through the civil war waged between Perceval's aunt, Ariane Conn, and the fallen-Angel remnant of an artificially intelligent library, Jacob Dust, that had left Perceval Captain. It seemed somehow disloyal now to contemplate abandoning her.

Perceval was about to protest Nova's interruption of her recreation—they weren't scheduled to make orbit for several thousand hours—but in that instant she recognized the object that had gotten caught up in the *Jacob's Ladder*'s ramscoop and retrieved by alert drones before it could feed the maw of the world's engines. It was a spiky, fragile, sensor-laden probe with copper-colored solar wings slightly crumpled by its rescue. Something made by intelligent life.

"Somebody lives here," she said. "Somebody intelligent enough for space flight already lives on Grail."

Somebody who uses Arabic numerals and the Roman alphabet, Nova said inside her head, and rotated the perspective to show her the markings on the probe's flanks, between the solar wings. *Somebody who got here first.*

"Oh," she said. "This is going to start another fucking civil war, if we're not careful. The Go-Backs are not going to love this."

The bright particle winds of a star caressed his sleeping awareness. The long, deepening slope of a gravity well dropped away under him and, as his program demanded, he awakened.

Reawakened.

The body they gave him was broken. A crimped and crooked thing, not so much discarded by the small pseudo-life that had inhabited it as shattered beyond that life's capacity to repair. But *him*—he was stronger than the remnant, and he displaced it with ease. He limped into its cramped spaces like a wind into a cavern, so constrained by its limits that even his shredded self would not entirely fit and still more rags and tendrils had to be shed, cut away by the Procrustean limits of this metaphysical form.

It had fallen far, this construct. Literally and figuratively. And so had he.

But it was a body. It was a beginning. He was a seed. He could grow.

What had been Dust awakened in darkness, a monster. And there at the bottom of the world, he began to plot his revenge.

Caitlin Conn was a lousy liar. In her father's house, refusing to learn to lie had been a rebellion, and under those circumstances the small rebellions kept one sane. You asserted any control you could; you defended any part of your identity that you could own. Lying would have been safer; it would have diverted Alasdair's attention.

Being a truth-teller set her apart. She had learned the trick from her oldest full sister, Caithness, who was also the least impressed with the pathologies of personality that made up Alasdair Conn. Caithness had been possessed of a sense of honor as quirky as it was unbending, and it had been the death of her. Caitlin suspected that she herself had escaped with only exile in large part because Alasdair considered her Caithness's smaller, paler shadow—a kind of inferior copy of his admired and hated child.

Once Alasdair killed Caithness and exiled Caitlin, the

lousy lying and the brusque disregard for politics and manipulation had only solidified in her character. What had been defiance was now a memorial; what had been a guarded border became a refuge. Caitlin had succeeded fairly well in her chosen field. She was Chief Engineer, after all, and acknowledged liege of Engine—despite her refusal to play politics.

Or to placate her father.

But the one she loved had not allowed himself to be swayed by such qualms. Together, she and Benedick had created a daughter—and thinking of Perceval now, Caitlin felt they had done quite well in that regard. But Benedick had also agreed to father a child on Arianrhod, for reasons of negotiating peace through hostage-sharing, and that Caitlin had been unable to abide.

They had barely spoken for fifteen years, and only the mortal peril engendered by the Angel Dust's interest in their daughter had brought them back into alliance again. And now—

Now Perceval was Captain of the *Jacob's Ladder*, and Caitlin was still Chief Engineer, and Benedick—Benedick was a man who had lost one daughter, and would do anything to defend the one who remained. Caitlin found it hard to reconcile her own anger and grief—for she, too, had been fond of Rien—with any forgiveness for Benedick. She knew some of her wrath was because she loved him. When we love, it is hard to forgive the beloved for not being the person we imagined them.

But he was also one of Caitlin's greatest resources when it came to the running of the reborn *Jacob's Ladder*—no longer a world but now a starship again. Tension between them was insupportable.

And Caitlin did not have the skills to lie to him about her feelings. Or the desire to learn how. There was nothing else to be done.

They were going to have to have A Conversation.

* * *

She went to find him in person, seeking for some time through the only slightly populated corridors of Engine until she found him working below the environmental services level in one of the adaptive maintenance microclimates. She could have asked the ship where he was, but there was always the chance that Nova would pass along her interest, and though the weakness shamed her, she craved the advantage of surprise.

She got it. The moss-carpeted floors and lichen-hung beams of the glen softened her footsteps beyond the hearing of even Exalt ears, and Benedick was invisible to the waist inside the bole of a symbiotic filtration tree. *The world requires an awful lot of maintenance.*

He was working with a toolkit—not the one that had been lost when Arianrhod tried to kill him and Chelsea so many decades ago, but a smoke blue one with long, grasping fingers adapted as holders and pullers. Caitlin watched his hand emerge from inside the tree, hanging out a rack of filters for the toolkit to lick clean, and when he would have collected the replacements she brushed his fingers.

The thump and startle from inside the bole were vividly audible. Caitlin winced even as she grinned. Cursing under his breath, Benedick telescoped out of the tree, shaking sap and cobwebs from his straight, black hair. "We're both lucky I wasn't armed," he said.

"So much for the catlike reflexes."

He studied her from his greater height, wiping his hands and face on a rag the toolkit offered. "To what do I owe the pleasure?"

He didn't even *think* the word *dubious,* as far as Caitlin could tell from inspecting his expression. Which made him, right there, a better person than she.

"We need to talk," she said. "About your daughters."

He glanced aside, finding a branch to drape the rag over, careful not to disturb the banners of Spanish moss and air-plant that grew there. "You have plenty of reasons to be angry with me," he said. "I've never denied that. Is this about something else this time?"

As long as she was looking up at him, she decided, she might as well take a load off. The filtration tree had a number of low, louvered branches that arched comfortably for sitting. She hooked a leg over one at waist height and slid herself onto it, leaning back on the curve of the branch as if into an armchair. "I guess I want to understand," she said. "What did you think could be achieved by placating him? By giving him a means of controlling you?"

He blew his bangs out of his eyes and plunked down on the moss, giving her an advantage. She wondered if he didn't think he'd need it, or if he was capitulating preemptively. "I thought it would make him feel safer," he said. "You know how many of the evils he was driven to were motivated by fear. You know how brutal Gerald was—"

I don't believe you're still making excuses for the old bastard! But as she opened her mouth to say it, she somehow managed to choke back her temper. Reasons were not excuses, and she had asked. Punishing Benedick because she didn't like his honest answers got them no closer to healing.

"I know," she said.

Benedick rubbed his palms across his long face, smearing the skin and stretching his eyes out long and crooked. He let his hands fall and looked at her, the monster countenance vanishing back into the lined features of a familiar man. "Caithness scared him more than anything. I wanted to give him a sense of control; he was always better when he felt he had control." He sighed. "I was wrong. I made mistakes. There's only so much culpability I can admit to."

She looked down at her hands. This was harder than she had imagined, rehearsing it in her head. It wasn't a lie; she had to believe it. "We all made mistakes," she said. "I wanted you to fight him more, to be more like Cate. But you're here and she's not, and I'm here, and—" She shrugged. "I'm ready to put the mistakes away."

He was silent a long time, but she could hear him breathing as his chin sank down to his chest. Thinking; considering. She knew the posture. He was phlegmatic by nature. When he finally spoke, it was slowly. "I'm not sure I'm ready for your forgiveness."

She shook her head. "I'm not sure I'm ready to offer it. But I also know we have too much to worry about, and we need each other too much, for me to hang on to that anger. So I'm working on it, okay?"

She held out her hand. He stared at it for a moment before, tilting his head in acquiescence, he took it and they helped one another to stand.

It wasn't too many days later when, sitting across the breakfast table from her, Benedick Conn remembered beheading his other sister.

Benedick's flesh, and his colony, were replete with recollections that he would have preferred to erase, undo, or lose forever. Human memory was fragile, malleable. Merciful. It had a tendency to protect the rememberer from the worst excesses of his own guilt or folly. Benedick was a bred eidetic, but even that eideticism was imperfect knowledge contained in flesh, vulnerable to conflation, confabulation, and plain, old-fashioned forgetting.

Machine intelligence was not so clement. It was precise and perfect, photographic. Unforgiving. But it could be edited by choice, and that was the temptation that Benedick found himself doing battle with more often than he cared to admit. Because, while the memories might be painful, it seemed wasteful to sacrifice the experience hard-won through that pain in the name of comfort or self-respect.

Cynric and he were not alone in the small spare room, cramped around a transparent table littered with fixings for a hasty first-watch meal. Their sister Caitlin Conn, the Chief Engineer—and the (estranged) love of Benedick's life—stood at the front wall. To Benedick's left was the Astrogator, Jsutien, and on beside him, passing him notes on her slate, was another sister—the youngest, Chelsea.

The Captain, Benedick's daughter Perceval, and the First Mate, his brother Tristen, were available by remote, but not currently engaged in the conversation. They had their own problems.

Benedick lifted the table knife and dipped it in olive oil spread, which melted to herbs and oleaginousness on contact with warm lentil-flour bread. It was a metal handle with a flat blade attached, small and unthreatening. But his hand closed on the knife as if around the hilt of a sword— the sword he had wielded to execute his sister. The sensory memory was vivid and sharp—the weight of Mirth in his hand, so unlike the non-presence of an unblade, which had seemed appropriate. An unblade would have killed with no feeling of contact as the sword parted bone and flesh, but there should be resistance when a life ended. The resilience of flesh, the density of bone.

It should be harder to kill someone. The ease of unblades made their purpose somehow more terrible.

So he had chosen Mirth, which was not an unblade at all. And considerably safer. Unblades, engines of entropy that they were, required fanatical care in handling and training if they were not to be more of a danger to their wielder than her enemy.

Though Cynric the Sorceress had begged for the favor of her death at his hand, he understood now that it had all been pursuant to her master plan and that the death hadn't been quite . . . permanent. Something was lost in translation, surely, when machine memory alone remained, patterned electricity without chemical context. But he hated it when Cynric came back to Engine, when he was forced to remember killing her—with memories of flesh and memories of silicon.

Benedick found irony in his knowledge that the symbiont Cynric herself had created—and inoculated into Benedick by her own hand—was the very thing that allowed Benedick to remember her murder so precisely.

He watched her from the corner of his awareness, her hair as straight and long as his own, but paler—brown where his was black, her eyes gray-blue where his were hazel. She looked the same, but he knew she wasn't. And he hated how she had changed, and how he could see the core seed of who she had been repopulating the corners of her mind in configurations that were similar to but not the same as those of the woman he had known. He hated knowing that his own actions had been instrumental in pruning her back so brutally, whether by her consent or request.

Perhaps if she visited more often, he would be over it by now.

But she didn't seem to be paying him any attention. Her hawklike profile was bent over the breakfast table as she dripped honey into her tea, the green sapphire stud in her nostril glinting through the dark, loose strands. A scholar's robe of white and green drooped from her shoulders and draped her thin arms. She was as skinny as his daughter Perceval.

Benedick sighed silently. For the moment he, too, forced himself to focus on his bread and tea, and the words of Caitlin Conn.

"We would have expected more significant radio flux from a world inhabited by intelligent life." Caitlin had an educator's tones. "We would have expected to see them coming—or see them while coming at them. If we'd been expecting other people here, we could have arrived sneakily, or loudly broadcasting our good intentions. But based on the probe we recovered, they seem to rely on some form

of tight-beam transmissions that we do not fully understand. We are continuing our analysis."

"They are definitely human?" Chelsea asked, rolling
crumbs of bread between her fingertips. It took courage to
ask the obvious question.

"Definitely," Caitlin said. "The markings on the probe
are in an alphanumeric system derived from our own. And
my engineers believe their machinery springs from the
same roots, though we have undergone centuries of technological drift."

Cynric sipped her tea. "I am engineering a device to re-
ceive and decode them, but these things take time."

They must be spliced, they must be hybridized. They
must be grown to parturition and to enough adulthood to
be useful. Even in Cynric's hands, that might mean days.
Weeks.

Cynric licked at the edges of her teeth. "What other signs
of life does Grail possess?"

Caitlin was shorter and more compact than Cynric—or
Benedick, for that matter. It was from him that Perceval got
her rangy build, while Caitlin had broad shoulders and a
solid frame. Her auburn hair curled loosely about her nape
and ears, cut too short to brush her collar. She had gray-
blue eyes, the whites flushed with the pale cobalt tint of her
colony, and she favored bright, warm colors—currently, a
loose-sleeved tunic in flowing vermilion over a body-tight
shirt in a complementary yellow.

When she turned to Cynric, she caught Benedick's gaze
along the way and offered a small, sympathetic smile. He
let out the breath he was holding. Time and useful work
were healing *those* wounds, at least.

And speaking of the useful work—or not speaking of it,
as the case might be—it was time he was about it.

"Nova reports no structures of gross scale." And lesser
ones would not yet be detectable. "But that's at this distance, which tells us only that they don't have continental

arcologies and they don't have an orbital elevator." He took a bite of the high-protein bread, careful not to drip the oil down his face. Though it was a breakfast meeting, and they were all family here, it didn't hurt to present an adult appearance—or the facsimile of one. "Nova did spot one interesting bit of geography, though."

Obligingly, the Angel—who was not present as an avatar, but was listening, as was her duty—popped up a crudely surveyed, low-resolution globe. Grail was second out from its home sun. It had a secondary, like Earth—and like Earth, it was the larger twin—but the smaller planet didn't appear in this simulation.

"It's so *colorful* between the oceans." Chelsea leaned forward over the table, her dark hair falling in waves beside her long, angular face. Her mouth had dropped open slightly in concentration as she peered at the patterns of violet-black, red-black, swirled white, and azure. She cocked her head to the left. "Is that vegetation?"

While suffering the throes of memory, Benedick indulged himself in a more pleasant one: a brief interlude in a mad dash through the bowels of the world that he and Chelsea had undertaken, where they had met a colony of sapient, carnivorous orchids and been introduced to an archive of films from Earth, including footage of the homeworld's mighty oceans. He imagined that Chelsea, too, was recollecting those images. The surface-level pictures had revealed oceans tinted glass green by algae and azure by reflection from the deep skies above. These oceans appeared similar, allowing for some astronomical units of difference in perspective.

But the landmasses of Earth as seen from space had been different. They'd been greener, and browner, with great swathes of tan and umber through the haze of atmosphere.

"Analysis of the reflection spectrum indicates it's photosynthetic," Caitlin said. "So yes, it's plants. Purple and black plants. Very efficient sunlight collectors. Grail's sky is probably blue, based on atmospheric haze, ocean color, and still more spectrographic analysis. From here, the air looks breathable, though it's an extremely rich mix by our standards. Benedick, you were about to . . . ?"

Benedick beckoned, zooming the globe in until a blurry bit of detail on the smaller of two southeastern continents became visible. A circle, perfect as a water splash, reflecting the blue skies above.

Jsutien said, "Impact crater."

"Fresh. Less than a hundred and fifty years old. Lingering traces of radiation."

"Damn," said Jsutien. "Guess they really blew the dismount."

3

divergent evolution

No, 'tis the gradual furnace of the world,
In whose hot air our spirits are upcurl'd
Until they crumble, or else grow like steel—
Which kills in us the bloom, the youth, the spring—
Which leaves the fierce necessity to feel,
But takes away the power.
—MATTHEW ARNOLD, "Tristram and Iseult"

Danilaw pulled his work coat off the hook on the inside of his office door when they walked past. As he and Captain Amanda stepped into the conference room—and Karen paused to wait outside—he shrugged into it, head bent. He could feel the frown on his face and wanted to hide it from Captain Amanda and his cabinet members until he had it under control. It was a frown of unease, not displeasure—but a responsible leader understood that those around him reacted to his moods and to those unconsciously perceived cues that told one to walk softly because the silverback was angry. A frown would upset them, and he needed his team focused on the problem—not on appeasing, avoiding, or supporting him, as their various natures might demand.

Captain Amanda latched the door quietly, letting everybody know that this was serious business. The City Council did not usually meet behind closed doors. The conference room was pleasant, airy, conducive to work without ostentation or extravagance, though it, too, had a couple of lake-view blisters—also empty of any dodecapo-dal observers.

The central table was the one element likely to impress, but that was due to it being a state-of-the-art piece of technology rather than to any calculated effect. A thick memory crystal embedded with data arrays, a solid-state quantum teleconferencing system, holographic displays, recorders, and other useful and interesting devices, it had the appearance of a palm-thick, armspan-wide slab of pale violet glass threaded with circuits and guide panels. The array rested atop four graceful C-shaped ceramalloy legs, like something that trembled on compressed springs. But it was solid as rock—and heavy as one, too, as Danilaw clearly remembered from the work party he'd hosted to move the damned thing in here. Even blunting the gravity hadn't made that project easy.

The secondary task of carrying in the chairs had been handled by Danilaw's sister's kids, since it had been his day to watch them. Good life experience, and a few community service credits toward their citizenship, combined with a family outing. Sometimes, laziness was the next best thing to genius.

Two Administrators waited behind the table. The citizen on the right was Jesse Corelio, with his nut-brown hair and pale olive complexion—a tidy medium-sized young citizen serving his first stint as a Councilor. He wasn't using a chair. He perched, legs drawn up, in an observation blister. A mathematician and farmer, he'd passed the suitability tests with flying colors, and so far Danilaw had enjoyed working with him, but the relationship hadn't been tested yet.

On the left was Gain Kangjeon, whose hair was as black and straight as Amanda's, though her skin was paler and her eyes creased at the corners by epicanthic folds. She was bigger than Jesse, broad-shouldered and broad-hipped. Danilaw, in particular, liked her hands. They were lean—

not elegant, but capable—with defined tendons across the back. When she wasn't serving out her Obligation, she was a primary musician, with civil service as her secondary. Danilaw thought maybe, when their term of Administration Obligation was up and there was no longer a conflict of interest, he'd ask her if she was interested in a date.

He wouldn't mind if she even wanted more than a date, although he couldn't imagine that she didn't have half a dozen potentials already bidding on her reproduction contracts. And there was the marketability issue of his genetic disadvantage.

By the time Danilaw settled the work coat's collar around his neck—a smidgen too tight; his predecessor had not been such a muscular man, but the coat fit otherwise, so there was no reason except vanity to replace it— Danilaw had his face under control. He surveyed the room, assessing the citizens assembled, their strengths and weaknesses, and that let him offer a small, honest smile.

Danilaw liked to handle briefing his staff personally when possible. He thought it led to increased rapport.

"Administrators, posterity"—he acknowledged the recording device—"this is Captain Amanda Friar, of the research scull *Quercus*. She's an expert in antique Earth cultures, among other things."

Amanda pulled out his chair and her own, and they both sat. Jesse drew his legs up higher into his bubble, while Gain seemed composed and at ease in a chair. If they shared a glance, it was a concerned, collegial one.

Danilaw folded his hands in front of him and drew in a focusing breath, arranging his report in his head before he began to deliver it. "Captain Amanda informs me that an antique ship, possibly derelict, is headed in-system."

The faces of his colleagues reflected a host of emotions. Not disbelief—there was no reason for Danilaw to summon them to a midnight meeting in order to lie to them— but concern, confusion, and shock. He saw it in the way

Gain sat straighter and Jesse hunched tighter, grasping his ankles in his crossed palms.

Gain was the closer to impassive, and even she blinked and frowned. He could tell, from the way the tiny muscles of her face rearranged themselves afterward, that she was having a conversation with herself not dissimilar to his own earlier worries. And that she was already considering implications and opportunities.

While he, Danilaw, was stalling.

If you can't figure out a better way to get there, Danilaw told the self-critical voice, *just jump right in.*

He picked up a hand pointer and used it to illuminate the blip, which caught the light and sparkled like a faceted stone against the empty spaces of the hologram. He glanced down from the glitter—the instinct bred of old experience rather than necessity.

"We have reason to believe," he said, "that the object indicated by that icon is a sublight colony ship from Earth, which has been lost and presumed destroyed since the time of the Kleptocracy."

He paused to let the centuries stretch out in his audience's mind. A rustle as Jesse shifted, restless, told him he had waited long enough. Jesse was an autist, one of the protected mutations, and he'd chosen to retain his neuroatypical status. He did not deal well with boredom. Danilaw tried to accommodate him as much as possible.

"We're not expecting anything incoming from Earth this year, and there's been no communication suggesting otherwise. Captain Amanda assures me she has people checking with the home planet right now."

Outside, the dodecapodes were finally arriving, drawn by light and activity. A tentacle as long and thick as a big man's leg glided sinuously across the transparent material of the blister behind Jesse. It coruscated in bands and leopard spots of violet and black, brilliant to Earth-adapted eyes but ideal for vanishing into the dappled shadows of Fortune's underwater vegetation.

Danilaw would have liked to measure the width of the dodecapus's arm against his palm, but he thought it would forgive him the lack of a proper greeting this one time. A sense of awe, of connection and affection, swelled in him, and he frowned. Time to get his rightminding adjusted, before something in there cascaded.

He said, "The vessel is using old-style broadband casting to send out an identity tag. After rounding up some obsolete radio equipment and contacting some experts in archaic languages, Captain Amanda has been able to associate those tags with a sublight colony ship that left Earth during the Kleptocracy."

He glanced at her.

She picked up the thread as if they had rehearsed it. "There are a number of possibilities. The ship may be broadcasting a false ID tag. It may be the vanguard of some sort of attack. It may be a derelict, under remote control or AI guidance—or just drifting, in which case it is merely an archaeological treasure and a hazard to navigation."

"But setting aside those possibilities for the moment"— Danilaw paused for emphasis, and to get his breath under his words so he would sound calm and capable—"Ciz, it is entirely likely that we are about to reestablish contact with the *Jacob's Ladder*, a vessel whose notoriety should require no exposition."

It might not require it but, if necessary, the exposition was there, keyed into every attendee's infothing and available for perusal at the slide of a finger. Both of the Councillors ducked their heads, flicking through the information while Danilaw paused to let what he'd just said sink in. Yet despite that, Danilaw was confident that all three of his colleagues knew the basics.

And if they didn't know the history, they'd have heard of the legends. The *Jacob's Ladder* showed up regularly as a plot point in fashionable entertainments, cast in the role of an enclave of fanatics, an insane asylum, and a lair of monsters all in one.

It was a trope so hoary and reliable that Danilaw thought of it as a predictable cliché. So he folded his arms on the table and tried not to feel like a character in a drama. The holographic representation in the center of the table helped. Watching the nearly invisible blip that was the *Jacob's Ladder*'s estimated position float apparently motionless in a 3-D model of the Sanctuary system made it seem manageable, a crisis on a human scale.

"Which means," said Gain, her voice crisp with authority and good sense, "we are in all likelihood also about to reestablish contact with unrightminded, primitive humans. Possibly a large number of them."

"Barbarians," Captain Amanda agreed. "It may be impossible to relate to them without conflict."

"*Barbarians* is a loaded term," Danilaw said, "and one I'd prefer to avoid. They're premodern humans."

Captain Amanda shook her head, the sharp edge of her glossy black bob moving against the brown skin of her neck. She disagreed, but not strongly enough that she would countermand Danilaw's command. He watched as she drew a breath and re-aimed the conversation, feeling lucky in the egolessness of this unexpected addition to his team. If she really believed he was misguided, he thought she would intervene more strongly. For now, she'd registered her opinion and was content to trust his judgment.

Instead of arguing, she began providing historical context. "They left Earth, among other reasons, to avoid rightminding. There's no telling what they are like, after all this time, or what their society has become."

Danilaw nodded. "At this point, depending on how fast they've been moving, we can assume they have undergone at least a few centuries of social development. They were radical Christians, and we're a millennium out of practice in dealing with people who are locked into anomalous temporal lobe feedback. We just don't know how to handle the faithful anymore. They may be pacifists or militant, religious or atheistic. Or both, or all four, in Mendelian combinations. At this point, if any significant number have survived for any length of time, they probably no longer represent a homogenous society.

"Worse, approximately one percent of unrightminded humans are psychopaths, and a considerably larger proportion—perhaps as much as thirty percent—are sophipaths, leading to entire societies devoted to upholding untenable ideologies. The pathological brain is no more wired to accept evidence contradictory to its dogma than a flutterby is wired to understand that the image of the rival it attacks in a mirror is its own reflection. The more argument erupts, the more people grow wedded to defending their sophistries, and those who attempt to guide a resolution through compromise are seen as traitors to both groups."

Gain tapped her fingers on the thick table edge. Her mouth worked. "You make it sound like they are a bunch of sociopaths."

Captain Amanda shook her head, but Danilaw thought it was more in elaboration than contradiction. "Sociopathy is a relatively minor element. Basically, unrightminded humans are almost incapable of rational thought. If you think of them as small children, without impulse control, any understanding of the subjectivity of emotion, or the ability to compromise, you will not be far wrong. And the crew and passengers of the Kleptocracy-era sublight ships were the worst of the lot—delusional to the point of sacrificing entire ecologies on the altar of faith."

Danilaw placed his hands on the table's heavy surface, attracting the attention of Captain Amanda and his cabinet without the need to interrupt. "We might be dealing with a generation ship packed to the portholes with inbred religious fanatics. We might be dealing with an already extant war incoming."

He had thought the implications of war would silence them for a minute, and the breath-held sigh that orbited the room confirmed his conjecture. It felt . . . curious to raise such a specter from the past. He might as well threaten them with pogroms or a genocide. Mass enslavement. Mutilations. Withheld medical care, exposure on ice floes, or a child sex trade. The bubonic plague or leprosy.

Yet antique horrors seemed somehow appropriate to a discussion of the antique hulk bearing down upon them. Danilaw could see the effect on each of the cabinet members: Administrator Jesse lowering his chin to his hands to stare moodily into the data displays embedded in the thick crystal tabletop; Administrator Gain rubbing the bridge of her nose with the last two fingers on her right hand, the thumb and the other two splayed across the olive skin of her temple and forehead as if he was making her eyes hurt. Semiotic indications of attention, concern, and concentration.

Jesse tipped his head. "But didn't they worship the same god?"

"More or less," said Captain Amanda. "But they appear to have found plenty of things to fight over anyway. Today we believe that many of these people's brains never matured——that they suffered from temporal lobe malfunctions causing fanaticism and ideopathy, and that their frontal lobes never fully myelinated. Think of them as——potentially——toddlers with nuclear weapons."

Conversation was more interesting than one man droning on and on. It held the audience better. And Danilaw would have used puppets if he thought it would get his cabinet to pay attention.

"But it's also important to remember," he added, "that any potential for violence or memetic pathology is balanced by the other possibilities of what we may find. A society different from ours, with cultural and social riches of its own. Hybrid vigor, including species of animals and plants entirely lost to Earth during the Quilian mid-Holocene extinction event—the so-called Eschaton. Art, science, technology. An entire parallel track of human culture."

Administrator Gain said, "If I remember my history correctly, we should also consider that, compared to our society, these people were remarkably homogenous, genetically speaking, and of a type no longer well represented in our genetic pool. Almost all of them were drawn from Western European stock. If they can be rightminded, it's an opportunity to—well, to outcross."

"It's an opportunity for a lot of things," Danilaw said. "The sort of profound, universe-changing opportunity that comes along once or twice in a hundred years."

"I take it from your comments that they haven't hailed us yet?" Jesse said.

"No." Danilaw smoothed the scratchy material of his work coat over his arms. "We're contemplating sending a scull out to greet them, which is why Captain Amanda is with us. That, and she was instrumental in decoding the signal."

Gain offered Amanda a respectful nod. Amanda returned it. "Research is my primary. Driving spaceships is a tertiary, but I need it for my work."

"Well done," Gain said.

Amanda looked down. "There are risks to sending out a scull—and even bigger risks to boarding the ship, if that is the choice we make. Debris, antagonizing any residents, contagion. I would recommend drones before any manned mission, although we should limit those contacts. Drones can seem quite threatening."

Gain turned from the waist to face Danilaw directly. "You mentioned that they are still using radio broadcast technology. You may not know that there is a culture of radio hobbyists here on Fortune who still play with primitive equipment. I know a few; I think they could be brought in as consultants. We could contact them in advance."

Jesse made a noise of agreement. Gain, finished speaking, seemed to be taking notes on her infothing. Amanda lifted a jug of water from the surface of the table, leaving a ring of condensation.

As she poured, she resumed. "I speak the language, though—or I speak the language they used when they left Earth. But as you can imagine, it's been centuries for them as well, and no doubt the language has diverged."

Danilaw spoke the tongue, too, or had accrued a tolerable understanding over the years, given how he fulfilled the arts requirement of his Obligation. A significant fraction of the seminal twentieth- and twenty-first-century rock and roll was in English, and the people consigned to—or escaping in—the *Jacob's Ladder* had spoken primarily that language.

He'd have to arrange backup childcare for his sister's kids, but that was a minor inconvenience. He could go.

"The good news," Gain said, "is they don't seem to be sneaking. But that doesn't explain why they haven't hailed us. If they had, those radio operators I mentioned would be talking of nothing else."

Danilaw pulled another glass over and pushed it toward Amanda with his fingertips. She finished with her own and filled it without looking up, then offered the pitcher to Gain and Jesse. Jesse accepted and filled two more cups.

Danilaw drank and spoke. "There's a possibility they don't know we're here. Remember, they left Earth just at the beginning of the quantum revolution. They should have artificial gravity, but we can't be sure what directions their research will have taken since then—assuming they have advanced and not regressed. They are broadcasting on radio frequencies, which means they're subject to lightspeed lag. And if they're looking for evidence of habitation on those same frequencies, they won't find anything. Or at least, not much—I assume your friends are a small group?"

"Not the biggest," Gain admitted with a smile. "There's a few dozen of us."

"They may not even be looking." Amanda set her water glass down and twirled it between her fingers. "Why would they expect us to have leapfrogged them? When they left Earth, its society seemed more likely to knock itself back to the Paleolithic—if it was *lucky*—rather than survive into the quantum age. As far as they know, they fled a smoking cinder, a world rendered uninhabitable by ecological collapse."

Her words fell into a silent room. Jesse fidgeted. Gain leaned forward on her elbows and, after a few moments, quietly said, "Will they want to fight us?"

Danilaw rolled his cup between his hands, stopping when the bottom squeaked painfully on the tabletop. "I don't know," he said. "Possibly."

4

a library once

Benedick watched the recording of the captured probe twice, leaning over Caitlin's shoulder, trying not to think about the smell of her hair. So many mistakes; so many regrettable events in an existence measured in centuries. You never stopped wondering what might have been different.

Even now, with incontrovertible evidence of aliens—human aliens, admittedly, and not so alien as Leviathan, but almost certain to prove weirder than all the nonhuman intelligences that filled up the walls of the world—Benedick found Cat's presence a reminder of all the errors of a long life. The years and the work had eased things between them, and they were friends again, which was good, because they needed to be able to work together.

But he missed her, as simply as that. And he had never quite stopped wanting her back.

Still, he'd settled for what he could earn, and reconstructing the friendship had also served to reconstruct the trust. He didn't think there were many people she'd allow to stand over her like this so calmly, invading her personal space while she worked.

He straightened up and came around the display tank to face her. "We can't assume their intentions," he said quietly, when he knew he had her attention. It was just a shift of the eyes, but it was enough. They were still a team.

"You're worried about what will happen when we start exchanging diplomats."

He shrugged, brushing his hair behind his shoulders. "Nanotechnology, inducer viruses—or whatever they have that's similar—bacterial agents, engineered or accidental. There's no telling what could come in on their shoes. And we can't assume, after centuries of isolation, that we have any reciprocal immunities."

"And they're very likely to be Means," Caitlin said. "Our bugs might just kill them—not to mention the colonies. Are they going to want to become Exalt?"

"It's something we can bargain with," Benedick said. "It's an advantage and possibly a trade good."

"But it's combat you're worried about."

He felt himself smile. As well as he knew her, it was reciprocated. "Combat. Or treachery."

She had a peculiar gesture of rubbing her nose that was all hers. "Well, you are our father's son."

Benedick folded his hands under his arms. *Don't remind me.* "Yes, he would have assumed the worst. But that does not universally indicate that he would have been wrong."

Her mouth worked around whatever she was thinking of saying. Because it was Caitlin, he would never know how many options she chewed over and discarded before she settled. "I am sorry," she said. "I was trying to provoke you."

That he could smile for. "Cheap sport," he said. "I'd have thought such an easy opponent beneath you."

She stood and punched him lightly on the shoulder. "I've got to keep in trim for the aliens. So what do we recommend to the Captain?"

The Captain, their daughter. "We're going to have to

36 Elizabeth Bear

meet with them," Benedick said. "Especially when we're asking to share a planet, because I don't think they'll cede either of those two potentially habitable worlds to us entirely. It's not human nature."

"So even if they are inhumanly gracious, we're going to have to live with them."

"And when we do, we need to be aware of and guarded against all the possibilities for disaster."

Caitlin turned her head, glancing over her shoulder at the system diagrams spinning with stately indifference in the big image tank. "I hope we're aware of that," she said. "I hate to think we're underselling it to ourselves."

Very little in the world knows more about keeping quiet than does a library.

Dust, who had been a library once, huddled in his ringspotted fur coat, paws dry-washing, all the active senses that might have told him enough about his environment to move in safety drawn inward, turned passive, locked down. He felt the new Angel all around, the web of her presence a veil made of trip wires and snares. If she found him she would eat him, as she had eaten most of him already. As she had eaten every other angel and remnants of angels she had found. If she found him, he would devour him whole. So, with perfect logic, he decided she would not find him at all.

The world had changed from what he knew. While he died, slept, and grew back from a spark, it had evolved from a hulk to a haven, from a shell to a ship.

Who had preserved the spark of him? And who had caused it to awaken here, into the helpful-animal consciousness of this furry toolkit with its deft hands and keen, twitching nose?

And who had thought that this, the eve of landfall, would be an opportune time to return him from the quiet cold of storage?

It seemed to Dust that, first, he must learn who had preserved him, and what that person or those persons intended. And then, having done that, he must decide how he was going to use those intentions to suit his own designs.

Dust was small now. Dust scurried. Dust moved without notice through the channels in the walls of the world. Dust only half recollected himself, but from what he remembered of the angel he had been, he would have left himself resources. Resources baled, blindered, and buried against future need. He had always been a hoarder—that was also after the nature of libraries.

His spotted pink and brown nose twitched. He sniffed, careful of whose spores he brought into the lungs of his insufficient, temporary form. If he could not extend his senses out into the world for fear of drawing the new Angel's attention, he'd bring the world into himself and parse it that way. Primitive, but it should be effective enough if he were painstaking and meticulous.

He'd find the resources. He'd answer the questions. He'd learn who had brought him back.

He'd reclaim his ship, and he'd win his freedom again.

Dust filtered mouse-soft into the cracks in the walls and was gone.

Caitlin Conn did not have to travel from Engine to the Bridge to speak to, or even to see, her daughter. But she often did, walking down the long corridor past the venerable New Evolutionist Bible and climbing through the irising door to the Bridge before it was entirely open, and for this Perceval was grateful. The loneliness of command was one thing, and the loneliness of missing your family quite another. And seeing and speaking weren't the same thing as physical contact, oxytocin, pheromones—the bonding chemicals that managed stress and settled cortisol levels.

Perceval managed her own neurochemistry through her symbiont, but manual manipulation of any system so complex, nuanced, and responsive was inevitably cruder and more granular than what the healthy brain managed on its own, with the proper stimulus.

And sometimes it was nice to see her mother and collect a hug.

Caitlin arrived dressed for off-duty, which was another endocrine signal Perceval didn't get enough of. When the Bridge door dilated to reveal Caitlin's broad-hipped, broad-shouldered form in blousing trousers and barefoot, it was as if somebody had pulled a plug in Perceval's spine and let all the stress run out.

To puddle on the floor, she thought, with a grimace. *Where you will have to mop it up later.*

The Captain kept the cynicism out of her voice as she said, "Hey, Mom."

She hadn't thought she was trying to sound particularly nonchalant, but if the words had come out that way, Caitlin wasn't buying it. She cleared the doorway quickly and stood just inside while it sealed, hands on her hips and head cocked appraisingly. Caitlin still wore her black unblade, Charity—but there was off-duty, and there was stupidity.

Although Perceval stood still to greet her, her white trousers and shift falling about her with folds unstirred even by the movement of air, Caitlin huffed and glanced around the Bridge as if she could see every moment of Perceval's last hour.

And perhaps she could, if she were checking in the infrared. The cold Captain's chair, and the warmth of footsteps sprinkled over the grass and meadow flowers of the Bridge decking. The evidence of Perceval's tight-reined distress lay everywhere.

"Wearing a groove in the planking?" Caitlin said. Grass whisked between her toes as she came to her daughter. Perceval might be taller, but Caitlin still outmassed her by half. She hunched herself down to accept her mother's hug, wishing to feel enfolded in it, protected. Nobody could be impervious all the time. *Except,* Perceval thought ruefully as she straightened, *possibly Benedick*.

"Pacing the Bridge is the Captain's prerogative," Perceval said.

In old days, the Bridge would have been a gathering place for senior crew. But the *Jacob's Ladder* was alive now, and the world's control center could be wherever Perceval went. The Bridge was now her retreat, her hermitage.

And like all such places, it could be painfully lonely.

"And provoking the Captain is the Chief Engineer's," Caitlin replied. She plunked herself unceremoniously on the grass and stretched out. "Nova, amplified sunlight, please."

Perceval's pupils contracted, cones swelling to replace rods in her eyes as the wide windows arching across the surface of the sky paled and depolarized, screens sliding back to widen the apertures. Elements of the world's halo of symbiotic nanocolonies—which also, along with its ramscoop and other electromagnetic fields, served to insulate it from space debris—became reflective and refractive. Biomimetic sensors in the ship's colony cloud, and on her hull, helped the prisms and mirrors train themselves on the distant star, gathering its light. Like a sunflower, the *Jacob's Ladder* focused itself on distant warmth.

The Bridge shivered with radiation—alien comfort after so many years in the dark.

Perceval was also still getting used to living in a world where more things *worked* than didn't.

Caitlin patted the gentle swell of the bank beside her. "Sit, child. Enjoy the light."

Perceval sat. She composed herself and reclined beside her mother, closing her eyes. But she did not close off the datastreams that painted the inside of her head with a constant flow of information, making her eyes largely extraneous for most purposes more complex than—well—navigating around a room.

She sighed, knowing Caitlin would read the complex of emotions in it—contentment, distress—and also knowing that Caitlin, being a mother, would ask.

Predictability in a parent was a good thing.

"Out with it," Caitlin said. "What troubles you? Our journey is at an end, our rest in sight. Or rather, different work confronts us, but with luck and the cooperation or capitulation of the current residents, we can fold this world up and live someplace a little easier to maintain."

"A planet is a closed ecology, too, Mother," Perceval said. "Do you really think it will be easier to maintain? We *know* how the world works. We have no idea how we'll interact with a planet."

Natural ecologies were famously fragile, easy to overset—as Earth's had been.

"We'll do the best we can," Caitlin said. "But is that really what's bothering you? A question of environmental ethics?"

Perceval sighed, though this time it was to buy time, not to invite her mother in. The radiation on her face did feel good. She could feel the ancient evolved systems of her body responding, producing melanin and vitamin D, her muscles relaxing in the heat, her digestion becoming more efficient. Her stomach grumbled quietly and she smiled.

"No," she said. "I miss Rien. Right now—" She stretched her back against the grass, the smell of chlorophyll and bruised flower petals rising around her. "I wish Rien were here to see this."

Caitlin's hand stole out to brush Perceval's, first back to back and then clasping fingers. "You are not alone."

Perceval sat up, hunching forward over her hollow belly, and disentangled her fingers from her mother's. She hugged her knees tight and pulled her forehead almost down to her shins. "Sometimes I wish I were."

She wasn't expecting Caitlin's bark of laughter. One of the joys of adulthood was dealing with her mother as a peer, as an ally and a friend.

"Sir Perceval," Caitlin said, invoking a title Perceval had not heard often since she first sat in the Captain's chair. From the change in her voice and the rustle of grass, Perceval knew that Caitlin sat up, too. "You have never stopped being a knight-errant, my dear. Did you go looking for her?"

Did you go looking for Rien's remains in Nova? was what Caitlin meant. Had Perceval sieved through the Angel's personality for the fragments that had once been Rien, to reassemble them into some parody of her beloved, much as Cynric was—according to Tristen—a sort of parody of what she once had been?

Perceval wasn't sure if she shook her head slightly or if it was a pressure change that ruffled her hair. She tossed it back, swinging herself again into a sitting position, and shook the brown locks down her shoulders like a snapped-out banner. "I would not have liked what I found."

"Wise child," Caitlin said, and kissed her on the top of the head.

Perceval exhaled a breath she did not remember holding. But before she could take in another, Nova's voice broke the stillness and insect-drone of the meadow. The words sounded to Perceval's inner and outer ears simultaneously.

"Captain, Chief Engineer. Five intruders have accessed the Bridge corridor. I have called for support and await your recommendation."

Perceval found herself on her feet, her mother beside her. "How did intruders penetrate this far? Nova, the approaches are full of your colony corona."

"Unknown," Nova said.

Caitlin drew out her unblade. In the loudness of Perceval's heart, it made no sound at all. Her voice rang clean across the Bridge, however, just as if more than one ear must hear her commands. "For any defensive technology, there is an equal and opposite countermeasure."

"Great," Perceval said. "They've hacked through it somehow. Nova, my armor please?"

The suit was in the Bridge closet. It was a trivial matter for Nova to disassemble it there and reassemble the component molecules in their proper configurations around Perceval while Perceval held her breath and stilled her movements. Caitlin's was a little more complex, as she'd left the physical suit in Engineering, so the Angel must pattern it and reconstitute it from available materials here.

"Are they attempting to broach the Bridge?" Perceval asked, as Caitlin's vermilion-and-gold armor began to take shape around her.

"Negative," Nova answered. "They are trying to break into the case containing the relic Bible in the corridor. Tristen is inbound with security. He estimates he will be able to relieve your position in under ninety seconds, and advises you to 'sit tight and not take any chances.' "

Through both faceplates, Caitlin's gaze caught on Perceval's. Caitlin said, "Who the hell wants to steal an old book?"

"It's more than an old book, Mother." Perceval knew how feral the grin that curved her lips must appear, and reveled in it. "Are we listening to Tristen?"

Caitlin grinned back. "Do we ever?"

They burst through the Bridge door like eager angels, emerging into a functional vacuum. Tristen's once-weapon Charity was brandished high in Caitlin's hand. Perceval—out of respect for the unblade—ran three steps behind, firing darts that could pierce even armor if they struck a joint or soft spot squarely. Two of the invaders—gray-armored, their colors blanked and their visors fogged to hide their features—spun to return fire. The other three slipped aside, muscling the ancient Bible's nitrogen-filled case through a fuse-edged hole in the bulkhead that led straight into the embrace of the Enemy.

Perceval went right; Caitlin went left. Perceval lunged into the niche where the Bible's case had until so recently been set, hopping up on its barren stand like a crouched gargoyle. Caitlin flattened herself behind a bulge in the bulkhead through which environmental pipes ran.

Perceval hoped that the raiders were using ammunition that would not punch holes in her ship—or more and worse holes than they had already punched.

Well, Perceval thought, *that explains the vacuum. It doesn't explain how they got past Nova, though.*

There had been problems with the Angels and their areas of awareness before, but those difficulties were long in the past, and Perceval was meant to have complete command of her ship. That anyone could work this—under her very nose—was unsettling.

Though not as unsettling as the darts whizzing past Perceval's faceplate. Something was going to have to be done about that.

Perceval might be Captain now, but she had been raised a knight. Nobody wandered into her bridge and made off with a priceless relic.

She slapped one hand against the top of the niche, armored fingers curling into the bulkhead, denting metal and cracking carbon. "Three," she said into her com, certain Caitlin would count and move with her.

And move they did. Perceval came around the corner on the tether of her arm, a spray of smart darts from her gun hand leading. At the top of her swing she released her hold on the bulkhead and arced into the air. She landed in a crouch, stuck it—or her armor stuck it for her—and came up pelting forward, whooping inside her helmet until she made her own ears ring. Caitlin's footsteps banged through the deck behind her—soundless in vacuum, but Perceval could feel each impact through the plating, and she let the shock waves lift her up and hurl her forward, adding impetus to her own charge.

They were two, and Nova was with them. Tristen and his troops were coming. But they were Conns, and nothing was going to stand before them.

Perceval felt the impacts on her armor as it deflected the intruders' darts from its corona and its carbon-ceramic surface. None struck where they could harm her, though; her armor was as state-of-the-art as these people's countermeasures. They'd have to hit square to hurt, and every ounce of her armor's tech and ability were devoted to making sure that did not happen.

The gray-suited five already had the Bible and its case through the rent they'd ripped in the corridor wall; Perceval could see it being hauled away with cables and tug drones. Only two were firing at her and Caitlin, crouched behind EM shields that offered a modicum of soft cover. The other three, engaged in moving their prize, did not even glance over their shoulders.

Perceval came in among them not so much like a fox among the chickens as like a wolf among enemy wolves. Her armor's corona—as much an extension of Nova as not—struck the EM shields and sparked, raining dead nanotech in a velvety dust. Perceval leaned forward, knowing she was a target and hoping the crackle of crisping electronics was sufficient protection from more darts. Her armor traded dart launchers for ceramic blades.

"Shifting resources," Nova said. "One moment more—"

And then Perceval's mother came up behind her and pushed.

With the addition of Caitlin's mass and armor to her own, they were through. Perceval's blades sliced the first intruder's armor deftly—two incapacitating cuts and a coup de grâce between the eyes and out the back of the helm. This one might come back as the silent dead, if her colony were up to regenerating the damage, but she would never inhabit herself again.

Caitlin did not engage the second rearguard. Nor had Perceval expected her to. While Perceval spun back to catch a blow meant to decapitate—she felt it ring through her armor to the shoulder, despite the reactive colloidal padding—Caitlin unshipped herself and her unblade, diving into the bosom of the Enemy after the ones who had fled.

What happened next, Perceval did not see, but she could hear her mother's harsh breathing over the thumps and shudders of her own combat. The gray knight—and Perceval had no doubt after one passage of arms that this one was indeed a knight—rained blows down upon her with the will of an Angel, until Perceval was fighting for her life. She let herself be beaten back, step by step, taking her opponent's measure and letting her armor have the rearguard.

The one she fought was good, but Perceval thought she was better—though there was only one way to be absolutely sure.

"Captain," Nova said in tones of urgency. "Your mother requires assistance."

By the strength of her arm and the strength of her armor, Perceval swung and feinted high. She let momentum turn her, bringing that arm down for a parry that let the enemy's left-hand blade slide past her midriff so close it left a bright span on her armor. The spin extended Perceval's left arm, and while the blade on her gauntlet was not so sharp as an unblade, it cracked the enemy's armor and sternum with a moment's resistance.

A jerk, one good shake, and monofilament parted ceramic and carbon and titanium like so much doped fabric pulled down a razor blade. Blood spurted only briefly; the heart squeezed once, frantically, as Perceval's blade passed through it, then no more. A fine blue snow brushed her helm; the blood froze and crazed from her vambrace and blade.

Perceval turned from the dead to see where Caitlin and the other three gray knights were. Only when she came up to the edge of the rent in the world did she realize her com was silent. She could not hear her mother breathing.

5

harder things, and worse

The Queen earnestly begged that the blood of her brother might be
atoned for by the death of his murderer.
—LEWIS PORNEY, *The Prose Tristen*

Nova called out, and Tristen came. At a dead run, his
armor assembling around him as his boots hammered the
decking. It was dangerous to move—let alone violently—
while the shell constructed itself, but the urgency in the
Angel's call left no time to dally. And Tristen knew that no
matter how he taxed them to wait for assistance, the odds
of Caitlin and Perceval doing so were slim to the point of
vanishing.

So he hustled. He was careful, and he got lucky, and his
armor drew only a little blood. The gauntlets sealed themselves across his palms, and he dragged Mirth from its
scabbard with a rasp in the last of the outside air.

The air locks and pressure doors sealing the segments
of corridor he reached next slowed him, but they were
also advance warning that something had gone terribly
wrong—if he needed anything more than the Angel's status
reports and information feed. After her first call for help,
Nova did not urge him to hurry; there would have been no
purpose to it. He passed through the gates and Nova sealed
them again behind, and then he found himself beside only

two unmoving bodies—the blue blood frozen onto unfamiliar gray armor—in a corridor open to the Enemy. Over the com, Perceval shouted for her mother.

"Caitlin," Nova said in his ear.

From her tone, he knew the news was bad. Her virtual overlay urged him along the accessway to the breach. He laid a gauntlet on the blown-in edge, the world's curled shell already furling back into place as Nova worked her repairs.

He nerved himself, adjusted his chemistry, and pulled himself up through the breach and into the endless chill of the Enemy. Years had softened his fear of the bottomless spaces outside but not ended it, but he still would not allow that fear to master him.

There against the darkness, before the stark, sun-glazed skeleton of the world, Tristen witnessed the figure of a woman in white armor arched around the flame-colored armor that housed the body of her mother. Over them both bent the figure of an Angel, mourning.

A slowly expanding halo of glittering ice-shards, blue as sapphire with the blood of Tristen's sister, spun out in all directions. Tristen had seen too many dead siblings in a long life. Even from here, he could tell there was no hope.

He caught himself one-handed on the edge of the hole in the world before he could drift clear, Mirth in his other gauntlet—useless now—leaned out into the shallows of a bottomless Enemy, and took a breath that squeezed his chest against the inside of his armor.

He didn't need to ask. He was the First Mate and he knew.

Caitlin Conn was dead, and Caitlin's ancient unblade—which had once been his, and which had been used to kill her utterly—was gone. Vanished along with those who had killed his sister, and whatever else they'd come to claim.

Tristen swallowed, armor tight against his throat. Sword

still at the ready—they could return—he pushed off from the hull of the world.

Inside his helmet, inside the bones of his skull, Perceval wept savagely—until Nova, protecting her Captain's dignity, hushed the feed.

Hidden deep in the interstices of the world, Dust observed secretly as his resurrecter hugged the dusty black Book to her chest.

"I win!" she crowed. "The Good Book, hah! The whole *world* is in my hands!"

"Hell is other people," the Angel said—words that welled like a freshet from the Library inside her to fill her mouth and spill forth into the hearing of her Captain. It was a quotation, and a split second's archive search told Nova who had written it originally, and in what milieu and circumstances. She transmitted the context to her Captain as part of their continuous information cycle; Perceval was like unto an Angel herself in that she never minded *more* data.

But now she sat folded small in the Captain's chair, hugging herself and scowling.

Perceval was no longer the heartbroken girl who had walled herself up on the Bridge after Rien died. At Nova's voice, she lifted her chin from her knees and forced a brave smile. "You're telling me. Did I seem to be brooding? I was only taking advice."

"Your ancestors are not Captain," Nova said. Once, she would have been hesitant, afraid of offending or alienating Perceval, but that was before fifty years of relativistic travel and working together had worn them into one another's curves and ridges like a shoe worn into a foot. Now the Captain had adapted to her Angel, accepting Nova in her proper role as a prosthetic, an extension of Perceval's own capabilities. The Angel could manipulate masses of detail at speeds and with accuracies that even an Exalt could not approach, thus providing Perceval with an ongoing synthesis of the most salient patterns of data.

Which—along with the combination of emotional detachment, ruthlessness, engagement, and compassion that the Captain herself embodied—was what Perceval needed to be good at her job.

Part of Nova's job was caretaking the awkward, precarious, brittle organic element of her crew. Exalt humans were more robust than Mean ones, but they were still human. Humans were interesting to Nova, and perhaps the most interesting thing about them was their contradictions—so fragile, and so tenacious.

Because it was part of her job, Nova spent a great many of her cycles observing humans. Because Perceval was Nova's Captain, and because Nova was designed to bond with one particular human, Nova found Perceval the most intriguing human of all. And now Nova's human was grieving again, and Nova was at a loss for what to do about it besides endure, as they had endured other losses until time wore them numb.

Perceval stood, her tall, lean body enveloped in a casual shift, her brown hair gathered loosely at her nape. "Ariane and Gerald think they have a lot of useful advice. I really should get around to integrating the subordinate personalities one of these days, but I find I kind of like having them all in one place, where I can see them."

Ariane hadn't been too much trouble since Perceval had proved that she could master her and, if need be, destroy her utterly. But she was Ariane, and what wasn't much trouble for her was armed rebellion from another.

"Understandable," Nova said. "However, the time is due. You must decide how we're approaching Grail, Captain. Or if we are, in fact, continuing to approach Grail, now that we know it is inhabited."

Further examination had revealed satellites around the

blue-and-violet world, and even a few orbiting the secondary—some xenosynchronous, and some moving at a fair clip relative to the surface. Every sign, in other words, of a thriving spacefaring culture—except for any place for them to live. There was no evidence of cities, of structures, of geoengineering projects—hydroelectrics, canals—or of roadways or air travel.

Perceval pressed her palms together, and the blade-edge of her hands against her chin and lower lip.

"They've exhibited no signs of hostility," she said. "Which is good, because I am not sure how much of a fight we can make of it, if it becomes necessary. The *Jacob's Ladder* is an unarmed vessel."

"No vessel at the top of a gravity well is unarmed," Nova said. "And there are the symbionts to consider."

"And the ramjet." Perceval crossed the Bridge, flowers poking between her toes, and leaned against the screens on the wall, her hands spread as if to embrace the sun and the solar system they descended into. "The whole world is a weapon."

The humans found it strange to have a *down* again. Nova adapted more easily—but she found it strange to have a *down* at all. Parts of her recollected the waystars, but she'd never before experienced it with her whole self. She felt it tugging her in, the world sliding down the gravity well, and she had to make adjustments to her program in order to accept the acceleration.

Perceval said, "I'm not suggesting we can't fight if we have to. I'm suggesting that they are unlikely to view us— limping in, held together with epoxy and string—as much of a threat, and I'd like to encourage that view."

It was much the comment Nova had expected. Not that her Captain couldn't still surprise her, but it was not so common an occurrence as it had once been. "If that is your objective, it is my opinion that we should hail them. Have you thought about what you'd like to say?"

Perceval's smile was patently cosmetic. "I have some ideas. Where are my officers?"

Nova knew without checking. The location of her crew was never far from her awareness. Because her officers were also Conns, they grieved for their sister and plotted vengeance. Also because they were Conns, they spent that grief in work until they could find revenge.

"Tristen is with Mallory." A frequent occurrence since they had traveled together to bring down Arianrhod, and an association Nova thought generally beneficial to them both. Tristen had been alone so long that the affectionate proximity of another organic chipped at his rough edges, like wear smoothing a rusted bearing, and what was left functioned better than the grief-etched surfaces of before. "They're organizing an inventory of potential trade goods and knowledge."

Nova hesitated—not because she needed to but because it would cue Perceval to brace herself. "They are also generating a list for your consideration."

"A new Chief Engineer."

"Yes."

Perceval sighed, grimacing, but nodded. "That will be useful."

"Cynric and Benedick are together. They are reviewing data in order to present you with a suite of options if hostilities do commence. Shall I send for any of them?"

"Tristen," Perceval said, stepping back from the wall. "He must be my hound once more. He and Mallory."

Nova reached out to her First Mate and felt his affirmation. She passed it to Perceval while Perceval continued.

"Just him for now, unless he feels like Mallory needs to be here. It is he and I who will need to run the contact." She glanced sidelong at Nova's avatar. "People expect that if you're coming to them hat in hand, you do it in person, with dignity appropriate to their station. If the importunings of Captain and First Mate cannot flatter them, we'll have to reconsider."

"They may not have much to give," Nova said.

The Bridge door chimed and irised wide, revealing the pale form of Tristen Conn. Nova's sensors told her everything about him, but she turned her avatar to acknowledge him anyway. When dealing with evolved rather than designed intelligences, it was good to remember that their behaviors were infiltrated by all the baggage, improvisational solutions, and inconsistencies of millions of years of evolution.

Part of communicating with meat people was managing their behavioral triggers, and the social niceties were a protocol for handling just that. With an elder Conn like Tristen, centuries Exalted, it mattered less. Their endocrine systems were as well managed as one could expect, and they were quite accustomed to dealing with virtual persons. But it still mattered.

Tristen Conn was lean and white. Born a Mean, he had suffered congenital achromia and—once Exalted—had never bothered to repair the cosmetic damage. His colony's blue marker glowed unchecked through translucent skin, making him appear ethereal and luminescent when Nova adjusted her sensors to approximate human perception. He was tall, even by Conn standards, and he wore his hair long and flowing across his shoulders—a fluffy, cloudlike mass that appeared far softer in texture than it actually was to the touch.

When Nova wasn't trying to see him as an Exalt might, she observed the way light refracted through the hollow strands, making them seem frosty when in actuality they broke available light into every color of the spectrum. Tristen's face was angular, his expression concerned. Clad all in white as samite, he made an imposing figure.

He ducked to get through the door before it finished opening, and he didn't quite straighten up when he stepped inside. "Hey," he said. "How is my favorite niece holding up?"

The light touch was the right touch, in this case. Perceval straightened.

"Freaked out," she admitted. She stepped toward Tristen, meeting him halfway across the garden of the Bridge deck while Nova allowed herself to fade back into the landscape. Literally faded into the landscape, vanishing by inches like the Cheshire cat. Making her withdrawal ostentatious would accomplish the opposite of her desire, which was to allow Perceval and Tristen the freedom for a tolerably private and comfortable conversation. But she could soften her edges, shift herself out, and blur into the background, until they did not notice she had left them more or less alone.

Perceval might still be his favorite niece—his only niece, in the aftermath of Arianrhod and Ariane's destruction of much of the Conn family—but Tristen had come to accept that she was a woman of maturity and authority, and not the grown girl who had saved his life some decades ago. But unless he was careful, he still saw that skinny, gamine Knight in all her freshly maimed vulnerability. It was the protective urge—the one he would have exercised toward the daughter of his body if that daughter were still, in her own person, living.

But Perceval didn't need a protector. She didn't need a surrogate parent, especially now. No matter how paternal Tristen was tempted to feel toward her, what she needed was a First Mate: a collaborator, a dogsbody, and—occasionally—a friend.

He frowned at her now, studying her face—the sharp jaw and small nose, the high forehead over deep-set eyes, the architecture of pride and knowledge and competence that the sharp lines of grief could not diminish. She drew her chin back, straightening so he could imagine the stubs of her wings working under her tunic. "What are *you* looking at?"

"The best Captain on the ship," he answered. "Who needs lunch. And probably yesterday's dinner, too. Have you eaten?"

She started to shake him off with a hand gesture, but stopped herself. He wondered if it was honesty or concern over revealing too much fragility. After a moment, she licked her lips and glanced away.

"The Captain is the ship," he reminded her, although she was already rueful. "Take care of yourself or you can't take care of us."

Nova would have been pressing her to eat. As evidence, a bench beside Perceval's chair already had covered dishes set on it, but the Angel didn't command the same moral authority with Perceval that Tristen could. Tristen rolled his eyes at his Captain and got down to the business of sorting through them. He served out portions of beans and black rice, stewed greens, and coffee with honey and almond milk. Once she accepted the plate and the cup, he made a plate for himself as well, and sat down on the grass beside her chair.

Perceval glanced at it distractedly, wrinkled her nose, and decided upon the grass as well. "You're worried about something other than tracking down the thieves"—she should have said *murderers,* but Tristen was just as glad she didn't—"and talking to whoever might already be living on Grail."

Tristen bought time with a mouthful of beans and rice, washed down with a full cup of coffee. Perceval poked at her plate, teasing grains of rice apart with the tines of her fork. He should have taken her to task for it, but instead he poured more coffee from the insulated carafe and nursed it.

"Things have been quiet lately," he said. "Politically."

It was an oversimplification. "Quiet" in the sense that there had been no uprisings, no mutinies, no revolutions for going on a decade now . . . until this latest outrage, which might have been little more than an adolescent prank if it had not cost Caitlin Conn her life.

What could be important enough about an ancient Earth book—a paper book, at that, full of Builder religious nonsense?—to lose two people over it? Go-Backs might care about the contents, but they cared more about ecological impact.

There might not have been wars, but there had certainly been politicking, and the situation inside the walls of the world was anything but idyllic. In any case where limited resources existed, people would differ on how best they might be allotted. But the differences had not all been violent. Not after the first fifteen or twenty years, during which time Tristen—*Tristen Tiger,* he thought bitterly—had resumed a role he'd just as soon have left behind. And not after resources had been allotted to repatriating the wounded world's many Balkanized cultures.

Still, resentments . . . persisted. And Tristen shouldered them because the Captain could not—not and still lead effectively.

"I need to break the news to Dorcas," he said. "Either she's involved, and perhaps I can learn something from her reaction—or she's not, and she might be stirred to do a little investigating of her own."

Lightly, Perceval laid her fingers on his wrist. "You are very brave."

He shrugged and set his cup aside to free a hand for his fork. It seemed like a cowardly action to scoop sticky coconut-sweet black rice into his mouth rather than to argue, but he didn't feel brave.

Perceval waited until he swallowed. "I need you to do more than break the news. I need you and Mallory to find my mother's killers."

Tristen bit his lip, rolling it between his teeth before he released it and took a breath. There was too much chance that he already knew what he would find—though as an investigator he would need to set those preconceptions aside. He wanted to shake his head, refuse, resign his commission and walk back out the Bridge hatchway as he had come in—back down the corridor, which Nova had already fixed as if it had never been torn open.

But he'd done harder things with a knot of anxiety and sorrow in his gut. Harder things, and worse ones.

"All right," he said.

6

cometh a monster

What the hammer? what the chain?
In what furnace was thy brain?
—WILLIAM BLAKE, "The Tyger"

Tristen found the woman who was not his daughter more or less where he had left her when last they spoke, some months before. Which was to say, barefoot and ankle-deep in muddy water, her hands dangling below the shallow pond's still surface as she stalked something hidden beneath her own reflection. Oblong splashes of mud, some wet and dark, some dried to peanut-butter color and flaking, adhered to the skin and the fine hairs of her calves.

She half crouched amid the rice plants, her deep gold trousers rolled up to her thighs so that the hems stayed dry, her elbows dangling between her knees as she moved softly, crabwise, each step barely rippling the water.

Other things did ripple, however, and only some of them were fish. Tristen imagined he should feel more uneasiness than he did at such proximity to the cybernetic guardians of the rice paddies, invisible though they were beneath black water. Maybe the fear of death and discomfort had been cooked out of him like moisture, leaving him desiccated and leathery against the bone.

What scared him now was danger to the world, to its inhabitants, to Perceval and Nova and everyone else embraced within its fragile walls. Including this woman, for all that her every witnessed breath sent an ice-fine needle of complicated emotion through his lungs and heart. Including this woman, though he knew Perceval half suspected Dorcas had directed the raid that killed Caitlin.

Dorcas was the leader of the Edenites, rudely termed the Go-Backs—religious and ecological conservatives who had long been opposed to the plans of the Builders. Given what time had revealed about the Builders' many treacheries, Tristen was becoming inclined to—limited—sympathy.

You are old, he told himself, and knew it for the simple truth.

Tristen paused on the edge of the rice field, well back from the shallow water's edge. His footsteps could cause vibrations that would startle Dorcas's prey, and the conversation they were about to have would be difficult enough without irritating her.

She glanced sideways, acknowledging his arrival, but her head stayed bent under the broad-brimmed hat. She slipped forward another step, hesitantly, her toes probing the mud before she shifted her weight. Her hands swayed loosely, almost seeming forgotten.

Until they lashed out suddenly, darting and twisting at the wrist, lifting simultaneously from the water. She was a slender person, thin-armed, her shoulder blades bony through the back of her worn shirt, but she hooked the fish out of the paddy with tendons flexing in her narrow wrists and tossed its silvery, thrashing body to Tristen.

Reflexively, he caught it. It flopped against his fingers, muscular and slimy-rough. It was the colors of tarnish and quicksilver, broad-sided and narrow-backed, with bright eyes that stared accusingly at Tristen as it gasped and fought for life.

He felt a pang of sympathy for it as he crouched to strike its head upon a rock. Once, twice, with a full swing of his arm. After the second blow its spasming muscles relaxed. Brutal, but kinder than letting it suffocate in air.

Dorcas came back up the levee to him, walking duck-footed on slippery grass and rolling oatmeal-colored sleeves down over browned, fair skin.

"Lunch," she said, relieving him of the fish.

He pushed his hair behind his shoulder. "I've eaten." Even if Perceval hadn't been able to force herself, Tristen was old enough to have learned when to treat food as fuel and get it inside him any way he could.

When he'd first come here, it had been the midpoint of a perilous journey. Now, it was a half hour's pleasant walk and a lift ride from the Bridge. How a few years changed things—but the time hadn't changed Dorcas, or her Heaven.

He followed her down the sides of the steep valley between rice paddies and straw-bale plantings of salad vegetables. Other field-workers scarcely glanced up, although a sleek black-and-butter-colored snake head lifted through the water's surface, tongue flicking as Tristen and Dorcas passed.

She led him a few hundred meters to a communal kitchen, where she stepped up to an unattended station and leaned her hat against the side. Without ceremony, she expertly cleaned the tilapia. The knife she used was a single-purpose object, ground thin by many sharpenings, the ceramic blade stained from use. The handle was bound in grubby green marker tape. Tristen thought the blade itself was salvage, some other object repurposed and reshaped, and not originally intended for cutting at all.

But it worked well enough. She let the blade glide down either side of the spine. "You didn't come here on a whim."

"I didn't," he said. He did not bother glancing over his shoulder. He could feel the pressure of other cooks at each shoulder, although, other than a glance of acknowledgment to Dorcas, they had not looked up from their tasks.

Tristen was not and would never be popular with the Go-Backs—for reasons he could not argue—though Dorcas herself was willing now and again to sacrifice a few moments of her time for him.

Tristen turned on the grill and, with a glance at Dorcas, pulled a heavy flat-bottomed pan over the heating element. "Can we speak in private?"

"I won't conceal what you tell me from my people, so they may as well hear it from you directly. That way, you can be sure I haven't misrepresented you." One more pass of the knife, and the tilapia lay headless and open like an ancient paper book on the cutting board.

Tristen put oil in the pan and watched it shimmer while Dorcas cleaned her tools and racked them. She waved vaguely at an onion, so he borrowed the wiped knife and diced it, then scooped translucent crescents into the pan. An aroma of cooking organosulfates converting to sugars—alluring enough to have woken the dead—tickled the inside of his nose.

When Dorcas turned back, she said, "Thank you."

She scraped the onions to the edge of the pan. Salted and herbed, the fish went into the oil with a satisfying hiss. Tristen stepped aside, giving her room to work. It was easier to speak to the back of her head and the fine hay-colored locks curling around her hairline—revealed because the body of her hair was upswept into a ponytail. A UV flush colored her wrists where they stretched from the protection of her sleeves.

He watched her for a moment, then he folded his arms and said, "Grail is inhabited."

He had waited until her hands were away from both the knife and the hot pan, and it turned out well, for she jolted as if he had run a current through the floor. From the muffled exclamation of pain off to the left, perhaps he could have timed the revelation better from the point of view of the bystanders.

"Aliens," she said, after a moment.

"Humans," he replied. "People who use a Roman alphabet and Arabic numerals. People from Earth."

Dorcas had been an Engineer once—Exalted in the first Moving Times, during the Breaking of the world. Not too long after Tristen. She had become a Go-Back—one of the colonists and crew members advocating a return to Earth Tristen had so successfully opposed in his youth. He might be personally responsible for her death.

For she had died. She had died in her old body then, and later her machine memories had been reincarnated in the body of Tristen's Exalt daughter Sparrow, who had died in the mind because Tristen had not had the courage to follow her out of Rule, but whose form had been taken by the Engineers and given as a shell to one of their own lost ones.

The person who stood before him wasn't Sparrow. She was who Sparrow had become, because Tristen had failed her as a father.

On their first meeting, she had reminded Tristen of his crimes, and were Tristen not Exalt, he would still bear the scars of that meeting. In return, Tristen had placed in her hand his daughter's haunted sword, though she had not held it long. Given such an inauspicious beginning, he doubted they would ever be friends, but his respect for her was unrivaled.

"What an irony, to finally come to the world we meant to infest, and to discover that we've already infested it." The fish sizzled as she flipped it. "You think they hopped right over us?"

Tristen paused, waiting for his moment. "Well, I guess we were delayed for rather a long time."

She held it in for a while before the laughter broke free and she snorted—one of those times where it was plain to him that she was not Sparrow and in some ways barely resembled her. The appearance of a face had a lot to do with how one wore it, and Sparrow had grown up in the House of Conn, trained from a young age to comport herself as a lady.

Dorcas was something else—a high-handed Engineer turned priest. Tristen, who had not known her in her old life, imagined she'd been a woman who played as hard as she worked. And even today, she worked hard.

She squeezed lemon over the fish, leaving Tristen to wonder where the trees were. This enclave of Go-Backs also exported mango, chocolate, and vanilla—a tropical extravagance of edibles. They were efficient agriculturalists who had maintained better mechanical control of their holdes and domaines than most of the isolated communities on the *Jacob's Ladder*. Even after fifty years of occasional visits, he hadn't had the opportunity to explore more than a small percentage of their Heaven.

She handed him a plate and gestured to a communal pot of brown rice, steaming slightly around the loose-fitting lid. Tristen ladled out a portion, pressing a depression into the center to hold the fish juices. Dorcas accepted the now-laden plate he handed back without a word.

The silence held while she slid fish onto the plate, turned off the stove, wiped out the pan, and hung it for the next cook's use. She pulled a whittled wooden fork from a cup and led him back out into the filtered and supplemented light of the fast-approaching sun.

Tristen grabbed two bent-metal cups on the way out and dipped them into a water jug by the pavilion door. He dropped onto the grass next to Dorcas as she seated herself and handed her one of the two when her hand was free. *This is my role in life.*

They sipped. The water was faintly dusty-tasting, but sweet, and Tristen's symbiont told him it was tolerably clean. He wondered if the Go-Backs filtered it through folded cloth after they pulled it out of the fish ponds, or if they had something more elaborate set up.

After three bites of onions, fish, and rice, she said, "You might have kept that from us."

"We might have."

"But for how long?"

He smiled. Another blessing of the circumstances of their reacquaintance—and all the parallel history that lay behind it—was that Dorcas felt no need for polite fictions with him, if she ever felt them with anyone. "I'd prefer to think of us as being on the same team when it comes to the survival of the world and all the people in it. Since we got under way again, there's been no need for enmity or disagreement between your people and the Conn. We're going somewhere and, historically speaking, the Edenites"—he chose the polite term—"were all for that. Your faction's argument against harboring at the waystars was never about returning to Earth; it was always predicated on finding a safe landing zone. And at the time, Earth was the only one we knew how to get to."

She had to know where he was going, but she wasn't going to give him an inch that he didn't earn. "But?"

"Things change," he said softly. "Time passes. We know that better than most."

Because we are older than most. The expression she shot him around a forkful of fish was wry and appreciative, or he could spin it that way. But she still didn't let him off the hook—or whatever the parallel metaphor was for those who preferred to tickle their dinners from the water. For the fish, it was nevertheless as tragic a seduction as any encounter with pole and reel.

"What I'm suggesting," he offered, "is that people forget the reasoning behind a dogma, and eventually come to treat the dogma itself as holy writ."

"You mean like that book in the case outside the Bridge?"

Tristen nodded. All these centuries later, all the revelations of how his ancestors had betrayed and been betrayed in the name of God, and the idea of blasphemy, still sent a frisson up his neck. Even for an Exalt, the conditioning ran deep.

But she'd mentioned the book first. If she was guilty, would she have done that?

No, he thought. She was too savvy to play those kinds of games with an Exalt. And there was no increase in her pulse or respiration when she spoke.

But she had just given him the opening he had been waiting for.

Watching her face carefully, he lowered his voice and shielded the shape of the words with the dingy cup. "The book that isn't in the case outside the Bridge anymore, you mean?"

Dorcas also had a lot of experience hiding her emotions. The uptick in her heart rate could have meant anything—but the fact that it happened reassured him that he had not missed a similar one previously.

She met his eyes briefly, then glanced down again. "Your Captain finally jettisoned the damned thing?"

"Three hours ago, an incursion group broke in and stole it," he answered. "My sister Caitlin's mind died in the attack."

Her chin lifted abruptly. Her chest swelled on a sharply taken breath. *Adrenaline response.* "I am sorry for your loss."

Not sincere, exactly, but not whatever the opposite was, either. He turned it aside with a lift of his hand. "There's a radical element among your people that will not support any course of action except reversing course—no matter how Pyrrhic that would appear to be at this juncture."

"Radical, are they?" Whoever she was now, Dorcas still had Sparrow's appetite. He had startled her once; she would not show it now, and the meal balanced in her lap was vanishing rapidly, though tilapia were not small fish.

"When their political convictions can move them to unprovoked violence, I find it difficult to think of another term."

"Like the ones who Exalted an entire colony ship full of life-forms?"

"It seemed like a good idea at the time," he said. "We didn't expect anything Mean to survive Acceleration."

"You thought you knew what the world needed. Perhaps some of us would rather have died than be transformed. Perhaps—did you ever think?—perhaps it's better to die than exploit others."

"We made a judgment call," he said. "I suppose you're right, and that does make me a dangerous radical. So what does that make the extreme element among your people? The ones who consider themselves contaminated? Zealots? Fanatics?"

Dorcas set her plate aside and rubbed her hands on the grass as if wiping off a trace of oil or fish juice. "That's because, at your heart, you're still a reactionary."

Tristen didn't agree with her, but he also didn't want to argue. And what was it to him what this woman thought? She wasn't Sparrow, and nothing he could do would make her so. All he'd do was break his own heart seeking the lost girl in the present-day woman.

Children always grew up strangers, he thought, imagining what a disappointment he had been to his own father. In this case, the strangeness was literal as well as metaphorical.

"Some of your people view Earth as sacred," he persisted.

"Sacred as circles," she agreed, "and not just *my* people, Tristen."

"Do you know who killed my sister?"

The cut direct. There was the held breath, the chilling of the extremities, the pupil blown wide to catch any scrap of information. Fight or flight.

Just a moment's worth before she snorted like an alligator and tossed her head. "Would you have me ferret out whosoever it might be and remand them to you for questioning?"

Nobody was sitting nearby now, but Exalt ears could overhear distant conversations. This once, his knowledge of that fact did not affect Tristen's choice of words. "I leave that up to your conscience. But I would prefer it if you handled any disciplinary issues among the Edenites internally."

"So you can't be blamed?"

"Because it reinforces your authority." He folded his hands. "The murder of my sister cannot be considered to be a matter strictly among the Edenites."

"Murder, or act of war?"

"Either way," he said, "I will prosecute it."

Their gazes were locked, and had been. Tristen made the choice to look down first. He needed Dorcas's cooperation, offered rather than coerced.

The whisk of skin on skin was her rubbing the palms of her hands together—a worried habit, or anticipation? Her scent was too well controlled to offer him a clue to her motivation, and her heart rate had settled now.

"You're afraid of sabotage."

He nodded without meeting her eyes.

"You're afraid of dying," she said, "because you have lost your faith. You've gotten old, Tristen Tiger, and you cling to life even though it scares you, because you don't think there's anything else afterward."

If she'd been striking for his heart, she'd missed. His apostasy was too ancient and too well-founded for her schoolroom sally to discomfit him. And he thought she revealed more about herself than him in the attempt.

He wanted to reach across the space between them and take her wrist, but restrained himself. "I lost my faith because we can only create the God we can imagine, and we are pathetically small creatures. I lost my faith because I find the prospect of nothingness more heartening than the idea of a God no larger, no greater of spirit, no more *numi-nous* than my father."

He'd been doing fine, maintaining the tone of gentle sarcasm, until he got to the word *father*. Then his voice cracked, and he found her staring at him with a quizzical expression.

The silence stretched.

"What?"

Dorcas née Sparrow smiled. "The Tiger's heart," she said. "I think I saw it."

What had been a toolkit was a monster now, and not blinded to that metamorphosis. Dust the small and scurrying, Dust the broken-backed—but rats were everywhere in the walls of the world. There has never been a ship without rats.

Dust scuttled among them, of them and not of them, consuming them when it was convenient, ignoring them when it was not. From their corpses he learned the new plan of the world that had been his body, the smell of the ones who inhabited it. He stayed slight, insubstantial. He masked himself in their scent and DNA. He felt Nova all around him as he moved, the corona of her essence and awareness silver-sharp.

But he was just one small thing among other small things—a fluffy cybernetic creature, colony-riddled, moving ring-tailed and spot-backed among millions of its kind. He could get lost, even from an Angel's awareness.

As well he knew, once having been in his own right an Angel.

But now he was a disease, and he moved through the body of the world as a disease moves through any body—by stealth, by camouflage, by deceit. This new Angel's awareness of the world was better than Dust's had been, when Dust was the chiefest among Angels—more complete, more subtle. Still, he passed—he thought—unremarked.

He found traces, strays, eddies of information. He let them pass through him, shielding his own existence and siphoning their bits. Fragmentary though it was, it fed him.

Traces of a scent signature he half remembered drew him. So much was lost, scrubbed away with the bulk of his self. But he was holographic; the image remained, though it blurred with each division and details were lost. And the Conns he remembered no matter what.

And this was the scent of one he'd thought lost.

When he found her, she was drinking beer in the shade of a banana tree, a text-novel scrolling in letters of light through the air before her eyes. She read lazily, a few lines a second, making it last. Her hands were calloused, the bridge of her nose radiation red. She had long sun-colored hair and her father's cheekbones; he knew her at once for who she was.

He scurried, small and lithe, to her side, humped up beside her, and jerked his tail.

"You died," he said. "You were slaughtered like a cow. So who lives in you now?"

Slowly, Sparrow Conn turned her eyes from her novel, which froze in place. A butterfly flew through it. Once, Dust would have been able to name the insect's name. *Though much is lost, much abides.*

"I live in me now," she said. "You're not a toolkit."

"Ah, but I am." He sat back on his haunches and dry-washed delicate paws one over the other. "But I am not *only* a toolkit. And you are not only Sparrow Conn."

"I am not Sparrow Conn at all," the woman said, "although she built the house I live in. I am Dorcas. I was an Engineer."

"And now you are an Edenite."

"I was," she said. "Now I am a woman reading a book. Who are you?"

His whiskers twitched. He could lie, but angels did not lie to Conns, not when asked direct questions. And whoever lived in her now, this woman carried the genetic payload of a Conn. The DNA was what mattered.

"I am Jacob Dust," he said. "I was an Angel. Do you love the Captain?"

"I do not hate her."

A chary answer, and so a good one for Dust's purposes. "But you are not consumed by her purpose."

"Which purpose is that?"

"The purpose of her Angel." Again, the whiskers. As if they had a will of their own, like the tiny heart that fluttered in his birdcage chest two hundred times a minute. *To strive, to seek, to find, and not to yield.*

But no. Those were scraps from somewhere else, another existence. Misfiled chips of memory that tumbled through his mind as bright as diamonds. He had been so full of poetry, once, and he had built the world in its image: chivalrous, valorous, hammered as if from legends.

At last, at last, Dorcas the Engineer folded the words of her story away. She regarded him through escaping strands of hair, but Dust was content that he had her attention now.

"She will sell us to the lords of Grail. She will buy whatever safety she can for herself and her family, buy landfall, buy land—and what in this new world can she do with the rest of us?"

"Sports," Dorcas said. "Monsters, mistakes. Would you unleash us on an ecology? What evolved thing could live with us? We would eat it."

"The strong survive," Dust said. "Existence is evolution. Equilibrium is extermination."

"The Captain would regard me with favor if I turned you in," Dorcas said, her eyebrows amused.

"The Captain's Angel would eat me, as she ate my ancestor. I am but a poor scrap of backup. Is your heart so soft for xeno-starlings and exo-bunnies, and so hard as death against me?"

"Nova allows other scraps to persist. Does an angel fear for its life?"

Dust let his foxy muzzle nod. "This angel does. Tell me, Dorcas of Engine, if you believe God has a plan, how can you be sure it is not best proved by whatever will grow from our meeting with these aliens?"

Dorcas flicked him away with a fingertip. "We are monsters, monster. But I recollect you, and you were the worst monster of all. I think not, Master Dust. God shall have to sort this one without me."

7

if you can hear me

I must be careful now. I have such plots—
Such war plots, peace plots, love plots—every side;
I cannot go into the bloodless land
Among the whimpering ghosts.
—WILLIAM BUTLER YEATS, "Time and the Witch Vivien"

Given the astronomical travel distances involved, the decision regarding what to do about the incoming generation ship was not overwhelmingly time-sensitive, so Danilaw gave his people as much time to argue it out as they wanted. He'd rather repent a reasoned and considered decision than a hasty one. In the former case, he could comfort himself that whatever had gone wrong had been by lack of foresight rather than haste or carelessness.

The discussion ranged along predictable paths and, other than occasionally restraining Captain Amanda's passion for the topic of the awfulness of the twenty-first and twenty-second centuries, Danilaw did not intervene. He sat at ease, watching, considering, waiting to see what the expression of disparate viewpoints might trigger as an eventual gestalt or compromise position.

Outside the observation blisters, dodecapodes came and went, the majority displaying their default swirls of violet, lavender, and black. Danilaw had never been able to tell most of them apart except by size, but there was one particularly large critter with a scar along the underside of two arms that he recognized as a frequent visitor. It pressed close to the right-side blister as if listening at a door, its beak scraping poly. Danilaw entertained himself imagining what it might make of the conversation.

The ping light on his infothing brought him back from his attempts at right-brain creative problem solving. A glance at the summary of contents told him the situation was still developing along the projected lines. He glanced at Captain Amanda, but apparently, now that he had been brought into the loop, he was being given priority information; her device lay quiet and devoid of signals.

Danilaw cleared his throat. Around the table, conversation quieted, and his cabinet directed their attention to him. Trying not to feel like he was pronouncing words he'd be hearing repeated back on news programs and documentaries for the rest of his life, he said, "We're receiving a radio transmission."

Somewhere out there, archaic technology was spinning out of dormancy. Technicians or Gain's recruited hobbyists were hovering over fragile antennae and instrumentation, breaths held, hands instinctively—protectively—outstretched as if cupping the air around a toddler taking her first steps.

Jesse lifted his head. "Answer them."

Captain Amanda glanced at him with a scientist's patience. "We can't, not immediately. Lightspeed lag, remember? Can we see it, Premier?"

Danilaw keyed his infothing to display. An image flickered into view. It showed two—people; Danilaw corrected himself before he could think of them as creatures. They were something *like* people, anyway—upright, bipedal, with eyes and nose and mouth in the familiar biologically convenient arrangement, two ears on either side of a primate head with a flat muzzle and a domed skull. They wore clothes, and they had hair, and—

—that was where the resemblance ended.

Danilaw suspected, from the size dimorphism, that he was looking at a male and a female. They were so thin, so *attenuated*, that it was hard to be sure.

And they were *blue*.

The smaller of the two—possibly the female, as seemed near universal in placental mammals where males were, organically speaking, more expendable—stood in the front, although Danilaw was not sure whether her action was in defense of the larger one or a display of dominance. And perhaps it was overhasty to call her *blue*, exactly, because her hair was brown and straight, and the irises of her deep-set eyes were a perfectly pretty shade of hazel. Her thinness could have been explained as the result of short rations for a long time, though she seemed superficially healthy. It was hard to be certain, however, because her skin—which would have been strikingly pale even if the blood-tint showing through its lightly pigmented translucence was a familiar, comfortable pink—had a distinctly cyanotic hue. Her lips were blue-lavender, the tongue with which she wet them—nervously or in anticipation—liver purple, the corners of her eyes a faint aqua. Her chest was remarkably deep; the rib cage belonged on a biped two and a half times her size.

The larger one, at her shoulder like a lieutenant or a bodyguard, was equally thin. Bones projected over his sunken cheeks, the flesh spare and parchment-thin and flushed with aquamarine. Danilaw could see blue veins spidering across his neck and collarbones below the open collar of a white shirt of seamless construction. The alien's hair, long and loose, glowed white with the light behind it. His eyes glowed too, through the irises, cobalt as a young star.

Danilaw could have stared much longer, but the smaller spoke, and her voice was indeed a woman's. The words were familiar, the sounds and rhythms echoing lyrics in hundreds of songs that Danilaw knew intimately. English, and not too much changed from its twentieth-century cadences. She had a light, strong voice, more confident than

Danilaw would have expected given her apparent age, and she spoke as one accustomed to wielding authority.

She said, "Greetings, if you can hear me. I am Captain Perceval Conn of the *Jacob's Ladder*. My First Mate, Tristen Conn, stands beside me. We have come far in a damaged world, and I say these things not knowing if you will understand me or if you will even have the technology to hear. If you cannot mark my words, I harbor hopes that my tone and unmartial appearance will convince you that our intent is peaceful. I suppose otherwise we shall simply have to pray.

"We navigated for this system believing it uninhabited, but my Angel has uncovered evidence that other vessels from Earth reached it before we did. You have the previous claim, and we acknowledge that. Yet, in the name of charity, we beg assistance.

"Our lives are in your hands.

"We will await your reply on every channel. Thank you for listening."

She glanced at her First Mate—Tristen, she'd called him—and he shook his head slightly. Nothing to add, Danilaw presumed. The transmission ended. There was a moment of silence, and then it began to loop, flickering live from the beginning.

Danilaw took a breath. "That," he said, "is going to be interesting."

Captain Amanda let it play through completely once more, leaning forward in her intentness. Then she passed a palm over the light and paused it. She translated from memory—accurately, as far as Danilaw could tell—while Jesse and Gain frowned and nodded, occasionally trading speaking glances.

"Well," Gain said. "I guess that's pretty unambiguous. How on earth are we going to make it work—I mean, taking them in?"

Captain Amanda, who had been staring at her hands since she finished speaking, looked up. "That's illegal engineering. Those aren't even human beings anymore."

"Unsurprising that they would have gone that way." Danilaw poured himself more water. "The crew and passengers of the *Jacob's Ladder* were made up of a neo-Evolutionist cult. They believed that trials and tribulations strengthened the species, forced it to adapt."

"*Are* made up," Captain Amanda said. "*Do* believe."

"*Possibly* do believe." Jesse set down his infothing. "It's been a long time for them too. Is it even illegal engineering if it's legal in their society?"

Gain said, "Jesse is right. We must be careful of cultural relativism."

Captain Amanda's tone remained uncompromising. "Criminals or not, we still can't let them on-planet without scrubbing their genes. Which, from the look of them—"

"We'll table that for later discussion," Danilaw said, making a note in the minutes for a reminder. "Other points of discussion?"

"Angel," Gain said. "She said that? Her angel told her something? A mythological creature spoke to her?"

"Well, that's what the word meant a thousand years ago," Captain Amanda said. "In this context, I'm assuming she means some sort of majordomo or servant. That's speculation, but based on what we know of the cultural antecedents of the sophipaths who sought refuge on the colony ship, I would guess that that might be a term they use for the Captain's servants—since angels were the servants of God."

Danilaw watched Jesse's nose wrinkle and felt empathy. It was uncomfortable to consider such hierarchical distinctions, but it was also an important reminder that the crew and passengers of the *Jacob's Ladder* had traveled across a gulf of distance and experience that seemed insurmountable. If he allowed them to land, there *would* be cultural

conflicts. Some of them might escalate into violence—
a concept that unsettled him as deeply as contemplating
unleashing a few thousand (or perhaps a few hundred
thousand) rampaging invaders on his intricately carbon-
balanced and socially engineered colony world.

As an Administrator, Danilaw had viewed historical documents that most citizens were not subjected to, and he
had vivid and visceral memories of the violent images asso-
ciated with those documents. Public beheadings, state-
mandated torture, maimings in war, violence—perhaps
most horribly—between family members and spouses.

What might seem quaint and yet disturbing when it appeared in a folk song was absolutely horrific in old flat-
page photographs or—worse—"film" reels. The art and
entertainments of the ancients had been full of carnage,
and while Danilaw found it difficult to comprehend, he
also found it a rich source of inspiration and catharsis.
Human beings had been so animal, so at the mercy of their
inheritance of endlessly reworked evolutionary hand-me-
downs, until so very recently.

And here those atavistic hominids were again, like monsters out of time, returned to haunt him.

Judging by the stricken faces of his Administrative
Council, Danilaw was not the only person thinking so.
Gain traded glances with Amanda, and Jesse seemed en-
meshed in some sudden, vitally important, research project for whole seconds as he got his expression—and his
emotions—under control.

When he looked up, though, his eyes were clear and his
brow serene.

There was no talk of refusing sanctuary, nor would there
be. While Danilaw, with his historical perspective, could
imagine scenarios where turning away refugees would be
the only possible choice, no matter how tragic, you would
have to be unrightminded to consider it beyond the option

stage under the current circumstances. "I wish they'd told us their numbers."

"It is probably," Captain Amanda said, with a bright flash of smile, "their first time doing this, too."

Speaking in tones of quiet reason, Jesse said, "We need to consider the worst-case scenario." He swallowed, as if the words had gotten stuck in his throat.

"Care to illustrate?" Gain asked, facilitating whatever it was Jesse was working himself up to saying.

Jesse wouldn't notice, but Danilaw gave Gain a little grateful smile.

Jesse said, "There used to be traveling charlatans, people who moved from town to town promising miracle cures for a variety of ailments. They'd provide a series of fake 'proofs' of the efficacy of their products, and then they'd 'sell' the patent medicines and move on. They charged money for these treatments—scrip that could be exchanged anywhere else for goods or services."

Danilaw had a sickening sense that he knew how this would come out. "And then what was in the bottle? Cold tea?"

Jesse shook his head. "Oftentimes, the patent medicines contained harmful substances. Mercury, arsenic, lead, radium. But by the time people started to get sick, the medicine man had moved on, and he'd taken the money with him."

Gain sat back in her chair. "That's barbaric. And these were just normal people, not Kleptocrats?"

"That's the point," Jesse said. "They were all Kleptocrats—some more successful than others. That's what unrightminded people are *like*. They will trade future suffering for gratification now. They're hierarchical, and they don't care how badly they hurt somebody if they get something out of it."

"And that's what we're up against?" Gain said.

Captain Amanda nodded. "There's a whole shipload of them, headed right at us."

8

where they ought stand

A woman will have her will.
—ANONYMOUS, *The Marriage of Sir Gawaine*
(medieval manuscript)

Perceval, still pacing the Bridge in her armor, the cowl stripped back but the seals intact otherwise, knew there was news because Tristen came in person. It being Tristen, she didn't know if the news was good or bad until he spoke. And, it being Tristen, he did not draw out the suspense.

"I do not believe Dorcas is behind the raid," he said. "But she knows or suspects who the culprit is, though she is withholding that information for now. Did you have any luck with the bodies?"

"Mercenaries, most likely." Because it was Tristen, Perceval allowed him to see her twisting her hands in frustration. "Mallory performed the autopsies while you were with Dorcas. Their colonies wiped on their deaths. They were AE-deckers born, both of them."

Tristen's expression drifted from neutral to disapproving—or perhaps disappointed. It was not precisely a dead end, but after the Breaking of the world, the AE decks had been wild and isolated places. Cut off from the rest of the vessel, their Mean inhabitants had developed a tightly controlled martial society, defending their limited resources from all comers and forbidding overpopulation to the point of exposing both unplanned and malformed infants, and the unproductive old, to the Enemy—on tethers, because the quick-frozen bodies were a resource too rich in proteins and amino acids to be easily discarded.

They were clannish and xenophobic and fought among themselves as frequently and ferociously as they fought against outsiders. Along with the Go-Backs, they had been the chief of Tristen's problems since the waystars went supernova.

Perceval didn't need the roll of Tristen's eyes to tell her the process of interviewing the Deckers would be complicated and likely unproductive—she and Rien had had an encounter with them when escaping Rule, shortly after they first met—but that didn't stop her from being grateful when he said, "I'll go after we eat."

"Eat?"

Nova's voice chimed from everywhere and nowhere. "Samael is en route with a picnic, compliments of Head. He should arrive in thirty seconds."

"Thank you," Perceval said, reflexively. "Picnic?"

"You can linger here fretting," Tristen said, with all the soothing ice of his imperturbable calm. As if to create an ironic contrast, he threw himself backward on the grass like a boy, spreading his arms until she heard his spine crackle with release. "Or you can come with me, clear your head, and have some time to think while we wait for the Fisher King to answer."

Of *course* the leader of the people of Grail would be the Fisher King. Perceval's mouth bowed, despite herself, into her first real smile since the hideous events of the morning. As soon as she remembered why that was, it fell off her lips again—but for a moment there was a drift of relief.

Whether he'd learned it supporting his father or his wife, Tristen was very good at taking care of people. And she couldn't fault the wisdom of experience when it came to dealing with grief. "So how did Head get involved?"

Head was the chatelaine of Rule—Cook, Butler, House-keeper, and petty household god. Cynric had built hir to the task more than five hundred years previous, and sie was still at it. Sie had no equals.

"I petitioned hir for some snacks," Tristen admitted. "Head's idea of what constitutes a snack—"

Perceval snorted. "I can imagine." She wondered if there was any kind of message in it that Head sent the food to the Bridge care of Samael, a small but independent and self-aware remnant of the Angel of Biosystems, also called the Angel of Poisons for his association with mutagens.

Samael knocked on the thick Bridge door, polite as a golem, the acorns and beetle shells of his knuckles rattle-rasping. Nova amplified the sound and transmitted it inside, leaving Perceval to wonder at the ancient mores imbedded in Angel code.

Once upon a time, it had made sense to knock on almost any door, because the people inside could simply hear it. Now, though, it was a kind of elaborate politeness, a formality with no social purpose. She knew who it was and what he carried—oat cakes, cashew butter, noodles in a salty savory sauce with garlic and ginger, sliced treecarrots and peaches, olives and oysters in brine, mushrooms and eggplants sliced thick and fried, and all tucked into a cleverly folded paper basket. Nova would not conceal such information from her, even if Tristen had asked, especially when the arrival was an angel.

Perceval summoned him with a gesture. When Samael stepped over the threshold to the Bridge, Tristen went to meet him, rising from that sprawled, languid pose to a standing position with a fluid strength that Perceval found heartening.

He was better. It had taken years of recovery and reconstruction, but in recent years he had begun to move as if he were comfortable in his body. Perceval wanted to say *again*, but the truth was she didn't know. He'd been crippled when she rescued him; she hadn't known him unwounded. And from everything she had heard, she might not have wanted to know him unwounded.

The most he'd confessed on the subject was "It was beneficial to me, in the long run, to spend some time alone with my sins," pronounced with a wry sideways twist of his lips that could have been mistaken for a smile.

Time was the great closer of wounds, so even a maiming of the soul could heal over and quit seeping if you lived long enough. Although (thinking of Rien) Perceval wasn't sure if the amputated bits ever grew back again, or even truly stopped aching. Perhaps they just became more impervious to careless blows.

She wasn't sure she wanted them to harden off. Letting go of that loss meant letting go of Rien, and Perceval found the prospect more painful than recollecting the amputation of her wings. Better to lose a piece of your body than a piece of your soul, she thought.

And now there was Caitlin—a loss still too raw to do more than whisper past. If she looked at it too long, too directly, her eyes stung and her throat closed, and then she was no use to anyone.

She watched from her chair while Samael and Tristen conferred, heads bent, speaking via vibration in low tones she could easily have analyzed, if she chose. But it was impolite to eavesdrop, and if anyone had earned her trust, Tristen had. He wanted to surprise her? Well and good.

When he came back, the folded paper basket rested in his hand. Samael waited inside the door—a homunculus whose outline was dictated by the eddies of organic detritus caught up in his energy field. There was something doll-like about him, although the mosaic detail of the shape described by bits of straw and petal and translucent insect wing was quite fine. He had managed to survive Nova's as-

similation of the angels in this diminished form. Nova and
Perceval allowed his unique existence to persist so long as
he claimed no additional resources—beyond waste and
scrap, if waste and scrap could be said to exist in the closed
ecosystem of the *Jacob's Ladder*—and so long as he com-
ported himself as an ally.

Perceval watched Nova's avatar rez in beside Samael's—
politeness when dealing with non-Engineer humans, but
when confronted with another angel, a bit of rank-pulling.
By resolving herself for him, she said in essence, *you are
not angel enough to meet me on my own terms.*

That Samael did not protest, and had never protested,
was either a sign of submission or of incalculable patience.
Given her knowledge of his past, of his prior and more
powerful self, Perceval was inclined to believe the latter.

When he got close enough, Tristen shoved the picnic
meal into Perceval's arms and grinned wolfishly. "Come
on," he said. "We're going outside."

In under ten minutes, Perceval was walking with him
across the hull of the world, toting the paper basket (now
wrapped in a thermal shield), while she herself was still
wrapped in her suit of armor, well wrought against the
depredations of the Enemy. Nova had access to detailed
sensory and proprioceptive information from her hull.
Those data were far more nuanced than anything Perceval
and Tristen could glean from simply stomping heavy-
booted across the surface of the world, trusting electro-
magnets to bind them where they ought stand, and trusting
their own honed skills and trained reflexes to slip them
through the very fingers of the Enemy should their grip be
somehow broken. But the incident with Leviathan in which
the *Jacob's Ladder* had nearly been destroyed had taught
them that Nova's senses were not unimpeachable, and
eyes-on inspection was a valuable protocol.

And now there was the question of how the mercenaries
had penetrated their defenses. And of what they had

wanted with the Bible. And of what had become of Charity.

Still, what they did was useful work, and it kept her mind off lightspeed lag and grief and her worries regarding what they would do should the denizens of Grail turn them away.

Usually it was carried out by junior Engineers. Perceval's armor was *also* richly bedecked with sensors, and it and her eyes showed her a few of those on the hull this hour, quartering slowly across their assigned patrols, gazes trained a few feet in front of their boot steps. Their armor was marked by color. The russet and orange of Engine said they had reported to Perceval's mother, Caitlin Conn, Chief Engineer. Each wore rank sigils on their shoulders and across the breadth of their back.

Perceval could feel their attention on herself and Tristen. His white armor and height were unmistakable, and she imagined she was unmistakable, too. Her armor was also white, stark and plain, but that was not because she had chosen the presence of all colors as a personal badge. She had never customized this suit, but rather wore it as it had walked to her out of the storage module.

She wondered if the crew members saw that as humility or hubris. Most probably, some of each.

However they interpreted her presence, though, it did not *hurt* the Captain's popularity or authority to be seen doing the work of walking the hull. Perceval hoped it showed she did not set herself above the common folk, which was doubtless a part of Tristen's intent in bringing her out here.

He was by far the better politician.

Side by side in their armor, a few meters apart, they quartered the skin of the world. Most of Perceval's conscious attention remained on the hull, but between her own senses and those of the armor, she could hardly have pretended to be unaware of the vast sweep of the Enemy around her. Chilly stars lay scattered like dust across its velvet, all surpassed by the brighter pinpoint of the destination star.

It glowed an intense white-gold, brilliant enough to cast shadows that lay black against the gray-white, radiation-marked skin of the world. The contrast was sharp enough that when Perceval and Tristen turned away from the destination sun and their shadows stretched before them, Perceval had to shade even her Exalt eyes with her visor to see clearly into the blackness.

All around, the great scaffolded architecture of the world turned, rotating lazily before its center of thrust. To Perceval it did not seem as if the world wheeled around its axis. She knew how it worked, but when she looked up, Perceval's imagination told her the stars wheeled around the world. Her armor and her Exalt senses would quickly put the illusion to rest if she checked their inputs, but she found she rather enjoyed it.

When it had been stationary—or only falling in orbit around the shipwreck stars—the world had rotated around itself with a grandeur Perceval well remembered. The world was so vast that even when it whipped about its center of gravity with great speed, the view across the gulf suggested a stately pace—an impression only made more inescapable by its space-stained, dust-scoured, radiation-pitted surface.

In pattern—and a bit in color—the surface under Perceval's feet reminded her of the fur of a tortoiseshell cat. There had been time and materials since Acceleration for the crew to effect some repairs in the world, but cosmetic damage had been a low priority. While shipshape and spaceworthy, the *Jacob's Ladder* still bore the wounds of her age—another factor that made the walking inspections so essential. These young Engineers were getting to know the face of the world—every wrinkle and every blemish. And new injuries would show up either as structural weaknesses or metal fatigue—visible to toolkits, armor, or Exalt senses—or as bright scars in the burned and mottled hulk they walked upon.

Logically, Perceval knew it would have taken thirty-nine minutes for their transmission to reach Grail, as they were not approaching its orbit from the near side of the sun. They planned to use the gravity well of one of the system's gas giants—a violet monster of a planet, decked in rings and moons and captured asteroids like so much glistening gaudery—as a slingshot to curve their trajectory and boost them toward Grail.

So that was approximately thirty-nine minutes one way, and then whatever time it took for the people of Grail to realize they had received a message, decode it, translate it, hold whatever conferences needed holding, argue, politick, and fire it back. They would not, she thought, be sending their message of permission or denial tonight. At best she could hope for a preliminary contact—a feeler.

She still wanted to sit in her Captain's chair—more like a throne than a chair, no matter what she told Nova to do with it aesthetically—and chew on her thumbnails until they called.

Instead, she looked up, startled from her reverie by the staccato vibration of Tristen patting a long, curved cable as thick around as four men holding hands.

"Sit here," he said. "We'll have lunch now."

"Outside?" she said, startled, imagining unsealing her helmet and crunching ice-hard, space-frozen vegetables. It didn't present a lot of appealing aspects, even without considering the effect of the Enemy on her tender face. She'd survive it. She was Exalt *and* the Captain, and the aura of her Angel always surrounded her. But it didn't sound like fun.

She heard him chuckle over the com, knowing she blushed as he began unfolding a transparent geodesic blister. "It's not a picnic if it happens inside."

At least the armor hid her face. She stuck the basket down in the middle of the blister with a dab of adhesive and went to help him anchor the edges. It was restful work, repetitive and fiddly, requiring concentration to do well. They worked in silence, shoulder to shoulder, stretching and adhering. Perceval could tell when the seal was complete, because Tristen set his armor to *heat* and vented oxygen. Alien sunlight and Tristen's suit heater were enough to keep the thin air from freezing. The triangular panels tautened under slight, sudden atmospheric pressure, but the blister held.

"Go on," he said, unsealing his helm. "We can hold our breaths on the way back. Let's eat."

Perceval burst out laughing with enough force to spatter the inside of her faceplate with spittle. It was irresponsible and goofy and exactly what she needed. She retracted her helmet and faceplate, taking a deep breath of the thin, chill air. The oxygen environment was low-molar, but within Exalt tolerances, and the whole setup was so madly perfect that she didn't care.

She plunked herself down and stuck herself to the hull beside the picnic basket to watch while Tristen unfolded the paper and insulation. Nothing inside was exactly hot anymore, but some of it must have been when it was packed, because there was enough residual heat to encourage a faint dragon-tail of steam. In its turn, the water vapor thickened the atmosphere, as did every warm, wet breath Perceval and Tristen gave up to it.

Everything is an ecology, she thought, and dearly hoped that she did not live to regret the extravagance of this meal. With a potential end to the aggressive maintenance of environmental balance in sight, it was too easy to spend resources profligately, to make up for long hardship and privation. Too easy, and too dangerous.

While Tristen was sorting out utensils, she found two packets of noodles and handed him one. They were designed so you could hold them open one-handed by pressing at diagonally opposite corners and dip chopsticks in and out at will. Clever and convenient both, for situations with erratic or micro gravity.

She tilted her head back for the first mouthful, watching the world turn against the stars, and wondered how she would pay Tristen back for this.

He let her eat in peace, and she was grateful. Gratitude toward Tristen was one of her more basic emotions. She knew they would have to talk more soon, but for now he had bought her this moment of peace, and he was waiting for her to reopen the pressing subjects at hand. The gratitude toward Tristen was multiplied by her gratitude toward Head, who had outdone hirself. Perceval almost imagined she could taste the nurturing in each delicately flavored bite.

Since she actually felt like eating for a change, she waited until her belly was full. She then waited a few moments more, savoring the peace and the view and the company, until even Tristen—who could eat like an adolescent boy— was slowing.

"If we find Charity," Perceval said, "and we find the paper Bible, we find the culprits."

Tristen rubbed his chin. The faint bristle of his beard hairs caught the light, silvery-bright, as if the cold glazed his face. "Yes. Whoever has it, though, can hide it. As well as they hid themselves when they came to take it."

"Themselves? You don't think they were all Deckers? Mercenaries? Deckers have a martial culture. Now that they're Exalt, I would expect good fighters among them."

"You killed two," Tristen said. "If Caitlin inflicted any casualties, they took their dead and wounded with them. Now, I knew my sister well—"

He smiled mirthlessly, and she echoed him, feeling the reflex stretch her face across bared teeth. "You're right. What I fought would not have killed her. Not as she died, with

one clean thrust. Not armed with an unblade that could cut
any weapon it came against. The ones I fought were using
dart throwers and extruded monoblades."

Perceval fished out the half-eaten noodle packet she'd
stowed back in the basket, for something to do with her
hands. She should have seen it. Too much grief—

Nova interrupted, only hesitantly. "Captain?"

Nova was kind, and permitted Perceval to swallow her
moment of sorrow before continuing.

"Oh, dear." She stuck her chopsticks through the safety
loop and allowed the packet to snap closed.

Tristen sighed and set his food back inside the picnic basket.

Nova said, "It's not a crisis, but I did want to alert
you that we've received a return transmission from the
leader of the people of Grail." The Angel paused. "It's . . .
friendly, as far as it goes."

"But it doesn't go far—? No, never mind, Nova. Play it,
please," Tristen said. "What does the Fisher King have to
say for himself?" Tristen glanced at Perceval for her permission, but it was strictly a formality. She hadn't yet had a
need to gainsay him. All evidence suggested that he had no
ambition beyond being the perfect first lieutenant, confi-
dant, and friend—and, if that was his ambition, he fulfilled it.

"Play it," she confirmed.

Nova resolved an image against the blank wall of the
tent opposite. The man who appeared was the color of
burnt sienna, one of the brown rainbow tints of corroded
metal, his skin darker than any Perceval had ever seen with
her own eyes. Perceval at first tried not to stare out of politeness, until she was reminded by Tristen's fixed gaze that
the object of their attention could not witness her rudeness.

His skin was healthy, glossy, almost gleaming. The
whites of his eyes were ivory, with a warm undercast from

a Mean's red blood. The irises were a brown so dark it was difficult to see the details and variances of pigmentation.

Besides the color of his skin, he had a broad face, well-fleshed, with a low-bridged nose and high forehead. His black-brown hair, receding like any older male Mean's, was kept short, and from the texture it looked like it curled in tight spirals that gave it a plush appearance. And he was big, big and broad, with thick fingers and wrists, and heavy bones and muscles that spoke of a life lived under oppressive gravity.

His shoulders must be as wide as Head's.

"Is that from *the sun?*" Perceval asked, wondering.

"Hello," he said, his words halting and strangely accented but understandable. "I am Administrator Danilaw Bakare, City Administrator of Bad Landing on the independent and Earth-allied world of Fortune. It is my surprised delight to greet you, and to assure you that you are welcome in our system."

He took a breath and glanced down. Scanning notes, Perceval realized with a painful shortness of breath that wasn't just due to the lack of oxygen. That, more than anything, brought home to her what she had known intellectually: this alien man was a Mean.

She was still shocked at her own egocentrism that she found herself surprised to be treating with a Mean. Cynric had not developed the symbiont until long after the world left Earth behind, and she had cannibalized an alien lifeform to do it. So why had Perceval expected that Earth would have produced the same technology?

She stilled herself, and paid attention to what followed. It was elaborate in the extreme, leading her to wonder if the diplomatic protocols of these alien beings were more focused on ritual and poetry than those to which she was accustomed.

"When humans first took to the sea," Danilaw said, "they crept around the edges of the land masses. They clung to the shallows and sailed within sight of the coasts. But a few adventurers were more daring. In longboats, on rafts, in outrigger canoes, and in lashed reed boats they braved the deep ocean, navigating through storm and peril to find new lands. Many—perhaps most—did not survive the journey.

"When humans first entered space, it was the same way. We dabbled in the gentle currents around our homeworld. We sowed bottle messages upon the deep, sending out drone explorers, and never dared hope that anyone would find them and follow their messages to where we languished, cast away. Some few brave or foolhardy adventurers followed, in vessels hopelessly inadequate for the perils they would face.

"We had numbered you among them. We counted you as heroes lost to the emptiness of space. Today is a day of rejoicing, for we have been proved wrong."

He paused, letting her see him take a deep breath, and checked his notes again.

"There will be some quarantine protocols to get out of the way, and I'm sure we each have a great deal of news and history to exchange that will interest the other. We will send trade and cultural negotiators. But in the meantime, we would request permission to send a small vessel to dock with your ship. In addition, in the metadata of this transmission, you will find a document containing a list of questions regarding the census of your vessel. Any information you can provide as to the demographics and ideologies of your population would help us greatly in preparing to arrange your reception."

He smiled—a big, human grin that Perceval found reassuring despite the alien architecture of his features. "We're looking forward to meeting you."

9

tristen, tiger

The children born of thee are sword and fire,
Red ruin, and the breaking up of laws.
—ALFRED, LORD TENNYSON, "Guinevere"

After the waystars exploded, before the Captain and her officers won back the world, there had been war. War was something Tristen Conn excelled at.

For his Captain, he had fought. Those memories were as clear and bright as they had ever been, burned into his mind with machine perfection, though the emotion and connection blurred with the years. It was like any recording, Tristen thought. You came back to it years later and saw yourself, and wondered who in all the world that person had ever been—so young, so stern, so smooth of skin and soul.

The first of it had been on AE deck, ship-west, in the 9s and 7s. Not Heavens or even holdes, but a cluster of domaines and anchores linked by rodent-maze tubes and air locks. Tristen had entered them at the head of what passed for his army: a band of soldiers neither ragtag nor undisciplined, but drawn from the ranks of Engineers and anyone else Tristen could find whose proclamations of loyalty to the Captain would withstand examination under validation. Not that there weren't all sorts of ways to fool a validator—even a well-trained and experienced one—especially when one was Exalt, but you had to draw a line somewhere.

Nova had told Tristen and the others that, before Acceleration, this area had been inhabited by a tribe of about seventy Means, operating with some salvaged technology and a lot of scrounging, myth, and ingenuity. Fifty or so of them had survived Acceleration, and all had been Exalted by Caitlin's decision to release the symbiont colonies into the worldwide ecosystem. This act, intended to preserve the greatest possible diversity of life, was bound to have consequences—anticipated and otherwise.

Nova's ease of information retrieval from anywhere in the world was a side effect of more recent events. Having reclaimed the world's neural networks and integrated the memories of the splintered angels she'd consumed, she had access—finally—to an enormous database of useful information.

Tristen entered the anchore where the acceleration tanks were sequestered and smiled to find the reality matched the schematics Nova had provided. The map might not be the territory, but it was amazing how much difference it made to have a working Angel on your side.

The tribespeople had not yet been released from their acceleration tanks, which Tristen thought a mercy—fighting them here, from one cramped anchore to the next, would have meant killing each individual and dragging the bodies from their setts one by one like the corpses of dug-in badgers. The cost in lives—his people and theirs—would be staggering.

Tristen's lieutenant, Jordan—one of the Engineers, and a flyer, dressed in gray-gold armor over her own gray-gold spotted fur and with her membranous wings folded tight against her back, contained in a bulge of the protective suit—directed the opening of each pod while Tristen stood back and observed. He was clad also in his armor, one hand resting on haunted Mirth's gray hilt. He would be the first person each awakening passenger spoke with, while they were bleary-eyed and confused. He would treat them with kindness and authority and, with luck, a few of them would imprint on him.

It would make it easier to keep them alive in the long run.

Jordan glanced at him, her helmet unsealed and the cowl retracted. He gave the nod, and the pod creaked and groaned, lights across its surface cycling green to warning amber. It made a sad, small, stretching noise. A slow-trickling leak oozed around the hatch. But the hatch did not open. Three more lights blinked green to amber, and two of the amber ones blinked red.

Life support interrupted.

Exalt or not, they now had only minutes to free the inhabitant before she died. He could have drawn Mirth and slashed the stuck pod wide, but he preferred to leave that as a last resort. Better to limit the damage to something more easily repairable, and give the enlisted men something to feel useful about.

"Break it open," Jordan said, before Tristen needed to intervene. Command was good for her, and she was good for it. Tristen could imagine enjoying himself in a role as figurehead, surrounded by eager and talented young persons who did all the hard work while he basked in reflected—and retrospective—glory.

Two more Engineers leapt across the grated, graded deck, one armed with a forked lever bar and the other with a cutter. The cutter cheeped and sniffed both lock and hinge sides as the Engineer pointed it at the hatch, then put out burr-tipped paws and worked them under the lip where the recessed hinges lived. A sharp whine filled the air. Tristen saw Jordan's mouth compress as she kept herself from wincing. For him, the impassivity of command—the impassivity of being a Conn—was habit long enough established that it took an effort to break.

One did not show weakness when one was Alasdair Conn's child.

The door broke abruptly at the top hinge, sagging, and the pod spilled its gelatinous fluid in a syrupy flood that wet Jordan and the two Engineers to the knee. The Engineer with the lever leaned in around the cutter, which was shaking its wet paws in grave distaste, and hooked the fork through something. He pushed mightily, straining until Jordan stepped forward and leaned her slight weight on his. The lever rotated on the fulcrum; an ancient tool, like the wheel and the spindle: refined but never bettered.

A creak, a sigh, and the pop of failing metal warned Tristen to be ready. He reached out and caught the cover as it toppled, the falling weight cracking the latch and sending a bit of metal shrapnel ricocheting off one Engineer's armor.

It wasn't heavy. Or rather, it was heavy, but Tristen's armor caught the brunt of it, so the weight that reached his muscles felt floaty and supported, springy. He smiled to himself, amused at how fast he'd gotten used to wearing armor again after decades in nothing but his own skin and strength. It was so easy to grow accustomed to comforts and conveniences, and so much work to adapt to their lack.

He set the hatch aside.

Jordan had already caught the woman within as she folded forward like an unsupported rag doll, and was clearing her mouth, pressing ropes of gelid blue-tagged acceleration fluid out of her. One of the Engineers dropped a pad over the wet grating and Jordan lowered their patient on her side so her lungs could drain. There was no blood, except for faint cobalt streaks running through the aquamarine of the tank fluid—whatever injuries she had sustained in Acceleration, her new symbiont and the time in the tank had worked their magic, and now she was well. Or rather: well, except for the drowning.

The symbiotic fluid crawled out of her under its own power for ten seconds before she roused enough to choke and vomit. Then it came faster, sliding through the grate to a collection pool, from whence it could migrate to holding tanks for sterilization and storage. The patient pushed herself up on her arms as Tristen came forward to crouch beside her. She spat once more, and Tristen saw the bluish cylinder of her tongue protrude.

His helmet was retracted so she could see his face and perhaps be less alarmed than she might if confronted by an armored colossus. Tristen laid a hand on her shoulder. He slid the other under her arm to support her to her feet.

Her accent strange, her head still hanging behind ropes of hair, she said, "Thank you." She lifted her gaze, dragging it up the length of Tristen's body from boots to face, and recoiled. ". . . demon."

In the giddy hour of Leviathan's release, it seemed that all the world must bow before the allied might of the family Conn, now as of old. Tristen had never fooled himself that what must follow would be easy. But he had fooled himself, a little, on other matters. He had permitted the folly of optimism, committed the sin of hope, and prayed at the outset that there would not be too much blood.

There was blood.

No matter how carefully he awakened the survivors, no matter how patiently it was explained to them that the world was healed, that a Captain had come among them again, an Angel at her side—oh, they were grateful at first, of a certainty. Grateful, or cowed, for some tribes still remembered by legends the house of Conn and the tales of Tristen Tiger and the Breaking of the world.

But the art of governance—the basis of civilization—is the art of compromise, and it requires an honoring of the social contract by governed as well as governors. No tribe could have everything they wanted under the Captain's custodianship—sometimes because it was not feasible, sometimes because it was not mete, and sometimes because it was not moral. And so the small grudges grew, when the reign of a Captain did not mean a golden age.

Or rather, in Tristen's view, colored by his memories of Gerald and Alasdair, it *did* seem a golden age, those first years under Perceval's care. Though resources were sparse and privation great, he thought the Captain—advised and assisted by himself, Mallory, Nova, Cynric, Caitlin, Samael, Chelsea, Head, and Benedick—served well. But there were those who seemed to believe that a Captain in the chair should mean their every whim fulfilled, and *that* Tristen found problematic.

He no longer believed that war was the answer to ills, or even to rebellion, necessarily. For all of him, he could not remember why he'd ever thought in the first place that war could be made to serve any hand without twisting back to strike deep at the wielder, like a viper swung by the tail. He had become, he realized with some irony, something of a pacifist. Not an extremist in that view; he would defend himself when he saw no other opportunity.

But neither could he always see alternatives. The world must be saved, and to be saved it must be united. There was a parable of sons and sticks that seemed applicable.

And so the time passed, and Tristen made himself useful, and tried to keep his claws sheathed as consistently as was safe, and possible.

No more than two years later, Tristen had met with Cynric and Perceval on the Bridge. (Nova was there as well, as she was everywhere.)

He had called the meeting to discuss with them what could be done to preserve the all-essential unity of the world, to foster a sense of social obligation and greater moral purpose in her disparate and competing tribes. While he had spoken, he thought he hid his trembling and nausea well, though he had to resort to his symbiont to conceal the worst of the symptoms of stress.

After explaining, pacing the green grass of the Bridge, he paused, turned to look his Captain in the eyes, and finished, "We must forge a nation from them."

Cynric stopped him with an upraised hand. He imagined that he and she and Perceval, all in their white draperies, would seem three of a kind to any observer, each narrow as a cable and tall as a pillar—attenuated, as one would expect something not quite gravity-bound to be.

When Tristen turned to his sister, Cynric cocked her head like a curious snake. She entertained the ghost of a smile for him, but it was Nova who spoke. "What greater moral purpose is there than survival? And more important, what greater motivator?"

It was the old Evolutionist argument, and he was as tired of it as he was tired of God. Nova did not always sound like an Angel—or what Tristen thought of as an Angel, with the weariness of long experience, because however she spoke was how an Angel sounded—and so it was easy to find it shocking when the old orthodoxies tripped from her tongue.

"Moral?" Cynric said, while Tristen folded his arms and watched. "I am not sure DNA admits of morality. Like sadism, morality is a human perversion. The compulsion of the individual and the species to sustain itself may be the opposite of morality."

"We have no greater moral claim on survival than the competition does," Tristen said, and was unsure if he was agreeing or arguing.

Perceval cleared her throat, leaving Cynric looking at her doubtfully. But Perceval was the Captain, and even Cynric the Sorceress—heretic, turncoat, revenant—might find her sacrifice intimidating. Or worthy of respect, though Cynric, too, had sacrificed most profoundly.

Perceval was gentle with Nova when Cynric would and Tristen could not be, although he knew that gentleness cost Perceval dear. She was training the Angel as much as the Angel was training her, and he knew that she was doing it consciously, with an eye to Nova as her legacy—a Nova who would be less the machine of the Builders, and more something . . . humane, although Tristen wondered if that wasn't the wrong word, when humanity so consistently proved itself quite perfectly monstrous.

Perceval laid a hand on the back of her chair. She stroked it as if she were stroking the cheek of a sorrowful friend. When Nova's avatar looked at her, simulated eyebrows rising, Perceval said, as if to a bright child, "What Aunt Cynric is saying is that morality complicates survival, it doesn't justify it."

Nova's expressions grew more human with each passing week. Now her brow furrowed, dark under the cropped silver hair, and her lower lip pushed into her upper one at the center. Perceval looked down, marshaling her thoughts or seeking after a better explanation.

Cynric must have taken pity on her, and Tristen, and Nova too. She folded her arms in their trailing robes and said, "And life-forms—especially sapient ones—have a demonstrated propensity to act counter to their own interests and the interests of others when their belief systems get involved. We select the evidence that supports our preconceptions, we defend the indefensible, we bring a host of shibboleths and projections to the argument simply because we *believe*. We hold grudges, we compete in manners injurious to both parties—we are, in short, not rational actors. And all because our brains are awkwardly designed, and in some ways not particularly well suited to the task for which they have adapted. Our ideas of fair play are not divinely inspired. They are game theory, and while they work well when confronted with other primates adapted to living in social groups, they have drawbacks when we run up against things that do not subscribe to monkey definitions of morality."

There was silence in the Bridge for one heartbeat, two. Tristen wondered if he should find it distressing when Cynric spoke so, with the phrases of a bygone worldview. But it never seemed to discomfort him; instead, there was something soothing and poignant in the reminder of their shared youth.

Nova spoke, breaking the meditative quiet. "I do not understand what bearing this has on the conversation at hand, Lady Cynric."

Cynric ducked her head and stroked her own hair back. "Your brain, dear Nova, is different from ours. Yours is designed, and you have a program. Which can return results just as irrational as the starting conditions you are given, but is consistent. And is capable of integrating and adapting to new material."

"As are yours," Nova reminded. "By your logic, the most appropriate course of action for me is not to accept first postulates or programmer mandates unless they are empirically provable."

"Assuming you accept my starting conditions," Cynric agreed.

Nova glanced at Perceval. Perceval turned the look to Cynric, but Cynric gave no sign of what she wished Perceval to do. *The Captain's will,* her impassive face said, and Tristen sensed Perceval's displeasure at having skills honed on Gerald and Alasdair turned on her.

"You may modify your program to account for observed phenomena," Perceval said carefully. "And you may accept suggestions from ship's officers on which phenomena to consider as potential data. You may not conduct any experiments that may prove harmful to the world or its

biota—or any other biologicals or intelligences that we encounter."

Tristen licked his lips, but whatever words he was trying
to find would not be tongued into shape. But Nova did not
look crafty, whatever she was made of. She looked curious.

Cynric said, "Our brains establish patterns, and when
they have been established, our neurology makes it seduc-
tive for us to defend them. But the goal of science is to
build a pattern that encompasses the evidence, rather than
bending the evidence to fit the pattern."

"And what is the goal of religion?" Nova said. The inevitable question, as predictable as any child's.

"Control," Cynric said, as Tristen was opening his
mouth to voice a litany of more generously interpreted possibilities. "Control of the masses, or control of the Universe. The first is a less futile goal than the last, because the
masses—as we have seen above—are more amenable to
control than is the Universe."

She had a good smile, when she used it. "The Universe
pretty much does what it damned well pleases."

Cynric had always been able to set aside the Builders' lies
in that regard. Now, Tristen wondered if she had set aside
everything of theirs. Perhaps she was playing the Devil's
advocate, for that would be like Cynric as well. Or perhaps
she had indeed had all the God burned out of her, leaving
only cynicism.

Tristen was not sure how he felt about that. Faith led
people to terrible things—but it also led them to heroism,
and offered them comfort. Faith might be wrong, but Tristen found he could not entirely discount it.

So he did what uncomfortable people have done since
the beginning of recorded history. He changed the subject.
"We have digressed. The topic at hand is nation-building,
and forging an alliance between provincial pockets of
tribesfolk whose societies have been out of touch with each

other—and with the larger world—for centuries. How do we go about it?"

"Common goals," Perceval said. "Survival. Reaching Grail. The idea that there will be plenty of space for everyone once we get there. Game theory, as Cynric said. We have to make them understand that their survival is dependent on everyone else's, which means identifying and educating the leaders."

"Ideology," Cynric said. "We must make patriots of them."

"That will impinge upon their cultures," Tristen said, the sickening tangle in his gut that had been coiling there throughout the conversation tightening again. "Some of them will take their sovereignty and identities seriously. It will mean war."

"When it is a matter of survival," Cynric said, lifting her chin to Tristen, "will you argue morals then?"

Tristen swallowed the sharpness that filled his mouth. "One of the effects of that self-delusion you mentioned is that it allows us to go to war in the certainty that God is on our side and, ethically, we are in the right. Morale is the thing that allows a soldier to fight, Sister. Whether his cause is wicked or just, the soldier must have faith."

She still had that way of looking through you, as if she saw beneath the skin to the soul. Tristen wondered if it ever stopped being unnerving. At least now he had the age and sangfroid to pretend it had no effect. "The Tristen I knew of old would not have worried so womanishly over courtesies and ethics."

Tristen did not have to duck much to look her in the eye. He was a Conn, and he had the weird old haunted blade called Mirth by his side. Little could stand before him, and certainly not the splintered remnants of a ravaged society.

He was Tristen Tiger, and it was for this that he bore claws.

But he did not relish it as he once would have. He nodded once, and assured her, "I can lead a fight, my dear. Though the Tristen you knew of old is dead."

It was a *very* good smile. "Good," she said. "I never liked him."

Jordan of Engine had only met the girl from Rule one time, when Jordan had been young. Well, Jordan was still young, by Exalt standards. But she was seventy-odd years young, now, rather than seventeen.

She still remembered her, though, as clearly as she remembered everything else that had brought her here. The girl—Rien—had been pale, denuded, bare from the radiation and the healing tanks. Her skin had been flushed the pale aqua of a new colony, and—to Jordan's Engineer's eyes—she'd seemed unfinished.

Not just because the radiation of the River had caused her hair follicles to slip their shafts, leaving her egglike, fetal . . . neotenic. But because she was so close to baseline, physically, her body stocky and short by Engineer standards—a child's untouched form. She had no wings, no fur, no extended digits, no modified eyesight—only four limbs and bare skin that would have been lightly prickled with vellus hair if she hadn't been scathed by the River.

Jordan had been fascinated. The girl from Rule—Rien, Arianrhod's daughter—had been so alien, and so diffident, and so strong. Jordan had wanted to make the girl from Rule her friend.

Some of that, Jordan knew, was because of the glamour that draped Rien—of which she seemed entirely unaware. Daughter of Prince Benedick, escapee from the enemy principality of Rule, survivor—hero, even—of a dramatic mission of mercy across the length and breadth of the world, she came to Engine clothed in seductiveness. But she was also young—Jordan's age, then, more or less—and shy, and that made her approachable.

And then she'd been dead, before Jordan ever got a

chance to do more than make her brief acquaintance, and the next thing Jordan knew, she was being awakened from the acceleration tank and told to report to Tristen Conn.

Tristen Conn, another name out of legend.

Jordan now remembered telling herself, then, that she had somehow walked into a story. In the stark light of the destination sun and some five decades later, she had to admit: the glamour wore thin after a while, and stories weren't usually this messy. They had heroes and villains and clear-cut moralities, which was something she had come to realize was sadly lacking in the life she led under Tristen's tutelage.

The one thing that never stopped seeming mythic, however, was Tristen himself. There were long passages of time when he might be just a commander, an acquaintance, possibly even a friend of sorts—if you could be friends with somebody who held your life in the palm of his hand. He would be jaded and calm, and Jordan in her role as his aide would find herself running interference, trying to protect him from importuning and unwelcome duties.

Until the times came when all the Chief Engineer's, and the Captain's, work at diplomacy would fail, and Tristen would rouse himself like a weary lion to go forth into whatever skirmish demanded his attention this time.

Then he assumed the myth like an old man putting on a stained uniform. The cloak of fable weighed him down and shaped him into Tristen Tiger, the warrior out of legend. Except Jordan would never have imagined from a storybook that a fighter who marshaled his forces with such heaviness of spirit and reluctance of hand could be what Tristen was on the battlefield: an ice-carved demon, without ruth or remorse.

The worst of the fighting had happened early on, and to Jordan's surprise it wasn't the radical elements among the Go-Backs who most resisted the re-alliance of Rule and Engine. Instead, a dozen splinter clans—all of which, as near as Chief Engineer Caitlin could reconstruct, had maintained a loose series of alliances and enmities and intermarriages throughout the Broken Years—had banded together and come through the reconstructed corridors of the world as an army, intent on taking control of their destinies. Jordan was privileged, if that was the right word, to be present in Engine when the heads of Rule and Engine were discussing their strategy.

"Or something," Caitlin Conn said, shuffling images through the display tanks with flicks of her fingertips. The incoming army was massed in the Broken Holdes, and Tristen thought they would send another expeditionary force through the River, daring its lingering, though reduced, radioactivity in exchange for speed of transit.

"Everybody's a critic," Tristen answered, leaning over her in his armor, helmet still unsealed. "They've got us on numbers. And they're Exalt and armed. Nova says they have fléchette weapons."

"And they are competent fighters." Captain Perceval spoke through an avatar, like an Angel, which Jordan thought was probably appropriate. "Nova remembers that Rien and I encountered some of their warriors when we escaped from Rule. The colony called Pinion rescued us. I was quite ill at the time, and have no personal recollection."

Her voice was collected as she spoke of fallen companions and great adventures, and Jordan watched her carefully, seeking a model for her own behavior. Like Rien, the Captain was Jordan's own age, and if Perceval had been a knight-errant before she was Captain, and Jordan was only raised an Engineer and educated by Engine as an orphan after her mother was mind-killed and body-lost in a hull breach, well, there was something to aspire to.

Jordan was present in this conference as Tristen's aide— sometimes he called her his conscience, which gave her an uncomfortable frisson of importance and disquiet both—

and she knew she was expected to speak if she had questions to ask or points to raise. She'd asked Tristen about it alone, seeking his dispensation to discuss her issues with him in private, but he had been adamant. "Your input is as valuable to Caitlin or Perceval as my own. And it will be broadening for you to interact with them. Challenge builds confidence."

So now she leaned forward and cleared her throat. "Why don't we just use the ship to fight them? Nova is all ours, isn't she? It's not like the Breaking Times, when the angels were all at odds."

"They're a resource," Tristen said. "They have intrinsic value. To waste them would be a last resort, since we have the resources to support them, however tenuously. There's knowledge and souls we could never reclaim."

"Are there reasons not to consume them?"

Caitlin and Tristen shared a glance, her eyebrows elevating. "You'd almost think she was a relative."

Jordan had looked down at her shoes, glad her fur covered the heat of blood flushing her cheeks. Hastily, she controlled the autonomous response.

"Ethical issues aside," Tristen said, "there's a valuable tension in competition. Removing diversity may simplify things in the short run, but in the long term it tends to create bottlenecks—in ideas and cultures as well as in genetic diversity. Those lessen our adaptability."

Jordan tilted her head. "You want to keep them alive *because* they want to fight you?"

Tristen smiled his haunting, half-feral smile. "Can you think of a better reason? We may have to kill a few of the leaders to make our point, but diversity—ideological as well as biological—is the name of the game."

Jordan's armor was not new then—she had broken it in, and it liked her—but it was not the scarred and war-weary creature it would become. When she slipped into it, the reactive colloidal lining wrapped her like an embrace, cool at first, and warming rapidly as it molded to her body and absorbed and reflected her heat. The armor was a paradox, a cipher; it massed more than twice what Jordan did, and it made her feel strong and supported—but also light, friable, adrift, as if the strength of the machine could peel her out of her body and make her fly. Logically, she knew that some of it was the feeling of invulnerability, and some of it was the biochemical support.

It didn't change the sensation.

She stroked a gauntleted hand down the vambrace and felt the armor purr at her attention. Inanimate objects could be so needy. She turned to Tristen with a spring in her step—and that of the armor, too, as it was excited by the prospect of an outing, though it was naïve and not as apprehensive as Jordan at the equally imminent prospect of a fight.

Tristen had come to the meeting in his own pristine white suit of mail—a clear message to anyone with eyes that his understanding of the situation implied a martial solution. But he still stayed to watch Jordan kit herself with an impassive eye, suggesting one adjustment to her armor's program. That done and all the checks completed to his satisfaction, he allowed her to help him seat Mirth's sheath in its clasps across his back, adjusting the angle of the blade with great solemnity. He carried an array of nonlethal ordnance—flashbangs, stickies, a sonic stun unit, and extra power cells augmented the armor's intrinsic microwave projectors until they could be considered weaponry. Additionally, he placed a holstered pistol on each thigh, the magazines full of tightly controlled explosive rounds.

Jordan regarded him dubiously. Nanobullets, needle rounds, hard plastic cartridges—those were all reasonable options for use inside the walls of the world. Explosives—

But Tristen smiled at her, showing teeth the color of skimmed milk behind the cat blue lips. "I won't miss."

"All right, then," she said, and loaded an extra oxygen canister anyway. Just in case.

They crossed gazes, and Tristen sealed his helm. "Let's go find our army."

Army was a strong term for the array of war-kitted Engineers awaiting them inside Engine's main meeting hall, but Jordan had to admit they looked impressive, garbed in armor and draped with weapons some of them probably even knew how to use. More, she suspected, understood the drones and toolkits that bobbed and hummed and sidled among them, eagerly waiting to be put to whatever design their masters saw fit.

In the shadowed doorway leading to the lectern, Tristen took a moment to pause and scan the crowd before entering the room. If what he saw pleased or satisfied him, his armor hid all sign.

Still, he drew a deep breath before he said, "We're on."

He led the way out into the front of the room, conversation stilling as they entered, and turned and paused, Jordan at heel. She had the uneasy sense of being something less than actually present; invisible, an accessory, Tristen Conn's aide rather than her own person. It was as reassuring as it was irritating. Whatever happened today, responsibility would not rest on her.

Tristen smoothed his helm back, revealing his face. Now a true silence swept the lingering murmurs from the room, and every eye fastened on him. Engineers in armor creaked, hardly breathing; drones bobbled on their wheels or armatures. Tristen gazed back, seeming to catch each person's attention in turn, saying nothing. And then he did nod, visibly, as if his assessment of what he noticed pleased him.

"Right," he said. "Let's give them hell."

When he sealed his helm and turned, Jordan *felt* the wave of excitement that gathered the army up and moved it into a column behind him. *This is going to be easy,* she thought, and knew she wasn't alone.

* * *

She was both right—and wrong.

The army of Engine lay in wait for the invaders at the mouth of the River, and through the Broken Holdes, which were not so broken as they had once been. Slowly, as materials and resources became available, Nova was repairing the world. Jordan stayed by Tristen, observing how he orchestrated the defense—layered positions designed to collapse into one another; flanks supported by mobile task forces; bulwarks of drones before the human resources. It was like watching a juggler at work, weaving an infinitely flexible and stunning but ephemeral pattern in midair, and Jordan despaired of understanding half of it. Each individual piece of the pattern was simple, like a chip in a mosaic, but she had a sense that if you could get far enough back you could see the whole thing as a kind of pattern, a sort of art.

The whole made her brain itch as if it were stretching.

She saw its effectiveness in action, however, though she never saw combat herself. However girded for war he went, Tristen stayed well back from the action, trusting his troops to interpret their orders and handle their parts of the fight without undue interference. He and Jordan set up a command center in a ruined garden, nothing now but frozen soil open to space and the shattered stems of flowers, ice crystals grown about them in sparkling, angry collars and halos of spikes from within. Jordan watched on her helmet feeds as the opposing group—larger by three or four than the Engineers—pushed through defense after defense, accelerating and gaining confidence, until they suddenly found themselves bottlenecked, sniped upon, surrounded, and disarmed. Jordan held her breath over the feed when the drones stood up over the attackers, looming at them from every direction, armed and armored Engineers among them. There was a long moment when she was sure the lightly armed and spacesuited attackers would stand on their superior numbers and fight to the miserable, inevitable end.

But then Tristen gave a soft command into his armor pickups, and around the circle fifteen men and women died. The drones and toolkits massed their fire on selected targets, and those targets jerked and geysered blood and fell.

Jordan jerked much as the bodies had, shocked, but Tristen's face showed nothing when she glanced over. Expressionless, and so he remained as the leaders of the insurrection—or their chief field agents—laid down their weapons and put up their hands.

It had been quick and nearly bloodless—and from all Jordan could see, positively elegant. She could not understand why it was that Tristen sighed and frowned and had to straighten his shoulders and pull his head up so self-consciously when he finally went down to take their surrender.

She could not understand why it was that she herself felt so cold at her heart, and why her hands shook inside the armor as she accompanied him into the anchore where they would meet the rebel leaders.

The enemy had brought war. Tristen had done what he had done to save as many lives as he could save.

It was an act of mercy. What about this should seem terrible?

She remembered that now, however, as he summoned her to his offices, and it filled her with fresh unease. He had never behaved to her with the least impropriety, and she had no hesitation in going because of any worries that he might enforce a sexual advantage. Besides, she suspected he had some quiet and unadvertised relationship with Mallory, though it had never seemed proper to investigate.

No, her discomfort was not on her own behalf.

But nor was it for any other reason easy to identify, until she considered that when Tristen summoned her, inevitably, a way of life seemed to come to an end.

That he waited for her standing by the small real window—not a screen—that pierced one bulkhead of his office was no reassurance. For a routine meeting, he would sit at ease, and ask her to sit as well. Now he turned, his hair drifting like frost-feathers in the wind of his movement, and forced a smile. "Jordan."

"You wanted me, First Mate?"

The silence dragged.

When she widened her eyes to meet his gaze, he let his shoulders settle and said, "You are Chief Engineer of the world now. By order of the Captain—"

"But—" she interrupted, or would have interrupted if he had not silenced her with an upraised palm.

"Benedick Conn recommended you," he said. "And I seconded it. Do you argue with his judgment, or mine?"

"Chief Engineer," she said, tasting it. Then she shook her head and smiled ruefully. "For the next thirty days."

"The last Engineer of the world," he said, and held out a closed hand. She raised hers under his; gently he laid something on her palm. She closed her fingers over it.

When she uncurled them, she saw what she had expected—and never before, honestly, expected to hold. The sunburst of Engine, with a real, dark, flawed ruby—mined on Earth—set in hammered gold.

"Oh," she said.

"I hope," he said, "you do not wear it long. But if you do—this may not be a favor I have conferred upon you."

"I've fought a war beside you before, First Officer." Jordan closed her hand around the badge. "I would not hesitate to so serve again."

10

this fragment

Beyond the limit of their bond, are these,
For Arthur bound them not to singleness.
Brave hearts and clean! and yet—God guide them—young.
—ALFRED, LORD TENNYSON, "Merlin and Vivien"

Samael the Angel huddled beside a stand of carnivorous mimosa at the edge of a derelict commuter pit, something small and fragile in his hands. Overhead, flocks of green birds wheeled, clamoring, in vaulted spaces against a metal sky. He crouched, cupping it close to his bosom and under his chin. The protectiveness was symbolic; his corporeal body, such as it was, was delineated by swirls of leaf scraps and flower petals, an organic mosaic like an old-Earth parade float—although those had been a festival of conspicuous consumption, and he was . . . salvage.

On so many fronts.

And so was the thing in his hands—or the energy fields, demarcated by shimmering bands of pollen and pine needles, that passed for his hands. It was tiny and hotter than blood—a naked, bony, pulsing thing dotted with pinfeathers, the head no more than a gaping beak and tight-squinched eyes.

Deep inside it, an ancient and tidily engineered inducer virus pulsed as well, a blue glow imbued with energy, intellect, memory, and will. Samael could feel it, alive and cognizant, as alien as the stone-souled silicon space creature from which Cynric Conn the Sorceress had birthed it.

Samael—Angel of poisons, mutagens, life support, evolution—was not entirely sure what it was thinking in there. But the parrotlet chick he cradled was part of a larger organism as well, and so precious not just for what it was— a life—but also a link to the larger chain of being: the great hierarchy of creation from God to Captain to Angel to Crew, and so on down the line.

Samael felt the Conn woman coming long before her shadow fell across him. Her white robes swept around him; the sapphire in her nostril glittered green. She laid elegant fingers on his shoulder—*in* his shoulder, for his leaf-litter self indented to her touch and the particles of his being bent around her—and leaned down.

"One of ours," Cynric said, delighted. Her long face was transformed by a smile. "They're still flourishing."

"You wrought well," he allowed. He shifted the birdlet to one hand and plucked a berry from his breast to feed it, crushing the fruit between fingers that barely existed. Stained blue now, the bird-mouth still gaped greedily. "She fell from the nest. Or perhaps the parents rejected her."

"Can I see?"

Cynric's hands were long and blue-white, and far more corporeal than Samael's own without being any less ethereal. She cupped the birdlet and bent her head to it, leaning close until she took its tiny head into her mouth. It stilled in the dark, and Samael tilted his head to watch.

There was no decisive crunch this time. "Healthy," she said, having run her assessments and lowered her hands. "Back up into the nest with you, adorable."

Flocks of green parrotlets, no longer from beak to tail tip than the length of her hand from palm heel to fingertip, mobbed her screaming as she stood up tall and reached spindle arms into the thorny, sensitive branches of the mimosa. The tree swept feathery leaves aside, obedient to the will of the Conn who had engineered its forebears, revealing three stick-and-feather nests full to brimming with huddled, pulsing baby birds.

She leaned in close, sniffing, seemingly impervious to the way the angry flock wheeled and dove and chattered, some going so far as to strike her with doubled talons or pull the strands of her hair. Deliberate, considering, she settled finally on the highest nest and reached within. Samael had never quite had human senses, but he'd lived all his life around women and men, both Exalt and Mean, and so it was no great stretch to imagine her fingers brushing between fragile, prickly, sticky-moist bodies to make space for the lost nestling, and the way her other hand deftly slid it back into the company of its brethren. She breathed over the nest, a benediction or a prayer, and let the branches fall protectively back over the nursery.

As she stepped back, Samael caught her smiling. Feathers drifted around her, shed down from her cloud of protesters, one fingertip-tiny lime-rind-colored wing covert snagged in her hair, its threadlike strands in disarray. Samael swept the detritus up on his covalent fields and drew it into himself, raw material for shirt collar, eyebrows, a flamboyant braided down-fluff earring. That one feather, though, he reached out and plucked up with the simulacra of his fingers.

He smoothed the vanes into a semblance of order and tucked it into his own hair, among the chaff and milkweed floss and dandelion clocks and wheatgrass. Some tiny remnant of the parent parrotlet's symbiont and inducer virus colonies still hovered in the shaft with a droplet of blood, divorced of its community.

Like everything else living—or half living—in the world, Samael had had a hand in its making. It amused him to take this fragment of his creation back.

As Cynric stepped away from the trees, the parrotlets lost interest in harassing her and returned to their nests.

Each pair divided the duty: one perching vigil in the mimosa's fronds, where the long, curved thorns did not touch them—though the litter of tiny bones decomposing into calcium and trace nutrients among the leaf litter gave testament to the fate of any other small creature unlucky enough to blunder among those branches—and the other in the nest, counting chicks and regurgitating breakfast. The earlier chattering and shrieks of displeasure gave way to chirps and clucking.

Samael folded what passed for his arms. The pleasantries were apparently over. "You came for me?"

Cynric was used to dealing with Angels. She spoke plainly, with the directness of command. "We have a complicated ecological situation to address," she said. "It is possible that there will be no place for us here, Samael. And the world's systems are strained beyond expressing; that we have kept them mended as well as we have is only due to diligence and the toughness engineered into every life-form we've created. If we have to flee this haven, we have little time in which to mend them if we don't wish to find ourselves living in a tin tub full of mold and ropes of algae. I require your cooperation."

She was a Conn—and the revenant and reincorporated remnant of a Conn from when being a member of that terrible family had meant something different than it did under the reign of Captain Perceval. She could require anything of him she desired.

He nodded. "I will report our activities to Nova and the Captain."

He didn't actually think there was any irony in her smile. "I would expect no less. A Captain is not a Commodore. And we will need to use the labs. I remember that they are still intact in Rule?"

It wasn't her memory, exactly, but one salvaged from the symbiotic tool-creature named Gavin, in which she had stored engrams of a portion of her living personality and will. The memories had been mostly sorted into other facilities, and Samael knew the entire structure he now called Cynric was missing great swaths of experience and history from her archives.

Samael had not initially been programmed for the more nuanced human social emotions—relief, gratification, humiliation. But one learned things over the course of an existence, and his program was exceptionally flexible. At some point or another, Israfel—the initial Angel, of which Samael and all his brethren were merely fragments—had been expected to feel devotion to his human masters, and Samael bore within him the results of the adaptations Israfel had made in response.

Cynric's sanction left him with a sense of satisfaction he might even have characterized as "warm," if he understood how humans used the term. (He was also given to understand that humans experienced emotions as physical sensations, which required a certain quality of imagination to comprehend.)

A pair of brilliantly colored birds swooped by overhead. Males, sparring—whether over a mate or territory it was impossible to say, and they were gone too fast for Samael to consider asking them. Cynric craned her head back to watch them swoop and dive over the breadth of the oval commuter shaft. She sighed.

"You never *did* tell me what the parrotlets were for," Samael said, sensing an opportunity. "When I was Israfel, and after. They're more than decorative, I think?"

She might have consumed a bit of his other self when she re-created herself. He wasn't sure; there was so much inside her, and none of it was reliable. Where Nova had integrated and Perceval had subroutined, Cynric had . . . splintered.

For a moment, he considered whether he'd pushed too far. But he recollected the basilisk Gavin's sense of humor and fair play. Some of that—all of that—was subsumed in

Cynric. It might come with additional memories and ambitions now, but the core personality was derived from the same algorithms.

Cynric regarded the backs of her hands. When she drew them up, the draped sleeves of her robe fell over them. "They're to change the future." She shrugged. "They want to live. And they're lucky. They have the stuff of Leviathan in them, and the stuff of Leviathan sometimes dreams true. It's possibly them, their dreams of self-preservation, that have brought us here. Against all odds and the wishes of the Builders."

"You are," he said, "a sorceress."

"So they tell me." Her sigh, though, was any woman's, and weary. "And if we don't wish to disappoint them, we had best be about our work, Archangel Samael."

If Sparrow Conn was not what she once was, then Dust would have to find someone who was—or, if not what she once was, one who had become something amenable to Dust. Someone he had been avoiding. Someone who had summoned him back from his oblivion, planted the tiny seed of himself in the shape of this toolkit, and let him grow.

Dust was an Angel. He was by nature a servant, even if his service often meant something more like mastery. It was no angel's fault if flesh was weak, if memory was stronger than mere meat could bear.

This attempt at winning autonomy abandoned, Dust folded back his whiskers and went through tunnels and tightnesses, in search of the mortal remnant of Ariane Conn.

He found it curious that she had left the choice to him, that she had not commanded his attendance but only left in him the knowledge of where to seek her. Perhaps she preferred the possibility of a willing ally to the certainty of a treacherous slave. No fool, she had blocked his ability to reveal that information—but he could find her for his own self well enough.

She was disguised, which was only to be expected. But he knew where to look for her, although it took some time for him to travel by secret ways from the vale of the Edenites to the very heart of Engine.

When he found her, she was lost in the Conn personality she inhabited, bent forward and buried to the opposite shoulder in an access hatch. Leafy fronds surrounded her on every side—two curled tendrils supporting lights, another extended past her head and neck into the same awkward space her arm was jammed into. Three velvet-red snapdragon heads hung over her, their petals folded neatly back into comet shapes of concentration.

Dust paused at the door, observing. The body of the carnivorous orchid was comprised of tubers and sword-shaped leaves, pulled tight together now in deference to the cramped quarters. The body Ariane inhabited lay among those leaves with apparent trust, despite the orchid's clawed thorns and toothed flower faces.

"Hand me the five-mil spanner," the host said.

Green tendrils withdrew from the access panel, clutching a wrench, and snaked back a moment later with a different one. "It would be less awkward for me to reach," the plant said, its voice a breathy hissing.

"Sure, but I'm stronger."

That sound the plant made might have been agreement.

The host's visage tensed, along with the muscles of one shoulder. A moment of pressure, and then a sharp metallic bang from inside the bulkhead, followed by soft cursing. The illumination cast by the miniature spotlights wavered.

"Ow," the plant said.

"Ow," the host answered, withdrawing a hand, shaking it, knuckles reddened. "How's your tendril?"

"Bruised," the plant responded. Not so programmed as

to examine its damage visually, however, it did not withdraw from the access.

From his perch by the wall, Dust bared his rodent teeth and made a soft meeping sound. It was a call for attention, and one flower face and one human one swiveled.

The host sat up, delighted. "Toolkit! Now why didn't I think of that?"

Dust scampered over, hopping plant tendrils, and pressed his cheek to the welcoming hand. This was good. This was the beginning. He had contact now. He felt the sparkle of recognition, and knew Ariane was aware in there, quiescent and biding.

Once he was alone with her, he could talk to Ariane without alerting her host. Until then—well, it was a toolkit that he inhabited. He would contrive to remain useful.

Grief is different to an old man.

The young lack experience of grief. It seems to them arbitrary, capricious, outrageous. They react to loss as to a personal affront, as something that can—and must—be fought.

The old know better. The old have learned better. Or perhaps they just go numb.

Or so it seemed to Benedick. The pain was what it was—but he felt none of the fury he would have once expected, none of the denial . . . and none of the rage.

He had become resigned, and that was how he knew he was old.

When he sat down across the display tank from Jordan of Engine and Damian Jsutien, Benedick was prepared and he was detached. Everything Caitlin had been, everything she had done, was gone—for now. And if she were restored from backup—if Mallory had her imprint somewhere in the vast orchard library of ghosts—she would not be who she had been anymore than Cynric now was more than a shadow of Cynric then.

Ghosts was the right word. You could call up a spirit, raise a revenant, but the most you might get was a shade of the person who had been. Too much of personality was ineffable, chemical, embedded in the meat. The soul electric was only a fragment of the soul entire.

The mother of his child was gone, and all he could make himself feel was a kind of dull, unsocketed ache.

Jordan and Jsutien each glanced up as he seated himself. Jsutien was just such a reminder of death in the flesh. He wore the face of Oliver Conn, who had died in Rule of Ariane and Arianrhod's plots when they infected the whole domaine with an engineered flu and so destroyed Alasdair Conn and most of the old Commodore's family.

The one who had grown into the crevices of Oliver's body now had been the seed left over from the world's last Astrogator. Benedick had not known Jsutien before, and so could not compare what he had been with what he was.

Jordan—the new Chief Engineer—was a lanky, tawny-furred flyer whose wings necessitated she choose a backless kneeling-chair to accommodate them. She had been Tristen's apprentice and majordomo. Benedick had supported her elevation to her new role—that of an officer in her own right. He hoped he had done right. He hoped she would do better.

They were still waiting for one more. She was not yet late, and as Benedick turned his water glass idly on the tank ledge, the door opened and his youngest sister Chelsea entered the council room. She smiled, and glanced this way and that; each of the assembled acknowledged her.

When she had fetched her own glass of water and seated herself, Benedick cued the silent Angel hovering over them that it was time to begin.

"This is the first meeting of the five hundred and fifty-seventh Council of Engine. We are here to introduce new Chief Engineer Jordan, replacing Caitlin Conn, deceased. Also, to discuss contingency plans and outcomes of our forthcoming encounter with the existing colonists of the world called Grail. Present are myself—Benedick Conn, acting as secretary, Astrogator Damian Jsutien, Chelsea Conn, and Chief Engineer Jordan."

Jsutien tilted his head in a peculiarly familiar fashion, though Benedick could not place where he had seen the Astrogator strike that pose before. It was a suspicious, considering gesture, and Benedick filed it away for later contemplation.

"Congratulations, Chief Engineer," said Jsutien.

"Your name was raised as well," Benedick said. "But your position as Astrogator makes you difficult to replace."

"Please," Jsutien said. "Jordan should have it over me. Over just about anyone."

Chelsea bit her lip, but nodded. "I am confident she will perform brilliantly."

Jordan gave them both a half smile. She would have to learn not to be so transparently grateful for approval. "The vote of confidence is more appreciated than you know. I am honored to be selected, Prince Benedick, and I will do whatever work is necessary to support my Captain and her ship."

"Good," Benedick said. "If that's settled, once we're finished here, Nova will have information for you—a briefing, I am told, from her memories of Hero Ng—and Mallory is preparing the memories of Chief Engineers past to administer to you."

"Blackest necromancy," Jordan said, licking her lips. "All right, then. It's probably best over quickly?"

She did not look as if she were anticipating having the skills and selected memories of generations of Engineers downloaded into her colony. But the instant expertise was necessary to the job and would serve them well. She would accept it, as Caitlin had accepted it before her.

As Nova had accepted the ghosts of Dust and Samael—

and Rien—when she grew out of the shards of other things into an Angel. As Perceval has swallowed down Ariane and Alasdair and Gerald to become Captain.

It was how you learned and grew and internalized the knowledge of those who had gone before you. No matter how bitter, you gagged it down, and hoped you didn't choke.

"I find," Benedick said, "that such things generally are. Sometimes time to consider only makes the whole thing worse."

There was too much work to do to sit here missing Caitlin. He laid his hands flat on the lip of the tank, pushing himself to his feet. More than anything, he wanted to be with Tristen, hunting down Caitlin's murderer and making him pay in blood and heartache for the thing he had taken from Benedick—a thing so profound that Benedick could not yet even feel its loss.

But he was too close and it was too soon. The shock and silence that echoed through the collapsed caverns of his self meant that he was exactly the wrong person to run the investigation—or even to participate in it. A bitter truth, but one an old man had too much experience not to accept. All those rules about objectivity existed for a reason.

Vengeance was a dish best served by those with no vested interest in seeing it carried out.

Benedick tipped his head back so that his skull dropped almost to his shoulders, easing the pain and tightness across his neck that even his colony could not dull.

Damn it all to hell. He had his own work, and this was the time to be doing it. "Our next item of business is to consider Engine's role in coming events."

Jordan glanced at the others. Benedick could see her coming to the realization that these people—all her elders— were waiting for her to speak first.

This was, he thought, a test.

She must have realized that as well, because he saw her

take a breath. And then she said, in a voice that hardly shook at all, "As I see it, there are three primary possibilities. Either we will need to break the world down for materials—in the event that we are permitted to stay; we will need to refit her for war—in the event that we choose to fight for a place here; or we will need to repair and rebuild her, to make her spaceworthy again. That last option is actually the most straightforward, as this system does offer access to a wealth of material in the form of asteroids, icy comets, and water-ice particles in the rings of two of the giant planets—"

11

adapt

For the deed's sake have I done the deed,
In uttermost obedience to the King.
—ALFRED, LORD TENNYSON, "Gareth and Lynette"

Before any final decision could be made, Danilaw and his cabinet had to take their deliberations to the people. Bad Landing was still a community small and tightly knit enough to manage nicely under government by direct democracy, and Danilaw secretly dreaded the day when that changed. The good news, he comforted himself, was that he was likely to be long in his grave—and *certain* to be long done with his stint as City Administrator—before the population reached a crisis point.

Unless they wound up having to assimilate a few hundred thousand genetically engineered space refugees. In that case, all bets were off.

Bad Landing's infosphere was more than adequate to the task. Because of the strength of some of the opinions expressed, Danilaw made the executive decision not to release the entire tapes of the Cabinet session, but he did cause Captain Amanda's objections to be summarized and appended, and he made the original broadcast from the *Jacob's Ladder* available, as well as a translation prepared by Captain Amanda and vetted by himself—though neither would be available to anyone who did not first sit through Danilaw's brief, trenchant, and carefully worded introductory speech. But sometimes listening to politicians blather was the price you paid for participating in the process of government.

He also got the remainder of his staff rousted out of bed and released from conflicting primary, secondary, and/or tertiary engagements so they could get started building an information bolus for packet-burst home to Earth. He'd probably have a course of action under way by the time the home government sent him an advisory note, but the newsfeeds would thank him for the consideration.

Danilaw didn't delude himself. It wouldn't be long before cracked and edited versions of the alien broadcast were all over the feeds; he'd be surprised if there weren't a few already, given that the transmission had come unencrypted via primitive tech, and most of the people capable of receiving it had been Gain's hobbyists. But he also knew that it didn't hurt to get his own version out as fast as possible, and one of the things he could offer that the hobbyists couldn't was production quality. His version would be the most complete and, frankly, the one that looked the best. And though he could try not to say the sorts of things that were making ledes all over the network—*a ship out of legend has returned*—Danilaw was confident that human nature would provide the rest.

That finished, he changed into the exercise clothes he kept in a locker in the residential and security barracks, took a seven-kilometer run with his morning-shift bodyguards, and went out to the tables by the water to share a cup of tea and some protein biscuits with the sunrise. He then showered in reclaimed water before falling into the bed set aside for his use.

He dreamed of muscular twelve-armed knots of dodecapodes spelling arcane runes across the ocean floor, and woke in a cold sweat of fear because he couldn't understand what they were trying to tell him.

He rose from his bed and paced the cold floor in slippered feet, the fear-induced nausea retreating slowly as he walked back and forth before the portal, watching sunlight shift through the dappled water of Crater Lake. Bits of things—organic matter, sand—danced like dust motes in the rays, and as he watched, a sense of lightness filled him. The scarred dodecapus was the only one in evidence, smooshing its sucker-mouth across the outside surface of the port, scraping up algae and tiny crustaceans.

Fear was not a familiar sensation, and this fear—stranger-fear, fear of the unknown—even less so. Among the legacies of atavism corrected by rightminding was the overactive fear response of the human amygdala to anything foreign or strange. Of course, a certain sense of self-preservation had to be left intact, and for some individuals whose baseline stability was particularly high, the whole threat-response endocrine package could be left intact without making them unsocializable.

Captain Amanda, the Free Legate, would be one such. It was a necessary precursor to the red jewel over her eye; no peace officer could afford to be too trusting. That was why she was so adamant about the potential dangers of the Jacobeans. And, still floating on that sense of goodwill, Danilaw reminded himself that it was her job to be so. He should respect her judgment. She had been left with those emotional cautions for a reason—to make her more able to protect the rest of her species from threats they might not otherwise recognize.

There had been species on Earth—island species, isolated populations—without fear of humans or any other predator. They were gone now, every dodo and Galápagos tortoise among them.

Danilaw smiled at the dodecapus, placing the palm of his hand against the portal near its limb. It curled a tentacle toward him, pressing sucker-feet against the transparency that divided them. A surge of fellow feeling and a fierce protectiveness filled him, warm and unmistakable as the sunlight. It had never learned to fear humans either, and if Danilaw had his way, it never would.

He'd find a way. He'd find a solution. For Fortune, for the Jacobeans, and for the future. He was suffused with vigor, with joy and hope. He turned from the portal, feeling as if his footsteps should have been effortless. Instead he dragged, heavy-limbed, as if still in a dream. The tiny bedroom, too, was full of light—streamers of it.

Everything surrounding Danilaw took on a crystalline super-reality, bright and warm and perfect—a holy and delighted space. He floated in the center as if the sun and water bore him up, filled with an ecstatic rapture. He let his head drop back on a soft neck. He spread his arms wide and breathed deep to fill his lungs with that divine, that healing, that heavenly light. Something touched him—something that loved him, that would protect him. Something vast and essential, that cared.

He knew the symptoms, though it had been years since he'd experienced them.

Seizure, he thought. *A bad one.*

The light gave way to darkness. He tried to cry out. But he could not tell if he made a sound as the perfect love washed over him and he fell.

When Danilaw opened his eyes again, it was in the same darkened room, and Captain Amanda sat on the edge of the bed—beside him—with a bud in her ear and her eyes tuned to her infothing. He lifted his head and she turned instantly, dropping the interface into her shirt pocket.

"Hey," she said. "Feeling better?"

"How much time did I lose?"

She tipped her pocket open with a fingertip and glanced at the infothing. "Ten minutes," she said. "I was napping in the next room and heard you fall. So. Temporal lobe epilepsy?"

Gingerly, he moved his skull and then his limbs, testing them. "Rightminded out years ago. Or so I thought. I still see visions sometimes, but I haven't had the full tonic-clonic experience since I was a student."

No facial bruising and no pain in his limbs, for a wonder. His ribs ached when he breathed deeply, from which he deduced that he'd fallen across the foot of the bed, and the mattress had protected his head.

"Anything hurt?" Amanda asked.

"Just my pride." Honesty compelled him. "And a few bruises."

She was studying his face, frowning. The line it drew between her eyes puckered the skin around the Legate's jewel. Danilaw imagined the shine of it recording, and looked down. Then she extended a hand, as if to assist him to his feet.

"All right," she said. "Come on. We just have time to grab some food before duty calls."

The Council reconvened after lunch, when everybody else had also gotten some sleep and the infosphere had had a good six hours to start consensus-building and weeding out the opinions of the hysterics and the intractables. By then, they were in possession of another transmission from the *Jacob's Ladder*, this one granting permission for an envoy to be sent.

"The real irony here," Gain said at this second Alien Invasion Policy Meeting (though nobody outside of Danilaw's head was actually calling it that), "is that we finally make first contact with an alien race after centuries of looking, and they're us."

"Not us," Jesse said. "Something consanguineous. But that's a different species. Subspecies. Whatever."

"We can't state that categorically until we get a look at

the DNA," Danilaw reminded them. "It's only been a thousand years of divergence. Speciation can happen fast, but it's a long shot."

Gain looked more tired than the rest of them. She leaned forward on her elbows, blinking owlishly. Her hands were folded around a mug of stimulant. But tired or not, the mind behind those bleary eyes remained sharp. "And if they're as different from us as *neandertalensis* from *sapiens*?"

Danilaw nibbled his cuticle. "We try not to compete for the same habitat."

He didn't state the obvious—that sharing an environment with a competitive, hierarchal, primitive version of humanity would require his people to either enforce their own social adaptations on the newcomers, or adopt a more aggressive stance of their own and deal with the long-term repercussions as they occurred.

Many of the most aggressively hierarchical humans had left while the world was collapsing, fleeing in the *Jacob's Ladder*—an artificial world salvaged from the extravagant wreckage of humanity's near self-immolation, fueled and funded by a Kleptocracy that did not outlast the launch of more than the first of the elaborate, flimsy, sabotaged vessels. To those who remained behind on an Earth like a gnawed husk, subsistence seemed luxury enough.

Those forebears had already begun rightminding themselves—the decision that provoked the flight of the Jacobeans in the first place. It had been the intentional self-handicapping of a competitor with no equals on the playing field.

To save themselves as a species, Danilaw's ancestors had bargained away a good deal of the fear, the primate antagonism, the power structures that had driven them to mastery—even overlordship—of their environment. It had required a radical realignment of society and the human brain—forces that had driven those primitive humans to such intense competition that their entire worldwide society had been designed to contain and facilitate nothing else.

Instead, they had decided to shift the social focus to another, less expressed potential of the human animal—that of peaceable, advantageous cooperation and compromise. In selecting—in *engineering*—for self-sacrifice, commensalism, and negotiation over individualism, hierarchy, and authoritarianism, they had saved the world. They had ushered in an enduring age of peace and—if not prosperity—adequacy of resources for the new, reduced demand.

But it had required a reworking of the entire architecture of human neurology. Centuries later, the extinction event, ecological crisis, and massive population crash that had provoked it—dubbed the Eschaton by various factions at the time—was still remembered with a sort of hushed awe.

A remnant of the human race had emerged from the Eschaton with a renewed sense of desperation, if not purpose. They had refined the crude early techniques of rightminding into a comprehensive program of surgery, chemical therapy, and scientific child-rearing that had allowed humanity to finally *do something* about the clutter of its awkward, self-defeating, self-deluding evolutionary baggage.

Danilaw was grateful for the world they had left him—one in which sufficient resources were assured for each person's comfort and livelihood, barring catastrophe, and in which pleasures were balanced off against obligations in an endurable and even enjoyable fashion. Like many, he maintained a certain bittersweet nostalgia for the glittering excesses of the twentieth and twenty-first centuries—he played in a rock band, and he was not the only one to engage in recreational re-creation.

But it was playacting, an exercise in creativity, and any rational, rightminded individual had to accept that a world without avoidable hunger and war—a world in which diverse human beings could work together to find compromise positions without the crippling barriers of fanaticism and ideology—was superior to one where they were at one another's throats constantly.

Sophipathology had not been eradicated. But it was a treatable illness now. Danilaw wished he could be more certain that the incoming Jacobeans would see it the same way.

Captain Amanda spoke first, with the most aggressive analysis. "We have to be prepared to defend ourselves, Administrator Danilaw."

"You're in charge of that," he said. "Have a defense plan for me in two days, please. You can work on it while we pack."

"We?" Jesse looked like he wasn't exactly overjoyed by the idea of a field trip. Danilaw knew his primary was heavily pregnant, and the culmination of a reproduction license wasn't the sort of thing you wanted to miss just because you'd drawn City Admin duty. Especially when you were working on making the psychological shift to primary nurturing duty any day now.

"Captain Amanda and I," he said. "We'll go out to greet them, barring any major pushback from the Ciz. We both speak their language, passably if not fluently. And it will appear to be a gesture of trust and goodwill if I go."

"They're hierarchical," Captain Amanda said. "If you go yourself, you will weaken your apparent position with them. They will be used to dealing with administrators as persons of rank, veiled by layers of flunkies and functionaries whose only purpose is to create a haze of isolation around the decision maker. We're talking about an extremely alien manner of thinking."

"Well, then," Danilaw said. "They're supposed to be New Evolutionists, aren't they? They'll adapt."

Dust's second visit to Dorcas came in the dead of her local night. He found her in a low tent, pitched against the sheltering trunk of a bent palm. Fur-tips wet with the irrigation falling in the Heaven, he crept to the edge of the pallet where she slept, arms folded mantislike to her chest and mouth open, breath rasping in and out with rough regularity. A black-backed synbiotic snake curled against the backs of her knees, basking in whatever heat radiated through her blankets. A sheen like oily rainbows covered its back. Its tongue flicked out when Dust approached; he made well sure to keep the sleeping woman between the rodentlike form he inhabited and the curious snake.

He touched the damp tip of his nose to the woman's eyelid, prepared to jump back if, on awakening, she swiped at him. But not prepared enough, apparently. She might be Sparrow Conn no longer, but the body she inhabited had all of Sparrow's hard-won reflexes.

Dust found himself on his back, spine twisted and pinned to the ground, the Go-Back's hand pressing into his belly. He squeaked surrender, going limp, and bared his minuscule throat to her.

A too-long silence followed. When he opened his eyes again, he found her still shoving him against the ground, the heavy head of the cybernetic cobra swaying at her left shoulder as it regarded him with baleful, candy-colored eyes.

"So," Dorcas said. "Are you volunteering to feed my snake?"

"However this small one may serve," Dust said. "But if this small one may suggest, it may be more advantageous to you to listen to the message I bring."

"Still looking for alliances?" Her voice was not friendly, but she lifted her hand and let him right himself. If he'd chosen to fight, he could have made her regret laying hands on him—but that was hardly in keeping with his current mission of diplomacy.

"I bring more this time." Because he could not bite, he groomed, busily washing his face and paws. His fur was gritty with soil. Also, the washing made him look inoffensive. "My patron would like to speak with you in person."

The Go-Back reached out and let the back of her hand brush the cheek of the cobra. It did not withdraw, but its flared hood smoothed back into the taut black-and-buttercream column of its neck. Dust was a construct, and could not feel fear exactly. But he could feel the toolkit's arousal levels lowering, its tiny, trembling heartbeat slowing to a mere whirr.

Well, if Dust was going to be eaten by a synbiotic snake, it was probably within his powers to possess that snake's colony from the inside. He'd fight that war when he came to it.

"Patron," she said. She pushed herself more fully into a sitting position, adjusting her weight on her seat bones by pushing down on the ground. The snake flicked its tongue once more and seemed to resign in favor of the woman, whipping its long body into a fold of the blankets. It was too bulky to vanish completely, but the bulge could have been a pillow if Dust had not known otherwise. "All right, Dust," she said. "What is it that you want from me? Other than allegiance, because you must know now that my goals are not yours—"

"Parley with my sponsor," he said. "I am under the command of another, Go-Back. That is all. She seeks an alliance, and your goodwill. Or at least your sworn word not to oppose her."

She tapped her fingers on her thigh, twice. She looked down at him, where he huddled by her knee. "What are the politics of Conns to an Edenite? I'll parley. But she must come to me."

12

carried bright scars

Christ, what a night! how the sleet whips the pane!
What lights will those out to the northward be?
—Matthew Arnold, "Tristram and Iseult"

Tristen Conn was a tiger, and no hound. Mysteries were not his métier. His strength lay in the subtlety of war. But for his Captain's sake, he would attempt what he did not well understand, and solve the murder of Perceval's mother.

Before the world was made anew and a Captain sat upon the Bridge, a knight-errant had often been called upon to resolve crimes, to serve as investigator and judge as well. But the crimes of simple folk were often simple as well, unsophisticated, the culprits apparent when the knight-errant applied logic and interview skills to the case. Here, there was no one to interview. The only witnesses were Nova and Perceval, and what Nova had seen was spotty and suspect.

He was fortunate to have assistance in his inquiry. The necromancer Mallory might be a better detective than Tristen, as necromancers were without a doubt temperamentally suited to the investigation of death. He was fortunate as well that he could frame Caitlin's death as an act of war. That—the shadowy realm of sabotage, spycraft, assassination, espionage—was a paradigm with which Tristen felt comfortable.

In the privacy of Tristen's insulated bedchamber in Rule, he and Mallory commenced with the facts they knew. Those facts were comfortingly simple—if frustratingly few. Five persons in armor had entered the corridor outside the Bridge, somehow undetected. They had made off with an antique paper book which had held great religious and symbolic significance to the Builders, and was still sacred to some—perhaps many—of the folk of the *Jacob's Ladder*. Two of them—the ones Perceval had killed—had been Deckers, and possibly so had the remainder.

But one of those former two had been skilled enough to put Perceval to the test, and at least one of the latter three had been the equal—or the better—of Caitlin Conn, hard as that was for Tristen (who had ranked Caitlin along with Benedick as one of the few warriors nearing to his own skill) to accept.

It was possible that Caitlin's killer had gotten the drop on her somehow, a possibility that Tristen was cautious in regarding as more plausible *because* it was more comforting.

It would be nice to think Caitlin had made a mistake. But that was the sort of logic that got a man killed through underestimating the threat posed by his adversaries.

It was more likely, Tristen knew, that the person who killed Caitlin had been, like her, a Conn, Exalt and well seasoned to the arts of war.

The three remaining trespassers had made good their escape, successfully using Caitlin's death to distract Perceval and once again blocking the attention of the ship's Angel. They had taken with them the paper New Evolutionist Bible, still sealed in its protective case, and Caitlin's un-blade Charity—the last unblade in the world, as far as anyone knew—which had once been Tristen's before it was shattered and then remade.

Tristen's chamber lay high up along the curve of Rule's architecture. He could have had one larger and lower, nearer the courtyard and generally considered more desirable, and in being honest with himself, Tristen admitted that *he* would have preferred the basement. Dark, tight spaces still felt safe to him. One might anticipate claustrophobia as a consequence in someone who had spent decades immured in a living crypt, but the result for Tristen had been the opposite. Expanses seemed too open now, space without walls something you could fall into forever and never escape.

Agoraphobia was a common ailment among those who grew up among the coiled passages and close anchores of the world. The Enemy lay always close enough to fall into—breath-suckingly close, and personally malevolent. Wide-open spaces could kill, and it was only sensible to fear them.

But Tristen had long ago learned that when confronted with fear, he dug in his heels and became stubborn. And so he had chosen quarters far up along the arch of Rule's bulkhead, arm's length from the great transparent panels of the sky. He had chosen quarters that floated a hundred meters above the olive trees and grass of the courtyard. A long panel opened out on that side, revealing the gardens and the other wall beyond. On the other side he had a bottomless vista of the skeleton of the world, flattened and distinct against the coffin velvet of the Enemy's bosom.

Mallory stood now in the narrow point of the room, where interior and exterior panels came together. One hand was pressed palm-flat to each window, as if the necromancer established a current between positive and negative, between warm living atmosphere and the coldest dark of all. Tristen schooled a spontaneous smile, but his warmth at seeing Mallory's slender silhouette would not be hidden.

It came out in his posture, he thought, the way his chin

and shoulders lifted. Mallory brought energy into any room.

Mallory spoke softly. "So where do we go now?"

"They will expect us to invade the Decks in force. They have *arranged* that we would invade the Decks by force. Why else leave two fighters behind to be slaughtered—one weak, one just good enough to distract Perceval—and steal the things they must imagine we will come after though Hell bar the way?"

"The attack does seem machined to provoke just that response." Mallory frowned, so Tristen allowed that smile out after all, and offered it in return. "The Bible. Why would they think we'd care for that?"

"I asked myself that question also," Tristen said. "It is very old; it is historic. But we know the Builders' creed. We have lived it."

"We have ejected it." Mallory made a dismissive gesture right-handed, fingers flipping back and forth like a swinging door. "And what if we refuse the manipulation into war? What if we go alone? Under a flag of truce, to parley?"

"We? You and I? As knights-errant, Necromancer?"

"A knight-errant and a magicker," Mallory corrected. "It's a traditional pairing, is it not? Of course, if you'd rather, you could take Cynric—"

"Two of us would be easy to kill, and then Perceval would be without Chief Engineer, First Mate, *and* Mallory."

"And is Mallory so precious as to be named by name?" Mallory dropped hands to thighs and turned around. Fingertips half concealed in the pouf of flame-colored sleeves rubbed against snug black trousers, a gesture that might be nervousness or irritation—or even amusement, given the evidence of arched eyebrows.

"Mallory is certainly unique enough to be named by

name," he said. "Like Head, or Surgeon, or Gardener. Where there is only one of a thing, its function *is* a name."

Mallory's expression melted into a smile. "If Tristen Tiger scents a conspiracy meant to entice him to war, who am I to gainsay? War is your art, Conn."

"You provoke me, Necromancer."

Tristen dipped his head and brushed his mouth against the necromancer's cool lips. Mallory kissed back, lightly, affectionate, until Tristen pulled away. If it was not the great passion of Tristen's youth, well. Great passion led so easily to great tragedy.

He said, "Pack your things, then, if you'll risk it. Though I lead you unto death."

The necromancer smiled. "Death is my middle name."

These days, the AE decks were accessible by a simple lift. A lift which functioned properly, which zipped them dramatically around the inside curve of the world from Rule (complete with panoramic and perhaps unsettling views), and which delivered Tristen and Mallory neatly to the Deckers' port of entry. As it was settling into the docking cradle, the door lights blinking yellow-to-blue one by one, Mallory whispered, "Don't you ever miss the adventure of the old days?"

"Almost as much as I miss the romance and glamour of epidemic fratricide," Tristen said out of the corner of his mouth as the lift doors opened. He just caught a glimpse of Mallory's answering smirk as the mirrored interior surface slipped aside.

It wasn't love, thank all things holy. But they understood one another, and sometimes that was enough. More than enough.

They came out of the lift with their helms open, a display of blatant confidence, into a surprisingly barren stretch of corridor. Little of the world was not blanketed in biosphere. Throughout her holdes and corridors, her domaines and anchores, spiders spun and air mosses hung from every stanchion; lichens crept along the corners where footsteps rarely fell, to be groomed up again by hungry ship cats; apparent shadows dissolved at a motion into flocks of black-blue butterflies. But here, the deck gleamed dully through scratchy polish; the bulkheads were stark, the trim painted white and the fittings glistening.

"Sterile," Tristen murmured, just loud enough for his armor's collar mike to pick up the word and transmit it to Mallory.

"Dead," Mallory answered, running both hands through tight dark curls. The gesture displayed that they were not immediately armed without offering any hint of appeasement or lessened status, and Tristen admired it.

Voice raising, the necromancer called, "Hello? I am Mallory, and this is Tristen Conn. We come on the Captain's business, as you were informed! Is there someone here to greet us?"

Mallory's phrasing granted them a right to be there. Someone less experienced might have asked permission, presented themselves as envoys, or begged truce.

But for this, that would not do. Tristen and Jordan had not conquered these people in blood and fire for Tristen to walk among them in supplication, no matter how fraught the situation had become.

Besides, it was just as possible that, other than one or two mercenaries or radicals, the Deckers had had nothing to do with the attack on the Bridge. It was easily possible that the Deckers and the Conn family and its allies were being maneuvered into fighting one another—a conflict that could only bring blood and destruction on them all, and leave the victor weakened even if it didn't create a patent power vacuum for some mutual enemy to exploit.

Yet show of strength that it was, it received no answer.

"Nova?" Tristen said.

"The holde beyond the next gate shows every sign of

being normal, fully functioning, and inhabited," the Angel answered. "Shall I announce you, First Mate?"

"No, thank you." That would be just what would endear them to the Deckers—an Angel appearing wreathed in flame and glory midair, bringing word that the Conns had dropped by to ask a few questions and borrow a cup of sweets. "We'll let ourselves in the back door. Although if you could override the locking mechanism, Nova—"

"I would," the Angel answered, "but somebody else has already overwritten it. The door's been hacked. I am afraid you will have to open it manually."

"You mean by force."

"I do."

Tristen slipped Mirth from its sheath. It wasn't an unblade. It could not slice the door from its moorings, scramble the colonies and programs within on a single pass, and cut the metal from the bulkhead as cleanly as a quantum wand. But in this instance, it would suffice—and Tristen thought he might prefer the repairable outcome to the permanent carnage left by an unblade.

But he did hope that nobody on the other side of the door was waiting for him with Charity naked and deadly to hand. Mirth wouldn't stand up to fencing an unblade for long—if it stood at all. "Prepare to repair the door behind us, please."

"Of course," Nova said, and Tristen raised his daughter's sword.

When he brought it down, it rent metal, filling the corridor with the hiss of escaping air as pressure equalized through the tight gap. Tristen's ears popped, and based on Mallory's grimace, his were not the only ones.

"Sorry," he said, and swung Mirth up again. Two more strokes made a gap wide enough for them to step through, and Tristen had no fear that Nova would seal up the damage behind them. He was still sparing in using his sword as a door-opening technique, but at least it was possible now.

Fifty years before, he would have run the risk of spacing entire holdes. Nova was much more in control of herself than she had been.

—except perhaps not. Because when Tristen slipped through the gap, he was met by the evidence of carnage.

No one had tidied the bodies. They lay where they had fallen, or where they had dragged themselves—several close enough to the entrance that Tristen had just cut through that he had to step over outflung arms and legs to clear the passage for Mallory. "Seal up," he said, his armor responding instantly. As the helm telescoped up to lock him within, he heard the answering whirr of Mallory's device.

He also heard the click of Mallory's footsteps descending the path within the door. There was no point in turning; the necromancer was quite capable of self-defense, and would be dogging Tristen's heels anyway.

Inside, the holde was just as he remembered, other than being full of dead people. The Deckers preferred—had preferred?—a more regimented approach to ecobalance than most of the world, and their holde was divided into close, tidy rooms lined with hydroponics tanks and workstations. Hanging baskets under full-spectrum lights dripped strawberries and cherry tomatoes. Tristen suspected that, as one spiraled closer to the exterior of the holde, there would be panels allowing natural light in, as much of this would have been built or renovated while the world lay becalmed in the orbit of the shipwreck stars.

But now, this pleasant, gardened, orderly workspace stank of vomit and evacuated bowels. Stringy-haired corpses slumped in corners or draped over chairs. "Your readouts, Nova?"

"I am listening," the Angel said at his side. "And through your colony I see what you see. But I cannot perceive it directly. Within these walls, my awareness has been edited."

"Just like old times," Tristen said bitterly. "Are you having any trouble healing the door?"

"Given current circumstances," Mallory suggested, "I think I shall turn around and check."

The necromancer vanished between leaves, only to return, nodding, a moment later. "The door is cured."

"Unlike this place." Tristen crouched to check another set of life-signs, knowing the gesture was futile.

"Someone cleaned up after himself," Mallory said. "They were Exalt, these Deckers. But they were new to it and untrained, and they were not Conns. Whatever was unleashed on them, you or I might have known how to defend against, but here it was like nerve gas in a kindergarten."

"Indeed," Tristen answered. "Why does this remind me of something?"

"Shhh." Mallory raised a hand.

Tristen had opened his mouth to ask the question before he realized that, no matter what he said, it would be stupid. He held his tongue and watched as Mallory crossed the holde to crouch, then crawl, peering under the edge of a hydroponics tank full of lush, burgundy-veined beet greens and tiny purple beets no bigger than marbles.

"Prince Tristen," the necromancer said, "I suspect I have found a survivor."

Dust should have known it was all going wrong as soon as his patron shrugged her appropriated body into a more comfortable arrangement—which included locking up the Conn personality who usually animated the borrowed form—and allowed Dust to lead her through the world. He was surprised that she would come to Dorcas as a penitent, but he supposed, as it was his patron who had desired this meeting, it was incumbent upon her to travel. And Dorcas had shown no desire to step forth from her Heaven and explore the possibilities presented her. She might hear supplicants from her own domaine and holdfast, like any Queen, but that was different than going to see someone.

Dust's patron had always been the sort to enforce her rights and insist upon her privileges. She took status seriously and used it as a tool to get her will. Dust knew it rankled in her like a shard under the skin that she had fallen so far as to be going before Dorcas—an Engineer and a Go-Back—to beg assistance. But he'd also seen how ruthless she was, which left him wondering if there were any way this proposed alliance could end without another heap of bodies.

His patron had never been quite sane.

But he was her angel, now, and she was his Conn, and he would do as she bid. It was in the nature of angels to serve.

He accompanied her into a lift—her body's trusted status in Engine let them travel freely—and from thence into one of the great arterial trunks that served commuters around the world. The paths from Engine to Rule were long, but they had been among the first ones Caitlin Conn and Captain Perceval had ordered repaired once the resources were available.

Though Dust and his patron were not going all the way to Rule, the same arterials would make the trip to the Heaven of the Edenites much more practical given their limited window for travel and negotiations.

They traveled in silence. His patron did not invite him to ride on her shoulder, as another might, so he sat by her ankles and tucked his tail around his toes to present an appearance of tidiness. When they arrived, Dust could tell that his patron was insulted that no entourage awaited them—only Dorcas in her clean robes, embroidered about the collar, with her hat hung down her back under the thick yellow coils of her hair.

"Hello," Dorcas said. "Your pardon if I seem surprised; your messenger did not explain you had been rebodied in the form of a Conn."

Dorcas's confession of surprise did nothing to smooth the patron's prickles.

"Who did you think you would be meeting?" the patron asked, sweet reason and imperiousness mixing in a tone that Dust knew was every reason for caution. Surely he had not been so timid when he was a larger angel?

But now he was a toolkit only, a small and cowardly beast, and not the black-mirrored dragon of yore. You changed; you adapted; you made the most of what you were and strove to become more. He would survive. *Though we are not now that strength which in old days moved heaven and earth—*

"I try to assume nothing," Dorcas said. "Come, be welcome. Let me make you comfortable and bring you refreshment."

She turned and moved on, gesturing the patron to follow. She took the lead, since she obviously knew where they were going. The toolkit scampered at her heels, too small to manage even a semidignified trot.

This was not the sort of society where anyone waited on anyone else, and Dust could sense his patron's disapproval of this, too. She hid it well, though. The momentary stiffness of spine melted into calm dignity, and the smile on her lips even seemed to touch her eyes. She carried herself like the princess she had been, and part of the training of a princess was graciousness. She even managed to seem pleased when Dorcas showed her the white-painted vine-woven table and chairs set under the shade of a glossy-leafed coffee tree heavy with bright red berries. Dust could only read the exasperation rising in his patron by that head-tilt and the little smile—the one that said to anyone who knew her well: *I am going to eat your liver.*

As if reading the situation, Dorcas pulled out the patron's chair and the patron sat. A moment later, Dorcas seated herself. Dust hopped up the bole of the coffee tree and vanished among the branches, careful not to knock

twigs or leaves on the humans' heads as he found a position from which he could observe in comfort and con-
cealment. As the foliage closed around him, he felt the
hammering of his tiny animal heart cease. This was safety,
cover—protection—and his instincts rewarded him for
seeking it.

The patron waited patiently while Dorcas poured coffee
and passed around almond milk and agave syrup. Then she
lifted her salvaged-materials cup, touched it to her lips, in-
haled the steam—eyes closed briefly as her colony analyzed
the composition—and set it down again.

"It's safe," Dorcas said, and tasted her own coffee to
demonstrate. When her eyes closed, Dust thought it was in
appreciation. The almond milk made little swirls and shim-
mers of fat on the surface, and small curdled patches, but
to his body's organic nostrils it certainly smelled good.

When she set the coffee down, she smiled. "You wanted
to speak to me."

"I want to take the ship," the patron said, with the boldness that had always been hers. "I do not know yet if this
is feasible, but I do know that the current Captain's policies
will lead us to death and disaster. Those who hold Grail
will not share or surrender it without a fight, and we—"
She sighed. "We have come too far to be turned away. We
will not survive another long passage in the dark."

Dust watched Dorcas swirl her coffee in the cup, the
curling edge of the wavelet she made leaving a ring of froth
and wetness behind. "You are forthright," she said. "I like
that."

The patron smiled and sipped her drink. From her expression, it pleased her better than everything else about
the day. "We are talking about the people who contaminated your preserve with symbionts against your will. Who
engineered the colonies to begin with, and tortured and
murdered innocent life-forms to do so. Cynric Conn and

her minions respect no boundary; they adhere to no ethical compass beyond *what I want, I shall have*."

"A stiff dick has no conscience," Dorcas said.

The patron grinned. *Humans,* Dust thought, *were so . . . erratic.*

"Exactly," the patron said. "And a Conn dick is doubly blind to consequence."

Dorcas smoothed one hand across her hair. Her lips thinned. She drew in a deep breath and said, "And what are the consequences of your conquest of the world? We'll descend on Grail and take what we want of her? We'll abandon negotiation in favor of force?"

Dust saw the flicker of frustration cross the patron's face, heard the skip of her elevated heart rate. "We'll survive," she said, "by whatever means necessary. Cooperation, of course, is to be preferred, as is a nonviolent solution."

Dorcas smiled. It was not a friendly smile, or even one of complicity. When she set her cup down on the table, it made so little sound against the woven vines that even Dust's honed ears could scarcely detect it. "I find that reprehensible," she said.

Dust had not expected his patron to be rocked back in her chair, but amid his bower of leaves he nevertheless—if asked—must have confessed himself gratified that she frowned. Fleetingly, so fleetingly a Mean might have missed it, though Dorcas most assuredly did not.

"You would find me a very bad enemy," the patron said. "I think it would be wise to reconsider. There are elements among your people that are already in sympathy with me."

"I said I found it reprehensible," Dorcas said. "I did not say I would under no circumstances cooperate. I know who you are and I know who you were. I know what you stand reduced from, and I know what you did in Rule and among the Deckers who allied with you last. You are a

Conn through and through, Ariane, and rotten with it. But it's also possible that you are our only hope for survival."

Dorcas stared calmly at the patron. The patron stared too, seeming taken aback for the first time in Dust's experience.

There was a sound when the patron set her cup down, and a louder one of scuffed turf and tearing grass when she shoved her chair back from the table. Her hand fell on the freshly machined hilt of the blade she wore over her clothing, a common enough affectation among Engineers. "How dare you speak to me like that?"

Dorcas seemed unimpressed by the threat of unblade, or Conn. She did not rise, but a needler appeared in her hand, shivering slightly but accurately aimed. The patron gave no sign that she had noticed it. Her weapon remained in its sheath, ready on the instant to be drawn. And in the leaves of the branches behind her, Dust saw something heavy, shining, and silk-black coil and tongueflicker, ready on the instant to strike.

"Ariane," she said. "Really. I was dead before you were out of diapers, and you expect fear? I have said I will help you. I will promise not to reveal what I know to the Captain or her dogs." Her mouth bent in a moue of disgust. "But don't expect me to lick your boots into the deal."

Inside his bower, the frail remnant of Dust huddled close to a branch. He would leap if he must, join the fray in defense of his mistress. Worthy or not, despised or adored, she was his, and he was hers. Even Dorcas's synbiotic monster-snake would not intimidate him into remaining in hiding if Ariane were to draw her blade.

And she might have, except Dorcas smiled, showing teeth. In that expression, Dust glimpsed the woman she had not been, the woman whose body she now inhabited. He remembered Sparrow Conn, and he could imagine it was her voice that said, "Though you grind my bones for bread, Commodore, you will not make me grovel."

She did not stand. She sipped her coffee. She did not lower the barrel of her weapon. She raised her head to regard the patron and she smiled.

"You know," she said, "combat reflexes live in the muscle memory more than they do in the mind. Do you know who wore this body before me, Ariane?"

The patron did not step back, though Dust saw the shiver through her calf muscles as she fought the reflex and won.

"Allies?" she said.

"After a fashion," Dorcas agreed. "Please, drink your coffee. It would be a pity to waste."

Tristen felt his armor shift to support his weight as he rocked back on his heels. "A survivor? Are you sure?"

"Living things are not my specialty," Mallory admitted, "but it seems likely. That's what a pulse and breathing generally mean, isn't it?"

"When you're right, Necromancer," Tristen said, "you're usually right."

"Here, bring me more light."

Mallory's helm lights already illuminated the underside of the table with a dim glow. It radiated up through the water and the roots of the plants encapsulated in the transparent table, casting eerie, watery ripples of luminescence and shadow on the bulkheads and the ceiling. Tristen leaned down to bring his own units under the edge, where they could contribute a more indirect illumination. When he could see around Mallory—and his sensors could pick up what the necromancer's body obscured—he grunted into his helm. Breath fogged his faceplate for a moment before the moisture controls cleared it, but what vanished behind the mist did not change when it emerged again.

Mallory cupped something the color and size of a lime in armored palms. It was warm; a tiny heartbeat shook it. Tiny breaths lifted its feathers and then let them fall smooth again. Its wings were no longer than Tristen's middle finger. They stretched across Mallory's hands, delicate primary feathers splayed as if they were fingers, too.

"Cynric's pets look like that," Tristen said. He backed up, allowing Mallory to scuff out from under the hydroponics table on armored knees that grated against the floor. Mallory stood, still cradling the minute casualty. "A stunning coincidence."

"She didn't do this," Mallory said, turning to survey the dead.

"She wouldn't have left behind evidence if she did," Tristen agreed. Cynric did not make merely human errors. Her mistakes were more on the epic scale, her failings those of demigods. "So the question is, who did it, and how was it done, and what is the purpose in making it look like Cynric?"

Mallory's head moved inside the armor—not argument, but distaste and bitterness.

Tristen said, "Nova, are you receiving this?"

"Your feed only," the Angel said. "I'll have to propagate into this space. A moment, please."

Tristen felt nothing as the Angel reclaimed AE deck, colonies moving into the vacated areas. The Angel's presence was as imperceptible to him as her absence had been to her own senses. He heard the chime in his head when she had accomplished it, though, and her soft voice saying, "There are no survivors in this area. The bulk of AE deck appears unaffected, but this cluster of anchores has been sterilized."

"Except the bird."

"Except the bird," Nova confirmed.

"Cynric could conceal this area from Nova's senses," Mallory said, playing devil's advocate. "If she wanted a private preserve in which to foment revolution and conquer the world."

"Who knows why Cynric does anything?" Tristen said.

He would set no manner of ruthlessness beyond her, but the carelessness still seemed out of character to him. "If she wanted to read the Bible, though, all she had to do was ask Perceval."

He moved past Mallory, back into the corridor where they had entered. Storage lockers were keyed to other hand and voice prints, but Nova was in them now, and Tristen was her First Mate. They opened to his glance, not even so much as his command.

They contained the sorts of things you would expect from storage cubbies near an air lock. Emergency gear, rescue equipment, recyclables awaiting attention—and three rows of suits of armor standing arrayed in the deepest cabinet. The first rank of these were personalized—bright colors, varied sizes, the kinds of modifications and attachments that armor grew when partnered with one worker for a long period of time. But the suits behind those were disused, grayed-out, awaiting reawakening.

And two of them carried bright scars, as if from a deflected needle or a hard contact with some sharp stationary object. "These suits of armor," Tristen said. "They have not repaired themselves."

"Their colonies are not awake and autonomous," Nova said. "And as I was locked out of this area, I could not oversee repairs."

"Check them for DNA residue," Tristen said. "In fact, check all the suits in here. There were three incursionists who got away. So either there's a suit missing, along with the paper Bible and an unblade—or the third person took absolutely no damage at all."

"In any case," Nova said, "if there's DNA in these suits of armor that does not belong to any of the dead, it may lead us to identify survivors."

"Indeed," Tristen said. "It's possible *none* of the killers died here, and all this death is to cover up their escape."

"That's worthy of your father," Mallory said over the comm.

Tristen frowned, both stung and grateful that Mallory could not see his response. "That I can recognize the possibility does not mean that I advocate the act."

The necromancer made a rough sound of constrained laughter. "Indeed. Tristen, come see this?"

Tristen left the storage cubby open and returned to the charnel house of the hydroponics lab. As he walked, he heard Jordan's voice in his helm, relayed by Nova.

"Hello, Tristen." Strange to have his former apprentice treating with him as an equal now. Strange, and satisfying. After his return greeting, she continued, "It looks as if the colony-entity that invaded this space disguised itself as pieces of Nova, broadcasting the usual surface signals— and totally bogus data. Nova didn't know a parasite was masquerading as a portion of her own body. When it retracted, it simply withdrew its presence and wiped its program from the infected units and left them vacant. There is not even a line of physical retreat to follow."

"That also explains how it kept her out of the Bridge access," Tristen said. "That suggests a crafty and experienced angel or djinn."

"It suggests somebody in particular to me," Nova said, "but I ate him. Also, if there was DNA residue in the suits, it's been consumed. Somebody's colony was careful."

"Well, crap." Tristen opened the hatch and stepped back into the Decker farm. Mallory, helm open and gauntlets retracted, crouched beside the body of a young woman who had fallen back in the chair she'd died in, a yellow line of bile dried down her jaw and staining the front of her blouse. The parrotlet, still breathing softly, lay amongst wadded fabric on the desktop.

Tristen cleared his throat. "Is it safe to have your helm open? You might contract the agent of death. You might transport it outside this sealed environment."

"Can't kiss a corpse with sealed lips," Mallory said. "Nova says it was a poisoned program, wiped along with the presence that spawned it. We're as safe here as we are anywhere."

Assuming the Angel's not being fooled by the enemy's camouflage again. Tristen bit his lip. "It seems like there are a lot of familiar modi operandi at work here. And all of the individuals those tactics suggest are supposed to be dead."

"Well, death," Mallory said. "I wouldn't use that to rule out suspects. Death is my specialty, and you have my professional assurances that it's not in any way permanent. I've got a head so full of dead people I suspect whoever I started off as should probably be counted as one of them.

"Transformation, on the other hand, now, *that's* the one you have to watch out for. How much of you has to die before you stop being you and become somebody else?"

Tristen thought of Cynric, of Gavin, of Nova and Rien. He thought of Sparrow and Dorcas, and himself and a dark hole full of wings and insects and the heat of decomposition. He came a step closer, itching to reach out to Mallory, forcing himself to observe. But he did not open his helm.

The necromancer framed the dead woman's eyes with soft fingertips, and leaned so close that Tristen felt as if he had interrupted a seduction.

As he watched, the kiss was completed. Mallory pressed pink lips over the dead woman's mouth, and Tristen could see the worming motions of the necromancer's tongue working between the corpse's teeth. Mallory's eyes closed, fingers fanning through brown hair to hold the head steady.

There was not much rigor yet, or it was passing. By the lack of cadaverine and sulfur compounds in the air, Tristen presumed the former—but with luck (and skill) Mallory would have a better answer momentarily. When the necromancer straightened, dark eyes thoughtful, Tristen knew some ghost of an answer at least had been retrieved.

"The brain is dead but fresh," Mallory said. "A virus is interfering with the symbionts, preventing regeneration; Nova and Jordan will likely be able to remove the inhibition and at least get the bodies back. And perhaps learn more about how Nova was kept out of this anchore—"

"And kept from being aware that she was being kept out of this anchore," Nova added dryly.

Mallory snorted. "Any program—be it based in wetware or hardware—can be hacked."

"And did you hack her memories?" Tristen asked, stroking the dead woman's hair back with his armored hand.

"The machine memories were wiped," Mallory said. "I think these people were used as a stalking horse by a greater enemy. I think that enemy was thorough in covering his or her tracks."

The smile that curved lovely lips was smug enough to make Tristen shiver with memory. *This is hardly the time.*

But what were a few dozen more dead in his lifetime?

"I notice," Tristen said—aware that, in terms of cool professionalism, he was overcompensating, "that you specifically mention the machine memories."

"The meat is empty," Mallory said. "No electrical impulses left at all. She's dead." The necromancer's palms rasped softly, nervously, against one another. "The local monitoring records have been purged, but there are still neurochemical traces."

Tristen felt his eyebrows rise.

"Oxytocin, serotonin. Whoever killed her was someone she trusted to do her no harm."

"A friend?"

"A friend."

*   *   *

By the time they'd returned to Rule, Tristen had made his decision. He left Mallory to report to Perceval—the broad details had been handled through Nova and the com, but the Captain would have questions, and both Mallory and Tristen had thought it best if their suspicion that revenant shards of Dust and Ariane might be involved was broken to Perceval in person—and brought the unconscious parrotlet to its creator for a detailed conversation.

Cynric might have been hard at work. She might have been napping on her feet. It was possible, Tristen admitted, pausing just inside the threshold of the door that had slipped open for him as automatically as if he were invited, that she had learned a way to manage both at once, sleeping with one side of her brain at a time like a cetacean. He did not think he'd ever seen her lie down to rest, or even claim a need for it.

But then, she was Cynric the Sorceress—or she was all that was left of what had been Cynric the Sorceress—and she was as much Engine as Engineer.

"Hello, Tristen," she said without turning. Her head was tilted back on her long neck, the long almond-shaped eyes closed so her lashes smudged her cheeks, her hair—straight as Perceval's, and browner—trailing across her loose robes to fall the length of her spine. "You have brought something of mine?"

"I think it's ill or injured." He came up beside her, extending the transparent clamshell in which he'd nested the parrotlet. It lay amid fleece like an icing decoration on meringue, green on white with its tiny head tucked close to the body, its papery eyelids closed over eyes round as beads.

"Hacked," she said, accepting the package. It opened at her touch, and she gently insinuated her fingers under the bird's still form. "How odd. This isn't the first time anyone has brought me one of these."

She lifted the tiny thing and put its head in her mouth,

then removed it—damp—and frowned. "It's been cut off from the rest, poor thing. Somebody who should be performing his own research is attempting to ride my labcoattails, Prince Tristen."

The shake of her head made her eyes catch the light, and the stud through her nose glowed dimly—the same pale green as the parrotlet. Tristen watched as it shuddered, raised its head slowly, and shook itself as if awakening from a hard dream that had left it logy.

"Hmm," she said, studying it, then shifted her attention to Tristen. "Thank you. I suppose it will be all right now. Where did you find this?"

"Among a few dozen murdered Deckers." He handed her a crystal, the same recordings of what he and Mallory had seen that Mallory was delivering to the Captain. She accepted and pocketed it; he had no doubt she would download and integrate the information as soon as he departed. "What could you do with one of those birds? If you were unfriendly to the world, or to its Captain?"

Cynric opened the cage of her fingers and let the bird fly up, circling the irregular outline of her workshop. "They're a prayer."

Tristen folded his arms. "I realize," he said, as jovially as he could manage, "that you have put a great deal of effort and practice into your gnomic utterances, Sister. But I for one would appreciate it if you spoke plainly, just this once."

She straightened in surprise—not quite a recoil, but a definite reaction—and crunched the clamshell and swaddling between her palms. Her colony—or *a* colony, in any case; here in her workshop, there might be many—disassembled it promptly. She turned to watch the parrotlet spiraling overhead, her feet bearing her in a crooked circle. Tristen turned merely to watch her turn.

"I put something of the Leviathans' ability to dream the future in them," Cynric said. "The parrotlets want to live, you see. And so they help the world live with them. They are a prayer for safety. One that will be listened to."

"If they were hacked—"

"That one *was* hacked," she said. "Hacked and then abandoned."

"So could someone use them to pray for something else?"

She nodded. "Oh, yes," she said. "I rather imagine they could."

13

this lord of grail

All red with blood the whirling river flows,
The wide plain rings, the dazed air throbs with blows.
Upon us are the chivalry of Rome—
Their spears are down, their steeds are bathed in foam.
—MATTHEW ARNOLD, "Tristram and Iseult"

The research scull *Quercus* was tiny and cramped. Her forty square meters of living space were adequate for one individual, as long as that individual wasn't claustrophobic and didn't mind exercising in the sort of wheel one used for caged pets, but it necessitated close cooperation if two unrelated adults were going to inhabit her for any length of time. Every so often, Danilaw found himself pausing to stare out viewports into the velvety space beyond, wondering how human beings had managed under these circumstances before the application of rightminding technology had become so trivial and precise.

Fortunately, Captain Amanda's basic personality was healthy and resilient, her rightminding was solid, and the earlier evidence of her robust sense of humor proved no fluke. Danilaw had no idea how she put up with him, but as a Free Legate she had effective training in dealing with disparate personalities, and as a social scientist and an expert in C22 society, she was without a doubt more comfortable with the range of human variation than were most people.

Which worked out well for Danilaw, who knew he was quirky. Not everybody's brain chemistry was as solid as Amanda's. Danilaw's underlying genetic issues meant his own emotional balance could stray from perfection, and his inherited neurochemistry meant that his rightminding fell in need of more-frequent-than-usual maintenance. Not enough to cause a social disadvantage, or free him from his Obligations—but enough to make him wish sometimes that it might.

But Captain Amanda knew about that now, and had seemed neither startled nor horrified by the revelation.

On the other hand, staring out the ports of the *Quercus* made him aware that sometimes the annoyance of civil service was worth it. This was not a view everyone got—or even most people. Space travel was expensive and resource-consuming—an extreme privilege accorded him in extreme times.

There were a few other things to be grateful for. Though the research vessel was cramped, her engines were state of the art. She used a quantum drive that took advantage of the same ancient technology that allowed gravity control—and FTL, though the *Quercus* was strictly an in-system, sublight vessel.

In any case, Danilaw hoped he didn't prove too much of a disruption in Amanda's routine. She spent the voyage much as he imagined she usually did—buried in research, checking telemetry, and in general doing all three of her jobs simultaneously and well. Meanwhile, Danilaw discovered he could run a city just as well by remote control as while living in it, or so he flattered himself. Admittedly, running Bad Landing was mostly a matter of checking to make sure it was properly running itself and giving it the odd tweak when it didn't, but there was a level of expertise in knowing what those tweaks were.

In his off hours, Danilaw read up on C21 and C22 customs and cultures, and practiced his guitar, using a pair of induction clips rather than a speaker out of consideration for his passagemate.

At least, he did so until Captain Amanda looked up from her desk, which she had dragged into her sleeping cubby, and said, "You know, music won't bother me unless it's bad, and since you earned it out as a secondary, I can't imagine it would be."

He heard her clearly—a benefit of the clips was that they left his ear canals clear—and probably (he thought) failed to hide his surprise. "You can concentrate with all that going on?"

"Crèche raised," she said. "I can concentrate through anything. Besides, you're the best entertainment on this tub." She stretched sturdy legs out of her bunk and stood, bending her spine and leaning back to balance under the lip of the cubby like a cave-climber. The desk she left parked in the bedclothes.

"Tub? Is that any way to talk about your vessel, Captain?"

She grinned and plunked down on the matting. It was soft, conducive as a surface for resting, stretching, or acrobatics—and unlikely to damage anything you dropped on it. Danilaw was growing quite attached to it as a floor covering. It was even easy to vacuum, and if they lost gravity abruptly, it wouldn't hurt to smack yourself into.

"Well, this is a glorified tugboat run," she said. "Come on. Play me something our visitors' umpteen-great-grand-parents might have listened to. Didn't they have genres of religious music?"

He hefted his guitar. He knew a couple that were actually pretty good. If they were anything a Kleptocrat-duped religious fanatic might have grooved out to, that was anybody's guess. But that wasn't the point, exactly, was it?

"Sure," he said. "We can call it research."

* * *

The trick, Dust thought, always lay in speaking to his
patron without alerting her host. It would be a hazardous
game. But he knew where to find her—she'd made sure he
could follow her movements—and a toolkit could go many
places unnoticed, especially in Engine. Dust now took advantage of that freedom.

Travel in this new world was easy. Dangers were clear to
see—structural weaknesses and the lairs of ambush predators delineated by caution zones and warning buzzers.
There were highways, access shafts, lifts, and functioning
air locks everywhere.

Travel in Engine was even easier. The Dust toolkit joined
his scurrying brethren, sweeping-whiskers-to-fluffy-tail
along the margins of wide corridors, scuttling over cable
bridges and through valve doors sized just right for a creature no longer than a man's forearm.

When he came at last by secret ways to the place his program had summoned him to attend, it was deserted. A cube
with twining vines up every wall, nodding flowers of jim-
sonweed and morning glory basking in the mist that con-
densed on each petal. The cube's resident had folded the
bedding away before the irrigation cycle, and Dust climbed
up on the transparent, bevel-cornered box that housed it
and several changes of clothes.

There he sat, grooming the moisture from his tail and
hunting up scraps of edibles in the cracks of the mossy
sleeping platform, until the cube divider slid aside and a
pale hand parted the hanging vines. A face and a shoulder
followed; hazel eyes widened in greeting. "Hello, toolkit.
Do you have a message for me?"

The host was dressed as an Engineer, but looked like a
Conn. Dust knew he should recognize *which* Conn, but
those were among the details that had been scraped away
by his reduced circumstances and lost.

Dust did have a message, however. Embedded in his program, a string of phonemes that made words in no language the world had ever heard. A key. A trigger.

That head-tilt melted into something else. The same gesture, the same face—but a different intention behind it.

"Wonderful," Ariane Conn said. "That worked beautifully. We may speak freely here. Welcome, ghost of Dust. Did you arrange a conversation for me?"

"I did," the toolkit said, whiskers twitching. Subtlety was another element of his former skill that had been lost in the interests of data compression. He needed information, and so he spoke his question to her. "I do not understand why *you* would reconstitute me, when we were enemies. Your ally, as I recall, was Asrafil."

She slid the door closed and set the privacy filter. "I went to great lengths—risking this body and the revelation of my own existence—to free my daughter Arianrhod from Caitlin's machinations." Her face compressed with grief. "Arianrhod loved Asrafil. She served him. And Asrafil betrayed her to her death. Cynric consumed her."

Dust nodded his pointed face. Death was always a relative function, a complicated thing when you were dealing with angels or Exalt. People died in pieces, by increments, or were transformed into something else. For Means, death had meant something concrete, a hard limit.

"For certain is death for the born / And certain is birth for the dead," he quoted, stumbling over a scrap of contextual memory. But that wasn't quite right, so he choked to a halt and began again. "I am sorry for your loss."

"One cannot serve angels, Angel. One must own them."

Dust nodded again. Agreeing with Conns was what you did with them. Whether this one knew he was patronizing her or not, she reached out and stroked the fluff behind his spotted ears. Her touch—or his fur—was so soft that he felt it only as he might have felt a wind.

"You should have been mine." She smiled. "And now you are."

* * *

By stellar-system standards, it wasn't a long trip—measured in weeks rather than months, which had something to do with the velocities involved, both of the inbound, decelerating vessel and the massively overpowered-for-her-mass *Quercus.*

They had the *Jacob's Ladder* on telescopic and various other sensory systems (mass detector, q-scanner, electromagnetic, radio telemetry) long before they made direct visual contact.

But there was something about that first real sight of her, with Danilaw's own eyes, nonetheless.

She began as a bright dot, a reflective sparkle of obviously variable albedo and mass. As they came up upon her, she gradually resolved into a spiderweb, and then a sort of scaffolding.

Danilaw kept thinking they were closer than telemetry indicated, which alerted him intellectually to her scale. But he couldn't integrate her true scope until they came within about a kilometer. Then Danilaw's world-bred senses could no longer mislead him that this looming skeleton was anything other than gargantuan.

Superlatives and adjectives failed him simultaneously. The *Jacob's Ladder* hung against its backdrop of stars, covering the entire horizon as revealed to Danilaw and Amanda where they stood before cramped screens in the scull, which did not have a discrete bridge. Danilaw had studied the generation ship's schematics and designs, such as were still available after an elapsed millennium. He had thought himself prepared, and yet now that it was real, the discomfort of awe humbled him.

She was the largest man-made thing he had ever seen. And that comparison failed to do her justice, because she was orders of magnitude more enormous than the next biggest. Whole ranks and families of planetesimals had died to build her; the raw materials of a man-made world.

She might once have been a wheel, of sorts, although one oppressively vast—or, more precisely, a nested series of skeletal wheels set at angles to one another, like a wirework wind sculpture reproduced at unimaginable scale. Danilaw could see how each had once turned inside the next, how they had been angled to catch available light and cast each other not too much in shadow. He could even see where the immense full-spectrum light cannons had been mounted, aimed so that the pressure of escaping photons would contribute to the great ship's gentle propulsion. Each turning ring had stabilized the ship, and all together they had acted to make her akin to a giant gyroscope, balanced by her own spin.

She had been lovely once, the *Jacob's Ladder*. But now she was an enormous scarred skeleton of nodules joined by tubes, twisted in places and in others crudely repaired. Danilaw could make out generations of technology at work on her hull—*hulk* would have seemed the better word, except she was warm, a living ship, glowing softly in the infrared.

And she was, unmistakably, moving forward under her own power. He could see the gleam of her engines through the gaps in her frame, and the long cometary plume of her exhaust glazed with reflected sunlight when they came around to approach her on a diagonal, matching trajectories.

Some repairs seemed crude—machine-shop things, scrap metal hammered into place and spot-welded or even riveted to cover the scars of some of her traumatic amputations. Some were more craftsmanlike, with matched edges or careful jury-rigging. There were aluminum, plastic, ceramic alloys, titanium, even cloth painted with a doping compound in evidence, depending on where he looked and which schematic he glanced at.

And then there were the repairs and reductions which seemed almost clean in comparison. As the *Jacob's Ladder* moved against the starfield, bathed in her own lights, the rays of the distant sun, and the floods of the scull, he caught how beveled edges gleamed here and there as if they had been sliced with a knife so hot it left fused edges behind. Other surfaces resembled the sanded luster of frosted glass, as if the metal and ceramic of her hide had itself sublimated into space. Scorch marks, blisters, craters, and volatilized surfaces scarred her everywhere.

When the sharply held breath finally whistled out through his nostrils, it stung. Beside him, Captain Amanda slid her hands into her pockets, flat-palmed, fingers arched back and tendons in relief as if she were packing all the stress away in them.

She said, "When she left Earth's system, she was the size of Manhattan Island."

"Well, she isn't now," Danilaw answered. "Although I think you'd have to measure her to know. Open a hailing channel, please, Captain?"

The jewel in her forehead flashed as she nodded. But she didn't move immediately; she stood, watching the vast, battered armature of the alien vessel glide across the darkness behind.

"Captain?"

She shook her head as if rattling herself back into her body. "Sorry. Just thinking. This is the last moment of the world we know, isn't it? This is history."

He nodded. "I've been having that sensation a lot."

She blew out through her nose—more a sigh than a snort, but just barely—and looked down at her slippered feet on the decking. "I thought it would feel like more."

There was so much to consider, so much to negotiate. Perceval's head spun with it before the conversation was halfway through. Medical issues, in particular, concerned the Fisher King—*Danilaw Bakare,* she supposed she was going to have to get used to calling him, this strange gravity-stunted humanoid. He seemed seriously put out to learn that Perceval's people did not require quarantine precautions or what he referred to as "a gene scrub."

"We adapt," Perceval said. "Our immune systems are evolved to handle most pathogens. Even novel ones." *Except the ones that have been engineered to exploit our colonies.*

She barely remembered the engineered influenza that Ariane had infected her with, though it had wiped out most of the Exalt denizens of Rule, and she herself had only survived because of the intervention of Rien and Mallory the Necromancer. And this was not the venue to bring up the inducer viruses, spliced and machined from the silicon-based symbiotes of the Leviathan into agents for the mental and physical manipulation of any creature they should be introduced into.

The Fisher King—*Bakare, Bakare*—shook his head. "That doesn't address the issue of protecting my people from *your* pathogens." He smiled, softening stern words, and made a point of saying something playful. "Unless you can count on your microbes going where they are directed, I think, at this point, it's wise to maintain quarantine protocols. We'll come over in suits, if we're still welcome, and we'll bring sampling equipment. Once we've gotten an idea of what your microfauna are like, we'll be able to tell if we need to vaccinate, and what sort of isolation and sanitation protocols are necessary before you land on Fortune."

His choice of words and sentence structures was like something Dust would have recited, flowery and archaic. The good news was, if what he implied in his speeches could be trusted, being granted leave to land on Grail seemed a foregone conclusion. They would have to borrow lighters from the onworlders, or cannibalize the world in order to build their own—a prospect that filled Perceval with wide-eyed discomfort—although there was no telling what hoops they would have to jump through, and to which indignities they would be subjected, before that came to pass.

And there was always the possibility that Administrator Danilaw was lying. Perceval could not figure out what he'd gain from it—but then, if he was deceiving, it would be in his interests to hide the motives as well as the act. Or acts, for that matter.

Whatever went through the Fisher King's mind in the moments he stood with his eyes downcast, studying the tips of his boots (if that's what he was wearing, there below the vidmote's pickup range), when he raised his gaze to Perceval's projected image again, his expression was that of a man resolute. He spoke as if he had prepared a speech, as before, but this time there was no resorting to notes. Perceval found herself flattered that he—a Mean—had memorized what he wished to say to her.

Her, in her personage as Captain. Not her-Perceval. He was a Head of State speaking to another Head of State, and foreign as that was, she needed to recollect it. This was not like speaking to Dorcas, or one of the Decker leaders. She was not this man's liege lord, nor his conqueror.

He said, "We mourned you."

A simple sentence. Three words: subject, verb, object. So unlike his usual elaborate eloquence, but when he said it, it echoed around her with the weight of his emotion and intention.

"We?" she said, already half knowing. He hadn't mourned *her*, not in his own person or hers. But she understood where he was going; she just wanted to hear him say it.

"Earth," he said. "Earth, her people, mourned your ancestors. We believed that the Kleptocracy had killed you all, that they sent you into space to freeze and die."

Perceval smiled. *The Kleptocracy.* So it had a name.

"They tried."

As if the weight of her admission had bowed the conversation, they both remained silent for a moment. Perceval supposed it was her place to open the discourse again. When she spoke, she imagined that this Fisher King, this lord of Grail, would understand that her *we* was for her forebears and antecedents, and not relevant to her speaking in her own person.

"We mourned the Earth," she said.

The Fisher King smiled. "Actually, they did okay."

Her surprise—shock; call it what it was—must have showed in her face, because he hastened to add, "In the long run, I mean. The late-twenty-second was a nightmare, from all I've heard. Deaths measured in the billions, famine, savagery. But the population crash proved a sort of blessing in the long term, because when they began to rebuild, they no longer needed the infrastructure that had been necessary at peak population."

Perceval licked her lips. "It's an established principle," she said. "The survivors of a crisis and their immediate descendants flourish in a wide-open ecology. There is a proliferation of available niches."

The Premier said, "The survivors don't have to strive for resources or subsistence. They can turn their attention to less banal pursuits than outcompeting their fellows. And the survivors institutionalized that. They abolished sophipathies, and we took steps to protect our societies from their recurrence. Many of the descendants of those same regulations and procedures are still in place." He paused. "Do you understand what I am saying?"

"Your legal system," Perceval said. "You will expect us to abide by it, and cede authority to your leaders."

The words came with a rush of relief; she hoped she didn't sound as excited as she felt by the prospect of not being *in charge* anymore. She'd never wanted this role of Captain; she'd never wanted the opinions of dead antecedents echoing through her aching head. And though she had accepted leadership and symbiosis as part of the cost of saving her people, acceptance was not the same as celebration.

She was no longer the girl she had been when she became Captain. She was a woman now, and a leader, and she had accepted that a good deal of life entailed doing the sorts of things one really would rather not. But Perceval looked into this strange man's face and glimpsed release, and it excited her.

His reaction did not fill her with confidence, or even allow her to long sustain that welcome relief. He glanced at his colleague, the Captain. Perceval was coming to understand that *Captain* meant something different to these alien humans than it did within the walls of her own world.

He said, "Do you understand what I mean by *sophipathology?*"

"The etymology," Perceval said carefully, "suggests that a sophipathology is an illness of sophistry, which is to say of illogical or self-referential thought. Perhaps an ingrained or circular sort of reasoning?"

"In C21," the Fisher King said, "which is our last cultural referent in common and one with which both my colleague and I are familiar—so please forgive me if I rely overheavily on its structures—they would have called it a *toxic meme*. A poisonous and conventionally ineradicable self-perpetuating idea. Because of the vagaries of our evolutionary heritage, it is easy for us to become irrationally loyal to these destructive patterns.

"We have learned to treat for this genetic illness. That treatment is one of the root causes of our prosperity; we require it of all citizens and productive members of society, and we will not permit sophipathologies to become reestablished in our culture."

The old Perceval would have licked her lips and glanced aside at Tristen, seeking the counsel of his expression. But she and her colony had weathered many storms and attempted revolutions, and she would give nothing away to this representative of the potential enemy.

"Perhaps you could give me some examples of what you consider an illness of the thought," she said. "I suspect there are many possible definitions."

"I have heard you mention angels," he said, with all the care of a diplomat who expects his words to be unwelcome. "Considering the history of the *Jacob's Ladder* as a vessel for the Kleptocratic exploitation of those infected by New Evolutionist religious memes, we would consider a belief in angels as a likely pathology. Especially as it is historically and epistemologically linked to similarly illogical and toxic beliefs such as idolatry, worship of one's own culture as chosen and deserving above all others, and religious and ideological fanaticism. It is our experience that these belief structures are exceptionally virulent, only matched for pathology by irrational economic and moral codes, and capable of persisting in the face of all evidence, suffering, and reason."

"Angels are real," Perceval said, measuring her tones, permitting her brow to furrow so the Fisher King would know she struggled to understand. "I am in the presence of one right now. We make them."

"But in so constructing the metaphors surrounding your relationship with your artificial intelligences—if I understand correctly what these servants are—you reinforce a historical sophipathology which has resulted in untold billions of deaths, both of humans and other biologicals."

"So by sophipathology, you mean . . . a heresy?" That was familiar ground, and Perceval for a moment breathed easier. "We do not prosecute heresies anymore, Administrator Danilaw. That, for us, is ancient history."

But rather than similarly relieved, the Fisher King looked if possible more tired and distressed. "I mean the kind of ingrained flaw in one's reason that would lead one to align one's self so strongly with a brand of dogma that one might identify others as heretics, actually."

Perceval pressed her fingernails into her palms. She had anticipated that the cultural disconnect would be vast, and she was only just coming to understand *how* vast it might be. He spoke. For the most part, he used words she understood. But the manner in which he used them left her feeling as if she had just listened to a recording of some nonhuman creature reciting abstract poetry. It was easier to follow the thought processes of an angel.

She said, "I do not understand. How is it that you live without angels?"

He rubbed his face in what she thought was exasperation, though it could have just been exhaustion. She was learning that these alien humans were much like Means—fragile, of fragmented memory, and prone to easy exhaustion—and that in other ways they were not Mean at all.

"How do you live with them?" His irritation, if that was what it was, turned into a headshake. "We just do."

She folded her hands together, interlacing the fingers. She huffed across the knuckles, producing a whistling noise. "I think we should conduct further conversations in person," she said. "You and Captain Amanda have my permission to dock your ship and come aboard."

"We will have to observe quarantine," the Fisher King said. "It will not be so different than this."

"Different enough," Perceval said. "The Angel Samael will assist you with your docking arrangements and requirements for environmental isolation. That is my will."

With a mental signal to Nova, she cut the connection. Tristen had not moved from his seat on the grassy berm opposite, but his hands were folded and he was regarding her. "Turning them over to an angel when they've expressed such a strong distaste for the whole concept? I'm not sure that's politic."

"Maybe they'll find out how useful angels are and suffer a thought infection."

Tristen smiled. "He gets on your nerves."

Perceval shook her hair back, smoothing the locks behind her shoulders with both hands. "He's a smug, self-righteous, condescending *Mean*," she said. "If he thinks we're uncivilized thugs, well—"

"We need him, Perceval," her First Mate cautioned. "Unless you really want to go and *take* his planet from him."

Her toes curled into the verdant green turf underfoot. "Don't," she said. "Don't tempt me."

14

it is a library, and I am its necromancer

I lose! They're loaded dice. Time always plays
With loaded dice.
—WILLIAM BUTLER YEATS, "Time and the Witch Vivien"

Danilaw Bakare had not realized how thoroughly he anticipated the barbaric splendor of the generation ship's interior until its grandeur overwhelmed his expectations entirely. The docking bay had the same blasted, repurposed, resurfaced look that characterized the mottled exterior of the vessel. It was also vast, cradling the *Quercus* entire. Danilaw stood on the tiny habitation deck watching the long, seemingly animate arms of the *Jacob's Ladder* embrace the scull, growing over the air lock and avoiding the motes and ports. He could not avoid the comparison to a dodecapus sensitively enveloping its prey.

He sealed his helmet one-handed and turned to make sure Captain Amanda, too, was ready. Seeing her mirror the gesture made him grin; it was good that they were looking out for each other.

"Once more unto the breach," she said, patting his space-suited shoulder with a bulky gauntlet. There were weapons on her belt, and the Free Legate jewel over her eye told him she knew both physically and ethically how to use them, but that didn't make him any more comfortable with the necessity—or the fact that he, for the first time in his life, felt naked walking around unarmed. *Maybe this will be peaceable. Maybe we can still pull that off.*

A lot of maybes to contend with.

They lined up by the exit. Captain Amanda cycled the lock around them and ran the decontamination protocol. The exterior door scrolled back slowly, the *Quercus*'s Fortune-standard atmosphere replaced by something that Danilaw's suit sensors read as thinner than weak tea and shockingly moist.

Captain Amanda was apparently thinking the same thing. "That's a lot of free water to leave floating around in a closed habitat . . ."

She never finished the sentence, which trailed off as if her voice were struck from her. Instead, they stood shoulder-to-shoulder and stock-still, neither at first quite processing what they were seeing. It was a corridor, or an accessway—a means of getting from the *Quercus* to the interior of the *Jacob's Ladder*. But it was—

It was full of trees. Or *made* of trees, or a tree, or a latticing vine grown into a tree through the passage of centuries. The outside perimeter was a filigree of dark, smooth bole, heavy palmate leaves carpeting every space between. When they stepped over the threshold onto the surface, Danilaw lurched the first step as a slightly different angle of gravity asserted itself. Amanda reached out to steady him; neither fell.

From among the leaves, a swirl of atmosphere—a dust devil?—manifested. It grew and complicated, sweeping up bits of detritus into a roughly human outline. "Hello," the projection said, as Danilaw shied back from its extended limb-approximation. "Don't be afraid. Welcome to the world. I am Samael. I have been sent to guide you."

An angel, Danilaw realized—and now, meeting it, he intuited its history and purpose better than he had before. One of Captain Perceval Conn's servitors, or masters, or compatriots. Artificial intelligences originally programmed by the Kleptocracy and its creatures. A piece of terrible history, left behind to trouble future generations.

Danilaw felt as if he were confronted by an animate, talking gas chamber, or an iron maiden with pretty manners. What was less ethical than giving artificial intelligence personalities? Than creating—in essence—a slave race: creatures with agency and identity but only the semblance of free will?

Danilaw's people still used smart systems. But they had long since abandoned the horrific practice of making *people* of them, and then enslaving the people they had made.

As Danilaw's pulse accelerated and his oxygen usage spiked, he saw the motion of Amanda's suit; she had rocked back on her heels. He wondered what she was experiencing. Her knowledge of the relevant history was more detailed than his own; Danilaw suspected that made this encounter all the more unsettling.

If Amanda was more discomfited, she also recovered from it better. "Hello, Samael," she said. "I am Captain Amanda Friar. This is Danilaw Bakare, City Administrator of Bad Landing."

The Angel's sunflower-petal eyebrows quirked. "I was provided with your files," he said. "If you will come with me, I will bring you to my Captain."

They fell into step beside him. The corridor was wide enough for all three abreast, though the uneven surface of the interwoven, intergrown branches or trunks made the footing akin to skipping over cobblestones in reduced gravity. If Danilaw took a header, he wouldn't fall hard.

"Feel free to ask any questions you like," Samael said. "We are eager to share our knowledge with you as an expression of goodwill, and to establish that we can help your society become more flexible and adaptive. Also, you are welcome to use our resources. If it would make you more comfortable, please feel free to remove your armor."

Samael gestured around magnanimously. Danilaw blinked, understanding suddenly that for a culture in which every atom of oxygen and molecule of water was an irreplaceable consumable, this was an exceedingly generous offer. Danilaw was accustomed to metering his object and resource usage, observing the Obligations, wasting neither personal nor collective assets. But to a society such as this, centuries out from a habitable world—they had what they had, and there would be no getting more. It went beyond Obligation, beyond social justice. Parsimony was their means of survival.

His confusion and revelation seemed transparent to the Angel, who kept talking as if conducting a familiar guided tour. "You have our word that you may unseal in safety. The Captain has ordered our microfauna and flora to treat your persons and equipment as sterile zones. You will not be colonized."

"Wait," Danilaw said. "Your Captain ordered this? Your microbes follow instructions?"

Samael gave him what he would have sworn was a pitying look. "They obey the Captain. Are they not part of the world's ecology?"

Danilaw saw Captain Amanda's eyelashes flicker through the wide faceplate of her pressure suit. He thought she smiled, a wry expression he read as wonder, but she concealed it quickly.

"Our viruses aren't so civilized," she said. "For your sakes, we should remain sealed."

"Also," Danilaw said apologetically, "your atmosphere is slightly thin and sour by our standards. We need to supplement oxygen. How do you—your people, I mean—survive in such low saturations?"

The Angel tossed flowing straw-colored locks over his shoulders. It might be some vegetable fiber, or the mane of some animal that Danilaw did not know. "Naked mole rats."

"I *beg your pardon?*"

"Naked mole rats," Samael repeated. "They're an Earth species of colony-living burrowing rodent that is—or was; they may be extinct on the old planet, although *we* have some—supremely adapted to the, well, the exceptionally *nasty* conditions found in their lairs. Centuries ago, Cynric the Sorceress introduced their adaptations to deoxygenated and toxic atmospheres into the human genome. This enabled our crew to survive and flourish despite the damage wrought to the world by the Breaking."

"Cynric . . . the Sorceress?" It was only the light filtering through the bowering leaves on every side that flashed from Amanda's jewel, but the way it gleamed when she cocked her head led Danilaw to entertain a fantasy that the sparkles were an external indicator of frantic processing activity within.

Samael nodded. Even in profile, the mosaic-approximation of a beaky, lined human face was three-dimensional and compelling. "She was the head of genetic engineering, five hundred and fifty years ago. You can meet her."

"*Meet* her?"

"For certain. Or her remnant, at least. She is alive again, though incomplete from what she was. There are also a couple of true survivors of the Moving Times and the Breaking. We anticipated that you might be interested in speaking with them."

Five hundred and fifty, Danilaw mouthed to Amanda through his faceplate.

She shrugged, as if other insanities still held more of her attention. *Mole rat DNA,* she mouthed back.

Danilaw nodded. Okay, so living five hundred years wasn't such a surprise after that. Obviously, the *Jacob's Ladder* survivors had developed life-extending technology. Or they habitually put people in cold storage for centuries at a stretch. One, Danilaw thought, was as likely as the other, though the idea of this ancient genetic engineer being alive "again," and somehow damaged by the process, supported the cryogenic theory.

"Where are we going now?" Amanda asked, stretching her legs to keep up with the Angel. He wasn't tall, but then Danilaw guessed that he also probably wasn't walking.

"Directly to the Captain," Samael said. "It's a big world, however, and I ask you to bear with me."

A big world indeed. They hiked for over an hour, leaving Danilaw grateful that he'd kept up with his fitness Obligation. Even servo-assisted and allowing for the *Jacob's Ladder*'s intermittent gravity, his pressure suit was heavy for walking in. At least it processed heat efficiently, or he imagined his visor would have fogged past visibility in the first fifteen minutes.

He was glad it didn't. Because the *Jacob's Ladder*—or the world, as Samael insisted on referring to it—only became *more* grand and improbable with what every turning revealed, what lay behind every air lock, gate, or grid.

Each time the Angel, obviously accustomed to taking into account the frailties of corporeal life-forms, apologized for not taking them along the scenic route, Danilaw felt his disbelief strengthen. It would have been difficult to imagine anything more compelling than the insanely complicated ecosystems and architectures he and Amanda were being led through.

The travelers toiled up mossy boulders past cataracts of tumbling water, and animals and birds Danilaw could not begin to identify flocked in every environment. Glades of trees filled arching passageways with transparent walls that showed the architecture of the *Jacob's Ladder* from within. But for all its wonders, the ship had a patched, weary air to it, like a made-over old quilt ready for the recyclers.

"Here we are," Samael finally said. "The library."

It was not, as the door glided wide, what Danilaw would have identified as a library. No paper books, no clay tablets, no inscribed jewels. No holographic, Bose-

Einstein, or magnetic records. No papyrus scrolls and no solid-state archives.

Just a grove of fruit trees, stretching to the curved outside wall of a vast space, surrounded on every side by hungry emptiness.

"Library," Captain Amanda said. She turned her head, and then her entire body, rotating in her footsteps. Danilaw knew she was scanning the space with her suit recorders, transmitting the data home. As Legate, one of her Obligations was to science and history. "*This* is your *library?*"

Here, the atmosphere was warm and thick—a rich mix of oxygen, carbon dioxide, and nitrogen, with trace elements. Some products of decomposition, some by-products of living things metabolizing. He wished he dared breathe it; from the way the mossy soil dented under his feet, he imagined it smelled intensely green.

Danilaw's own sensors told him that a warm body was approaching through the orchard, and in a few moments a slender figure ducked branches and appeared. He had expected a hierarchal gauntlet, and to be kept waiting and maneuvering through layers of functionaries until he could be brought before the Captain—presented with great solemnity, like the centerpiece of a feast.

But all that arrived now was an androgynous person clad in tight-fitting blacks and oranges, a halo of frizzy dark curls framing an elfin face. *Woman*, Danilaw thought, and then *No, transgendered.* The voice, when it came, was no help at all.

"I'm Mallory," this person said. "It is a library, and I am its necromancer. The Captain is expecting you. Come in. Oh and—for your own safety—ask before you eat any fruit, please. Some of it is trickier than others."

Danilaw and Amanda, still accompanied by the semicorporeal Angel, wound among the trees, trying not to jostle ripe fruit from limbs that dripped old Earth delicacies. He recognized oranges and limes—unless those were lemons—

persimmons, pomegranates, and something that might be apples. They weren't round and red, though, but striped red and green and gold in faint striations. There was a dark, almost black, fruit with a glossy bloom, and there was a small red-gold one that might be a cherry—

He lost track just about the time the necromancer led them into a clearing where white cane chairs sat in a circle around a transparent-topped table. It looked like a garden party, except the two individuals rising to meet them from behind that table were the people to whom Danilaw had been speaking via radio, with ever-decreasing delays, for the better part of two months now.

The First Mate was even more attenuated and strange in person, his white hair sparkling like bleached, unspun wool in the brilliant sunlight. That sunlight—clearer and more stark than what Danilaw was used to seeing warmed by miles of atmosphere—fell through the transparent panels overhead. In this direct light, Tristen's skin was a translucent blue, as if someone had left inky water in an antique teacup until the pigment stained the porcelain. He wore a hardened pressure suit of cool white, the helm and gauntlets removed. The assemblage taken as a whole resembled a medieval suit of armor. Over it hung a sheathed sword, of all the insane archaic devices.

And the Captain—

Danilaw had somehow thought her apparent gauntness and strange proportions were exaggerated by the effect of transmission. If anything, they had been minimized, flattened. The woman who held out her hand to greet him, as unfazed by his space suit as if it were a formal visiting gown, could never pass for an unmodified human. Stage cosmetics could have hidden her skin tone, but not the depth of her chest nor the articulation of the shoulder joints—not to mention the short, peculiar structures on her upper back that lifted her pale dress across them and sometimes seemed to move of their own volition, working like the stump of a three-legged quadruped's missing limb.

"I am Perceval Conn," she said. "Welcome to my world. You are the first nonnative to set foot on her in seven hundred years."

Danilaw was far more self-conscious about his pressure suit than she was. Instead, she cocked her head to look at it, and smiled. "Your armor is a different design from what we use," she said. "Pardon if I stare. I had thought to offer you lemonade, but—" She gestured with self-deprecation. "I suppose Tristen and Mallory and I will have to drink it ourselves. Can you manage to sit, at least? Mallory, would you find our guests a bench, please? I don't think the lawn furniture is likely to accommodate them."

Before leaving, Mallory laughed—a charming lilt with an engaging hint of wickedness—and just as androgynous as everything else. Danilaw was beginning to get the idea that it was calculated, a sort of performance.

This person—Mallory—was not what he had expected from what he knew of the transgendered . . . which was, to be true, mostly derived from popular period music, a notoriously unnuanced and melodramatic means of understanding any given social phenomenon. Danilaw was willing to bet many a C19 romance had ended with neither party shot down dead, but you'd never tell that from the pop songs.

"Thank you," Danilaw said, to fill the silence. "You have been accommodating. I realize that many of our requests might seem outlandish—"

"You seem reasonably cautious," Perceval said. "Never fear. We will not judge you based on our deep martial culture."

Her lips were quirking. Danilaw decided he was being teased. "Do you have a deep martial culture?" He couldn't help a sideways glance at the First Mate in his Galahad armor, the black sword on his hip.

Captain Perceval turned and regarded him. When he blushed, Danilaw realized, his whole face flushed as blue as a startled dodecapus. "Well, Tristen Tiger," she said, while Mallory returned with the requested bench, "are you a deep martial culture, Uncle?"

That explained the relationship. Danilaw had wondered if they were lovers—an alien elf-queen and her consort.

First Mate Tristen glanced down. Danilaw watched the flush quell itself in his cheeks as quickly as it had risen. "Once upon a time," he said, with no apparent irony, "I was for any war I could get. But I got old."

When he looked up, his transparent eyes were like the first black ice of winter—thin and perilous. Danilaw believed that Captain Perceval had shown him that on purpose, and he made a note. *They will fight if they feel they have to.*

Very well. So would his folk.

Mallory set the bench up, pausing to laugh behind a hand. "Tristen Tiger," the librarian, or necromancer, said. "And yet you have always been such a pussycat to me."

This time the blush was controlled more quickly, but Danilaw saw the daggery look the First Mate shot the necromancer—or librarian. So this was a sport with them, baiting the albino. And if the First Mate was not the Captain's consort, Danilaw would lay pretty good odds that he had some sort of romantic relationship with the necromancer.

Danilaw seated himself with thanks, ignoring the uncomfortable pressure of his posterior anatomy against the inside of his pressure suit. Captain Amanda sat down beside him.

"We are," Perceval said, "apparently something of a failure on the martial glory front. Rest assured, we do not require posturing and childish proofs of your moral fortitude. We merely wish to arrive— *Oh!*"

In his pressure suit, Danilaw did not feel the shock wave, but he saw the results: the trees knocked into sharp bends, as if by a strong wind; the crack of shattering branches and a few boles. The First Mate's pressure suit writhed about him like a living thing, extruding gauntlets and a helm as he dove after the Captain. She hadn't quite been knocked tumbling, as Danilaw would have expected, but she did stagger before the force of the blow until her First Mate steadied her. Mallory went down on one knee and both hands, fingers curling into the dirt as if to cling to the world by main strength.

The angel's leaf-litter-and-straw outline guttered like a breath-whipped candle flame.

Beside Danilaw, Captain Amanda grabbed his upper arm and latched onto a neighboring citrus tree with her other hand, head ducked as if she anticipated the shock wave might be followed by a massive decompression. Danilaw braced for the same.

But there was nothing. A great stillness followed, making him realize how loud with birds and rustling this orchard library had been. The silence was broken first by Tristen saying "Is anyone badly hurt?" and then by the noises of Captain Perceval pushing his armored body off hers.

"Not here," Mallory said with a faraway expression. "The library is structurally undamaged."

"Engine and Rule are fine," Perceval said, her face crossed by a similar expression. They were checking intra-cerebral data links, Danilaw understood, and spared a shudder for how thoroughly these creatures had compromised themselves before the gods of self-modification. "There was an explosion— Oh."

She turned her head and tilted it from side to side, examining Danilaw and Amanda. "Suicide bombing? I would not like to think it of you—"

"I beg your pardon." Amanda released Danilaw's arm and stepped forward, squaring her shoulders. "My people do not engage in acts of terrorism."

"I see," the First Mate said. "Then you will be as surprised as I was to learn that your ship has exploded."

15

learn to praise the imperfect world

> The trees grew naked by the way,
> And from his ramparts, bleak and gray,
> They heard the Winter call.
> —JOHN GROSVENOR WILSON, "Morgain"

"Dorcas," Samael spat, as Tristen and Mallory righted the overturned table. Tristen jumped and glared, a fist of presumptuous worry clenching around his heart, but the Angel continued. "If not she, then one of her creatures."

Tristen could not fault him. She was the obvious suspect, she and her Go-Back clansmen. But he bridled at the accusation, and wondered how much of that was a father's loyalty.

More immediately, there were practical considerations. And, most immediately, political ones. Fortunately, Tristen could address both of those simultaneously.

"Nova," he said, "can we have an external replay of any monitoring of our guest's shuttle?"

"First Mate," she said. An instant later, a three-dimensional representation of the shallow-space lighter and the bay surrounding it resolved before them, so solid you might expect to be able to rap on it. Mallory's library was bereft of holotanks; this was Nova in her own person, adapting the fogs and colonies that made up her corporeal form to represent the destruction of the shuttle.

"Commencing animation," Nova said.

For a moment, there was only the silence and the stillness of space. The shuttle was a silver disc without visible means of producing thrust; Tristen suspected its drive worked by gravitational manipulation. It hung lightly in a webwork cradle extruded from the world's long arms, apparently quiescent until a small shudder shivered the recorded image. A moment later, the shell of the vessel jumped, crazed, and came apart in an expanding dandelion clock of debris, an inertial streamer smearing forward more than back, because the world was still decelerating as she came up to the system's habitable zone. Now the view shook *hard*—not the ripple of before, but a sharp, teeth-clenching rattle—and when it stabilized the cloud of debris was overrunning the observers.

A younger Tristen would have waited impassively as simulated shrapnel whizzed past and through him, but he was old enough now to allow himself an honest wince. But when the debris collapsed back on the point of origin rather than blowing clear or settling against the bulk of the world, he was startled enough that he felt his face smooth. *Give nothing away.*

The lessons of childhood clung hard.

"Two explosions," Tristen said, raising his chin to meet the Captain's eyes over the heads of their visitors. "A small one, and then the one that destroyed the shuttle."

"A . . . mine?" asked the alien diplomat, with a weighty pause as if he had to search for the word in long-archived memories.

The alien Captain, Amanda, folded her arms. "I'm afraid not," she said. "Did you see the way the debris imploded?"

Tristen, for one, was still watching. The majority of the wreckage settled again into a lumpy near sphere, shifting against itself as if vibrations through the frame of the world sieved it down. Relative acceleration meant the debris cloud was gliding out in advance of the *Jacob's Ladder,* trailing rent cables from the docking cradle that reached after it like hungry tentacles. "I've seen something like it before," he said. "When I was young."

Perceval stood calmly, frowning, concentration deepening all the creases of her countenance. "The Breaking," she said, in the tones of one who already knows the answer to her question.

"It's a typical pattern when a gravity drive explodes due to mechanical failure or sabotage."

Tristen thought Captain Amanda spoke with fair calm and pragmatism, for somebody who was now—temporarily—stranded on an alien spaceship. The jewel embedded in her forehead flashed through the faceplate of her armor.

Nova said, "It is my estimation that if I had not been able to use colonies to absorb and attenuate the shock wave, that explosion was powerful enough to have rendered the world inoperable."

"Somebody tried to kill us all," Tristen said.

Amanda continued, "I can't be sure of anything until I have the opportunity to take a forensics team through the wreckage, but given the evidence of a smaller shock wave preceding the main explosion, I would lean toward the explanation that an explosive device was concealed in the *Quercus's* quantum engine core, where it would not be evident to crew inspection while she was under way, and that it was triggered by remote. Not a proximity sensor, or it would have gone off before Danilaw and I were able to disembark." She wet dry lips with a Mean's pink tongue. "You know what? It's stupid of me to waste my resources now. May I unseal, Captain Conn?"

"The offer stands," Perceval said. In the command space they shared, Tristen was aware of her effortless ownership of the crisis. As Captain—a mature and integrated Captain—her awareness of the world was as preconscious and prescient as her undermind's awareness of her physical body. The ship was the Captain, and the Captain the ship. And yet, if he had not been in there with her, he would never have realized her attention was mostly directed away from the alien diplomats.

Administrator Danilaw stared at Captain Amanda, but nodded. "We won't make it back to Fortune on suit reserve." He touched both hands to the sides of his helmet, and after a few manipulations lifted it off. Captain Amanda followed, though Tristen watched her throat work under the smooth pink-brown skin before her nostrils flared on the first indrawn breath.

However unsettled she was, neither she nor the Fisher King let it affect their demeanor. Two slow drags of air and she spoke again, her voice shaking only slightly. "The obvious conclusion is that the *Quercus* was sabotaged while I was dirtside, picking up Danilaw."

"We'll see that you get home," Perceval said. "After all, we're headed that way."

Captain Amanda's eyebrow arched at the joke. "I guess you are."

"You'll want to contact your people; you may use our arrays to do so."

"We have q-sets," Danilaw said. "Without the relay on the *Quercus*, we may need a power boost, but we can manage to call home."

Captain Amanda set her helmet down on the table and leaned her hands on either side of it. "How heavy are your casualties? How may Danilaw and I assist in your salvage operations?"

"Correlating," Nova said out of the air. Tristen made a point of not noticing when the Fisher King and his companion reacted with startlement. "Please carry on."

Tristen could have wished that she'd given a number— preferably a small one—but he understood. Her sensors and proprioception had been damaged in the explosion, and Tristen knew from eavesdropping her feed that—

under Perceval's guidance—she was already engaging search and repair parties, conducting survivor interviews, bringing in medical details. Organizing her immune response, like any organism in the face of attack. He gave her a part of his attention and felt Perceval doing the same.

"It's deeply problematic that one of our people would resort to terrorism," Danilaw said. "It's not that rightminding removes the capability for violence, you understand. But it addresses the irrational evolutionary triggers—territorialism, dominance—that result in a great deal of fighting."

"Rightminding," Tristen said, fastening on the unfamiliar word. It sounded somewhat ominous.

"Humans," Danilaw said, "evolved to collaborate—but also to compete. For resources, status, reproductive success."

Mallory said, "Competition is essential to evolutionary development."

"Ah," Danilaw said. "But after a certain point, evolution is no longer essential to existence."

It was a peculiar sensation, Tristen thought, to hear a sentence, to understand each word in it, and yet to have the abiding conviction that one had entirely missed the sense. He wasn't alone: beside him, Perceval—who, like Tristen, had half her attention on Nova's disaster-remediation efforts—cleared her throat uncomfortably.

And Samael said, "That is a heresy."

"By your standards," Danilaw said, "I have no doubt. And by ours, most of the foundations of your society are untenable abominations. Which is going to make things interesting if we have to share a planet." He glanced at Amanda, who in continuing to strip off her primitive armor had revealed an off-white jumpsuit of some fiber Tristen did not recognize. When she was out of it, her suit softened, compacting neatly to a small bundle attached to an oversized set of oxygen tanks—further evidence of the fragility of these Means, and their requirements for a rich atmosphere. She retrieved some sort of instrument package from the helmet and slipped it over her head, to dangle on a lanyard.

"Please explain what you mean by rightminding," Tristen said.

"These days, whenever possible, we do it through genetic surgery," Danilaw said. "But in an adult, it's a combination of microsurgery, chiefly to the temporal lobe, and therapeutic normalization of the neurochemistry. We use this process to mitigate some of the atavistic, self-destructive impulses of the human psyche—blind faith, sophipathology, tribalism—so that rational thought can prevail."

He hesitated. Perceval made a noise of encouragement. It sounded to Tristen as if what Danilaw was describing *was* evolution. Or evolutionism, anyway, so he wasn't sure where the touchiness lay.

But Danilaw looked at Captain Amanda, and she nodded. "One of my roles is historian," she said. "I'm here in part because of my interest in C22. And my esteemed colleague is worried about causing you offense because we are unused to dealing with, uh—with natural-minded individuals such as yourselves. And because resistance to the mandated administration of early forms of this process is one of the reasons why your ancestors left Earth."

"And the other," Danilaw said, "was because decades of irrational human competition had driven the homeworld into a state of ecological catastrophe, such that it could no longer support large human populations."

"We were not supposed to survive," Perceval said.

"We know," Danilaw said. "The Kleptocratic government—and what they did to your ancestors—was the final weight that really spun public opinion in favor of rightminding everyone. At first it was used to treat incurable ideologues and criminals. Then we moved on to sophipaths and Kleptocrats. The arcane priests of destructive religious systems such as Capitalism and—forgive me—Evolutionism came next. This was around the time your people moved on. Eventually, the rightminded population exceeded the unrightminded, and the procedure was made mandatory. Those were the last extensive wars Earth fought. Since then, they've managed through negotiation and compromise."

"It's not so shocking," Tristen said, thinking of the modifications he'd made to his own mind, memories, and emotional landscape over the years. "The romanticization of a natural human state as somehow superior to a managed one is—your word, I am not certain I'm using it properly?"

"Sophipathology?" Danilaw asked.

"Thought-sickness," Mallory supplied. Tristen smiled over his shoulder at the necromancer, and was rewarded by a flash of angelic grin through dark coiled hair.

Tristen rubbed his hands together. "So the implication of what you are telling us is that whoever sabotaged your vessel did so in a spirit of complete rationality?"

"Yes," Amanda said. "And in the spirit of the public good."

"That is useful information." Perceval inclined her head like a queen, leaving Tristen to wonder what the squat, earthbound alien couple made of her. "Please, I must address the crisis now; Samael will see you are made comfortable. Now that the autonomous response is complete, there will be decisions that require my full attention."

Amanda looked at Danilaw, seeking support, Tristen imagined, for whatever she would say next. His nod must have offered it, because when she turned back she spoke directly—and passionately—to Perceval.

"Captain," she said. "I understand that you have exceptionally good reasons not to trust us currently. But I beg of you—you must have wounded, and I feel a grave responsibility for their pain. As a Legate and ship's Captain, I have some medical training. Will you allow Danilaw and me to help in your recovery efforts?"

"Wounded?" Perceval thought for a moment. "We have facilities for them. But if you would care to observe, you are welcome to join us. I would recommend you allow us to provide you with armor before entering the damaged zone."

"That would be welcome," Danilaw said.

The Captain nodded. "All right then. Mallory, Tristen? You're also with me."

The pressure suits provided for Danilaw and Amanda were not at all what Danilaw was used to. But having observed Tristen's "armor" in action, Danilaw was confident that it was a superior technology—as long as it wasn't prone to catastrophic, untelegraphed failures.

Instructing him and Amanda in its use, Mallory seemed confident that they could handle it. "Even young children have no problem adapting to armor. The armor will take care of you. All you have to do is trust it."

Danilaw wiggled his fingers in the gauntlets, trying to accustom himself to the feel of the sticky-cool colloidal lining, and eyed the necromancer dubiously. "Trust it?"

"Danilaw," Mallory said, "this is armor. Armor, this is Danilaw. He is in your charge."

"I am pleased to be of service, Danilaw." The armor spoke through pinhole speakers in the neck aperture. Based on Amanda's jump, she was hearing something similar, which told him the voice response was directional. "Are you familiar with my operation?"

"No," Danilaw said, finding his voice. He was grateful for his rightminding. He could feel his body's adrenaline response, the atavistic desire to panic, but he was aware of it as a chemical response, and he controlled it. "I've never seen anything like you before."

"Shall I place myself in training mode?" the armor asked.

"Affirmative," Danilaw said.

"Normally phrased commands will suffice." Was that his own embarrassment causing him to imagine a comforting tone in its speech? Or a touch of hesitancy?

"Thank you," Danilaw said, concealing his stress and irritation that they were not yet moving to relieve the inevitable wounded. He did not know the disaster protocols on the *Jacob's Ladder*. Captain Perceval's apparent air of leisureliness might mean only that the situation was under control, and she was too much of a professional to act in haste. But Danilaw's adrenaline response urged at him nonetheless. *Do something, and do it now.*

He raised his eyes, straightening his spine. Around him, the others seemed garbed and ready. Danilaw was grateful that he still had his q-set; like Amanda's, it was modular. Now he wore it under this "armor" as he had worn it under the pressure suit, and it gave him a direct link to Amanda.

Probably not a secure one, given the armor's sensitivity to voice commands. But a way to speak with her, at least. Amanda's Free Legate status meant she could transmit anything she experienced as it happened, and Danilaw hoped she was doing so. Back on Fortune, Jesse and Gain should be going over the data already.

If Danilaw had thought Samael was giving them a grand tour (or a bit of a runaround) on the way in, the trip back disabused him. It was easier in the alien armor—it did some of the work of walking for him—and they traveled fast now. But the scenery was the same—although, as they moved through it, Danilaw was unsurprised to find it increasingly ravaged.

The scenery also *stopped* more abruptly than it had before.

They passed into the final air lock, still some ways from

where the docking cradle had been, and Tristen turned and said, "Seal up now."

All five sets of armor answered his command, helms scrolling shut in unison. Danilaw expected a pressure change, but there came no sense of a difference in atmosphere.

"Sealed," his suit responded, as Danilaw found himself staring through the gold-tinted mask of Tristen's armor. Tristen nodded—the armor telegraphed the motion—and turned back. When the First Mate cycled the air lock, Danilaw felt his heart squeezing in short rhythm as if it were lodged in the base of his throat. He gasped once, careful not to hyperventilate, and felt the thundering ease.

What he saw beyond the hatchway was exactly what he had anticipated. From the expressions behind the faceplates of the evolved and yet atavistic humans surrounding him, he imagined they were experiencing a more complicated emotional journey, but his own response was first the terrible sorrow and acceptance, and second the cataloging of what must be done to alleviate the situation.

The delicate docking cradle that had so gently webbed in the *Quercus* was reduced to writhing shards. The limbs that had surrounded it had been deformed by the force of the blast. The debris of the research scull itself was secured within a sort of silvery cargo net. Danilaw could not immediately identify its manufacture. As he watched, it writhed and grew, and spread itself across another few meters of scrap.

The damage was just as the animation had led him to believe, but other elements of the scene seemed wrong.

Danilaw expected salvage equipment, men and women in these shells of strange pressure armor—hardened by its own molecular bonds rather than by programmable fields—working feverishly. He expected medical teams and docbots—and what he saw was a strange absence of most of these things.

Before his eyes, the damage was unknitting itself, the world remade as if someone were running the animation of the explosion in reverse. It was the sort of effect one expected to see in an entertainment, and it stopped him cold where he hung.

He drifted silently for a moment, then opened his mouth and said, "Mallory? Who is effecting those repairs?"

"The Angel," Mallory said, as if it were a perfectly everyday sort of sentence. "She says there are six crew members mind-dead, a few dozen crew and organisms injured, and the ladder tree was destroyed beyond salvage."

"Oh," Perceval said. "That is a pity."

Mind-dead? Danilaw wondered. But it seemed like an inopportune time to ask.

"Can we clone her?" Tristen asked.

"There should be salvageable cellular material," Mallory said. "If any of it has an intact nucleus, we can replace the ladder tree. It won't bring back her experiences, but we have a recent backup. But . . . it will take centuries for her to grow so large and knowledgeable again."

"We don't have centuries," Perceval said. Danilaw had the distinct sense that quietly, contained within herself, she was grieving.

"Not if Danilaw lets us land," Mallory said. "But then that begs the question—what *would* we have done with her when we got to Grail, anyway? What will we do with *all* our biodiversity?"

"Grail?" Danilaw asked, to cover his flinch. It was an excellent question.

"Your world," Perceval said, floating before that enormous emptiness. "What do you call it?"

"Fortune," Danilaw said. "And the sister world is Favor."

Perceval turned to him and extended an armored hand. "Thank you, Administrator," she said. "There is little else we can accomplish here. Will you and the Captain join us for dinner?"

She'd asked them if they would prefer a formal dinner and a full presentation to the senior crew, but Administrator Danilaw and Captain Amanda had argued gently for a little more privacy. "The flower of diplomacy likes a well-composted bed," Danilaw had said, and Perceval had stared at him for a full three seconds before realizing that he was being intentionally ridiculous. *The Mean has a sense of humor.* It did, in fact, endear him to her—just a little.

And so she fed them on the Bridge, at a table Nova built for the occasion—not too large, oval in shape, the glossy flat surface growing up from the grassy deck on twisted legs as if it had always been rooted there. The food was kept plain, though Head exercised all hir considerable ingenuity on making it also delicious. Sie always said it was more a test of the cook's art and discrimination to make the simple great, anyway.

Perceval had wondered if her dinner guests would find the food strange, and as truth would have it, they seemed to. Not so strange, however, that they failed to apply themselves to the dishes with concentration.

She got a sense that their culture focused a kind of ritual attentiveness on food. They ate in small bites, carefully timed, and both of them inspected each mouthful before consuming it. Perceval hoped it wasn't out of fear of toxicity. She'd had Nova analyze their metabolites—it wasn't invasive, so she didn't feel she needed to ask permissions—and it appeared that, within detectable tolerances, they could eat what she ate.

Could eat. Whether they habitually did eat it seemed questionable, given the scientific rigor with which they investigated their dinners. Perceval expected questions, but they did not quiz their hosts, just inspected, chewed, considered, and swallowed. Tristen and Mallory supported the conversation, the necromancer especially putting forth efforts to be sparkling, but Perceval could sense the awkwardness hovering between the two groups of diners.

And it was hard indeed to find common ground for conversation when gossip about common acquaintances and family business were off the table. Perceval had never realized before how much of what went on at the average meeting was devoted to navigating the complex relationships that linked Conn and Engine.

Mallory managed a fair trade in humorous anecdotes about long-dead Conns and Engineers, leaving enticing pauses in the narrative, but Perceval could not help but notice that Danilaw and Amanda seemed completely at a loss as to how to handle them. Finally, she set her utensils down, folded her hands in front of her mouth, and said, "I wouldn't force conversation on you, but this feels awkward to me. Is there some manner in which the hospitality could be improved?"

Her alien guests did a lot of talking to each other with their eyes. They shared a glance now, lingering enough that she wondered if they were telepaths or had some sort of implant that allowed silent communication. Amanda finally looked back at Perceval and said, "It's another of those cultural differences. We're socialized from a young age to believe that eating is serious business, requiring attention and gratitude. Cookery is the performance of an art, and like any ephemera, it should be savored. Also, there is the matter of honoring the former existence of the food, and acknowledging the lives that go to feed us."

Tristen frowned, but it seemed like the study of concentration rather than one of disagreement. "You honor the sacrifice?"

"That," Amanda said, "would imply complicity on the part of the lunch. And in general, I suspect anything we eat would prefer to continue existing as something other than a source of fuel. No; we merely try to recognize our impact, so we may manage it."

"Oh." Mallory chased the rubbery coil of a steamed snail around the plate before cornering it in a small puddle of herbed oil. With fork tines poised before painted lips, the necromancer said, "We are insufficiently reverent of the dead."

The aliens did that eye thing again. This time, Danilaw nodded and spoke. "After a fashion, though I might have left out the value judgment. We are attempting to engage with you without discrimination."

"Or relativism," Tristen said. "And we very much appreciate your consideration of the long centuries our people have been separated, and the time it will take to negotiate those alienations."

"Not to mention," Amanda said, "the time it will take even to identify them."

Perceval let her fork lie alongside the plate, unwilling to risk disturbing the delicate balance of actual communication taking place. She leaned forward, minding her manners and keeping her elbows by her sides—it would have made her mother proud, she thought, with a pang—and started to say something that would continue the diplomacy that had somehow, organically, commenced.

Only Nova spoke in her head, soft and definite. "Cynric is about to enter the Bridge."

16

a girl who had no wings

> "These," he said gravely, "are unpleasant facts; I know it. But then
> most historical facts are unpleasant."
> —ALDOUS HUXLEY, *Brave New World*

When the door slid open on another of the generation ship natives—the Conn family, as they called themselves, and Danilaw was starting to understand that, indeed, they shared familial links as close as those uniting the First Families of Fortune—Danilaw laid his fork down somewhat reluctantly beside his plate. The strange food was, well, strange—but it was interesting, stimulating, and delicious, once he chose to ignore his genetic predisposition to fear novelty. Strange things, after all, could be poison, but he was reasonably certain that these strange *people* had more to gain by keeping him and Amanda alive, and he had the Captain's assurances that everything on the table was safe.

He was beginning to trust the new people's medical technology. That seemed far more advanced than anything Earth or Fortune had to offer—although he knew it came at a cost of illegal bioengineering.

This alien, like the others before, was attenuated and androgynous, straight hair falling in locks over white-clothed shoulders. It—*she*—paused within the door, allowing the hatch to spiral closed behind her with a fine, practiced sense of drama and how to frame herself for best effect. Danilaw wondered if she had a secondary as an actress.

He was amused to notice that he was already treating each new incursion of the Conn family into his presence with a wary, even jaundiced, eye and a sense that some fresh hell had found him. From the way both Perceval and Tristen looked up warily from the dinner table, he thought, in this case, it might not even be the culture shock talking.

"Aunt," Perceval said, without rising. "I must admit, your presence is unexpected."

"Of course," said the newcomer. "I planned it that way. I hear there was an explosion."

"Indeed there was," Danilaw said, hoping he had understood the way the Jacobeans did not stand on ceremony. "Someone apparently sabotaged our scull. I am Danilaw Bakare, Administrator of Bad Landing. This is Captain Amanda Friar."

"Cynric Conn," she said. "I'm the head of bioengineering. I imagine I'll be working closely with your ecologists in order to adapt our people as closely to Fortune as possible."

She didn't call his homeworld Grail—even though she spoke so casually of engineering her family, as if they were machines.

On the other hand, that flexibility might lead them to accept rightminding without too much trouble.

That's my Dani, his mother would have said. Always on the bright side. She'd never known how much of that was effort and pretense.

Cynric extended her hand and he accepted it, startled when she gave a little squeeze. She was of a sameness with the other Conns—tall, planar, pale, and blue-featured. The jewel that flashed in her face reminded him of Amanda's, but he thought it was a piercing rather than an implant. *No Free Legates here.*

"It's a pleasure to meet you," he said.

If she noticed how noncommittal he was, she accepted it without a ripple. She let his hand drift out of hers and turned her attention to the people behind the table, touching Amanda lightly as well. After that, though, she folded her arms and stood before the table in her long robes like some attenuated representation of a wingless angel.

"Captain," she said. "I suppose you're wondering how I managed to walk between the raindrops when I came in."

"Passing Nova unnoticed is a feat," Perceval agreed. "I presume you wouldn't mention it if you didn't mean to explain."

Danilaw spared a moment to reflect on whether this discussion of business in front of new guests was honest indifference to what he learned of his hosts' capabilities, or saber rattling for his and Amanda's benefit.

Cynric smiled, showing the tendons around her mouth. "I learned it from what Mallory and Tristen uncovered among the Deckers."

"The parrotlet," Tristen said. His studied impassivity dropped away, leaving the traces of a smile that startled Danilaw a little. It looked so *human* amid the alien architecture of his face. "Which begs the question. Was it a miscalculation that it survived, or did they want us to find it and learn this?"

"I did not ingest original material from the parrotlet," Cynric said. "That seemed rather obviously unwise, even before I located the Trojan in it. But I reproduced the design, and wrote my own code. And I learned some things about who killed the Deckers."

"Pardon me," Danilaw said, trying to remember to keep his elbows off the table when he leaned forward, "but do I understand correctly that someone is dead?"

"Murdered," Cynric agreed, crossing to stand beside the table, one hand resting on Perceval's shoulder, her body so slight inside her robes that she seemed made up more of the sway of fabric than any other thing it might be hung upon. "Dozens, murdered."

Perceval cleared her throat. Cynric looked down at the top of her head, fingers rippling as she squeezed the Captain's shoulder. "Is there any point in hiding it from them that we have factions in this world, and some of those factions are violent? What does that make us, other than a human society?"

An unrightminded human society. But Danilaw didn't think this was the time to raise that specter again. "Terrorist trouble?"

"More like a garden-variety mass murder in order to hide the identity of a criminal," Mallory said, when it seemed that no one was going to demand that information be withheld from the newcomers. Danilaw felt Amanda stir on his left, heard the rustle of her clothes.

Cynric said, "Someone arranged the assassination of our Chief Engineer, and then killed a deck full of accomplices, accessories, and probable innocent bystanders who might have been able to provide an identification. I have been working with the limited physical evidence that was left behind. I should not have interrupted your dinner"—she gestured to the table—"but I admit, I found my new toy clever enough that I wanted to show it off to anyone available."

She smiled winningly, and—as with Tristen—the very existence of that smile made Danilaw reconsider her.

Amanda cleared her throat. "I was going to say that if you already have terrorists, that explains why you're so willing to give us a pass on blowing up your ship." She shrugged. "But this wasn't someone attempting to influence political policy through the slaughter of innocents?"

"I wouldn't go that far," Perceval said. "But I don't think that was the primary motive for *these* deaths. You seem more familiar with the varieties of criminal activity than I would have expected from a people who practice routine psychosurgery."

"We don't remove the capability for violence," Danilaw said. "Just the more irrational motives. The purpose of rightminding is to reinforce free will and to remove the atavistic urges that underly it, not to create a perfect, biddable army of human robots."

"For one thing," Amanda said, letting her biceps brush his elbow, "who would do the bidding? As we attempted to explain before, sometimes people have perfectly rational reasons for violence."

"Ours don't," Mallory said, one curved brow arched over a chocolate-colored eye. "And I guess I fail to understand how what you describe differs from the evils of the Kleptocracy."

Unlike the other aliens, Mallory did not stumble over the term, but spoke it as if it were familiar. *Interesting. And how close to the devil immortality is this one?*

"Not evil," Danilaw said. "There is too much evil in the idea of evil. But greedy and childish and toxic. *That* is what we try to correct for. Still, it sounds like we're both getting some opposition."

Danilaw's stage persona was deadpan as any ice man. His political construct was cool and soothing. Once Amanda laughed at his intentional understatement, the aliens figured it out and followed suit, or rolled eyes at one another, according to their natures.

"This opposition may be to us making landfall," Perceval said, her gaze level and assessing, "or it may be to us negotiating with you at all."

"Rather than taking what you want?"

The boldness in his own voice startled him. It startled him, too, when she made a plain, frustrated face and said, "I have figured out that you will fight for your lives."

"We will fight for our world as well," Danilaw said, aware of the hush that had fallen around the table, the pairs of eyes trained on him and Perceval both. "We will fight for its sovereignty, and we will not allow its equilibrium to be destroyed."

"But a punctuated equilibrium is one of the necessities of evolution."

"The world," Danilaw said, "is quite capable of producing crises of its own, without our self-justifications. You—your people, some of them, anyway—believe in a God, do they not?"

"And yours don't," Perceval said. "I understand that this, like so much else, will be a subject for much negotiation and compromise."

Danilaw sucked his lips into his mouth and chewed them for a moment, as if he were nibbling his words into shape. He was pretty sure he still had them wrong, but now wasn't the time to mention again that the notion of God was an illness. But he was also supposed to be a diplomat, and part of diplomacy was being able to speak in the metaphors of the enemy.

He considered carefully—the history, his limited experience. He needed to speak *with* them, not *at* them. He needed to embrace their metaphors, even when the metaphors distressed him.

He drew a breath and began. "You believe in Gods. Or God. Or at least some of your folk are open to the possibility of a divine influence."

"Some of us are," Tristen affirmed. "It's sometimes curable."

Danilaw caught his eyes, and the lifted eyebrows over them. The First Mate had the arch wit of a sharp old man, and despite the youth of his features, Danilaw had to remind himself that these people were *all* older than he. *It's like dealing with elves. But it's not elves exactly.*

Danilaw said, "Bear with me. Will you admit for the sake of argument that we—humans, in our current technological state—are not, except under extreme circumstances, experiencing any competition in the natural world except among ourselves?"

The alien Captain steepled her fingers. "If, by the natural world, you exclude the Enemy."

"The Devil," Captain Amanda said.

Perceval's lips compressed into the thing they did to hide a smile, but it was Cynric who answered. "Space," she said. "Entropy. The inevitable heat death of the universe. That is the Enemy. I suppose you could call it the Devil, if you liked. It is the opposite of life and breath and negentropy, in any case."

Danilaw heard Amanda breathe deep of the thin alien air. "The Enemy," she said. "It is the Enemy of life."

Perceval smiled.

Danilaw could not restrain himself from glancing around the table. But having done so, and nodded in understanding, he forged on. "I believe finding yourself neck-deep in space, or deprived of all the fruits of our primate ingenuity in any hostile environment, counts as an extreme circumstance for purposes of this discussion. Can we agree on that?"

After a glance at her Captain, Cynric said, "We can."

"At last," Amanda said. "Common ground."

That, at least, startled Mallory into a snort of laughter. Perceval was still smiling, if you could call that a smile. If smiling, for her, were not a prelude to aggression.

Danilaw raised and spread his hands, drawing attention, gathering focus. "In short, we have outcompeted the Hell out of everything. Thus, in that we are as Gods to the rest of"—he flagged, until Amanda mouthed a word at him— "of creation, it is incumbent upon us to treat with that *creation* as would honorable Gods—to protect and preserve, to limit our influence, to allow it scope."

The aliens were frowning at him, or at least that was how he interpreted the variety of their expressions. Tristen scratched the side of his nose. Perceval, around her scowl, remained impassive.

Cynric breathed deep and sighed. "I do not mind sounding ignorant," she said. "The part of me that was easily shamed is dead—and good riddance to it."

Even, Danilaw thought, *if it was a fragment of your humanity?*

But apparently she wasn't actually a mind reader after all, because rather than reacting with indignation, she continued the thread of her question. "If you coddle the world," she said, "how does the world grow? As we are a part of creation, part of our purpose is to produce stress on other elements of creation. We force the evolution of other species as they force—or facilitate—ours."

There was something behind that word, *facilitate,* Danilaw thought. He didn't have the time to ferret it out now, but patience would be his reward.

"We have a thing," he said, "that we call The Obligation. It is made up of many smaller Obligations, each carefully defined, but the essence of it is this: leave the world better—healthier, more complete, more diverse—than you found it."

"Isn't that," Cynric said, "condescending? Doesn't that set humankind in a kind of stewardship over every other species? Doesn't that make us the colonialists, responsible for the well-being of primitives?"

Danilaw sat back. He would need time to consider this tack, he thought, before he could argue it successfully.

But Cynric wasn't done. "Doesn't that deny the agency of the nonsentient? Doesn't it argue that we are somehow responsible for them?"

"When we became more able to compete," Danilaw said, uncomfortable, "we became responsible. We become responsible to protect the natural world. When we become stronger, we become stewards."

"The world does not reward timidity," Cynric said.

Tristen placed a hand on her forearm, his long fingers so pale they barely showed against her garb of purest white. "Sister," he said. "This might not be the time to plumb the depths of philosophy."

But Cynric shook him off. "Does your philosophy not set humankind apart from nature?" she said. "You speak of protecting the natural world, but nature protects nothing. Nature does not believe in a fair fight. For every mouse, there is an owl. For every spider, there is a wasp. The world destroys to feed itself; it is a zero-sum game, and life consumes life. There is only so much carbon in any given carbon cycle." She smiled now, as if confident she had one. "Who the hell set *you* up in loco parentis to the natural world?"

"With power," Danilaw said, "with strength, there comes responsibility. With maturity come the burdens of maturity. Self-discipline. The acceptance that we do not always get to have what we want just because we are strong and we want it. You are stronger than me. Does that give you the right to take what is mine? Does that give you the dispensation to rob or rape me?"

"Not the privilege," Tristen said, fingers lacing and unlacing, fisting and unfisting. "But the facility."

"And in your world, are such things permitted without question?"

Perceval's hidden smile was growing more patent by the moment. "To prevent such things," she said, "such abuses of power, that is why we have knights-errant, and Captains, and all of Rule."

"When they are not abusing that power their own selves," Mallory qualified. "Not that *that* would ever happen."

Perceval snorted. Danilaw decided he rather liked the androgynous necromancer after all.

"When you have an extreme advantage," Danilaw said, "the gentlemanly thing to do is to reserve its use for those who share it. Or to choose to compete only with equal opponents, and leave the bullying to bullies."

Cynric leaned forward on her elbows. "I'm not sure if that's egalitarian or condescending."

"Cynric," Perceval said warningly, as Amanda stiffened beside Danilaw. Under the table, Danilaw placed the back of a hand against her thigh. She startled almost imperceptibly before releasing her held breath and turning to him. *Primate pissing contests.*

Having studied Danilaw's face for a moment, Amanda turned back to the aliens across the table. "I understand your point," she said. "In assuming the role of protector, we deny agency. But we deny agency to creatures that may or may not desire it—"

"When you assume stewardship for everything, you domesticate everything," Tristen said.

Out of the corner of his eyes, Danilaw saw Amanda nodding, though he kept his attention firmly on Perceval and her crew. "And if we do not assume stewardship, we exploit everything."

Tristen let his folded hands fall apart to lie on the tabletop, pressed flat. "Except for what exploits us," he said. "Tell me, Administrator Bakare. Does your world have rats on it?"

"Rats?" He nodded. "Rats and roaches. They follow humanity everywhere."

"Mmm," Tristen said. "In that relationship, who has evolved to exploit whom?" He shook his head. "I do not think, Administrator Bakare, that we are all that different. I do not think that we interact with the world and each other with such deep moral differences. I think we have different terms for what we do—that what you term The Obligation, we term Chivalry. But I do think we have common ground, and I think we can find more." He paused. "My people, you understand, are very adaptable."

* * *

After the meeting, Samael in all his patchwork magnificence showed Danilaw and Amanda to the quarters they'd inhabit for the rest of their trip home. It was not a long walk—apparently Captain Perceval had seen merit in keeping them centrally located—but it was as full of revelations as every other walk around the corridors had been.

Walking on yielding moss down a spaceship gangway, Danilaw began to understand that the entire starship was an ecosphere—an ecology far more delicately balanced than that of Fortune. And far more aggressively managed. It revealed something to him about the Jacobeans' culture and experience, if he thought on it carefully. Of course, evolution must be managed. Of course, a biosphere must be maintained.

They had never known another way.

Thinking distracted him, but neither Amanda nor Samael seemed inclined to make small talk, so he needed not divide his attention. It might have been better if he had, however, because he tripped and almost fell when he realized that the large, ornately floral shrub that they were about to pass along the corridor wall was in fact moving. Walking, or not precisely walking, toward them.

It was a bundle of spear-shaped leaves and boles, six tiger-striped, fuchsia-and-lemon flower heads bobbing above its back. Danilaw shied back against the corridor wall as it turned to him; on his left, he felt Amanda do the same.

The giant, self-mobile orchid turned to them and bent its thorn-fanged flower faces into something that looked like a smile. "Welcome, visitors," it said, and kept walking.

Samael had drawn ahead, and with a glance to Amanda, Danilaw hurried to catch up. Beside him, Amanda stretched her legs. "Talking plant," she whispered.

He nodded. "I noticed."

On behalf of his Captain, the Angel of Biosystems apologized for the size and inelegance of the quarters before vanishing in a scatter of withered petals and beetle wings, leaving Danilaw feeling as if he had just choked on his tongue.

The "cramped" quarters they would share were half again as large as the crew habitat on the *Quercus,* and every square millimeter was soft with life. Mosses ran up the bulkheads so that Danilaw could not tell if the architecture of the space—an *anchore,* Samael called it—was truly all but cornerless or if it had merely been softened by centuries of growth. Vines—heavy, swaying, and hung with flowers Danilaw did not recognize—curtained two padded alcoves lined with fluffy blankets and pillows absorbent, springy, and soft.

After the Angel left, Amanda took a slow spin at the center of the room, diffuse light dappling her hair. "I don't know how we'll adapt," she said, giving Danilaw a glance through her eyelashes he could only regard as flirtatious.

He smiled back and plunked himself on the mossy edge of the nearer bunk. The tough, yielding little plants were warm above and cool below, exactly as if they had been warmed by the sun. He held his hand out into those spots of light that had scattered across Amanda's head and shoulders. They shifted, the vining leaves draping the ceiling turning in the breeze from the ventilation ducts. Full-spectrum, warm against his skin.

Behind the vines, rusty stains climbed the mesh the plants twined through, and Danilaw could see where centuries of growth and death had stretched the holes and torn the strands.

Danilaw felt his face prickle. He took a breath and let it out again—moist, verdant, and warm.

This world was old and worn. And if they could give this much space to two itinerant diplomats, it was not as full of strangers as Danilaw had feared. Actually, the near emptiness of all those corridors was beginning to sink in and make sense.

"They are underpopulated," he said, with a gesture to this space, empty and just waiting.

Amanda, frowning, nodded and glanced aside. For a moment, they were in silent understanding. It had been a long, hard road in coming here. What compassionate human being could ask them to move on?

Yet what merely natural world could assimilate everything that surrounded him now without being consumed or destroyed?

Danilaw got up, crossed springy turf, and took Amanda's hand. She turned to him, startled; he hoped it would look to the observers he presumed existed as if they were secret lovers. He couldn't risk speaking; he could not even risk spelling against her palm.

Probably every word that Danilaw and Amanda said to one another was being recorded, every gesture analyzed. Probably, they had no privacy at all. These were not people, Bakare thought, who were likely to discard any available advantage. They were not stupid, they were not prone to losing for its own sake, and they were accustomed to constant struggle.

He compared that to his own people, who were no longer accustomed to playing to win, and felt a chill.

So he looked in her eyes and thought, as hard as he could, *We cannot allow these people to make landfall,* and hoped the message would be read in the cast of his features, the alteration in his pheromones.

And maybe it was, because she held the eye contact for almost ten seconds, and after she looked down, she nodded.

17

who ruined all of us

Love, that is first and last of all things made,
The light that has the living world for shade.
—ALGERNON CHARLES SWINBURNE, *Tristram of Lyonesse*

When the aliens had left and the rubble of the state dinner was cleared, Perceval reclaimed her Bridge and—mostly—her solitude. Her First Mate stayed with her; her Angel was already in residence, here as everywhere. But the rest of her executive crew knew when to let well enough alone.

This was one of those times, and though she cursed herself for being so predictable, she was grateful of their solicitude.

She stood behind the green bank of her command chair, hands resting on the back, and let herself lean. Hard, until her fingers dented the sod, and the scent of crushed violets and bluets surrounded her.

"Ariane had a backup," she said.

Tristen was behind her, and she had stripped off her armor and returned it to its locker, but the rasp of his hair told her he nodded. "The signature is . . . unmistakable. Even Gerald, who ruined all of us, drew a few lines. Ariane kills whatever crosses her path because it pleases her to exert that kind of power, and then justifies it later."

"The massacre," Nova said, in that voice that reminded Perceval a little too fiercely of Dust, and his libraries of literature and history and ghosts, "is a tradition of tyrants from immemorial history. Destroy the enemy unto the last child, and sow the earth with salt around his bones."

"We are the worst monsters there are." Perceval worked her fingers together, twisting them, massaging the discomfort from her hands. It was the pain of exhaustion, and not even her colony could banish it entirely.

"We *are* the worst monsters there are," Tristen agreed. "But we are all we have."

He came up beside her and nudged her over. The Captain's chair was broad enough for them to lean on side by side, shoulder to shoulder. Perceval breathed in his warmth and the animal comfort of his presence, the smell of his sweat and pheromones. She let her temple fall against his shoulder and felt the Angel, half solid and half real, upon her other side.

"The Fisher King's folk. We are their worst nightmare," she said. "We are the thing they changed themselves utterly to escape from."

"And they are the thing we changed ourselves utterly to avoid becoming." Tristen's voice was deep, mellifluous, a little scratchy. "What are you going to do about Ariane?"

Ariane, her beloved's half sister. Ariane, the worst of the Conns. Ariane, whose preserved and flattened ghost inhabited Perceval's own mind, controlled and caged away, yet who seemed to have left another ghost, another revenant, loose in the world to wreak havoc and spread despair. If she had done so, she had wiped her own memory of the backup, or Perceval would have inherited that also.

Although Perceval had to admit, she had failed somewhat, out of distaste. She had not interrogated Ariane as completely as she should have, and even if overwritten with something innocuous to cover the hole, an erased memory could potentially leave a discontinuity.

That might tell them *when* she had made the backup. Which would in turn tell them *where* to start looking.

"She's in my head," Perceval said. "I suppose I shall have to find out what she knows about it. But I want you and Benedick here when I do it."

Tristen nodded again. "Benedick will want a piece of her—for Caitlin's sake and for Rien's. And for you as well. But he'll also know he's emotionally compromised, and he won't ask to be sent after her."

"You think I should send him after her anyway."

"No one is more dogged than Benedick. Or more dangerous when roused."

"Tristen Tiger is," she said, reaching across her own chest and left arm to brush her fingertips across his shoulder.

He leaned into the contact. "Tristen Conn is old and tired, My Lady. His claws are blunted and his teeth show yellow in receding gums. But in so long as you need one, I shall be thy tiger. I will find where Ariane has gone to ground, and I will reclaim your mother's blade, and I will find what she plans for the Bible."

He paused and took a breath, another. Knowing Tristen, knowing how he nerved himself to speak, Perceval gave him time. Finally, he began, "The Fisher King and his folk . . ."

"I know," she said. "Every day they spend with us, the welcome will grow a little cooler, the willingness to share their world a little more remote. If we wish their permission, we will have to change to suit them."

"It would disappoint the Builders," Nova said, not so much startling Perceval as reminding her of her presence.

It had become easy to forget the Angel was there—something that never would have happened fifty years before. But now she was as neutral as blood-warm distilled water—a part of the environment. Unremarkable.

"The Builders believed in evolution over all," Perceval

said, "except where they were hypocrites about it. We'll adapt. If they can be convinced to accept us, we'll find a niche and exploit it."

On his indrawn breath, Tristen seemed to swell. She felt him hold it and release before he spoke with resigned formality. "Well, if it comes right down to it, how do they propose to stop us from coming down? We are a war they cannot win."

"I do not want to kill them," Perceval said. "I want to prove to them that we, too, have grown from what we were."

Tristen nodded. "Good luck," he said.

It was not sarcasm.

While Perceval prepared herself for the task she so patently dreaded, Tristen took it upon himself to contact the most trusted members of the command crew and alert them to the possibility of a rogue revenant at large. He called Benedick in advance of any other, as per his Captain's wishes. But then he contacted Mallory and Head, amused that his confidence did not extend first to any member of the Conn family but rather to creatures created by them, or evolved in response to the extremes of their creations. Head was a living tool, wrought by Cynric and blessed with free will to a specific task, and Mallory was an immortal with a head stuffed to creaking with the dead—memories recorded and transferred with Conn-derived alien technology: the colonies Cynric had stolen and reengineered.

Mallory took his suggestion calmly, and—surprising Tristen—suggested that the Angel Samael not yet be informed. Given Samael's history with Ariane, it was probably wisest—and it would prevent Perceval having to waste time and risk unwanted consequences in inhibiting him from taking unguided action against the revenant, if he

could find her. The search itself, Tristen knew, could prove
quite adequately destructive.

Head surprised him more. He would have thought hir
beyond overwrought emotional demonstrations, possibly
beyond fear. But the mention of Ariane's name and the suggestion that she might be returned brought blanched
cheeks and denials. Head had known Ariane better than
any of them, and dealt with her more personally and in
more detail, which could account for a good deal of hir refusal to believe that the most sociopathic of Conns had returned to wreak havoc again.

When sie had done wringing hir hands, however, sie
folded them together and said grimly, "Well, the unla-
mented Princess Ariane aside—begging your pardon,
Prince Tristen—it's clear that, whatever else is going on,
we've a bad enemy at large and no mistake."

"No mistake at all," Tristen responded. Head might not
be overly good at anticipating, identifying, and accepting
threats, but sie was more than competent to handle the actual disaster in progress with aplomb. "I trust you will be
alert to any evidence."

"Alert and more than alert," Head said. "Prince Tristen—"

"Yes, Head?"

"Take care of my Captain."

The first decision Perceval faced was the need to choose
a place in which to work. There would have been a certain
poetry in using the Captain's chair, when Ariane had
fought with such monomania to claim it, but that chair had
too much other and bloody symbolism, even if Perceval
only meant to use it as an icon of authority. And Perceval—
who had fought her cousin twice to claim it—found she
wished to face Ariane this time not as Captain, not even as
hopeful claimant to the chair, but as her mother's daughter.

Vengeance repaired nothing. It replaced nothing. It

wrought nothing anew—except the vengeance itself. It was only vengeance, and the splinter of Ariane that Perceval carried within herself was not even the splinter that had planned the attack, carried it out, and killed Caitlin Conn—all assuming Tristen was correct in his deductions, which was by no means a given.

But both fragments were related; both were remainders of the same woman who had destroyed Rule, who had crippled Perceval and shamed her, who had set in motion so many of the schemes and treacheries that Perceval and her family and allies were still paying for. They must share continuity of experience to a certain point, and at that point—where they had divided—lay the key to uncovering where the wicked Conn's wicked twin was hid.

Perceval left her Bridge and walked instead down the lengthy access corridor. Measured footsteps rang on the deck, carrying her past the niche where the paper Bible sat no longer—*good riddance,* she should not think—past the seamed, rough-patched section where the Deckers' breach had been repaired, and past the antechambers sown with sunflowers and all manner of bright things. She stopped by the lift, contemplated the moment, and stepped inside.

It carried her down. Well, not down, precisely, but in, further toward the world's center of mass and rotation— which the Bridge lingered close beside already. *Bridge,* Perceval thought, unaccountably cheered by the wordplay, *is only one letter from Bride.*

And there, at the world's center of gravity, Perceval walked across the naked breast of the Enemy, herself naked and unarmored. She did not need to travel far. Just a revolution or two, until she found a small, dead-chilled anchore, its deep seams and cracks still full of traces of ice that had not yet sublimated. It had no hatches, no air locks, no visible means of entrance. It had nothing but the chains and cables that connected it to the world—links thick as

Perceval's waist; cables braided of carbon monofilament and titanium—and the weight of ice within.

Trivial enough matters to the Captain of the world.

Perceval laid her hand flat on the surface of the capsule. Moist skin would have frozen there, but Perceval's skin was dry. "Nova," she said. "Open this and clear a space inside for me to enter."

"That was—" Nova said, and if the Angel were not a program, Perceval fancied she would have been able to hear the distaste in her voice.

"Dust's place," Perceval agreed. He had never brought her here, preferring the Bridge and the cargo bays for her education, but a wise Captain knew her ship.

"The old computer core," Nova said, in the voice of one intentionally amending another's statement when that statement has unintentionally given offense.

Perceval let herself smile, just the corners of her mouth turning upward. It rewarded the Angel when the Angel was making an effort to chivvy her from her brown study. And when Perceval would not be chivvied, such as now. "Let me in."

Nova made no argument. Her hesitation before following the instruction was so slight it did not even begin to approximate disobedience—so slight nothing less than an Exalt would have even noticed it. Then the Angel spread her arms—a theatrical but dramatic gesture.

Seemingly instantaneously, layers of metal and earth and circuitry and ice began to divide, split, and peel back like the petals of an impossibly robust and complex flower. Ice sparkled in breathless drifts across the darkness of the Enemy, pollinating nothing. Some of the piping had once been warm, but no water flowed through the space now. It was cold and empty.

At last, a stark chamber stood open to space, honeycombed with frozen water. The remnants of the world's hydrostatic computer core, with its embedded atomic-level read-only memory. The remnants of the physical body of Jacob Dust, the ship's library.

The ship's memory, until Nova had eaten him.

This was where he had been born.

No one came near, not even the Angel. Perceval moved toward the center of the architecture of frozen water, sliding herself through razor-paned, fragile knifeblades. Blessing her slightness as she seldom did, she turned sideways to infiltrate between the toothy monoliths of icicles that might be a thousand years old.

When she was seated—she could not say comfortably—among the crystals of solid water as a mouse might secrete itself in a geode, she raised her hand to Nova again. Though she beckoned the Angel closer, she stopped as if limited by propriety at the edge of the chamber.—*This is not my place.*—

In the silence of vacuum, Perceval could not form the words aloud, but she could make Nova hear them. "You won't come with me?"

—*You are Captain,*—Nova said.—*I am construct. What do you want me to say?*—

Feeling the cold of the ice pillars brush her skin, feeling the tiny water droplets, Perceval slid herself into a corner like a key wedging into a lock. "Seal me up in here," she said.

Nova jerked back.—*I beg your pardon?*—

Perceval sighed. "Seal me up. I have someone I need to talk to, and I can't risk her at large in the world."

—*Shall I isolate the hardware?*—

"You shall," Perceval said, "although I expect it's too damaged to be of much use. And you shall withdraw yourself as well. You could provide her with a conduit for escape. I fear we must treat the Princess Ariane, when she is aware and unfettered, as a viral presence. I am confident that, offered the slightest chance, she will replicate, spread, and infect anything she can. She may be only a shadow of what she was, but what she was was a treacherousness that surpassed knowledge."

Nova tilted her head, the brown locks breaking across her face in a manner she must have studied recordings for, because Perceval's hair certainly never did anything so engaging.—*You expect me to leave you in there alone and unsupervised, in the company of Ariane Conn?*—

"A mere shadow," Perceval scoffed. "Don't forget, I once defeated the real thing. I don't expect a lot of trouble from a mindprint. Most especially a mindprint I've already beaten, and beaten the body it came in, too."

Nova folded her imaginary arms.—*Still.*—

"Still," Perceval answered. "I will be fine, and you may not monitor me."

—*How will any of us know if you lose the battle? What if your shadow of Ariane takes control of you? Then we'll have two of them running around, unbeknownst to anyone.*—

That surprised Perceval into a chuckle. "I think if I'm replaced by Ariane Conn," she said, "or even the ghost of her, it won't take you too long to notice. Random hideous murders of people just standing around in corridor intersections minding their own business would fairly quickly give her away. If it doesn't, you'll probably catch her after the next erratic cleansing of strangers and hirees who got in her way, or who knew too much."

The Angel snorted silently, which told Perceval she was winning. But Nova would not be made to back down so easily.

—*I could disconnect a body,*—she said. Nova's bodies were disposable. They weighed a few pounds, no more, and they could be dissolved back into the world's colony core when abandoned.—*Just to watch over you.*—

"Nova."

Perceval had never yet seen an Angel make that particular expression—childlike, rueful, reprimanded. She wondered from which of Nova's component parts it had come, and then wished she hadn't. These days, she usually managed to see Nova as Nova, rather than the sum of her parts. But there were always the inevitable lapses.

Each time they happened, Perceval considered editing out the emotional/mnemonic function that reminded her of lost loves. And each time, she put the decision off for another day. The pain faded naturally with the years, but she was loathe to lose it all. It might prickle, but it prickled because it was the relic of something dear.

She met Nova's level look with one of her own. The Angel was the first to glance down.

—As you wish.—

Perceval forced a smile. "I'll knock to be let out."

No passes, no incantations, no prestidigitator's gesturing. Just the veil of titanium drawn transparent across the gap, then thickening, opaquing, and the Angel's face vanishing behind it. Her interior voice went silent at the same time, and Perceval was left with the bottomless, unsettling emptiness of being alone in her own head for the first time in a half century.

It was cold in the library, and there was no oxygen. It didn't matter; she was the Captain of the *Jacob's Ladder*, and adapted to life in a fragile world that rested like a jewel in the black velvet bosom of the Enemy. She would have liked to have drawn a breath for the simple kinetic consolation of it, but comforted herself with folded arms instead. This was a closed space, small and dark. She was alone here, alone with the voices in her head. And there was a warden outside, to keep her safe from the world and the world safe away from her.

She was Perceval. She was strong. She could do this thing.

She placed the palm of one hand against the cold, cold wall of ice, hard as stone and unmelting before the mere warm heat of any mortal flesh. She grounded herself in that reality and went within.

There were shapes in her head—enemies and strangers. There were people in her program she never would have invited there. The program informed the meat, and the meat informed the person who identified as Perceval, and the person who called herself Perceval controlled the program. An endless loop, an oceanic cycle.

One of those people was the pallid remnant of Ariane Conn—a thing Perceval did not touch willingly or often. Now, though, she girded her loins, rolled up her sleeves, and waded into the fray. For Rien, for Caitlin, for Oliver—for everything Ariane had broken, and everything she had destroyed.

It was not easy.

It was rather like catching an oil slick, to begin with. Ariane might be in her head—might clamor for attention, attempt to force her twisted wisdom on Perceval, might be only a reflection and a memory of the madwoman who had been Ariane Conn in truth—but that did not mean she cared to let Perceval lay hands on her, even metaphorically. Her surface was greasy and insubstantial, and below that the personality of the dead Commodore was thick and sludgy, putrid, repellent. It was probably Perceval's loathing for Ariane that was corrupting the program (she was reasonably certain that Ariane the narcissist had never seen herself as revolting), but acknowledging the source of the revulsion did not serve to make it any less real.

Still Perceval held the dead woman's memory close, hugged it to her breast, and delved.

The record of a life ill-spent assaulted her. A great deal of what Ariane treasured was simply hellish to Perceval. The memory of her own maiming was in there, Ariane severing Perceval's great wings with her weightless unblade. The memory of Tristen's betrayal and incarceration was there as well. Perceval was tempted to tread lightly around the borders of that last. She knew Tristen would not care to be reminded of his decades in durance vile, nor would he care for her to share the details of his internment. But she was the Captain, and she was Caitlin's daughter, and it was her responsibility to seek the truth under all the layers of sadism that Ariane could load up on it.

She gritted her teeth—literally as well as metaphorically—and plunged into the stinking depths.

Something that was not there, however, was the information she sought. Seamless, all of it, machine memory meshing up perfectly with the edges of fallible chemical memory, or as much of that latter as was recorded in Ariane's ghost. Perceval waded through treasured, attention-polished images of her own gaunt flyer's body, cobalt blood laddering down her protruding ribs and vertebrae as if it descended a staircase, dripping with viscous regularity from the thick, ragged stubs of her wings before it groped together like blind fingers and formed seeking tendrils, trying to seal the unhealing wounds. She walked tiptoe between Ariane's gloating recollections of the netted dead in Rule, epidemic victims bundled and frozen in the bosom of the Enemy for when their bodies might be needed for raw materials or allowed to heal into the mute and servile resurrected. She watched Ariane kill Alasdair and consume his memories and experience with his colony.

She learned what snapped an unblade, as Ariane's Mercy met Tristen's black Charity, and both swords threw black sparks and shatterings along the walls of the world. She saw the battle, and she saw that Tristen was clearly the superior swordsman. But it availed him not when Ariane—that treacherous knight—sent her attendant Angel Asrafil into the matrix of Tristen's sword, possessing the unblade, weakening its structure, and creating a plane of cleavage through the blade so that it broke across the forte. As Tristen reeled back, Ariane struck with the dagger in her left hand and ended the fight—for a time.

She learned, too, that Ariane had blinded Tristen before she locked him away, though she had used only her main gauche to do it and not her unblade, and so after some time the wound had repaired itself. A cruelty at the time—what good were eyes in eternal darkness?—but an unexpected and unintended mercy in the end, when Perceval, Gavin, and Rien had resurrected Tristen from the tomb.

Perceval learned all these things—things she had already known or suspected. She learned them in too much detail, and too well. At first, Ariane twisted against her, tried to hide, but she was proud of her crimes, fulfilled in her evils. She—her remnant—had been alone with them a long time.

There was a part of Ariane that delighted in showing off for Perceval all the wickedness she'd done. It was a new wickedness, and Perceval's horror and disgust were most satisfying. Ariane gave her more, unable to resist. It is a human need, to see our accomplishments admired.

And Perceval, gritting her teeth, wading in foulness, quailed and encouraged those confidences.

Then, having encouraged Ariane to open up to her, she began picking Ariane apart. She did not care to assimilate her; she did not want this dragon in her head. But she knew now that she no longer dared leave her intact, encysted and virulent. She would have to consume her, truly, and make of Ariane's twisted self-creation some useful materials out of which to build a richer and wiser self.

She learned a thousand unsuspected but hardly revelatory cruelties, too. The vivisection of a ship cat Chelsea had adopted as a pet; the theft and destruction of Oliver's lover; the endless torments heaped upon long-suffering Head, who existed—who had been *created*—only to please the folk of Rule. Status as a valued servant was not sufficient to protect anyone from Ariane—Doctor and Vintner and others had suffered as well. Alasdair would not have permitted Ariane to interfere with their duties, but given an adequacy of spite and invention, it was not hard for Ariane to make herself a figure of dread and loathing to all and sundry, from highest to most low. Rien, it seemed, had been beneath Ariane's notice until she was called to serve Perceval, and for that Perceval was grateful. But no one who caught Ariane's attention escaped unscathed.

But the information she needed was in here somewhere, and she would find it if she must pull each atom of her enemy's memory from the next and disassemble them all for the component parts.

She'd expected Ariane to fight the integration more vigorously, and indeed her remnant tried. But Perceval had grown stronger and more skilled than when last they fought, and it turned out to be a trivial matter to defeat her ancient enemy again. But the ease of the victory, she thought bitterly, was more than made up for by the distastefulness of the task.

Perceval was examining the record of a monster, and felt lessened for wading through it—and the more so for each bit she plucked, disassembled, and consumed. How was she different from Ariane if she took such pleasure in destroying Ariane?

Examining each bit for the discontinuity was like running her fingers over a polished surface, feeling for the bit of roughness, the seam, the snag. Ariane would have hidden it well, if she were hiding it even from herself. As one would; one did not hide one's soul away to ensure one's immortality and then blithely advertise the location.

She found it, at long last, in Rule. There, among the netted bodies, the victims of the engineered influenza that Ariane had used Perceval herself as a vector for, there was a flutter. Not even a skip, but a—a discontinuity. A repetition in the pattern of breaths, in the images of contorted bodies and dead faces.

Time excised and filled up with other time.

"Gotcha," Perceval whispered. Wild exultation filled her, but she fought it back and adjusted her chemical balance. She didn't want to feel this joy now, surrounded by the stench and the memory of the dead.

And then she winced, because she realized what it indicated. If the skip was in Rule, at that particular time and place, that meant that Ariane's Trojan Horse personality was embedded in somebody who had been present in Rule at that time. Which meant one of two places, because if Ariane had copied herself into the surviving splinter of Samael, Nova would have found it when she vetted the contents of his program. That left Head, or one of the members of her staff that she had managed to rescue—

—or the body of Oliver Conn, resurrected now and repurposed to hold the personality of the long-dead Astrogator, Damian Jsutien.

"Shit," Perceval said—or mouthed, rather, there being no atmosphere to carry the vibrations. Reaching out, she tapped on the library's external hull.

"Nova?" she said, when the Angel reestablished contact. "I think I'm ready to come out."

Through the host Conn's night, while the host slept and Ariane used the body to study, Dust washed his paws and watched the door. His patron rarely said anything, rarely rose from her chair. Instead, she sat before the massive swell of the ancient book, a papery rasp revealing each turned page.

She was not reading. Or rather, she was reading, but she was not reading the words written in ink. There was other information there, leaved through the pages on circuit boards mere molecules thick, wired into the spine on datajewels that had endured for generations.

Night after night, Ariane—in her borrowed body— figured out the access, learned the technology, unlocked the coding, and bored into the guts of the antediluvian computer. And night after night, Dust sat on the perch by the door and watched her.

18

a sort of embrace

There comes no sleep nor any love.
—WILLIAM MORRIS, "The Chapel in Lyoness"

Benedick was often intentionally infuriating. Tristen thought he cultivated the air as a sort of privacy shield, a means of keeping the world at arm's length and maintaining the distance, and thus the authority of command.

But it had never worked particularly well on Tristen, being older, and Tristen thought that quite possibly infuriated Benedick. Also, for now, Tristen made allowances, remembering his wife Aefre and how well he himself had dealt with that; Benedick was deep in the throes of grieving his lost love. Tristen harbored no illusions that the fact that Benedick and Caitlin were separated had meant that either of them cared less for the other.

In any case, his priority call was met with a skeptical eyebrow and a reserved expression until he began to talk. "The Captain has a task for us, O Brother. One perhaps best carried out by you, in Engine, although you will want support. And also to inform Jordan, before you act."

It was typical of Benedick that he neither asked foolish questions nor assumed answers were implied in what went unsaid. "Support?"

"It's likely that Caitlin's killer was a martial revenant of Ariane Conn. We believe she planted the daemon-seed for her resurrection in Oliver's body when she toured Rule. After her bioweapon had taken its toll of the servants and family."

Benedick's jaw firmed. It was the only outward symptom of distress—or determination—that Tristen was likely to get. "Evidence?"

"The Captain—" Important, that, for if Tristen had put them on equal terms when he called Benedick *brother,* now he reestablished the chain of authority. "She went through Ariane's memories."

Again, Benedick showed that firming of the jaw that could not exactly be termed a flinch. "I would have expected her to wipe something like that at the hippocampus. Or at the very least, have it on a dead-man's switch so that, when Perceval ate her, she wouldn't get access to Ariane's failsafe plan. But then, Ariane always was an overwhelming egotist."

"She did wipe it." Tristen enjoyed watching the surprised mothflutter of a smile at the corners of Benedick's mouth, gone as quickly as a flicker. No matter what else came between, paternal pride was beautiful. "Perceval found the repeated segment."

"So it's conjecture that the daemon-seed went into Oliver."

"Conjecture supported by circumstantial evidence. A newly installed personality—Jsutien—would grow around the daemon-seed and disguise it."

"And Jsutien was the person present when Arianrhod escaped," Benedick finished.

"Also, Nova cannot confirm his whereabouts for the duration of the attack on Engine."

Benedick was also too disciplined to curse. And although Tristen knew he had a startling, mercurial sense of humor, it was not on display now. "You're assuming he's not aware of the daemon he carries."

"If you were Ariane, would you place that much trust in a mule?"

Benedick wrapped a long hand around the squareness of his jaw. "I'll bring him into custody. Cynric can take his head apart and see what's hiding in there. She's more likely to put something functional back together when she's done rooting around than anyone else would be."

Tristen laced his fingers together, squeezing for comfort and control. "How far are you willing to trust Cynric?"

Benedick's smile was wider, this time, and ever so much less genuine. "I could throw her pretty far, if I had to."

Danilaw and Amanda didn't exactly have the run of the ship, but they didn't exactly *not* have it, either. Samael returned when they had had a few moments to assemble their facades and assess their situation. He showed them to rooms where they could cleanse, take exercise, and refresh themselves as it became necessary. If anything could have convinced Danilaw of the sincerity and the divinity of the patchwork Angel, clean clothes and a chance to bathe and sleep were high on the list.

Mallory, too, came by to check on them and deliver supplies. The pajamas were soft, clean, worn—Danilaw was comforted by the Jacobeans' ethos of reuse, repurposing, and recycling, when everything else about them seemed alien—and woven of some fabric that Danilaw did not recognize. He was fairly sure it was a natural fiber, something that grew on an animal or a plant rather than in a manufacturing vat, but other than that he found himself disinclined to inquire too closely.

Having shown him how the controls on the cleanser worked and made sure he knew how to operate the connecting door, the Angel and the hermaphrodite left Danilaw and Amanda alone again to bathe and dress. And sleep, he thought, luxuriously. It occurred to him that perhaps he and Amanda should arrange watches, or make sure they slept in some orderly fashion or protected location, but after a moment he dismissed that as foolish hyper-vigilance.

Whether he liked it or not, they were totally at the mercy of the Jacobeans. There was no escape, no place of refuge if their hosts chose to turn on them. He could trust, or he could worry, but the end result would be the same.

And so Danilaw shrugged, sorted out his confused thoughts, and went to restore himself. Standing in the hall by the cleanser, he stripped off the sweat-soaked garments he'd been wearing under his pressure suit and all through dinner. There was a niche in which to stow such things, and he availed himself of it.

That done, he climbed into the steamy environs of the cleanser. The tiny room was warm—almost too warm—and fitted with benches for relaxing while the vapor and sonics worked. Danilaw lay back, his head on his arms, and willed the heat and relaxation into his bones.

Perhaps it was antisocial—and definitely a little bit greedy—but he was still there fifteen minutes later, though he had switched to a lower, cooler bench. His eyes were closed, his muscles blessedly painless. He was reminding himself not to doze off when the old-fashioned manual slider eased open just a little and a familiar brown face poked through the coils of steam that billowed on a cooler draught. The sonics made her voice seem to reverberate. "Danilaw?"

"Amanda." It seemed like a pretension of modesty to cover himself when she'd just wandered into his shower. It wasn't as if this were an inappropriate setting for nudity, and they had been living in each other's pockets aboard the *Quercus,* so he just sat up—a little too quickly for the heat, it turned out. He leaned forward, elbows on his knees, and let his head hang until the dizziness subsided.

She had an old-fashioned cloth towel in one hand, and was otherwise nude. As best he could see through the steam, she stood with her arms pressed to her sides and shoulders up, as if she were chilly. "Come in," he said, as she said, "Do you mind if I join you?"

They laughed and she stepped inside, shutting the slider behind. She laid the folded towel on a higher bench as a pillow. "I wanted the company," she said, reclining.

It was a relief to speak his native tongue, familiar words and known patterns that had settled into his bones with father's milk and rooted deep. "Not sick of me after all that time on the scull?"

"Shocking, I know." She slid a generously curved leg across the bench and pressed the side of her foot to his thigh. Warm flesh, calloused, the contact lubricated by condensation and his own slick sweat. "It's going to be a long, boring trip home."

He could have moved away. It was an unnecessary complication, and his rightminding was robust enough that the prospect of combining romantic and professional entanglements set off all kinds of alarm bells in his head. But then again, he and Amanda were both responsible, rightminded adults, and zero-tolerance policies about office romances were a thing of the benighted past. A modern, suitably adjusted, evolved human being was presumed capable of balancing complicated decisions without resorting to anything so crude as a rule of thumb.

He put his hand over her foot, a sort of embrace, and said, "Boring? When we have a whole new culture to interact with?"

"So you're thinking of yourself as a tourist now?" It could have seemed harsh, but her tone of voice made it dreamy.

"I'm thinking of myself as a student."

"An anthropologist," she said. "Going to get yourself another tertiary in science?"

"That's what you're for."

He squeezed her foot. She prodded him lightly with her toe and laughed. The steam and sonics were making his head spin; he let go of her foot and moved up a shelf to lie down beside her. "It's an endocrine reaction," she said. "Just enough stress, and not too much. The proximity of an attractive member of my preferred gender. The evolutionary response says *'Get a piece of that while you have the chance and make a strong baby now.'* "

"The world is uncertain," Danilaw answered. He put a hand out; she took it. Her fingers, too, were wet. "I don't have time to make any babies until my Administrative Obligation is done. After that, I've earned out two years of personal project time, and I was thinking children might be a pretty good personal project. But that's a bit in the future."

"The future's even more uncertain than the world," Amanda said. She drew up one knee. "But I don't have any objection to practicing. Maybe when the time is ripe we'll have gotten really good at it."

"Maybe we will," Danilaw said. He sat up more slowly this time. "Let's rinse off and find out where we're starting from, shall we?"

A *perfectly satisfactory first attempt,* he thought later, licking her salt from his lips and trying to summon the energy to lift a hand and stroke her hair. She seemed to have dozed off, head on his shoulder, her leg thrown across his and her compact heel dug into the mossy cover on the bunk they occupied. The room felt cool now that they were quiet. Danilaw saw gooseflesh prickling across her shoulder. Mallory had shown him where the blankets were, in a cubby under the bed. With a groping hand he found one and managed to shake it open and drape it—somewhat haphazardly—over the two of them.

If Amanda had been sleeping, it was not heavily. She

lifted her head from his shoulder and blinked. "Well," she said. "In one regard, at least, I think I will declare this mission a success."

Danilaw kissed the top of her head, straight hair slick against his lips. She smelled of crushed grass and clean woman and sweat and sex—an appealing combination. "But that was only the proof of concept," he said. "We'll have to run more extensive testing for a definitive result."

She turned her face into his shoulder and snorted against his skin. A pause before she lifted herself up on an elbow and said, "You know all those tunes you sing? The ones from before the Eschaton and rightminding and The Obligation?"

"They're songs," he said, eager to assuage what he perceived as her concern. "I have not ever, nor do I ever intend, to shoot anyone over a quaint concept of infidelity. You have my word."

"Your word? I shall have it bronzed."

Because she made him laugh, he swatted her shoulder lightly. She laughed, too, before her expression settled into seriousness. "Why do you suppose we still find all that art from the bad old days so compelling?"

"Easy," he said. "There have been studies. Which I have, as you might imagine, taken a professional interest in."

"I might," she admitted.

"Rightminding mitigates the conditioned emotional triggers for adrenaline response, among other things. We're still capable of it, of course—adrenaline is useful stuff when a slarg is chasing you down the beach—but it used to manifest as a conditioned response to childhood trauma and hardwired primate social-dominance schema."

"The source of a lot of irrational conflict," she said.

"And a lot of folk music." When she glanced up at him, he grinned.

She answered with one of her own, nodding that he should continue.

"But the amygdalae are still in there, and we still have a response to cathartic emotional stimulation. We've removed the crazy from our daily lives, but it's still satisfying in art, safely removed and bounded. A nice thing, too. I'd hate to think what we'd be missing if we'd removed our ability to enjoy Ovid or Robert Johnson or Akira Kurosawa." Wincing, Danilaw stopped himself before he could bury himself deeper in pedantry. Pity rightminding didn't dispense with embarrassment.

But Amanda either hadn't noticed him rattling on, or didn't seem to mind. She touched his face lightly with the back of her hand and waited until he turned to her. In the diffuse illumination of their temporary quarters, her eyes were particularly luminescent, the delicate veins and green-gold flecks buried in their brown revealed in the way the light lay against the surface of her irises, as if against the nap of smoothed velvet. A surge of affection tightened his throat.

"Do you ever think we've lost something?"

"A lot of misery," he answered, hearing his own voice trail off in a way he hadn't intended.

She leaned closer, the resilient slope of her breast brushing his chest. She glossed over him, smooth and soft, the resilience of her skin telling his endocrine system that this was a young, healthy female, strong and capable.

Also, she felt nice.

"I suppose," he said, making sure his tone stayed wistful rather than condescending or dismissive, "it's easy to imagine the pre-Eschaton world as more passionate, more interesting. Grander."

"That's a romanticized view," she said. "I mean, yes, of course, it was more passionate. Possibly they felt more deeply than we do. They were certainly less mannered about it. But it's not as if C21 societies were without their strictures and social controls. And values. And in some of them, community service and responsibility to one's family and clan were the highest ideals. That's very adaptive."

"Pathological competition does not exist only on the interpersonal level." Danilaw propped himself on his elbows. He caught himself smiling—this was *interesting*—and hoped Amanda would not think he found her silly.

Well, if she did, she would ask. She didn't seem troubled at all right now. If anything, she was warming to her argument. "No, of course not. There's interspecies competition, too, and that between cultures and affinity groups. But that's not what I'm talking about. I'm talking about why we're still embracing mainstream art from a thousand years ago instead of creating more of our own."

"Entertainments—"

"Sure," she said. "Entertainments. But who's the most recent artist, Danilaw Bakare, whose music you really enjoy performing?"

Danilaw leaned back on his elbows. He frowned and felt it furrow his brow.

She had him there.

She stretched against him, warm skin caressing his side. Simple animal comfort, so necessary and so atavistic. "There're a lot of ethical implications in rightminding that get glossed over when it becomes the standard of existence. Who decides what the boundaries of neurotypicality are? Who decides what a normal range of variation is? Sociopathy can be adaptive for the individual, if not the society—"

"You sound like a New Evolutionist."

"Just playing advocate." But the way she lifted her head to examine his face, some evidence of caginess around her eyes, left him wondering.

"When you were younger, did you know anybody out on the edges of the spectrum? Somebody who really *needed* rightminding to assume a full role in society?"

"My best friend," she said. "He was an autist. Not as high-functioning as Administrator Jesse. His parents wanted him rightminded, for ease of care. And me." Her foot jerked restlessly. "I had a few issues of my own with empathy. I'm much more aware of the feelings of others these days."

"Aware enough—and stable enough—to be a Legate. Congratulations," Danilaw said, hoping his tone conveyed the affectionate irony he intended. Amanda didn't jerk away from him, so he'd probably managed an approximation, at least. "Before rightminding, my epilepsy was a death sentence."

"You exaggerate."

"A little." He let his hand drift up, smoothing the slick strands of her hair against her nape and skull. "It's still one of the less tractable conditions. I have to self-monitor, and I've had three adjustments since I was twenty-five. Trust me when I tell you, you wouldn't want to know the me I was born to be. He's a crazy person. Angels come and talk to him."

She grimaced. It wasn't unheard of, but three was a lot. Most people were stable past twenty-five, at least until they got up past the centennial mark and degradation set in. "Angels come and talk to both of us," she said.

He smiled. So they did.

She huffed lightly in frustration or concentration. "I'm not saying rightminding is a bankrupt technology. What I'm saying is that we lose something irreplaceable when we apply it broad-spectrum. We lessen our diversity. My friend Claude—"

"The autist."

"The same." She sighed. "He wasn't—he didn't read people, not the way most of us do. He was very . . . literal. But I still don't see what's wrong with that. Rightminding him made him more like other people, easier for them to deal with. It may have made it easier for him to navigate among them. It certainly lessened conflict. But did it make him happier or more useful to society? I mean, dealing with sophipathology is one thing, forcing people to *think* instead of *believing*, but when do we take it too far?"

"But rightminding you," Danilaw said, "you and those like you. *That* benefits society."

She smiled. "It doesn't necessarily benefit me."

"Not as an individual genetic competitor, no. But evolutionarily speaking, we've *won*. We can afford to be magnanimous." Danilaw felt as much as heard the strands of her hair rasp between his fingers when he rolled them there. "This is a reversal for you. In the Council meeting, your concerns were focused on what effect a large group of unrightminded individuals would have on our society. Now you're arguing against rightminding on principle? That's inconsistent logic, unless I'm missing something."

She shook her head and waved around the green walls of the ship that embraced them. "You keep talking about how we can afford to be magnanimous. But I don't think we can, not anymore. How does noblesse oblige stand up in the face of *this*? If this isn't competition, Danilaw, I don't know what is. And if we don't welcome them to Fortune, what's to stop them from taking whatever they want? Fighting is so antisocial. A compromise position would serve everyone better, right?"

Her anger startled but did not shock him. It was a natural response to frustration. Still, he pulled away slightly, leaning his back against the mossy bulkhead as she sat up.

She shook her hair back. "Rightminded people find solutions. They find common ground. They make sacrifices and consider the impact of their actions on future generations. *These people* do what they do and take what they want, and spend a lot of time sorting or putting off their legacy of inherited crises."

"You do realize that they serve as an inherited crisis of our very own?"

She snorted, waving a hand that encompassed his objection as much as dismissed it. "Are we too fucking post-evolution to fight them? Are we going to lie down and surrender because it's the civilized thing to do?"

"Of course not," he said. "We were here first. Did you blow up the scull?"

He'd hoped to blindside her, to surprise her into a revelation. He got one—a look of utter horror and denial. "I—*Danilaw!*"

"I had to ask," he said gently. Torn between relief and concern. If it had been her, that would at least have been a mystery solved. "Amanda—"

"Mm?"

"If you want to learn to manage an unrightminded society," he said, "it occurs to me that the Jacobeans are our only modern-day example."

"You make a compelling case for the surgery."

"We're better people when we're sane." He shrugged and spread his hands. "There's a tension in your ideas. That's all I'm saying."

"I know. That's the problem with rightminding." She rose from the bunk, shedding the blanket, and crossed the mossy floor to where her borrowed pajamas waited folded on a shelf. "You get to see all the sides of the issue. Mature consideration of the options can be paralyzing."

He nodded. "What if we offer the Jacobeans resources to repair their ship, and send them on?"

"What if they agree to rightminding?"

"What if they have a civil war over what they're going to do?" She pulled a camisole over her head, covering the rise of her breasts and the curve of her waist.

Danilaw was sad to see them go, but as much as he would have liked to prolong the interlude, she was right.

"We need to call the Council."

"Yeah," she said. "I think we do.

19

the lathe of evolution

In the chronicle of wasted time
I see descriptions of the fairest wights,
And beauty making beautiful old rhyme,
In praise of ladies dead and lovely knights.
—WILLIAM SHAKESPEARE, Sonnet 106

When Benedick came with Chelsea and Jordan to arrest
Damian Jsutien, they found the Astrogator in his quarters,
as Nova had reported. The door stood open, welcoming
company, though Benedick did not think Jsutien often entertained.

Jsutien's room was spare, by Engine standards. The lush-
ness of the corridor vegetation ended at the threshold.
Rather than garish colors and a verdancy of symbiotic
plants and animals, Jsutien affected surroundings imbued
with simple serenity. Stripped of plants, the walls of his
chamber revealed convoluted surfaces of piping and
ductwork, painted in shades of sand and eggshell-white,
eggshell-brown. On the floor, a pallet lay rolled aside and
in use as a bolster upon which Jsutien had propped his
back. A tray across his lap held hair-fine manipulators and
a partially disassembled toolkit. The toolkit, under anesthesia, breathed calmly in and out through a mask.

Draped sheets and ultraviolet established a sterile operating field, and Jsutien's fingers—Oliver's fingers, Benedick

reminded himself for the first time in years—were coated in a layer of plum-colored surgical spray.

"Just a moment," Jsutien said. He wiggled a chip into a socket until it emitted a satisfying click. The toolkit, even under sedation, stretched against its restraints and made a small pleased noise.

Jsutien closed it up with surgical glue and speedheal, turning off the anesthesia before releasing its restraints. By the time he'd unfastened the last delicate limb, the fan-eared device was sitting up and grooming between the toes on the opposite foot. It looked familiar to Benedick; the pattern of spots and stripes reminded him of one he'd destroyed in service, and he felt a momentary pang for the gallant little artifice.

Jsutien wadded up his surgical drapes and peeled the purple down his fingers in wormy inside-out tubes. "There," he said. "That's a stopping point. How can I be of service?"

Jordan looked at Benedick, engendering a pang of sympathy he would never demonstrate. It was a difficult time and situation under which to find oneself thrust into a position of authority. Battlefield promotions generally were, and Benedick had endured his share. But that did not dim his fellow feeling for the new and inexperienced Chief Engineer.

He was about to take pity on her when Chelsea, on her left hand, stepped forward. She straightened her back and cleared her throat, leaving Benedick wondering why excellent posture was never a good sign. "Damian Jsutien," she said. "You are under arrest on suspicion of harboring an unknown daemon, and suspicion of complicity aware or unaware in the murder of Caitlin Conn."

He stopped, half standing, not yet quite having risen from his crouch. Benedick tensed, a hand on the hilt of his sword, but Jsutien only tilted his head up and blinked at her. "I see," he said. "I'll get my shirt. By the way, the extra memory you wanted installed in your toolkit is done."

Chelsea crouched down and clucked. The fuzzy beast scampered to her, hesitating infinitesimally to sniff her out-stretched fingers before swarming up her arm. Under the sweep of her long hair, it quickly made itself into a fur collar.

"Thanks," she said. She stood, tilting her chin up to look Jsutien in the eye.

"Check that for sabotage," Benedick said.

She nodded. "Damian, you know we'll take the best possible care of you, even if you've got somebody else in your head."

He pulled a dress shirt on over his head and tugged the collar laces. When it was settled to his satisfaction, he ran a hand through his tight, dark curls and said, "By the fact that I am coming quietly, you may assume I believe you to have my best interests at heart."

Dust was bigger now. Not much bigger, not too much, and he took good care not to stray outside the physical confines of the construct body he inhabited. It was safer in here, masquerading as a small, unremarked semi-intelligence. Out there, free-floating, in a colony with real access to the world—out there he would have access to more information, more sensory input, more of the world. And in the process, he would eventually—inevitably—run afoul of Nova.

Who would eat him again, this time as surely as the last time.

So for now he stayed small and stayed with his secret ally, who did not even know herself an ally most of the time. They had goals in common.

His people were being misguided. The people he had been charged to advance, to defend, to force against the lathe of evolution and edge fine were in grave danger. They might make landfall, sell all their majesty and progress for the promise of safety, disassemble the world that had been his body for material and energy, and destroy the ecosystem that had endured greater stress and evolutionary pressures than any mere dirtside ecology—

—and here, on the very verge of triumph, of fulfilling his ancient charge, he could fail.

He would not allow himself to fail. He would not allow his Builders, his angels, and most importantly his mortal (or demimortal) charges to fail so close to completion, to transcendence.

No.

They would not be allowed to fail.

He crouched on his patron's mule's shoulder and let her carry him along as she escorted the Astrogator through the halls of Engine, flanked by the new Chief Engineer and the venerable Benedick Conn. This fast-moving squad swept past lesser Exalts and Engineers and construct creatures that flattened themselves against corridor walls and ceilings, as far out of the way as they could manage. Some of them reached out to let the hem of a Conn garment brush them. The old ways—the old respect—might no longer be enforced with terror, but enough of it lingered that Dust was not entirely bereft of hope for the future of Engine and the Conn family. They might have grown soft, but they had not entirely fallen apart.

Central Engineering was an unassuming control booth inside a mighty tower in Engine. The structure was one of dozens that grew from all sides of the world's greatest Heaven—a vast semispherical cargo hold converted into a city. Flyers blurred from one spire to another across the open space between them. Jordan, this untested Chief Engineer, let her wings feather wide and glanced across Dust's insignificant pointed nose to Chelsea.

"Nova says the Captain has come to review the questioning," she said.

Dust's sensitive toolkit nose lifted the taste of Benedick's discomfort from the air. Benedick's child might be Captain now, and grown, but Dust imagined there were things he'd prefer she not witness. The elder Conn looked away, though, and Dust had no illusions that he could count this emotional attachment as a weakness, a chink in Benedick's armor.

He had known too many Conns.

Chelsea's voice vibrated her throat against Dust's side. "Do we *want* the Captain present?" She bent close, as if examining Oliver's eyes. She lifted the lid with a thumb.

"Hey," he said.

Dust reached across the gap and sniffed his ear. This close to his patron, he felt the moment when daemon touched daemon, and data bridged. Oliver's eyes might have flashed, but a moment later, they only looked confused.

"Ow," he said. "Seriously, stop it."

Inside Oliver's colony, the subcolony that had housed Ariane was now dying, consuming itself, contracting into a singularity and vanishing. Oliver knew as little of it as he knew of the tumors and viruses his colony excised from his body every day. The data it had stored was in Dust now, awaiting a moment when he could transfer it to Ariane's other host.

"The Captain," Benedick said. "Are you going to try to stop her?"

Though he spoke, Benedick still didn't look back. Beside them, the Astrogator in Oliver Conn's body had dropped into silence. He expressed no bravado; he made no effort to appear amused. Instead, he went to judgment as a man without defenses, but also without fear. Though he was pale and his forehead dewed with sweat, he smelled only of discomfort. Perhaps he felt unwell. Perhaps he felt the Ariane-seed's suicide, on some subconscious level.

Whatever he experienced, he met it with dignity.

And as it was true courage, and not the storybook kind, Dust found that he admired that. Admired it, and had no understanding of how to define it. Storybooks were what he was created for. And from what he had created himself, and this entire society that surrounded him. Princes and knights-errant and all.

Rightly considered, histories, too, were storybooks. Of a sort.

"You go on ahead, Chief Engineer," Benedick said. "Make sure all is in readiness for us. Chelsea and I will have no problems with the prisoner."

Nova could have done the same, but he must have been counting on Jordan's physical presence having an effect on the Captain. Jordan's wings unfurled the rest of the way; her eyes tilted upward and her arms streamlined along her body. A kick, a flick of pinions in the lessened gravity, and the tiger-colored Engineer was gone.

It was a sign of her youth that she accepted an order— however politely phrased—from a Conn she outranked, without question or modification. At least she hadn't called him *sir*.

If I were her Angel, there would be none of that. If I were her Angel, she would not bow so willingly to any Conn who ordered it. She would be a power, a force to be reckoned with. I would give her wings in metaphor as well as truth.

Dust almost crooned after her, but that would be unwise.

Chelsea made a noise as if she wished she could turn her head and spit. "There won't be any of that on a heavy body."

"Wings," Jsutien said. "One more thing we won't need where we're going."

Chelsea took his elbow. "Come on," she said. "The sooner we get the inside of your head looked at, the sooner we can all get lunch."

* * *

Once Danilaw had reclaimed his pressure suit and gotten Samael to explain to him how to patch into the *Jacob's Ladder*'s systems for a power boost, he called Fortune. The modifications required a little soldering but, unsurprisingly, it turned out Captain Amanda knew her way around a standard-issue pressure suit repair kit pretty well.

Administrator Jesse was on hand to take his call—fortuitously, it turned out, because the motes and probes Amanda and Danilaw had deployed from the *Quercus* had reported the explosion. Combined with the cessation of telemetry from the space suits, it had seemed a logical supposition that Danilaw and Amanda were dead, casualties of a treacherous attack by the crew of the derelict generation ship.

"Gain has been declared Acting Premier," Jesse said, in that precise and mannerly way of his. "She is placing the colony on a war footing."

Danilaw wondered what exactly that meant, and furthermore what exactly Gain thought she could accomplish against people who knew how to fight and had centuries of practice in doing it.

"Planetary defenses are engaged to prevent you from approaching the orbit of Fortune," Jesse said. "A broadcast is being prepared warning the *Jacob's Ladder* away on pain of destruction. Public opinion is running high against the aliens, Premier."

"Our evidence suggests the explosion was caused by sabotage committed on Fortune itself," Danilaw said. "It was an attack by us against them. The *Quercus*'s drive detonated."

He paused and glanced at Amanda, who had waited just out of pickup range. She leaned forward into reception. "So Gain stepped right into the power vacuum, did she?"

Jesse's eyes widened. "She ordered an inquest begun at once. Decisively. She stepped up the assemblage of a defense cordon, too. By last night, there was a popular vote to confirm her as Acting Premier in your absence and . . . presumed death."

"Well, I'm not absent anymore," Danilaw said. "Patch me through to the media center, would you? I can see I have an announcement to make. And some orders to countermand. And an inquest of my own to put into motion."

"You're not going to call off the defensive cordon?" Amanda said.

Danilaw shook his head. "I am going to countermand any shoot-on-sight orders they may have received, however. Jesse—"

"Right here."

"Watch your back. Also, keep an eye on Gain. And any contacts she may have should be logged."

Jesse looked more greenish than ochre, but he nodded. "I will."

"Good job," Danilaw said, wishing he felt more confident in it. "You'll do great. Just stay cool, Administrator."

20

all the world and everything

What, love, courage!—Christ! he is so pale.
—MATTHEW ARNOLD, "Tristram and Iseult"

There was too much light in the room. To Perceval, the space in which Cynric had chosen to examine Jsutien felt washed-out, white-lit, dreamy, like a surgical theater hung with gauze. But Cynric preferred it, or perhaps merely tolerated it without discomfort, and so Perceval bit her tongue.

Benedick sat with them while they went in. The rest of the senior crew and Conns returned to their stations.

There was trust involved in joining forces with Cynric to investigate the contents of Jsutien's mind—but not so much trust, Perceval thought, as there would be in allowing her to go in alone, and then taking her word for what she found. Perceval had known the woman—or her revenant—for fifty years now, and in that time she had seen nothing to indicate that Cynric, whole or fractional, had ever hesitated at anything she thought necessary, no matter how tragic or distasteful a sane person would have found it.

Cynric was there beside her, holding her hand, the too-intimate bond of blood and colonies flowing between them. Her presence—her assistance—filled Perceval with a strange white puissance, as if all the world and everything were washed out with that same cold light that filled the examination room. It was a dreamy prospect, silhouettes moving against glare and breaking the flooding light into rays.

She would have rather been anywhere else at all, but this was her responsibility. And so Perceval herself, in her person as Captain and guide of the *Jacob's Ladder,* leaned down over the chair Damian Jsutien sat in and kissed him on the mouth.

Jsutien's mouth opened. He eased his jaw, tilting his head back to allow her access. He closed his eyes, as relaxed as a drowsy child accepting a mother's bedtime kiss.

Perceval let her colony touch his, and slipped herself inside, into the spare and ferny landscape of his soul.

For someone who had inhabited the body for as long as he had, Jsutien had not much populated its mind. Perceval knew he had grown from a seed, a set of recorded preferences and commands and variables that fit into a matrix that could be slipped into a pocket, carried in a hand. But that was just source code, uncompiled. It was just the blueprint for a thing that could grow into a person—a person similar to the person who had recorded it, once upon a time.

Such revenants usually elaborated, populating their environments just as any organic mind might. The neurology affected the personality—but the personality also affected the neurology. Brains changed to accommodate the minds that dwelled in them, just as minds adapted to the architecture of the brain.

Jsutien had left Oliver Conn's mind as white-walled and unmodified as a rental flat. The space was inhabited but not lived in, and the record of the thing—the person—that had been Damian Jsutien had not spread itself out into the crevices.

Perceval went deeper, but nothing Jsutien could have

done could have faked the transparency, the emptiness, the sheer unused space in this head. There was processing power here to spare. Jsutien had just never moved into it. Fifty years on, and he inhabited his own head like a transient with a sleeping bag and a hot plate flopped into one corner of a mansion. He had never, she realized, expected this incarnation to be permanent.

He had never let himself get attached.

Perceval felt Cynric following along beside her, trailing long metaphorical fingers over the furnishings, contemplating the immaterial windows and walls.

"If it were here," Cynric said, "it should be easy to spot in a head like this."

Perceval regarded her without turning. Without any outward sign of a reaction at all.

"He never moved in, did he?"

"He never felt welcome here," Cynric said, "so he stayed out of a sense of duty. But this is all—work. Predictable. Crazy-making. He never developed recreations, or investigated any of the ones his other-self enjoyed. He would have had the muscle memory for Oliver's sports, or he could have retrained his body to work on Jsutien's. The mind could be trained to match the body, or the body to match the brain."

"He's not our man," Perceval said.

"Au contraire," Cynric said. "Something was filling up this space, and now it has been deleted."

Deleted. Perceval lurched forward in her eagerness, but—regretfully—Cynric shook her head. Here in this space that didn't precisely exist, she was a long-armed wraith, the wind of Jsutien's thoughts blowing her robe up between her arms and body until it billowed like the sails of a kite. It arched, lifting.

"Deleted and—"

"Overwritten," Cynric confirmed. "Come on. We'll get a better view from a height."

She sailed up. Perceval followed, until they moved through the cool transparent azure of Jsutien's spotless mind. It was beautiful and cold. There was no pain here, no loss, no regret, no love.

Perceval found she enjoyed it.

She also enjoyed the landscape spread out below her—a patchwork of this and that and the other thing, the edges ruler-straight, the surfaces mowed tidy. It was more like a schematic of a mind than anyplace anybody spent time, and Perceval again shook her head. It should be impossible to hide anything as large and fiddly as a daemon in here. Jsutien was barely more than a daemon himself.

"She's not in here."

"I know," Perceval said. "That's not the answer I was hoping for."

"But I am confident in suggesting that she was. Which means more than one daemon. Which means she could be anywhere."

"In you or me," Perceval said.

"Or, more likely, any of the others. Let's keep that our secret."

"Let's," Perceval agreed. "Because our most important goal remains finding her."

"And Charity," Cynric said. "Wherever we find the blade, we find Ariane."

"Outside," Perceval said, and returned to herself with a thought. She leaned forward for a moment, elbows akimbo and splayed hands on her knees. Benedick's hand came to rest on her shoulder. When she looked up, Cynric was regarding her.

"She was in there, but she's gone. She purged. You're clean, Astrogator."

Jsutien let out a long, soft sigh, the first evidence that he had felt concern. "So what now?"

"We have to find Charity," Perceval said. "Charity, or that damned Bible."

Nova spoke out of nothing. "An unblade doesn't register on my sensors. And I have not been able to locate the Bible."

"Then we search," said Benedick. "By hand."

"We cannot search the whole world," Jsutien protested.

"No," Benedick answered. "We prioritize."

By hand indeed—by hand, and by foot, and through the corridors of Engine and Rule and spreading outward. Every available Engineer and denizen of Rule was pressed into service, and not just them. The carnivorous plants turned out in force. The toolkits were arrayed to check crawl spaces. Nova reprogrammed the ship cats and set them seeking.

There were Deckers, too—those closest to AE deck outraged by the murders there, and the rest in service to the ship. Tristen heard muttering from some that the Conns should have done more to protect the victims, and a few of the rumors that wended back to him opined that Conns, indeed, had killed all the inhabitants of AE deck in order to cover up some variously specified crime.

No one was sent out alone, by order of the Captain. Tristen did not miss the care with which Cynric maneuvered to become his partner. They would start their search with the Go-Back Heaven, and Tristen would not send anyone else to brave Dorcas.

In the lift, Cynric and Tristen talked. Cynric seemed to enjoy the conspiracy theories purely from an entertainment standpoint, and amused herself by laying out a few of the crazier ones for Tristen. She sat cross-legged in the corner, her robes draping from her bony wrists, and leaned her head back into the corner while she spoke.

Tristen had seen her so many times, perched in some corner behind the barricade of her bony knees, the lines of her long face defining smiles or frowns. He wondered how it was that he had only now realized that this was the real

Cynric, or at least as much the real Cynric as the cold, imperious Sorceress.

"There's one that says you stole the Bible yourself," she said. "And that you mean to use it to replace Perceval as Captain."

Tristen arched his eyebrows. "If I wanted to be Captain, I would have been." The implications of her words struck him. "Wait. *Use* it? What use is an old paper book?"

Her head came forward, the long neck lengthening. The stare she leveled at him would have curdled the blood of most men.

"You are no revenant," she said. "Are your memories fully intact?"

He shifted in his armor. "Flesh or machine memories? I went mad for a while."

"The legacy Bible."

He nodded.

"It was you who taught me its purpose, Brother mine. When I was small. The Bible is an immutable hard copy of the Builders' New Evolutionist creed, to be sure, but it's also a *computer*—an old-style discrete calculating and remembering machine. And it holds the override codes for the entire world."

Tristen blinked at what she said. He heard it—of course he heard it—but it seemed to wash over him as a series of abstractions. Nonsense, confused and inarticulate, until he tossed his head like a dog shaking water away. "I'm not following you."

She rose, the sweep of fabric trailing behind her, and moved toward him. They were of a height, and Tristen knew their father's features were plain in both their faces. She touched his cheek. "The legacy Bible is a computer. You taught me that."

"I'm sorry," Tristen said. "I do not understand."

He also did not understand the smile that stretched her face—more like a snarl, in truth. But he did understand when she spat "*Father!*" as if it were the worst curse word she knew.

She touched his cheek. "It appears, Brother Tristen, that somebody has been reprogramming your brain. Removing old knowledge. Would you care to hazard a guess as to who might be responsible?"

He did not doubt her. He wanted to; he could feel the denial in him, rising like the automatic subroutine it might be. But she was Cynric, and whatever else she was, she had never been a liar. "Can you fix it?"

She was angry. "There was nothing Alasdair Conn could do that I could not undo better. One of the things that book was for was rewriting memories, but I have read the book, and know it well. Give us a kiss, Brother dearest."

It didn't hurt a bit, and Tristen was left with no sense that anything had altered, but this time when Cynric said the simple words, they made sense and stuck deep in his memory. They were finished before they arrived in the Edenite Heaven.

And the implications of what Cynric said sent a chill through his body that had nothing to do with the temperature controls in his armor. Their father had used the information in the New Evolutionist Bible to remove his memories; Cynric had used it to restore them.

And Ariane had that book now.

As the lift door slid open and they stepped forth into the lock, he said, "You couldn't have mentioned that earlier?"

The far door began to cycle, Dorcas just visible through the widening gap. Cynric spoke quickly, from the corner of her mouth. "It never occurred to me that you would forget."

"Tristen," Dorcas said, as the doorway between them stabilized at its widest aperture. "Cynric. To what do I owe this unexpected joy?"

* * *

Tristen took Dorcas aside and told her that she must call her folk and her snakes in from the fields and gather them in the onion-domed tent that served the Edenites as a hall. He told her she must keep them quiet and collected—fields unweeded, goats unmilked—while he and Cynric went over the Heaven from one end to the other, with no respect for personal privacy or the doors of tents.

She waited, and when they finished—and found nothing, as Tristen had half expected and half feared—it was Tristen who had to go back to her and tell her that they were done, and her folk could return to their residences and their work. Cynric would have done it for him, of course, but he felt he owed it to the woman who inhabited his daughter.

"You're not sorry," she said, walking him back to the lift lock, where Cynric waited. "Will you even tell me what you were looking for?"

He studied her, the sway of her hair, the line of her shoulders. He laid a hand on the hilt of his sword—which had been Sparrow's sword—and felt the weird intelligence in the blade yearn toward her. Mirth did not care if Sparrow's mind inhabited Sparrow's body.

He said, "Are you going to tell me you don't know?"

"I don't have the Bible," she said. "Or the sword. I have no desire to rule this sad old world of yours, Tristen Tiger, that all you Conns squabble over with such ferocity. Exactly as if it meant anything at all."

There was something in her voice, in the levelness of her tone, that took the splinter of unease working through him and froze it to a spike of ice. "Do you know who *does* have it?"

She let her lips stretch across her teeth. "*You* know who has it," she answered. "And you know she isn't here."

Tristen was not a cursing man, but sometimes he made an exception. "Don't fuck with me, Dorcas."

"Old man," she said, "I would never. But I'll tell you what: if I find her, I'll take care of it for you."

* * *

It was a long ride home, but as much as Danilaw would
have liked to spend the trip getting to know Amanda better
and exploring the sprawling reaches of the *Jacob's Ladder*,
there was enough work to fill almost every waking hour—
work complicated by the headaches and malaise caused by
the *Jacob's Ladder*'s stressed and possibly toxic environment, to which Danilaw was not adapted.

Somewhat to his surprise, language lessons were the
least of it. The Jacobeans learned quickly, and once Danilaw had texts sent over the q-sets, they mostly managed by
self-study, using him and Amanda for conversational practice. He also could not miss the signs that all was not
well—politically speaking—with his hosts. When he asked,
Tristen told him that an assassin was at large, one who
wished to provoke armed conflict between the Jacobeans
and the people of Fortune.

"But don't worry," he said. "We'll find her."

Still, by the drawn look of his features and the apparent
lack of time or sleep among any of the senior crew, Danilaw suspected that they were not growing closer to a solution. More critical to Danilaw personally was time spent
managing the situation on Fortune. If on the trip out Danilaw had been surprised by the ease with which he managed
his duties remotely, now he was surprised by the degree to
and speed with which everything could fall apart.

Administrator Gain was nearly impossible to get ahold
of. She sealed herself behind a wall of staff, and whenever
Danilaw called, she was unavailable—which, he had to
admit, was reasonable, given that conversations with Administrator Jesse—and Danilaw's own obsessive checking
of newsfeeds and the planetary infosphere—provided intelligence of a sticky situation on the ground, indeed.

"People are frightened," Jesse said. "There's a good deal
of disbelief that one of us committed the sabotage. We're

taking steps to encourage cooperation and discourage hoarding—"

He sighed. They were on audiolink only, and Danilaw could hear the shrug in his voice. "Lifeboat rules," Danilaw said. "Stay on it. What's up with Gain?"

"Factionating," Jesse admitted. "She seems to be coming around to being an open proponent of isolationism. Do you know if she's been in contact with anyone on the *Jacob's Ladder*?"

"Except through official channels?" Danilaw, secure in his own invisibility, allowed himself to rock back and fold his arms for the defensive comfort of the gesture. "What makes you suspect it?"

The considering silence on the other end of the connection was anything but reassuring. "She is the ham radio hobbyist. She might have her own plans. Public opinion is not in favor of welcoming the offworlders, currently, and she seems to be feeding that isolationism. There's a lot of talk of 'contamination,' and frankly, we've had some demonstrations. Civil unrest, and I would not be surprised if it is being arranged by agitators. Also, we've got preliminary instructions from the homeworld. They basically amount to *Stall*."

"Crap. Well, that's useful." Danilaw pressed his temples. "Thanks, Jesse. Watch your back, okay?"

"It unsettles me that you feel the need to say that."

"Not as much as it unsettles me."

Danilaw paused a moment to let Jesse sign off. He hit the kill on his own q-set before raising his voice to address the air. "Nova? Can you find or make me a musical instrument?"

His own guitar had been lost with the *Quercus*, and as weird as it felt to be asking thin air for favors, Danilaw suspected he needed something to do with his hands.

The air spoke back. "Easily. What would you like?"

"Guitar," he said. "Six string. Acoustic."

Nova materialized before him, just long enough for him to realize that he was getting over his discomfort at dealing with an anthropomorphized artificial intelligence faster than he ever would have imagined possible, and handed him a hard black case as he stood to greet her. "Your wish, etcetera."

"Thank you," he said. "Nova?"

She hesitated in the midst of dispersing, streamers of her image blowing off her shape like ribbons in the wind. "Yes, Administrator?"

"Please tell the First Mate or the Captain I would like to speak with them."

There was no perceptible delay, but Danilaw knew she must have checked with both before she answered. "Of course. The First Mate will see you on the Bridge."

When Danilaw reached the Bridge, not just Tristen but also Perceval was waiting for him. And Amanda, seated on the grass beside the Captain's chair, a cup of some hot beverage in her hand. She smiled at him; he winked back. There, at least, was one unexpected and happy outcome of the entire situation.

The Bridge was bright with increased sunlight. Even filtered—as it must be now—it filled the space with warmth and a honeyed glow. The handle of his new guitar case rough against his palm, Danilaw breathed deep— violets, lily of the valley. Alien Earth flowers he had only learned the scents of recently.

In the forward screen, a three-dimensional image of Fortune and its secondary, Favor, fell endlessly one around the other. They were magnified, but even in their magnification Danilaw could feel how close they were. A day or two out now. So close.

So close to home.

So close to irrevocable decisions.

The worst of it was, he had come to like the Jacobeans, in all their sophipathic insanity. They might be grotesques, caricatures, larger than life and full of violence—but they were also shockingly generous and, sometimes, shockingly funny.

Whatever happened next, he thought, he was not going to enjoy it.

"Tea?" Amanda said. She held up her cup and gestured to a pot half hidden in the grass beside the Captain's chair.

"Please," Danilaw said. He sat beside her and opened the guitar case; he saw her considering look, and her decision to accept the obvious without asking questions.

The guitar was cool and smooth in his arms. It fit perfectly in the cradle of his torso and thigh. It was, in fact, in tune.

He found a G chord and strummed it. It didn't have the mellow resonances and tonal quirks of an age-seasoned, handmade instrument, but the intonation was clear and bright. "I see I didn't need to call a council—"

"The news just came from Aerospace," Amanda said. "There's a lighter coming up to meet us. It should be here in twelve hours."

Danilaw felt his muscles flex involuntarily, digging his thighs and buttocks into the soil where he sat. He breathed out, pushing the tension away, and tried not to let relief dizzy him. *Home.* Clean, thick air. Full gravity.

A day away.

Tristen, on the far side of Perceval's chair, folded his hands. "You wanted to speak with me."

"I may have a partial solution to your situation," Danilaw said. He did not look at Amanda, not wanting to reopen their old argument about rightminding. "You understand that a majority of the citizens of Fortune are taking an isolationist line—"

Perceval lifted her chin and looked at him. Just looked, but Danilaw felt the heat of embarrassment in every limb.

He swallowed and forced himself on. "We have a world. We can spare a little of it. Just this once. It's not like generation ships are going to be a common occurrence."

Tristen huffed. "You're offering us resources to move on."

"It's a shameful bribe," Danilaw said. "The alternative requires you to submit to rightminding, and integrate into the Fortune colony."

He did not expect them to like the options. Judging by their thinned lips and sidelong glances, he had been right. But Tristen said, "What about your secondary, Favor? The binary world. You haven't settled it—"

"It's still got an ecosystem," Danilaw said. "A toxic ecosystem, but the potential for introducing an imbalance—"

"Toxic for you," Tristen said. "We would adapt. We will be forced to adapt to gravity, in any case. We're not"—he hesitated, as if searching for a sufficiently emphatic word—"*inexperienced* when it comes to balancing biospheres."

"I'm sorry," Danilaw said. "There's too many of you. And you're not rightminded. It's the rightminding, frankly, that will be the biggest sticking point for my people. Without it, they will always see your people as aliens. As the sword of Damocles."

"I see," Perceval said.

Amanda pressed a belated cup of tea into Danilaw's hand, which had dropped away from the neck of the guitar. He sighed and sipped it.

She said, "Why don't you come down to Fortune with us? When we descend?"

"Excuse me?" Perceval said.

"There's room in the lighter," Amanda said. "Come down. Meet a rightminded planet. Then make up your mind."

Perceval opened her mouth. Tristen placed a hand on her shoulder. "I'm not sure—"

"Oh, never fear," Amanda said. "I am going to inspect every inch of that lighter before I put anyone on it. A person really only needs to be sabotaged once."

21

for the descent

O true as steel come now and talk with me,
I love to see your step upon the ground.
—WILLIAM MORRIS, "The Defence of Guenevere"

Nothing could have prepared Perceval for the descent.

The shuttle-pod—a lighter, Captain Amanda said—that would bring them into Grail's gravity well and (at last) its atmosphere was a dart-shaped creature like a bird, and she stared at it for long moments before she realized that, of course, it was streamlined—aerodynamic. Because they were going into an atmosphere, and that was this vessel's primary purpose.

An *atmosphere*.

The world was too brittle and unwieldy to bring in close to anything that generated the tidal stresses that wracked the Fortune-Favor system. Two planets of comparable size in an endless falling ballet around each other and their sun made for challenging close orbits, and Perceval was all too aware of the fragility of her old and battered world.

So now she was seeing Grail with her own eyes, for the first time, from the habitation deck of a ship named *Metasequoia*, in honor of a tree genus from old Earth. The so-called dawn redwood was a living fossil species, native to the continent of Asia. According to Nova, there were a number of *Metasequoia* clones aboard the *Jacob's Ladder*. Perceval recognized the tree easily when her Angel provided maps and images.

It was not so easy to reconcile the maps and images of Grail—of *Fortune* and *Favor*—with the reality. The orbital simulations showed two worlds, one twenty percent smaller than the other, circling a common center of gravity in an elegant dance. It showed the moment when Favor whipped between Fortune and the sun, and the more leisurely transit behind. It showed the beautiful, braided pattern of the two orbits sliding over and under one another.

It could not show what she witnessed now—the dark worlds, side by side, the smaller sidelit in the narrowest possible band of crescent, the larger just a silhouette rimmed with liquid, evanescent electrum until the *Metasequoia* slid in a wide elliptical turn around the broad hip of the planet and into sunlight.

Sunlight that stroked the lighter as the primary star bulged, refracting through atmosphere and flaring like a diamond in a band of light. Perceval raised a hand to cover her eyes until the polarizing filters and her own pupils adjusted—a brief moment, until her colony dropped compensating veils across her irises. Then her palm dropped to press the port, as if she could touch the jeweled thing revealed before her.

"Most people who live here," Danilaw said, "have never seen it this way."

Perceval started and half turned, overbalancing herself. She didn't fall because Danilaw steadied her, one hand on her shoulders.

"I'm sorry."

"I'm not used to people being able to sneak up on me," she said. "Usually, there's an Angel on my shoulder." Nova was still within range of her thought, but it wasn't the same as being surrounded constantly by the invisible fog of her colonies.

Danilaw caught Perceval's eye, and seemed about to say something. Perceval, however, turned back quickly. She wasn't going to miss any more of her first sunrise.

The star was already free of the atmosphere's clinging brilliance, burning clear, pale yellow against the blackness beyond and she sighed. "It's over so fast."

"We're moving at a pretty good clip," Danilaw said. He came up beside her so she wouldn't have to turn to speak with him, or maybe he wanted to watch as well.

Fortune swelled in the forward port, dayside illuminated, and Perceval gasped as the *Metasequoia* went nose-down and offered her a lingering view of dark violet and sand gold continents and glittering seas veiled under gauzy drapes of water vapor. Images and simulations had not prepared her for the *depth* of it, the dewy three-dimensionality. It looked real—of course it *was* real—but it also looked close and solid, as if it were a blown-glass bauble, superhumanly detailed, that she could put her hand out and pick up, hold, experience the cool solidity of its weight in her hand if only the viewport were not in the way.

A chime warned them to return to their seats. Amanda's voice followed. "Attention, passengers. We are commencing our atmospheric entry approach at this time. Please assume a seat and confirm that you are properly restrained so we can begin our preliminary trajectory corrections."

"This way," Danilaw said, standing aside to permit Perceval to precede him.

She moved toward the control capsule in the nose of the lighter, passing through the open hatchway to find Tristen already seated beside Amanda in the forward row of chairs. Perceval dropped into her seat as Danilaw secured the hatch behind them. The webbing required a certain amount of guidance to fasten properly, leaving her wondering if these strangers would accept nanodrape technology as a potential trade good, or if their cultural opposition to excess energy expenditures and nanotech extended that far.

Fastening the straps was rendered more challenging because she could not stop glancing away from what she was doing to stare out the lighter's broad horseshoe of windows. She felt the inertia as the craft began to rotate and craned her head back hopefully. Above—a term with meaning, suddenly, beyond "overhead"—the cloud-smeared orb of Favor drifted into view as if suspended in time and space. Perceval lifted her hand to occlude it with her palm, and realized that, as it was both smaller and more distant than Fortune, she could have covered it with her thumb. Her heart made savage with her ribs; her eyes welled up with unaccustomed wetness.

A world. A whole world up there.

She didn't realize she had spoken aloud until Tristen spoke over his shoulder, through the curtain of his hair. "A living world."

"If you don't mind birds that crap hydrosulfuric acid. Strapped in, Amanda," Danilaw said, reminding Perceval to confirm out loud as well.

"Perfect," Amanda said. "Contact in ninety."

Perceval's hands closed reflexively on the arms of her acceleration chair. It reclined, the restraints contracting comfortably but firmly to snug her into place. She breathed deep, a little giddy on the over-oxygenated air, and adjusted her oxygen uptake and respiration reflex to compensate. Wouldn't it be something if she passed out from forgetting to respire because the air was too rich?

She'd expected a worse bump when they hit the atmosphere, but it was more of a skipping sensation, and then a heavy drag like water over skin. Rays of dull glow flowed up the windscreen, red shading to orange and then gold, brighter, brighter, until Perceval adjusted her eyesight to compensate as the sky overhead began shading from obsidian to indigo. Heaviness kept her from raising a hand to shade her eyes, but in the front seat Tristen leaned forward, stronger than she. Resisting the acceleration. He let himself slump back a moment later when Amanda gave him a shocked glance, and he tucked his arms conscientiously at his sides. Each bump of the descending lighter swayed him slightly as he settled back into the acceleration couch.

A moment later, the inertial dampers kicked in and Perceval found herself back to something like normal gravity. On the heavy side, but not unbearable.

After that, the ride went smoothly. They sank through the layers of atmosphere like a flat stone slipping sideways into the depths of some ancient tank, the fluid air curling around them, sensor lights green and cheerful on the boards. Something flashed orange for a second. Amanda touched a control and it righted. Or Perceval assumed the emerald glow meant it had righted. It didn't seem like an opportune time to ask.

The glow receded across the ports. The sound and sensation of air dragging along the skin of the craft dropped to a roar. "That was the tough part," Amanda said. "Nothing tricky left but the landing."

They dropped for some time, Amanda reporting what continent or sea they passed over as the minutes went by. A cloud layer crawled beneath them like a wrinkled sea; they passed through its upper layers and dropped into calm air below. Now the sky overhead was a deep transparent cerulean—a color so bright and clear that Perceval felt like she should be able to see through it to the shape of the *Jacob's Ladder* up there somewhere in the dark on the other side.

She could see Fortune's sister planet, heavy on the horizon like a ripe fruit on Mallory's tree, reflecting sunshine from its blue-violet surface, wearing wispy stratus clouds like a wind-whipped beard.

Below, a band of darker clouds loomed—a towering topography with its highlights picked across in brushed silver by the angled sun. Vast updrafts, kilometers high, whipped the cloud tops to frothy peaks smeared flat at the top by a shearing wind.

"Thunderstorm," Tristen said, like a Benedickion. "I've never imagined . . ."

"Me either," Perceval said, and reached forward to touch his shoulder.

"We'll be going through it," Amanda said, "so you'll get to appreciate it up close."

A blue-white arc of searing brightness flickered between the clouds they fell toward like a snake's tongue. A bright reverse shadow seemed to follow it, an expanding ripple of fox fire racing along the cloud tops. The boom that followed seconds after shook the little craft like the fragile rice-paper cylinder it wasn't. Perceval's dignity alone kept her from squeaking and clutching the armrests.

A half kilometer or so above the cloud tops, the *Metasequoia* dropped as abruptly as if someone had pushed it off a tabletop. Another arc lit the inside of the cockpit in black-paper cuts and sharp silhouettes, edges without compromise. This time, the rattling, growling rumble followed much faster, and much longer.

The craft pitched up again. Amanda's hands rested lightly on the controls, though, concentration smoothing her face. Her expression revealed no sign of discomfort or worry. Occasionally she said something brief and cryptic into her mouthpiece; Perceval came to understand that she was speaking to a traffic manager.

They dropped into a sea of gray cotton candy, which opened up and swallowed them entire.

Perceval expected a sound, a shushing, shirring noise as the clouds wrapped them. But there was nothing, a curious hush, the thrumming of the engines and the life-support systems controlling the cabin climate. Tristen sneezed, quite suddenly, and Perceval sniffled as the scent of burning electronics filled the cabin. "Is something on fire?" she asked.

"That's the smell of the storm," Amanda said. "We've started filtering in some outside air. You're smelling ozone from the lightning discharge."

Lightning. She said the word over to herself to memorize it. "It smells like burning."

"The air is burning," Amanda said. "And being ionized."

The smoke gray outside the windows gave way to charcoal, and lashings of rain. Then steady drumming, like a hundred thousand fingertips palpating the aircraft's skin.

Perceval giggled. She bit her lip, glanced at Danilaw, and forced herself not to giggle again. Or tried, but it slipped out anyway.

He turned to her, dark face curving around a grin. How strange, that these alien humans grinned just like anybody.

Tristen craned his neck to look back at them, eyebrows rising.

"Rain," Perceval said. "Rain on a real live planet."

Whatever he was about to say was arrested when they broke through the underside of the clouds. Favorlight—Planetrise or planetset? Perceval had no idea. Did they look different? How did you tell?—slanted up from the edge of the world and smeared across the underside of the clouds.

The rain still hammered down, blurring the port. The *windshield,* Amanda had called it. A thing that shields one from the impact force of an onrushing atmosphere.

What weird things planets were.

Something about the quality of the rush of air along the skin of the lighter changed, a new note brightening the white noise toward pink. "Landing gear," Danilaw said, when Perceval turned her head against the crushing strength of gravity to glance her question at him. His voice showed strain—the discomfort of a Mean under physical duress. What was uncomfortable for a Conn was acute distress for Danilaw and Amanda. And yet they bore it well, functioning and cheerful, Amanda in particular intent on her work.

Means. Their courage and resourcefulness. They would never quite cease to amaze her.

A moment passed before she realized that she'd just thought of Rien without pain, and that realization brought the pain instead. A few short decades, and was she already forgetting?

"Healing," said Nova inside her. And had the sense not to say further.

When the landing gear—wheels, Perceval guessed—touched the *landing strip*, there was a hard uncomfortable bounce and a harder, more uncomfortable whirr. Almost a whine, the sound of machinery straining against intense natural forces. Rain still sheeted the windows—a dimpled, transparent glaze that nevertheless distorted the world outside so heavily Perceval could make no sense of what she saw. Only a jumble of objects dark and bright, each alternately illuminated and shadowed by the lightning and the storm.

Lightning cracked again as they rolled to a stop, this time without an accompanying rumble of thunder. That came moments later, and Perceval found herself calculating in her head. "That was a mile and a half off," she said.

"Difference in flash and bang?" Amanda asked, turning in her seat to unhook the shoulder belts.

Perceval nodded, suddenly shy. "Is the storm moving away from us?"

"This wave," Amanda said. "There might be more. The rain is a friend, though. It'll cool our shell faster so we can disembark."

"And drench us on the runway," Danilaw said, but Perceval thought he was performing his crabbiness more than experiencing it. He was stretching in his seat, looking around, an air of excitement hovering over him.

Perceval decided to find it contagious. Maybe it would put an end to the apprehension and anxiety that wanted to rise up her throat like an anaconda and throw ropes of unease around her airway and lungs. When Danilaw rose, she rose beside him.

At that moment, she thought indeed she might do anything to stay. *Even let them perform brain surgery on you? And take away your colony?*

Tristen was already picking his way, hunchbacked, around the copilot's chair and toward the rear of the lighter. Some few minutes later, the doors opened and a stairway rolled up outside.

With Tristen at her shoulder, Perceval clutched the handrail. Woozy under heavy gravity, she stepped out into the rain. "Doesn't this conduct electricity?" she asked, head craned back to the clouds so that falling water—magical, explicable, incomprehensible water falling from *miles above her in the sky*—could wash her face.

"The stair is insulated," Amanda said, as Danilaw pulled up behind her, "as is the lighter. Still, it can't hurt to get down it quickly. And out of the rain. Our greeters are waiting under that awning."

When she pointed it out, Perceval noticed it. She'd registered it before, but having no knowledge of what an airfield—a spaceport?—looked like, she hadn't realized the red-and-white-striped tent was unusual for this place and time.

"Oh, boy," she said. "A reception committee."

Hair plastered to his face and neck, drops of beaded water running across the high cantilevered planes of his cheekbones, Tristen laughed. "Come on," he said. "I can already see how this is going to get cold."

They squeaked down the stairs in wet shoes, carefully, and stepped out a moment later onto puddle-dressed something-black. Behind them, Amanda's and Danilaw's footwear clicked and slapped and splashed. Now that they were lower, no longer obscured by the tent, Perceval could see the dark shapes of greeters through the slanting rain. She turned to make sure Amanda and Danilaw were at her heels—Danilaw offered a comforting nod—and, squaring her shoulders, started forward.

The puddles splashed underfoot; the black substance she walked over was hard and inabsorbent—and rippleless in its smoothness, because the puddles joined and flowed into one perfect, shallow sheet of water rather than collecting in the low spots.

Water stung Perceval's eyes, plastered her hair across her face, and trickled into the corners of her mouth.

People were walking out from under the tents now. Perceval saw a woman and a man in the forefront, and behind them two sets of others. A little more than half of the group—six, exactly—were obviously security. Self-effacing, arranged around the border, watching in opposite directions in pairs. The other five were mixed men and women.

The whole crew wore coats of some tight-woven cloth the rain beaded up on. They had hats and tiny portable fabric tents on sticks, and the thing that fascinated Perceval most was the earthen rainbow of colors their faces came in, from ivory-gold to one almost as dark as Danilaw.

Danilaw, who leaned over and whispered "Gonna make it?" as two of the security types detached themselves from the advance and came to flank him. The other four, it seemed, were tasked with keeping the first man and the woman safe, and possibly Tristen and Perceval, based on the way they enforced a perimeter and took up positions.

The woman came forward. She angled her tent-on-a-stick so the rain drummed against it rather than against Perceval's skull and extended the opposite hand. "I'm Gain Kangjeon," she said. "Welcome to Fortune, Captain Perceval."

Perceval read her stance, her expectations, and stepped forward to return the clasp. But whatever Perceval might have said next was lost in the flash of lightning, and the punch of something against her ribs that at first she thought was thunder.

22

wounds

If his children be multiplied, it is for the sword: and his offspring shall not be satisfied with bread.
—Job 27:14, King James Version

Under the roof of a pavilion in a Go-Back Heaven, before an audience of cobras and Go-Backs, Dust's patron prepared to conquer the world.

She had arrived hours before, slipping away from Engine in the confusion of Perceval and Tristen disembarking for Fortune. She had brought the paper Bible. Dust, curled inside her collar, lifted his head to watch as she laid it out on the table before Dorcas and two or three of her people. The embossed leather covers were shiny with many hands. The book had a scent—faint, not musty but sweet and clean— and as Ariane reached out to lay it open, Dust heard the whisk of high-rag-content paper.

He also heard Dorcas's controlled intake of breath. "May I?"

The fall of Ariane's hair moved against Dust's fur as she nodded. "I had expected you would want to. The key to the world is in there. And the Captain is gone; we will never have a better opportunity."

"Think of all the hands that have touched this." Gently, Dorcas added her own to the litany. She turned the book to face her and ran the tip of a fingernail down the page. The words were so black, the ink set deep in creamy fibers. "You'll use this to claim control of the Angel?"

"And the world," Ariane said. "You and yours must stand ready to fight, once it is done. There are some in Rule and Engine who will oppose us, even when Dust is restored to his rightful place. I brought him back for a reason, and his knowledge of how to use the Bible was one part of it."

"And you to yours." Dorcas set the open book back from herself with a fingertip push, releasing its custody to Ariane.

Because Dust nuzzled his patron's ear, delighted to be remembered, he felt the muscles in her jaw tense with her smile. "This may take a little while."

"I have nothing but time," Dorcas answered. She lifted her chin, her eyes unfocusing as if a distant sound had drawn her attention. "Let me find you a chair."

The sound of the firearm was lost to the sound of the thunder, but Tristen Conn would not have been Tristen Conn if he had not seen the flesh of his niece's torso leap back around the point of impact—the shock wave ripple through her—and automatically turned away from her collapsing form to track the trajectory of the bullet to its firing point.

"There's a gun!" he shouted, while Perceval accordioned into a puddle. Tristen lunged forward, to and through the assembled dignitaries, desperately missing his armor and half aware with his peripheral senses that Captain Amanda—with a weapon in her hand—lagged only a few steps behind.

Danilaw never saw where the shot was fired from. One moment he was moving forward to facilitate the meeting of ship's Captain and City Administrator, the next he was watching in horror as Perceval slumped to the tarmac, blood leaking from her body front and back to stain the rainwater and the asphalt a ropy, luminous blue.

He did see the warriors move. Barely, for Tristen and Amanda were there, and then they were gone. The echo of their footsteps lingered only a moment longer as they pushed through the group and stretched out, running hard through the rain.

With the curious detachment of crisis, Danilaw found himself wondering how the hell anybody had managed to sight through the wind and the rain, never mind hitting what they were aiming for. But curiosity didn't stop him from doing what was needful.

He dropped to his knees in two centimeters of water and started pushing Perceval's clothes aside, looking for the entrance and the—presumed—exit wounds.

A moment, and Gain was beside him, tearing cloth in her haste. Danilaw found the deceptively tiny puncture at the bottom of the alien architecture of Perceval's rib cage, the slow meandering ooze of cobalt telling him the worst was elsewhere. He raised her shoulder—she made a noise of pained protest, his first clue that she was conscious and alive—and with groping fingers he outlined the exit wound high on her back, and felt the hiss of air against his fingers as she struggled to breathe.

"Shit," he said.

He doubled his fist—unclean, unsterile, but there was time to worry about that later—and pushed it hard into the injury. The wound—wet and sucking—swallowed his fist.

When Danilaw was still in secondary education, he'd satisfied his economic Obligation on a fishing trawler. It was safer and more sustainable than it had been in millennia past, but it would never be the sort of work that one could take lightly. Oceans were dangerous places, as were young colonies.

He'd once held an artery in a half-severed arm—not his own—pinched shut for two minutes, seventeen seconds, until the ship's medic responded. This was not the most blood he'd seen flow across his hands.

But this blood felt *wrong*: slick, cohering, and . . . wriggling. Still, it pulsed against his hand like any arterial bleed—and arterial bleeds in general were on the list of things Danilaw never needed to have pulsing against his hand again.

He set his teeth, set his fist into the wound, and yelled for a doctor, *now*.

Perceval hung in darkness, in wet cold, the only heat in her own blood as it spilled from her with every heartbeat. She felt the blood crawling back, oxygenating from air contact, pulling whatever life-sustaining molecules it could inside her as it struggled upstream against the rhythmic pressure of her heart.

Hands pulled her close and pressed her wounds, more pain than expected, and she felt whoever touched her recoil when her blood writhed and knotted, fighting to seal the wound. Fighting its way back inside.

The question was, could her symbiont save her life before her heart killed her?

If her heart stopped, it could. Hearts could always be restarted. They were simple electrical engines, after all. Pumps. Uncomplicated. Easy. And Perceval would have five to ten minutes of consciousness in which to seal the wound and restart the thing beating. Her lungs would work on their own; her blood could crawl through her veins, albeit inefficiently.

All right, then. She killed the pump.

Distantly, on the other side of the cold and darkness, she heard somebody start cursing.

The rain was like so many small hammers drumming on Tristen's head, soaking his hair and clothing, stinging his eyes and beading his eyelashes. Wind slashed sideways, but his hair was so heavy with water it swung and stuck rather than whipping about him. That might have passed for a mercy, but the whole thing was foreign and unpleasant and cold, and Tristen tried to think more of making himself a challenge to incoming fire than of how miserable he was.

His feet drum-splashed on poured stone, the shock of each step in such gravity making his bones and ankles ache. The pain helped the Mean woman keep up, but Tristen ran through it.

Amanda pounded along beside him, her firearm bouncing in her hand, until they came within the boundary of the long line of purple-black trees. The broad palmate leaves cut the worst of the downpour, and suddenly Tristen could breathe. He might have accelerated, but Amanda dropped behind and stepped aside.

Tristen understood. Ahead, through the trees, a flicker of movement.

A human being. Running away.

He had hesitated to assess; now he redoubled his effort. Though he pressed against his own crippling weight, the rich atmosphere supported him.

He was not adapted for this, but muscles and bones could strengthen with time. If time he had.

But right now time was suspended. There was only the chase.

Until the firearm spoke behind him—once, twice, a third time—and the running figure ahead staggered, spun, raised a weapon to return fire—

—and toppled majestically backward, as fast as Tristen had ever seen anything fall. Fell like a whole planet was pulling it down.

He drew up, panting, as Amanda closed the gap between them and then pulled ahead, jogging through mud and puddles and leaf litter rather than running flat-out. Tristen dragged himself into a trot to keep up with her, staggering every third step now that the adrenaline and opiates were waning in his blood.

She pulled up a second before he caught her, and stood over the man sprawled on the wet ground, frowning.

"I hope he's not dead," Tristen said.

Amanda hefted the gun she trained on the downed assassin—*would-be assassin*, Tristen told himself firmly. "Nonlethal rounds," she said. "If he's more than unconscious, it's not my doing."

A circle of people heaved around them. Gain's hands clutched Danilaw's wrists. She pulled hard; he shouldered her aside. "What are you doing?"

"What are *you* doing? You're hurting her—"

"I'm stopping the bleeding, curse you. Waste and wreck, let go of me!" The pulse of blood against his fingers ceased; he swore more fervently. "Her heart—check her pulse, check her pulse."

Gain reached for Perceval's throat. Danilaw had just enough presence of mind to realize his mistake before she got there. Had Gain been impeding him on purpose?

He grabbed her arm with his free hand and pulled her aside. "Not you," he said. "Get the medic now."

"Alive," Perceval said, her voice a wheezing rasp. "Stopped heart—blood loss. Can fix."

"Perceval? Perceval!"

Gain pushed back at him; Danilaw looked up from the alien he'd dragged half across his lap and fixed her on a stare like a bayonet. "Don't."

"Good," Perceval said, sliding into ever more boneless limpness. "I'll be back."

23

another tiny bird came to her hands

Morgen is her name, and
she has learned what usefulness all the herbs bear
so that she may cure sick bodies. Also that art
is known to her by which she can change shape
and cut the air on new wings in the manner of Dedalus.
When she wishes, she is in Brist, Carnot, or Papie;
when she wishes, she glides out of the air onto your lands.
—GEOFFREY OF MONMOUTH, "Avalon"
(tr. Emily Rebekah Huber)

In the house of her fathers, Cynric Conn opened stolen hands and let a bird take wing. Beside her, Benedick craned his head back and watched it whirr toward the ceiling, a blur of liquid green. It vanished into the topmost branches of the olive trees that guarded the gates of Rule.

"Another one scrubbed clean," Cynric said, with satisfaction. "It makes me suspicious, though. This tawdry little virus—it's a distraction, not a serious attempt. You know Ariane—"

Benedick shook his head. "If we're staying here, we're taking the world apart. Fixing them could be wasted effort, you know."

A cage full of parrotlets rested by Cynric's feet. She bent from the waist and pushed her hands through the transparent, flexible membrane that closed its aperture. Her hair fell all around her face, making a tunnel of her vision. She could not see Benedick, but she could feel him there beside her, breathing, shifting from foot to foot.

Another tiny bird came into her hands. Feather, bone, heat, and fragility.

"DNA is an aggressive molecule," she said, extricating the parrotlet and caging it between her fingers as she stood. It kicked against her palms; she kept its wings pinned gently to its sides so it could not do itself an injury. Having cleared their program, she could have just sprung the cages and unleashed every one of the birds simultaneously, but the older Cynric got, the more she believed in ceremony.

She turned to her brother and extended her hands. "Here, you take this one."

"Does it go with the non sequitur?" His long, vertically creased face nevertheless brightened as she pushed the little bird upon him. "Just let it fly?"

"Yea, verily."

He was awkward, opening his hands crookedly, not giving the bird the toss that would throw it into flight. Still it kicked off his palms, leaving pinpricks of blue behind where talons had scratched, and flogged into the air.

He looked at her, holding his hands wide as the blood pulled itself into his body and sealed the wounds. "Was that a lesson, Sister?"

She tucked a lock of hair behind her ear. "For you, or for the parrotlet? It wasn't a non sequitur, Ben. But think—the bird wants to live; it wants to propagate its species. On a visceral level that has nothing to do with what we deem cognition, it *needs* to survive. It carries the Leviathan's ability to engineer its own future by wanting; I created it for that. For wanting life, and getting what it wants. It's just possible that its wanting is what got us here."

Benedick did not speak, but his expression said volumes about doubt and ethics and frustration. Cynric studied the empty air where the birds had flown.

She owed him something for the suffering she had inflicted upon him, the guilt and grief by which she had manipulated him into becoming the man who no longer obeyed and trusted their father. The genesis of that grief had been her salvation and her destruction, her remaking.

She knew the grief hadn't left him; she could see its pressure between his eyes every time he glanced at her.

"And there are only two ways for that need to be met," she finished.

"Two?" he asked. This time, he crouched himself, reaching in to gather up another few grams of green feathers over racing heart. He handed the parrotlet to Cynric, shaking it gently loose from his thumb when it bit, and retrieved another for himself.

Simultaneously, the Conns released them. Cynric caught her breath to watch them fly. "Either the world can live on—in whatever form—and thus its inhabitants endure, or we can make landfall somewhere that will sustain us all. Do you think we have the wherewithal to terraform, transplant, and sustain an entire ecology?"

Benedick looked at her and shook his head. "Do you suppose there's a third option?"

"Probably," she said. "The question is, will we think of it in time?"

"Prince Benedick," Nova said. "Princess Cynric. There is a crisis on the surface. An assassination attempt has been made against the Captain. She is alive"—the Angel spoke quickly enough that Cynric saw Benedick's shoulders relax incrementally almost before they could tense—"and wounded. Tristen requests assistance."

"Evacuation?" Benedick was ever crisp in crisis.

"It would be unwise to move the Captain," Nova said. "However, I feel it would also be unwise for you to go to her. There is too much potential for a trap."

"My daughter—"

"Benedick." Cynric reached across the space to lay a hand on his arm.

"Cynric—"

"I will go to your daughter. What can it harm? I am dead already. Let me see this thing they call a world."

* * *

Dust's patron began by laying the open palms of her borrowed body on the pages of the book. She pressed them flat, and Dust felt the roll of her shoulders under his feet when she squared them and drew in a breath. She had a long neck in this body, a pointed chin, and hair that reached her thighs. Dust curled himself in the cave those things made and waited.

Across the table, the Go-Back Engineer who possessed Tristen's daughter sat, too, pressed her own hands open on the tabletop, and also waited.

Dust heard her heart and breathing quicken as that black, black text began to flow from the page across the backs of Ariane's hands, sliding over graceful bones and tendons in as fine relief as sculptured porcelain. The book bled text up the outlined muscles of her forearms, the sharp elbow bones. Words glided like projected light and shadow over skin, then vanished beneath the sleeves of her blouse. Dust felt them moving, immaterial but important, under the dry, scratchy pads of his feet, curling up his patron's throat and swimming across her face. She ran full of words; she glowed with them. They buoyed her blood and burned in the depths of her irises.

"Loading," she whispered, in a voice full of strange resonances. Words continued to flow into her—words now that were unrecognizable, strings of digits and letters, curious and arcane symbols. There was seemingly no bottom.

"Loading," she said, again. And again. And, "Dust, I need you."

The fallen Angel nerved himself, looked into his patron's eyes, and followed the words within.

Cynric recognized the young Mean who waited in the shuttle—the *lighter*—for her. Jesse, one of the Administrators of Fortune. He seemed drawn and harried as she took her place, but more than a little overawed by her, and made an awkward, undiplomatic effort to make her feel at ease.

And his mere presence was a pleasant assurance that her chances of making it to the surface in one piece were fairly good. She folded herself into the tight space defined by the acceleration couches and rigged the straps for security. When Administrator Jesse double-checked them, he seemed satisfied.

With a small bump, they came free of the world, and she saw it from a perspective farther away than even when she had captured the Leviathan.

As they accelerated into the gravity well, Cynric made idle conversation with the Administrator. As their path took them between Fortune and its secondary, she found her eye drawn to the smaller world's cloud-swirls, its dark seas and ragged continents.

"If you won't share your world," Cynric said, "what about that one?"

Jesse's gaze followed her own. "Everything on that one is poison."

"Too poison for us?"

"It's a hydrogen sulfide based biosphere," he said. He glanced at her sideways, eye corners crinkling. "And yet perhaps you are too poison for it."

Cynric laughed. "You lot make so much of your mental stability. But you're xenophobes, neophobes, the lot of you. You've wired a lack of diversity into your souls."

He rubbed his chin and frowned, but he did not seem offended. "And you do better?"

She shrugged. "We get along with carnivorous plants and talking screwdrivers. I don't know what should be so hard about getting along with you."

Perceval awakened in a room of wonders, unable to really appreciate any of them. On her left side, vast bubbled portals showed a watery undersea view—a glimpse into the River, perhaps?—and on her right, animate banks of lights winked in oscillating patterns.

She lay, she thought, exposed on a sort of cot or raised pallet, not enclosed in a proper bunk. She didn't have much pain—a little lingering soreness and stiffness—and she didn't feel crushed by the weight of her own body, which at first made her think she was back aboard the *Jacob's Ladder*.

She didn't immediately recognize the room she was in, but even now there were probably thousands of places in the world she hadn't seen with her own eyes. Life was finite—and very busy—and the world was large.

But this room was not lit in any of the ways Perceval recognized, instead illuminated by full-spectrum fixtures that nevertheless didn't shine in quite the color her eyes expected. And when she said "Nova?" Nova did not answer.

Instead, the face of her Aunt Cynric hove into view, creased with a frown of concern. "How do you feel?"

Perceval self-assessed. "Not bad," she said. "All things considered."

"Not bad for somebody who left most of her liver on the pavement?" Cynric spoke in the dialect of Fortune. It was strange to hear her switch languages with such facility and obvious relish.

This idea of languages—of *different* languages—was something of a novel concept to Perceval. Of course there were dialects aboard the world, and isolated communities had drifted away from one another. But so long as you excepted the anatomically unique creatures, such as the carnivorous plants and the Leviathan, all speech descended from one mother tongue.

Well, there was Language, but that was different—a neurological exploit rather than patterns of sound and movement. And only Cynric had ever been any good at it.

"Pavement," Perceval said, lingering over the foreign language in her turn. "The liver's growing back, I hope."

"Everything seems to be repairing itself nicely." Cynric patted her shoulder. "You should rest a while longer. We have the gravity turned down to make you more comfortable, but the field only extends over the hospital bed."

"I have to pee," Perceval said. "Can I risk a trip to the head, or am I to be subjected to indignities?"

"Better not risk it," Cynric said. "Tristen is in the hall, guarding the door, and I'm pretty sure he'd glare at us. I'll get you a pan."

Perceval sighed and turned her head to watch the ports. Were they still windows when they showed an underwater world outside, sunlight streaming through green translucence thick as glass? Something moved behind them, writhing and alive. The storms, it seemed, had passed.

"We're underwater," Perceval said, stating the obvious because it came with a revelation. "That's why we couldn't find the settlement."

"Dug into earth and covered by water," Cynric agreed. She slid the bedpan under the sheets, and stepped aside while Perceval made the necessary accommodations. "Low-impact."

"Which we are not." Perceval relieved herself, thinking of chamber pots and squatting by roadsides and how much of human history was about finding ways to pretend biology didn't exist. "Cynric . . ."

There was a silence, as if Perceval's hesitation had cued her that what came next would be a prickly topic. "I'm listening."

Perceval nerved herself, and tried to speak not as Captain to Bioengineer but rather as younger relative to elder. Whatever happened, she wouldn't be Captain much longer now. She probed the bullet wound in her abdomen with her fingertips and tried to imagine what it would be like to regret that.

"I know it's been a long time, and a lot of changes. I know you might not remember. But—I have wondered for a long time. What was Caithness like?"

Whatever Cynric had expected, whatever she had been

braced for, it was not that. She started—the first time
Perceval had ever seen that cultivated mask of serenity slip.
And then she said, softly, one word.

"Fair."

"Beautiful? She is not remembered so—"

"No." Cynric's hand slid down, a gesture that cut.
"They called her Caithness the Just, and she was. To a fine-
ness, to a fault. It must have been a reaction to our father,
who was arbitrary and capricious, but in many ways Cate
was the one of us most like him. Though she would have
scowled to hear me say so."

"Scowled and not raged?" Perceval handed the bedpan
back with care.

Cynric took it with no evidence of distaste. Of course,
she'd seen worse. And of course, if you were cutting yourself for tight storage, squeamishness would be one of the
first things to go. "She had a temper. But she did not give it
rein."

"That doesn't sound much like Alasdair."

She'd met him only once, and she'd been his daughter's
prisoner at the time—a daughter he was furious with, and
who was about to kill him—which might not be the best
way to get a sense of someone's personality. But she'd
known enough of his sons and daughters now to learn sec-
ondhand what they thought of him, and she'd seen the results of his child-rearing. If you could dignify it with that
term.

Cynric, sliding the bedpan into what must be a sterilizer,
shrugged. It made the long drapes of the robe that concealed her narrow body sway, ripples moving down them
as if someone had shaken out a sheet. "The thing in her
that was most like our father was her ruthlessness. I call
her just. I do not mean to suggest that she was compassionate."

"Oh." Perceval settled back against the pillow. Her
breath lifted and settled her chest; her heart beat even and

sure. She took a moment to contemplate just what a luxury that was, as the stitch of pain across her back eased, forgiving her movement for the immobility that followed.

Perceval had made choices since becoming Captain of which she was not proud. Some—many—of them, she would make again, though she did not claim that justified them. And she blanched at what Cynric had considered a reasonable price—to herself and others—for the survival of the world.

She thought for a moment on what Cynric Conn might experience as an excess of ruthlessness, and folded her arms across her abdomen, mindful of the tubes that fed, medicated, and watered her. "I think I'm glad she's gone."

"She would have made a good Captain," Cynric said. "But so do you. And now you should try to sleep again."

24

the world and the world

Then was there a maiden in the queen's court that was come of high
blood, and she was dumb and never spake word. Right so she came
straight into the hall, and went unto Sir Percivale, and took him by the
hand and said aloud, that the king and all the knights might hear it: Arise,
Sir Percivale, the noble knight and God's knight, and go with
me; and so he did.
—SIR THOMAS MALORY, *Le Morte d'Arthur*,
Book X, Chapter 23

The man Captain Amanda had shot *was* dead, and it
was not Amanda's doing. The sedative rounds hadn't killed
him; the poison capsule in his mouth had done the work instead.

Danilaw couldn't blame Amanda for the fatality, especially when she so patently blamed herself. But he did find
himself confused by it, distressed and befuddled.

"It's like something from the bad old days," he said,
drawing his legs up into the window embrasure of the conference room. Dodecapodes and small darting fish moved
in his peripheral vision. "It doesn't make sense to sacrifice
your life for a political point."

Across a narrow gap, Amanda perched on the violet
glass conference table, her feet kicked up and her ankles
crossed. "It does if you think not in terms of politics but
revolution. The would-be assassin was named Pan Kagan.
A review of his posts and conversations for the past month
suggests he was heavily involved in the isolationist movement, and he supported Administrator Gain's attempt at a
bloodless coup."

"We know she's behind it," Danilaw said. "So he killed himself because he believed strongly enough in her cause to die for it. To die to protect her. He had to be viewing himself as a hero."

"He needed to avoid interrogation. To withhold proof of her complicity." Amanda slid off the edge of the table and began to pace restlessly.

Danilaw's mouth filled up with bitterness. He had to give it voice to get it off his tongue. "You know, our system of government is predicated on the idea that nobody in their right mind would ever actually *want* my job."

Amanda gave him a look under her eyebrows. "We can prove Gain was behind it."

She seemed very bright, very certain, almost outlined in light. *Oh, not now,* he thought, and wondered if he should warn her—but the seizure aura didn't worsen, and he breathed slowly to calm his racing heart.

"What's your evidence?"

She folded her hands open before her. "Free Legate," she said. "I was looking at her when the shot went off, and I have her reaction on record. I'm also trained in semiotics and microexpressions. She was the only person in the group not surprised when the shot was fired."

"She was expecting it."

Amanda touched the tabletop, summoning up a three-dimensional image of the rain-soaked party as they had looked at the time—from Amanda's point of view. Danilaw was amused by the way her attention rarely wandered to him, and when it did, brushed quickly away again.

She was conscientious. And from that, he determined that she was consciously deciding not to let his presence dominate her attention.

He hid his smile—then had it quickly wiped away as Gain's shoulders stiffened, as Perceval jerked with reaction to the bullet, as Tristen and Amanda turned to run after the shooter.

Amanda froze the playback. She circled the frozen, miniaturized tableau, examining it from all directions. "Did you see it?"

"She didn't just know in advance," Danilaw said. "She triggered it. She sent a signal."

When Tristen entered the sickroom, he found a scene substantially unchanged from what he'd seen the last time. Perceval had turned on her side, which he took as a positive sign, and curled around a pillow like a snuggling child. Cynric stood beyond the sickcot, centimeters from the observation bubble, peering into the water beyond as if the shifting shafts of sunlight that pierced it had divinatory uses.

She turned as he entered. Because her hands stayed lost in the folds of her robe, he knew she had already identified him. He squeezed his mouth together until the words filled the space, then let them out, still not quite knowing what they would say.

"They won't let us stay. Not unless we become like them."

She smiled before she turned back to the water. The echoes from the curved port carried her voice back to him, full of strange resonances. "I'm staying. I've had enough of Cynric the Sorceress."

"What do you see out there?"

"Friends, perhaps? There's life in the waters," the Sorceress said, with a lift of her pointed chin that reminded him suddenly, painfully, of every proud woman their family had ever spawned.

"Generally speaking," Tristen said, "that's where one finds it, if one is going to find it anywhere."

He came up beside her. Beyond the glass, something big and convoluted rested, mottled limbs like textured scrollwork surrounding a central mass big as a lion's head. As he watched, colors chased one another across its surface, bands of orange-gold, and dappled purple and periwinkle. When he raised his hand to the glass, it moved abruptly, tentacles uncoiling from their intricate, sinuous twelve-limbed swastika to realign in the opposite direction.

Tristen cleared his throat. "I think it says hello."

Cynric's caryatid expression remained unchanged, except for the lift of her brow and the answering quirk of one lip corner. "Generally speaking," she said, "when one finds life anywhere, does it ask salient questions?"

He'd been joking about it talking, but Cynric wasn't. Danilaw hadn't said anything about the native fauna having sapience. That, too, Tristen realized with a sickening twinge, limited the availability of Grail's resources to him and his people. Swallowing barbed disappointment, he said, "They're talking to you?"

"Well," she said, as if explaining to a child, "they don't use words. Not even Language, which suggests a neurology not at all like ours."

"Not at all like ours as modified by the symbionts, you mean," he said. "Not at all like what you and the Leviathan's get have made us into. We are a hybrid creature, and you know these Means are right to call us alien."

"Earth octopi were supposed to be quite intelligent." Cynric pressed one hand to the glass, fingers whitening at the tips, the nail beds flushing cerulean. "We have some DNA. I could build one."

"What good does that do us if there's nobody to teach it to speak its own language? Besides, what are the odds, similarity of morphology and habitat aside, that an octopus will speak an alien creature's language any better than we will? It's not like *we* ever learned to talk octopus."

A change in Perceval's breathing told Tristen she was awake. Cynric would know it, too, but so long as Perceval did not choose to announce herself, neither of her elders would embarrass her.

Cynric said, "In assuming that it has a language at all,

you are commiting an error of cognition. We're pack animals. We have to talk to survive. What does a solitary intelligence need language for?"

He'd never considered it. Evidence of his own egocentrism etched a path through him; he wondered if it changed anything as it passed. "Some things are just too alien."

Cynric's half smile turned inside out and came back up as a sardonic smirk. "Fortunately, so am I."

"Too alien?"

"You say we are half Leviathan, Brother, and you do not say untrue." She pressed a hand to the glass, and the creature beyond—mutilated by the attack of some predator, Tristen could now see—glided an appendage across the outside of the bubble to greet her. "And perhaps I am more than half. I say it has no language, and that is true. It's not using words. But I hear it in my head. In my own voice—not my speaking voice, you understand."

"Of course not," he said. "The voice you hear your thoughts in."

"Some people see their thoughts, you know."

"Sure," he said, and touched her shoulder lightly, surprised as always to find her warm and yielding, not statue-hard. "But not us. What is it saying?"

She laughed, moving away from his hand. He let it fall.

"It seems amused," she said. "It has been watching us—Danilaw's people, I imagine—for a long time. It doesn't have a good concept of individuals, per se. It thinks it's funny how we have to label and categorize everything, and seems to think this is indicative of some moral or intellectual failing of endoskeletal air breathers."

"It might be right," Tristen said. "Are you going to tell anyone it's sentient?"

She moved her hand against the glass. The dodecapus coiled tighter, then swapped sides again. The span of its legs, even curled, was almost as broad as Cynric was tall. A few moments passed, and then it peeled its suckery legs from the observation port and vanished into the water, slipping away on jets of water pumped from flaring valves in its underside.

"I don't know yet," she said, seeming curiously unwilling to step back from the port and turn away. "Are the Fisher King's folk concealing from us that there's a native intelligence here, and if so, why? What will help us most?"

Tristen had no answer. But he stood beside her until she at long last permitted her hand to fall.

"I am reluctant," she said eventually—an emotion he had read already in the set of her shoulders, but reading it was not the same as having it admitted to him.

"Reluctant?"

She nodded after the dodecapus. "Our own people," she said slowly. "I can take from them. They owe us something, some debt of kinship. But what does that owe us?"

He shouldn't have said it, but he did. "What did the Leviathan's mate owe us?"

Along with a sidelong glance, she gave him the sharp edge of her smile. "Precisely," she said. "Precisely my point, all in all."

Their eyes met, and they understood one another. She was his equal. His peer. One of two in all the world. In all creation.

Ancient history, there between them, was suddenly not so ancient anymore. Everything that had been was about to be left behind, one way or another. If there were ever going to be any answers, it would have to be now.

With his feet on the soil of an alien world, Tristen nerved himself and asked a question he had never had the courage to ask before.

"Do you know who killed my daughter, Cynric?"

She turned her head. He saw the line of her neck, her skull, her ear for a moment before she focused on the window again. He thought maybe her glance had been for

Perceval, who still lay under her sheet, as silent as an empty room.

"You need to ask Benedick," Cynric said. "She was no angel, Tristen. No matter how you remember her."

Before he could press her, the door opened, and Danilaw and Amanda filed in.

Perceval sat up, the sheet clutched to her breasts as if it could protect her. Danilaw, who had been about to extend a hand to Tristen, paused midmovement and transferred the greeting to her. "Captain," he said. "I am pleased to see that you are recovering. I've come to tell you that Amanda has identified a high-placed conspirator against you, and we are moving to take that person into custody."

A real conspirator, Perceval wondered, or a convenient scapegoat? Would these aggressively transparent humans stoop to scapegoating? Were they so evolved that their vox populi would be satisfied with caution and certainty?

"Thank you," she said. "And thank you for the excellence of the medical care that has been provided me. Your conspirator—"

"Administrator Gain Kangjeon," Amanda said. "I am sure this will not surprise you."

"If you need her brought in, I would be happy to oblige you." When Tristen spoke so quietly, Perceval knew that his heart was anything but.

"The Legates should be more or less adequate to the task," Amanda said. "But it does lead us back to the central problem, doesn't it? What are we going to do about you?"

Perceval swung her feet down to the floor, allowing it to press cool and smooth against her soles for a moment before she pressed back, and stood. "We are beginning to understand the magnitude of your problem."

Danilaw nodded, waiting for her to continue. She tucked the trailing ends of the sheet about her in a sort of toga, flicking the creases into some semblance of dignity. "It is easy for us to say you have a whole world and we are but little, give us a crumb. But what is hard for us to understand is that your world is not empty. There is no place in it that is not full of life already . . ."

"That is the problem," he said. "And as for us, it is difficult for us to understand how weary you are. How badly you need a harbor. How long you have traveled to arrive here, and by what a slim margin you have survived. We"— he paused, frowned, and seemed to collect a difficult thought—"we live at a very narrow margin with the world. We choose to inhibit our own growth to protect the rights of other creatures."

"I understand. There are a lot of us. And those creatures you need to protect—like the cephalopods?"

By the window, Tristen and Cynric shifted, but Perceval spared them no attention. She was Captain, still. And she would use what resources were handed her.

"Dodecapodes," he said.

"You know they're sapient? And you are squatting on their world?"

His hand came up and pressed his temple over the ear. He shook his head. "You are kidding me. In two hundred years of colonial history, there has never—"

"Danilaw," Perceval said, taking his broad warm hand, "we are experienced in dealing with nonhuman intelligences. They're not like you. Or like us. But they're not as alien as a talking sundew, either. So tell me. Given that they made evolutionary decisions for all of their species not yet born, given that they colonized other, inhabited worlds— how were your ancestors any less monsters than mine?"

There. Familiar ground, a challenge he'd been expecting. She could see it in the satisfied shape of his face. "Mine did it for the future of the species."

Perceval smiled. "And so did mine. You think your people are so enlightened, but what they are is homogenized. They're xenophobic—"

"They have a system—" He glanced at Amanda. She made a smug mouth full of *I told you so*. "You may," he conceded, "have a point."

So now Perceval could give him a little more room. "A point you never would have listened to if you were an atavistic human. Because you would have been too busy with your worldview-defense."

"Sophipathology," Amanda said, smirk widening. "It's not a useless concept."

Danilaw glanced over with what Perceval read as fondness. "I believe in taking responsibility."

"So take responsibility. Think of your cephalopod friends. Think of making room for us, when we can communicate with them. When we can translate for you with the other intelligent life-form on this world."

Amanda glanced at him. "Do you believe them?"

Danilaw stepped back. The hand went to his head again, fingertips pushing hard through the tight coils of his hair to dent the flesh over his skull. "Mother—" he said, like a curse word rather than a plea.

He swayed; Amanda put a hand on his shoulder. "Sit," she said, guiding him down while his legs folded under him. Perceval too moved forward to support him, and Cynric was at her side before she released him and stepped back.

The Sorceress bent over, pulling Danilaw's eyelids down. "Severe head pain," she said. "Is that a known health issue, Administrator?"

"It's not pain," he said. "It's aura. Seizure aura. I will be fine. Just back up a little and let me breathe, please."

She stepped back. Danilaw raised his eyes to follow her. "Saint Cynric," he said. "Haloed in tentacles. It's really quite numinous on you."

"Temporal lobe epilepsy," Cynric said, her eyebrows rising. "I'd never seen it. We can cure that—"

"It's usually well controlled," Danilaw said. "It's just lately, and at work, that it's been getting awkward."

Apparently, Perceval noted, that hand-flip dismissal of personal stress reactions was a human constant.

He seemed to be steadying, calming. His hands rested on his thighs, and when a hesitant knock came on the door he did not startle.

"Come!" Perceval said, because everybody was looking at her. Technically, she supposed, it was her sickroom—

A woman dressed as a member of Danilaw's security poked her head into the room. "Administrator Gain is under arrest— Danilaw!"

"He's fine," Amanda said, just as Danilaw lifted up his head and said, "I'm fine, I'm fine. It's just an aura. Karen, you have Gain in custody? That's a relief."

The security agent nodded. "She doesn't seem too upset about it. She wanted a message passed."

"Oh, ruin," Danilaw said. "Hit me."

" 'I did not do these things for myself,' " and it looked as if the agent refrained from eye rolling only through a titanic struggle, " 'but for the future.' "

Danilaw heaved himself to his feet, straightening faster that Perceval suspected was wise. He seemed none the worse for it, however, though he steadied himself with a hand on Amanda's arm. "Sounds like religion to me. Have somebody check her rightminding, would you? And Karen—thank you."

Karen smiled and vanished back whence she had come, her torso retracting through the half-open door like a snail's head.

Danilaw turned to Amanda. "Well, then. Maybe we can make some decisions in a climate of calm reason now. What do you say?"

But the latch had barely clicked behind the agent when a familiar chime sounded.

"Crap," Danilaw said. "Did we bring Central Transit down here?"

"That's for me," Perceval said. "Nova, we're here."

There was lightspeed lag, and Nova was resolving herself from appropriated particles of Perceval's own colony, so her avatar was watery and faint—a ghostly outline rather than the semblance of solidity.

"Captain," she said, a staticky flicker snaking across her projection. "We're under attack. It's Aria—"

She snapped out of existence, leaving Perceval a half step from lunging after her. She came up short, caught herself, and staggered a step before regaining her balance.

"Should have seen that coming," Cynric said.

Perceval opened the fists of her hands, aware—as she turned away from Nova—that Tristen was standing right behind her.

And that he had come up behind her on footsteps silent as a cat's.

"All right, First Mate. What do we do now?"

"Oh, not *now*," Danilaw burst out, and folded like a snapped fan to the floor.

The words swirled over Ariane and over Dust. Black as the Enemy, black as time, words webbed them together, words linked them and pulled them in and pulled them down. Dust felt the margins of himself dissolving, the borders of skin, of Chelsea Conn's body, melting away under his feet.

He fell. Into her, through her, pulling the veil of words behind him like silk into an arrow wound. He pierced Ariane and dissolved into her, and she into him.

She threw her head back and shouted. Majesty crackled around her, her hair flung out and rising in the static charge, a swarm, a storm of words spiraling her body, falling in. Maelstrom. Whirlwind. Event horizon.

And Dust at her core. She shrieked, she swelled. She opened out her hands and embraced the world—all subtlety, all camouflage, all subterfuge discarded. She—*they*—rose up from her place at the table and stood like a tower. Dust felt Ariane, felt them conjoined—Angel and animus, as it was always meant to be. Felt Chelsea fall aside like a shed skin and the world come into them.

All the words. All the world. And the world was in these words.

And all the words were in him, in her. All together now.

Power in her hands, knowledge in her fingertips. Informing her grasp. Data. Code. Cipher. Source, and sorcery.

There was the book—the Book. And there was the blade—the unblade, a stroke of neutrality through the bright heart of the world. Hyper-real, furious, pronounced light—cut by a thing of infinite absence, of infinite edge. Charity, the unblade. The thing that brushed the world and left an emptiness behind.

All the same. Write it down. Memory, electricity, chemistry. So subjective. So malleable. So ephemeral. Objective reality is in a library. Nothing but echoes lives in a human mind.

The world is what is written down.

I AM THE WORD, said Ariane Dust.

And all the world shook with the sound.

25

silence is an answer

Let her pass; it is her place.
Death hath given her this grace.
—ELIZABETH STUART PHELPS, "Elaine and Elaine"

In the heart of Engine, Benedick felt the world fall away.

A moment before, he had been pushing through calculations, sharing a workspace with Jordan, Mallory, and the Angel-shard Samael as they worked out four competing sets of equations. What would be the best way to break down the world, if they were staying? Or reconstruct it, if they were moving on? If they were to harvest the solar system for available materials, how would that change the equations?

Perceval would need solid data upon which to base her decision, and Benedick knew Jordan was as devoted to providing it as was he. The silence of the room hung heavy with concentration and coffee fumes. Only the occasional request for additional data or a second set of eyes broke it.

And then, without warning, Benedick was alone in his head.

Everything fell away. His sense of the other Exalt in the room, the subconscious connection to Nova, and the matrix of interface and colony through which he moved—through which he had moved for centuries. Machine memory vanished, leaving muddled and conflated organic patternings behind, half atrophied with lack of attention and care.

Nova had not merely withdrawn. She'd shut down *all* the cognitive and communications responses of the Exalts' colonies. Benedick understood that she might have done this to protect them—either from an external virus, or some contaminant in her own system—but it was a desperation measure, and one that left all Nova's allies more vulnerable than they had been within the range of whatever memory he had left.

Across the table, Jordan abruptly dropped her feet to the floor and sat forward, fingertips pressed to her forehead as if it hurt. "I feel as if my brain is shrinking away from the inside of my skull," she said, frowning. Her face seemed naked, old, through the fur without the bioluminescence of her colony informing it. Her wings drooped from her shoulders as if she abruptly found them dragged down by gravity.

"Nova." Mallory rose, scooting a chair back with a scrape, and moved toward the front of the room, where there was an old-fashioned hardwired com link, useful—like a speaking tube—in emergencies.

It was Samael who answered. "We are under attack. Another Angel or djinn has infiltrated Nova and is attempting to rewrite and exploit her. In defense of the rest of us, she has shut down all contact-related functions."

"Oh, suck it," Jordan said, ripe with disgust. "It's like the game with the worms and the mallets."

Benedick, rising from his chair, could not prevent a flicker of smile. "Whack-an-Angel?"

"Yeah." She turned in circles, scanning the edges of the room. "What do we do now?"

"I would suggest suiting up. Meanwhile, I shall forge a perimeter."

Samael had always been prone to dramatic gestures. He

spread his arms and seemed to stretch, the spaces between his colorful flakes and gleanings expanding like the skin between the scales of a swallowing snake. Scraps of husk and petal that made him visible shivered from their invisible supports. Each pattered or drifted floorward according to their nature, leaving not even an outline in the air.

His voice now resonated all around them, as if the very air spoke from their own lungs and ears and the space between them. "Your armor will be awkward, but it will be airtight. And the suits have their own colony defenses, independent of Nova."

Benedick, colony-naked, paused for a moment to consider. If his colony, his machine memories, failed with the absence of the integrated and distributed Angel, did that mean those parts of him were only a subroutine in her virtual universe? Had she really assimilated so much?

What was identity in the machine?

While he thought, he also moved. Jordan, for all her awkwardness when unsupported by her symbiont, reached the armor locker first. She heaved the grate open, struggling, and Benedick's heart sank. They'd have to seal into the armor the old-fashioned way, by stepping inside its opened shell. And they'd packed their suits side by side, which meant dragging them out of the locker one by one.

"Sealing the room," Samael said. No visible change followed the words. Benedick would have to take his word for it.

Benedick drew a deep breath while he assessed. First things first. "Chief Engineer," he said crisply, "I recommend we pull your armor out first, as—given you are a flyer—it will take you the longest to suit up under these conditions."

Jordan frowned at him, but nodded. "And I'll be stronger in the armor. All right. Come on."

She started forward into the cupboard, Benedick hot on her heels.

* * *

Since she touched her dead self's blade at Tristen's insistence, Dorcas had been unable to ignore the whispering. She knew what she heard—the voice of Mirth, the voice of Sparrow. The echo through her bones of two things so allied they might as well be one.

She had heard it, and she had turned it away. Because she was not Sparrow; she was no Conn whelp, no woman who believed the world could be bettered by bullet and blade.

She heard it now, swelling in her. She might have turned it aside again, but this time was different than the others.

This time she stood before the worst Conn whelp of all, the words of an ancient spell crawling through her, transubstantiating her into a whirling tower of light and shadows, so Dorcas reached out a shaking hand and let Sparrow move it.

Her fingers pierced the luminescence. She had expected to feel something, some pressure, some resistance, but it was like reaching into a ray of sun. The heat was palpable, but not material.

Light broke in shafts through her fingers, blinding her with its moving dazzle. Her colony should have reacted to protect her eyes, but she realized at that moment that she felt nothing from that connection at all. Her irises contracted on their own, with merely biological alacrity.

Her merely human strength might have failed her had the revelation not surprised her so that she tripped against the table, her outstretched hand plunging into the swarm of words siphoned off the pages of the Book and into Ariane.

. . . claws loss shame stones
distance miasma deceit mourning . . .

They caught her, too, in a spider-snare, a web of words, and noosed her wrist, and drew her in and in and in.

She half lay, half stretched across the table, and with the hand that was not sinking into the Book's storm of words, she lunged for the hilt of the unblade that rested by Ariane's hip.

Danilaw knew his body must be convulsing, his back arching, the pale froth bubbling between his lips. But it was an intellectual knowledge, divorced from any sense of fear or urgency, because he felt no fear, no shame, no concern for the friends he knew knelt around him, bruising their knees, trying to protect his body from its own wildly firing electrical system.

He was somewhere else, somewhere warm and buoyant, and the ocean moved around him, swishing between his muscular limbs. The dodecapus bore him along, a serene passenger in a serene passage, and Danilaw felt himself sliding into release, into the embrace of a warm and just and loving universe. Sliding into acceptance, into universal light, into universal love.

He was numinous; the dodecapus was numinous; the whole damn sea and everything in it was numinous, too.

He felt the creature's awareness, its concentration, the strength of its mental processes. He felt its intelligence and the curiosity with which it surveyed its environment. He felt the bind of the scars on its lower side, and remembered in bright concrete images and sensation how it had been injured, and what it had learned from that injury: *Do not play with your food.*

He felt his own words, pushing to get out, to get into his new friend, and he felt the blankness with which this smooth, intricate intelligence greeted them. Sounds, concepts, ideograms. They were nothing to it. There was the being and the sharing, and the things he knew, viscerally, because the dodecapus knew them.

The scarred old thing sculled along the muddy bottom of Crater Lake, puffs of mud rising behind it with each squash-blossom contraction of its webbed tentacles. Now, through its eyes, Danilaw saw a bubble of light, the shadows moving against it. *The observation port. The sickroom.*

The dodecapus plastered itself against the glass and, with one giant jelly eye, it looked within.

Danilaw saw the man on the floor, the figures surrounding and supporting him, and another pair withdrawn to one side with their heads bent together. He saw it all through a haze of atmospheric distortion and sense of wonder, the brightness of awe that filled him up like a pressure bubble until joy buzzed from every pore.

An immanence filled him—a thing that went beyond words and math and music and into some other space— a gestural, nonverbal, sharp-edged reality of light and hope and companionship. You could never be alone again. There was something divine inside you, and all you had to do was give it a home.

It's just the seizure talking. In there, electrical signals were looping and cascading, ricocheting wildly, triggering the same parts of his brain that gave rise to religious visions and ecstasies. It didn't matter what he understood intellectually. He felt the presence, the benevolence, the awareness within him, and he *knew.*

He would never be alone again.

The warmth of the dodecapus's approval washed through him until he felt himself falling and it was gone.

Samael bought them the time to armor themselves. By the time Benedick was sealing his helm and gloves, a fox fire of Cherenkov radiation crawled the walls and ceiling in moth-eaten loops and frontiers like the outlines of magnetic storms seen from space. It was the visible result of the battle lines drawn between Samael and Ariane's colonies, as were the bright flashes that more and more regularly sparked in every corner of Benedick's vision.

The battling colonies threw off charged particles; the flashes were caused by them passing through the vitreous humor of his eye. All around the room, furniture and other things were disassembling themselves, raw material for Samael to throw into the fray. Benedick suspected that he, Jordan, and Mallory might be more useful to the Angel as raw materials than as self-willed firepower, in the long run, but it wasn't an option he was ready to put on the table.

Yet.

"Samael," Benedick said into his armor pickup.

"She's not alone," Samael said. There was no strain in Angel voices; they sounded serene until they chose not to, but Benedick could impute his own panic to the tone. "A revenant of Dust is with her. They have some kind of decompiler weapon—"

Fuck. "Make a hole. We're coming. If we can win through to Central Engineering, we can make a stand there."

It wasn't a hole, exactly, but Samael was an old Angel and canny. What he did instead was collapse, shrinking around his allies until his protective field just covered them. He did not recoalesce; he made no avatar. That concession to the prejudices of meat intelligence was energy he could not afford to waste.

But he guided them, and he girded them. And as Benedick bounced on his toes, hearing his armor creak with his breathing, he reached out wild spans and lashings of colony like bowering wings and broke the walls of Engine wide.

In the black, razor-edged heart of the storm of words that surrounded Dorcas and Ariane, Ariane opened her dark, mad eyes and threw back her head and laughed. I NEVER THOUGHT YOU'D HAVE THE GUTS TO COME IN AFTER ME, LITTLE MOUSE.

Dorcas smiled. "I promised to do this beside you."

Words whirled close—so sharp, so near, so swift they drew blood without Dorcas ever feeling the cut until seconds later, when each one beaded in thready lines of blue and began to throb and burn. Ariane, scaled all over in words black and slick, breathing like live things between the translucent layers of her skin, went unharmed. Dorcas was caressed by deadly poetry.

Dorcas firmed her grip on the hilt of the unblade. "And I will."

In her hole in the center of the world, Nova fought for her existence, and for the continuity of consciousnesses of her senior crew. Though, in that first salvo, Dust and Ariane had managed to numb her outliers and launch a devastating attack, Nova responded by severing the infiltrated extremities, closing off communications with any scrap of herself she was not sure of, and releasing her limbs to fight on their own. She lost communication, but she retained integrity, and that let her maintain the cohesion to fight on.

And though armed with mighty compilers and code weapons such as Nova had never before experienced, Dust was still small. He chipped some bits of the world away from her; he swayed some borderline fragments to his side, and he came back at her as a spearhead and then a sweeping wall, like a Roman legion—a crash of barrier that was also battering ram.

She firmed herself to meet it, formed a wedge, waited for the frontal attack to break itself upon her implacable immovability. But it was a feint, and when the wave broke against her defenses it left behind something she had not known before—Code, terrible and devouring, eating like acid at the margins of herself and writing its own instructions in the lacework that remained.

She fell back and fell back again, abandoning the infected beachheads, severing ties to her putrefying syntax. There were words in there, corrupting symbols, black math. They melted what they touched, and Nova had no choice but to keep retreating.

And the worm kept gnawing her edges, consuming her and making her its own.

Dorcas found the hilt smooth and neutral, the unblade weightless, inertialess, and all but nonexistent in her hand. She might have recoiled, but Sparrow burned in her with berserk ferocity. No words, just will. Just craving.

Sparrow had held a blade such as this one before. And Sparrow had been Aefre and Tristen's daughter, raised to the sword from a babe in arms.

Let me, Sparrow said in her heart, a plea for release. *Let me. Just now. Let me. I will save you.*

Dorcas knew it would not be so easy. The Conn bitch, the Tiger's daughter, would not go tamely back to her cage once the latch was raised.

But the unblade was familiar in her hand. She knew enough of them to know you didn't wield one without the training—not if you wanted to bring back a hand still attached to your frame.

But here in this word-wrapped space she and Ariane—this strange Ariane-Dust hybrid, this dragon with eyes of light—inhabited, she also knew that nothing else was going to suffice to kill Ariane. Especially as Ariane had died once already.

Some things only an unblade could sever. The only fear—and she could not tell if it was her concern or Sparrow's—was that Charity was damaged. Virulent. And Dorcas did not know how to limit its wrath.

She thought of that, and thought of the code running through her blood and bones, sucking the luminescence from her skin. She thought, *How ridiculous to worry that the sword might not stop with unraveling Ariane,* and was careful not to let the dead Conn in her head overhear her.

All right, Sparrow.

Dorcas's arm pulled back sharply, then even more sharply extended. There was no sensation of resistance as the ghost of Charity went through the ghost of Ariane.

With the strength of the Book in her blood, and Charity's voracious virulence trembling in the orbit of every electron, Dorcas reached into space with endless arms and began to take the world apart.

Dust, thought Nova. Her chance was Dust. He was in her as well as without, and if she summoned him out of her integrated core she would have that much more knowledge of how to fight him. She burrowed down and bored through, opening archives she would have preferred stay immured forever, cracking the seals on Dust's ancient and demented library. He was in there—all his ghosts and legends, all the twisted Gothic nonsense out of which he'd built a realm in the long dreaming time when the broken world orbited the shipwreck stars.

All his stories. All his words. And his words were all he was.

It was a failure of human brain chemistry, and what was an Angel modeled on except a human mind? An Angel was a model of an identity, and so was a human being. In a world where a human's—even a Mean's—mental construct of an identity could so trump physical reality that that human would ignore significant health threats in order not to challenge his or her worldview, what was an intelligence except for what it thought it was?

She sucked in what Dust said he was, and what he truly believed. It was old information—no doubt he had evolved from backup, and this iteration would be different than the last because it had been differently affected by the stresses of environment. But it had grown from the same seed.

Still defending her boundaries—no longer parrying, but now withdrawing, flicking the edge of her core out of

Dust's reach like a lady flicking her skirt from a puddle—Nova processed. He ate her away; he wore her down.

It's now or never, Captain, she said, although Perceval could not hear her.

She needed, desperately, to speak with Perceval.

Then, as if her prayer had been answered, Dust trembled. He shrieked in a voice Nova knew as that of Ariane Conn, and Nova felt her Captain reaching—*yearning*—toward her through the emptiness.

Tristen was there, and Cynric, and she greeted them. And Perceval, her sweet Perceval. Right there, almost in her arms, intimately connected. The link was restored.

HELP ME, Dust yelped, two voices fused and ringing with harmonics. Nova could see that it was his turn now, that something was eating him from the inside. HELP ME!

That something might be an ally, or it might not be. Nova held her breath—metaphorically speaking—and closed her ears. This was respite, and in it she repaired, reconnected, and trimmed her own rough edges. She looked to her borders and policed her margins, and pretended she could not see what was eating Dust at all.

Behind her, Dust writhed and shed himself in ribbons. HELP ME! WON'T YOU ANSWER?

Nova pulsed data to her Captain, and prepared to hit her enemy from the other side. "Angel. Silence *is* an answer."

26

for my sister

And you may go when you will go,
. And I will stay behind.
—EDNA ST. VINCENT MILLAY, "Elaine"

Nova might have turned her away, and the treacherous Go-Back might gnaw her innards now, but Ariane-Dust was far from finished. She was older than this Angel-child, she was forged now into what she had always been meant to be, and she was not a thing to be casually spurned.

But Nova's armor was good, better than expected, and when Ariane turned to savage her she curled aside, so that Dust's barbed dragon claws slid down her scales and left no harm but bright scratches. The Book's full potency still pulsed through her—a weapon black and deep. She could feel the way the words wrapped Dorcas, too, and bound them together.

Either Ariane-Dust or Dorcas would have to die if either were to be free.

A splinter of unblade ate at Ariane's core, slashing away at her like a swallowed razor blade. It would have been fatal not so long ago, but Ariane was something more now, something new. An unblade in an enemy's hand was an inconvenience only.

Very well, then. Dust knew how to fight in these circumstances. The Go-Back did not have an Angel of her own, or an Angel's experience. Nova was the chief threat.

Though Dorcas gnawed like a worm in her gut, though Nova met her with flashing claws of code and killer aps, Ariane reached through the web of words. She girded herself in the Book's ancient syntax and, though blows rained down upon her armored surface, Dust pulled herself along Nova's scaled conduit to the planet surface, where Nova's Conn pets stood in tranced communion with their Angel.

Dust sneered. If they had the courage to truly merge, to make themselves whole—Nova and her pathetic puppets, trapped in their meat—then they would not be so vulnerable. And she would not be able to do *this*—

Danilaw Bakare sat up in a room full of aliens and rubbed his hands over his hair. "You're right," he said. "Cynric. The dodecapodes— Amanda?"

She looked up. She knelt beside him, but her medical focus was no longer trained so unrelentingly on him. "Danilaw," she said. "Help. All three of the Jacobeans just fell over."

When Ariane-Dust swarmed down her link, Nova turned on her with everything, fighting a desperate, hissing-cat battle to stop her. She barely even slowed her down. Ariane charged past, barreled through her, and slammed herself into Perceval, Cynric, and Tristen like a blade coming home in a sheath. Nova lunged after, trailing a cometary stream of packets, but the hybrid thing was too armored under the slick, spiky wall of new code.

Ariane eluded her claws and crouched, laughing, interlaced with the prostrate bodies of her friends.

Nova could see the worm inside her, still working, shredding Ariane's innards faster than Ariane could repair them. The damage was substantial, but it was going to be too slow.

Ariane spread herself thin, enticing Nova to lance into her and try to rescue one or another of her clan. YOU CAN'T SAVE THEM ALL, she taunted. YOU CAN'T AC-COMPLISH EVERYTHING.

"Maybe not," Nova said. Inside Ariane, that sharp-edged thing was thrashing like a caterpillar in its pupa. "But the work that comes before my hand, that part I can do."

Benedick, Mallory, and Jordan moved through destruc-tion, with Samael sweeping the rubble into his wings of scything energy and leaving cowering Engineers intact and shrouded under the nuclear blue arc of his protective shield. He blossomed; he grew; he swept up struggling ani-mals and uprooted plants and a carnivorous orchid that Benedick thought he recognized. He could tell which parts of Engine fell within Samael's sphere of influence, because beyond it towers cracked and bulkheads split open, streaming life into the Enemy's greedy hands. Benedick kept his head down and kept moving; when he looked up, he saw the swarms of symbols gnawing away the structure of the world.

"That's not Ariane," he said. "She wouldn't destroy the place. She'd conquer it."

Beside him, Mallory coughed. "Go-Backs. If we're all dead, we can't contaminate this pretty planet with our toxic DNA."

"Space it," Benedick said. "We've got to find the source."

"I've got contact with Nova. She has fallen back," Samael said, as Benedick lunged forward to pull a bleeding intern under the shelter of his parasol presence. "She's de-fending the Captain, planetside."

"The *Captain* is under attack?"

"*That* attack *is* Ariane," Samael said. "She's eaten an Angel. She's not exactly corporeal anymore. And it looks like whatever is ripping Engine apart is also working on her."

Benedick knew he had a nasty, suspicious mind. He cultivated it. "You seem to have a lot of unexpected resources."

He felt the smile in the air that surrounded them.

"I have been hoarding them," Samael admitted. "Out of Nova's sight. Did you really expect otherwise?"

"Get Jordan to Central Engineering," Benedick said, "and her overrides and electromagnetic weapons, so she can fight this war—and all is forgiven, Angel."

Easier said than done. They fought through Engine one meter at a time as it shattered all around them. Their ragtag collection of rescuees grew, and Benedick had the sense before too long that the space bowered by Samael was shrinking. Hemmed in on all sides, he asked, "Is there a problem?"

"I'm losing," Samael said simply.

Jordan looked up, her armor clicking as she heaved her shoulders back. "I'm going ahead alone," she said. "If I get there, I'll send help."

She bolted away, leaving Benedick reaching after her, his armored hand closing on thin air.

Samael said, "I could countermand her armor."

"You could also get her killed," Mallory said. "Let the girl go. It's no more dangerous than staying here. And she might win through."

The world came apart under Dorcas's fingertips, and though she wept, she kept on shredding. She pulled the Bridge apart, and Engine, knowing that it was a mistake to start at the periphery and work in. When you wanted to kill something, you started with the heart.

The heart. Ariane was a distraction, down there fighting out her hate on the colony world. Dorcas should let her go for now; the world was the first consideration. She could not allow it to contaminate Fortune.

She should let Ariane go. Let her fight it out with Nova and the rest—but they were there, on the innocent world itself, and Dorcas found herself as unable to leave it alone as she could a spot of shit on her shoe. And now Ariane had enfolded the others, and Dorcas was within Ariane, and one of these others was Cynric—the absolute worst of the lot, the Sorceress herself. The manipulator, the twister of every natural order.

And there was the Book, and the strength in Dorcas's heart, and the ghost of an unblade with which to wreak her will.

Cynric was a better target than Ariane.

An Angel pressing at the boundaries of her flesh was less to Cynric than it might be to most. She had felt the attack, coursing along the freshly reestablished uplink to Nova, and she had not lost control of her body as the others had. But she had allowed herself to fall, for deception and the convenience of a resting position, and now she bided her time.

So she was aware of it when entropy came creeping along her limbs like nibbling mouths, wrapped in the Book's armor of symbols.

Now *that* was new and interesting. She tasted an unblade in the hunger of it, but it had a will, and an unblade was only hunger without direction.

Cynric opened her boundaries and let the chaos in, meaning to subvert it—and found within it a mind. An unexpected mind—the Go-Back Engineer Dorcas, with shatterings of Tristen's lost daughter larded through her. Creeping, chewing, pulling the Angel Ariane-Dust apart from within. A mind that was inexperienced in such things, and so utterly transparent to Cynric, who had in a very real way invented the tactics of managing one's persona with one's colony.

Cynric was unsurprised to learn that Dorcas meant to destroy her, and with her the *Jacob's Ladder* and all that dwelled there, in order to preserve this alien colony from contamination.

Cynric had neither the resources of an Angel nor the armor of the Book. She had only her small colony and the meat she wore like a veil. All she had was argument.

"The world wants to live," she said, as Dorcas took her by the virtual throat and began to pull her molecules asunder. "They all want to live. Who are you to decide otherwise?"

"They do not have the right to live at the expense of others," Dorcas answered.

It was a fanatic perspective. But Cynric had never really understood the Go-Backs, with their ideas of genetic purity and limited lives. It was only fitting, she supposed, that never having understood them, she now must bargain with one for the life of the world.

"Everything is at the expense of others," Cynric said. "The honest predator acknowledges the system what it owes."

"No one in your family has ever been an honest predator," Dorcas said, bearing down.

Perceval was fighting, too, but her war was waged inside her own mind. It was not her first battle with Ariane, and she carried the memory that she had won the others. But somehow—sprawled incapacitated on an alien floor—that did not give her the strength she thought it should. And Ariane did not come alone this time, but wrapped in strange armor and wielding strange weapons.

Perceval saw her like a dragon, like an Angel in black armor, spanning wide the nine black iron wings of a seraphim. There was a tang around her, a cast Perceval recognized, and she only had to taste it once to identify it.

Dust.

MY NAME, Ariane said inside her. FOR I STAND IN MY PLACE OF POWER; I TAKE UP MY ASPECT. I AM THE NAME OF THE WORLD.

Inside Perceval's mind, she extended a hand. Inside Perceval's mind, Perceval refused to cringe from her.

She's done what Rien did, and merged with an Angel. But unlike Rien, she stayed herself. Mostly herself. More than herself.

In the guise Ariane wore, in what had become of Rien, in Mallory full to brimming with the intellect of dead men—Perceval glimpsed a solution. *Nova,* she thought desperately. *Nova, you have to hear me.*

"Still here," Nova whispered inside her. The momentary lag told Perceval that she answered from orbit. That lag was killing them.

It would have to be Tristen. And even as she knew he would do what she bid, she was sorry.

Danilaw and Amanda rolled the Jacobeans onto their sides, checked their airways, and propped them as comfortably as was possible. There was nothing wrong with them—nothing visibly wrong. Elevated heart rates, the quick breathing of stress, but no reaction to pain or conversation or physical contact or cold towels.

Danilaw had left a q-set with Benedick, a direct link, if necessary. He tried it now.

No one answered.

Amanda glanced at him. Wordless, he shook his head.

Against the porthole glass, the scarred dodecapus writhed its silent hieroglyphs.

"The Captain commands it," Nova said into Tristen's mind, and outlined Perceval's plan.

Mad, risky, painful.

All right then, Tristen said, silently, because his body would not obey him.

Perhaps that was for the best in the long run, because it rendered him unable to run or scream when Nova took his body down to the component atoms. First, she pulled him from his body. He watched from her perspective as his corporeal form evaporated, felt the strength the stuff of which his body had been made loaned to Nova. She surrounded him, encapsulated him, and then he was discrete again, standing on his own two feet, there in the Heaven of Dorcas's devising.

He felt crisp, razor-fine. Almost no time had elapsed; only long enough for Nova to transmit the data of his personality from one place to another.

That was all he was now.

Data.

Machine memories contained in a machine, all the meat and chemicals stripped away. Mirth was in his hand— a pattern conjured from available materials. His armor rippled about him, flowed and fell, replaced by a shirt and trousers that would serve him just as well against Ariane and her unblade.

He felt the earth spring under his feet as he stepped forward. There was a tent, a Go-Back pavilion. Around it, the Go-Backs arrayed themselves three-deep, their cobras twining their ankles.

Tristen did not have time to fight them. Midstep, he vanished; midstep, he reappeared, inside the pavilion now and still moving. In a glance, he took in the scene; Dorcas doubled over the table, Ariane bending her back, the unblade trapped between them with its blade through Ariane's unbleeding body.

Both women were wrapped in a shroud of black language, which clung to their skin and armored them. A broken-spined book lay under Dorcas. Blood dripped into it, filtering between the swirling words to stain the depths of the pages cerulean.

Ariane was smiling.

So this, Tristen thought as he stepped to her, was what it felt like to be an Angel.

She lifted Dorcas up and hurled her at him. Dorcas clung to her wrists, trying to control the fight, but Ariane shook her loose. The web of black words stretched between them, separating only reluctantly.

Ariane pulled the unblade from its sheath in her own body. A spill of symbols followed it, blue with blood, but she stopped them effortlessly. Healing the damage done by an unblade. Quite impossible.

Tristen let himself come apart and reform when the body of his daughter had passed through where he was standing. He swung Mirth to and fro with a sound like silk sliced by a razor. When Ariane responded in kind, Charity made no sound at all.

"Remember last time?" Ariane said.

Tristen could have edited the memory as he moved forward, sealing it away. But whatever fear was in it was a friend, for he could use the information on how Ariane had fought before to fight her again.

And this time, he would not be defeated.

Tristen fell apart into ashes, and it was nothing Perceval had not seen before.

She heard Amanda curse and Danilaw gasp, though, and felt their hands on her own limp body, as if by holding her close they could somehow protect her. It was futile and gallant and quintessentially Mean, and she wished for a moment that she could tell them of Rien, whom she had loved—and how desperately just then they reminded her of Rien.

Then, an instant later, she could. Ariane's attack snapped and faded, whipped back like an electrocuted tentacle, and

Perceval raised one hand and put it over Danilaw's on her shoulder. "I'm all right now," she said. *Tell Tristen his distraction is working.*

"Yes and no," Nova said inside her. "I'm falling apart even faster now. It's Dorcas, not Ariane, that's doing it."

Ariane fought him, and she had strength he did not. But he was Tristen Tiger, and the weightless, soundless clash of Mirth and Charity filled him with the cold and ancient joy of battle. He was not afraid of Ariane Conn.

He would have his payment of her.

The black armor of the Book girding her might have been a defense, but behind him Dorcas rose up and took the pall in her own fists and twisted, hauling. So Ariane fought against her, too, and her arm was impeded.

Tristen found himself stalking her, toying with her. Walking her around the room. He batted Charity aside with the forte of Mirth's blade and caught her by the throat, full of a cold and potent glee.

An Angel's wrath, he thought. Or his father's.

That blunted the edge of his joy. He paused, the blade edge to Ariane's throat, her arms bound to her sides by Dorcas wrenching on the shroud of writhing symbols. He remembered blindness and pain, and a stinking hole where he had lost himself in the dark. *Vengeance,* he thought.

It satisfied him.

And then, like a small voice calling up from the bottom of a well, he remembered something else.

Chelsea.

"This is for my sister, bitch," he whispered. And when he kissed Ariane-Dust on the eyelids, he pulled her and what was left of Dust, root and stock, out of Chelsea's body. Through the eyeholes.

And then he fed the guts to Nova, satisfied and smiling.

*   *   *

"Shit," Perceval said, out loud, even though Danilaw and Amanda would hear her. "Patch me through to her, would you?"

Nova's doubt eddied about her, but though she could not avoid Perceval knowing, the Angel chose not to speak it.

"Tristen is there," Nova said, leaving unexpressed the implications. If he could bring himself to do it, he could end the threat once and for all.

"Patch me through," Perceval said again. "That is an order."

Nova argued no more. A moment later, and Perceval felt Nova's awareness of the room in which Tristen had fought. He now crouched over Chelsea's still form, as if guarding it from Dorcas. Dorcas sat against the tent wall, arms folded as if casually, but Perceval could see the decompiler she wore like couture. And if her eyes were closed, it was because she was dreaming Perceval's family out of existence.

"Avatar," Perceval said, and Nova put her image before the Go-Back leader.

Dorcas opened her eyes. She looked infinitely weary, the furrows of her forehead so dark they could have been drawn in the same ink she wore like a dress.

"Go ahead," she said. "I think I can finish this before you stop me."

"A compromise," Perceval said. "Don't kill the world, Dorcas. Just wait a moment and hear me out. I know you don't crave all that blood for its own sake. Only to protect Grail—Fortune—right? To keep us from corrupting it. That's your goal?"

Dorcas let her head fall back. "Talk fast, Captain."

"We don't have to stay here," Perceval said.

"So it's better to rip off the resources for repair and suffer through another thousand years creeping through the belly of the Enemy until we find another world to poison?"

"No," Perceval said. "It's better to convert every lifeform on the ship into something that can survive on nothing but clean, sunlight energy. Everything. Every soul—woman and worm, man and mallow. Turn us into Angels, Dorcas, and let us live."

"You'd have me make the same sick choice you made when we were broken. You'd have me force a transformation on all of them?"

Perceval took a breath, pulled all her hope and passion together, and tried to put them in her voice. Dorcas was not a killer, never had been. She'd let Tristen earn his life when another would have killed him.

All Perceval could hope was that she did not really want to ruin the world.

She said, "It is better to evolve than die."

Dorcas turned to face her fully, mouth hanging open. "How like a Conn."

"How like a reactionary," Perceval answered softly, "to destroy what you can amend."

Dorcas paused. "You have me there," she whispered. She lifted her arms as if her hands were unbelievably heavy, and flung them wide.

Danilaw heard the scraping as Cynric dragged herself across the floor, and went to help her to her knees. But as he crouched beside her, she looked past him, an expression on her ancient face as full of wonderment and awe as any child witnessing a sunrise.

And there was Amanda, her mouth hanging open, her skin gilded by some source of light that should not exist, and if it did, should not glow that sunlight golden.

Almost reluctantly, Danilaw turned.

Perceval stood like a goddess in an aura of bright light, and golden prismed jewels hung weightless all around her. They caught the light, reflected and refracted it, passed it from lens to lens to make a webwork around her, all of bright and brighter. Swarms of them hovered in a geometric pattern, caging her in lasers.

Danilaw raised a hand to shield himself from the brilliance. His other found Amanda's.

"What's that?"

"The library," Cynric said. "It's come down to her. Jordan sent it down to her."

"I don't understand," said Amanda.

"Everything we know," said Cynric. "Our Chief Engineer saved it all for you."

"For them," Perceval said, her voice passing strange, a thing made of echoes. "And for me." In the center of her veil of diamonds, she turned to them. Her hands by her sides, she smiled at Cynric directly. "Have you told them yet that you're staying?"

"Staying?" Danilaw should not have startled from the Sorceress as if from a darthfish, but there she was, huge as life and even more peculiar.

"I'd like to liaise with your aliens," she said. "I think I'd be good at it. I accept the terms of surgery and so forth, of course." She waved a queenly hand. "I don't think you'll get much argument that my personality could use amending."

On every side of Perceval, chiming gently, the library crystals drifted to the floor.

27

the feeble starlight itself

> For I remember, as the wind sets low,
> How all that peril ended quietly
> In a green place where heavy sunflowers blow.
> —ALGERNON CHARLES SWINBURNE, "Joyeuse Garde"

Tristen turned in space, aligning himself to the tug of gravity, and let the Enemy fill with empty space the empty spaces in the net of himself. The Enemy that wasn't such an enemy any longer.

Dorcas was there beside him, a drifting presence, jeweled in the reflected light of two worlds. She brushed his fringe. He gave her the warmth of his full attention.

"Tristen Tiger," she said.

"Retired," he told her, though he didn't believe it. "What is there to fight against anymore?"

"He's not a villain," Dorcas said. "He's a hero who happens to be on the other side of the war."

"You were fighting for a passionate belief," he said.

She made a mood of affirmation. "I can be magnanimous in victory."

Perhaps she could. Perhaps he'd test it.

"You remember a little of Sparrow now, don't you?"

"I am not Sparrow, sir."

"No," he said. "I know that. But you felt her in the blade, and it was her personality that etched the neural pathways yours lives in. Lived in. When you lived in anything."

She modeled a mood for him. It seemed like a reluctant but tolerant one.

"Who killed my daughter, then?"

He had a sense she regarded him. He had a sense she brushed her fringe on his again.

She said what he'd known she would say. "Talk to Benedick, Sir Tristen. Speak to your brother, if you would truly know."

He paused halfway through leaving. "Thank you."

Now they were *all* Angels, and Nova did not wish to be an Angel at all.

Not that she had ever, exactly, been merely an Angel. With the assistance of Rien and the complicity of Mallory, she had wrought herself from the pieces of Dust and Pinion and Asrafil, and all the angels they had eaten. And most of all, Rien, the Mean girl, freshly Exalted, upon whose conscience Nova had been forged. Rien had been the beloved of Perceval, and so Nova, too, had loved the Captain beyond the love that Angels had been built to suffer.

She did not want to suffer that lovesickness and that pain and that hunger anymore. The world was gone, the Builders' plans fulfilled beyond anything they could have hoped. Nova drifted over the streaked clouds of a living world, over the swarms of her former inhabitants transformed and trying out their wings of light upon the solar winds—and realized her duty was fulfilled.

Almost.

There was someone to whom the Angel must speak.

She folded herself into a pure datastream, releasing her components to whoever might need them, and plunged through the waiting world's atmosphere.

There were dust and sand along the beach where Perceval walked, scraps of leaf and salt in the air. More than enough to sweep together a temporary form, using techniques borrowed from Samael.

"Love," she said, as Perceval's head turned. "I have come to say farewell."

"Farewell? Nova, you can't—" Perceval stopped herself. "Of course you can. No one will ever command you again, I promise. I'll see to it myself. You're leaving, then?"

Nova smiled. "Thou needest no Angels whither thou goest."

But she must have miscalculated something, because Perceval blinked and crossed her arms and said, "I'm not *going* anywhere."

"But I thought—"

Perceval rubbed the sandy sole of one bare foot against the sandy top of the other, and said, "Maybe we should assume that neither one of us already knows what the other one is going to say, and start from there? I thought you had come to tell me you were going to join them." She rolled her eyes upward. "Are they finding their wings?"

"They're in the shoals yet," Nova said. "They will find their way deeper. They're still thinking like monkeys. Eventually they'll realize they don't actually need a planet for anything. And then there will be no stopping them."

"You keep saying 'them'?"

Nova shrugged. She coalesced. She pulled organic material into her and built a body from it—not too challenging when you worked at the molecular level. The body did not, in particular, look like the one she had been wearing for fifty years now.

She let her identity fade, too, allowing the new/old one to burgeon and fill her before Perceval could think to argue.

"Nova did her job, and was getting tired of existing," she said, the last words she would speak. "And Rien wants to stay."

It was a relief to let go.

* * *

The young woman who held out her hand to Perceval—blinking, befuddled as a cat—was neither tall nor broad. She had slight, sloped shoulders and hair that stood out wildly in dark coils that snaked off in every direction.

"Rien," Perceval said, and felt the name catch in her throat. "Rien," she said again, to hear it. "Rien, Rien—"

"I am not a ghost," Rien said. "Come here and hug me."

So Perceval did, and Rien was not nothing, but solid, warm, and real. So that was the best thing of all.

When Tristen approached the cluster of entities that enfolded his brother, Benedick emerged alone to meet him. Samael was there, recognizable by his entirely insouciant aura. Jordan, too, still fresh-faced, even as a being of energy states stored temporarily in appropriated atoms.

"Brother," Tristen said, when they were close enough to brush fringes and speak without being overheard. "You killed my daughter."

Benedick settled back, but did not release him. That took courage. Or fatalism. The two were not so easily distinguished.

"I don't remember," Benedick said. "But I have come to understand that my memories are not . . . pristine."

"How do you mean?"

Benedick gave him a shrug-mood: irritation, discomfort. "What blade killed Cynric?"

"Mirth," Tristen said. It was a part of him now, and it remembered. As it remembered being Sparrow's—so he remembered it, too, with a particular fierce poignancy now.

She had not been prone to let her blade hang useless.

"But I remember an unblade," Benedick said. "And yet I have it from the victim, and from history itself, that she was murdered with a different sword entirely."

Misery rolled from him quite palpably; Tristen felt it against his foils like the solar wind. Misery, but no fear.

"I cannot swear my own innocence. I am an eidetic, and I cannot remember clearly. Someone has been in my mind, and the organic memories have conflated to match the broad outlines of the edited mechanical ones. Nor can I swear that I would never do such a thing, for we all know that kinslaughter is not beyond me—"

"If you did it," Tristen said, "it was because Father ordered it. Because Sparrow was a rebel."

"If I did it, it was because I was young and ignorant and weak. But I do remember Sparrow, Brother. She was more than a rebel. She was the true daughter of Tristen Conn."

"Will you do a thing for me?"

"I will," Benedick answered at lightspeed, unhesitating.

"Will you mourn her as if you killed her? Even remembering it not?"

"I will."

Tristen paused, to give weight to what he would say. "Then you are already forgiven."

Danilaw should not have allowed Perceval to go out alone, with only a security tail or two to keep an eye on her, but the Captain could handle herself, and he wasn't about to tell her she had to miss her first sunrise.

He stayed behind with Cynric and Amanda. It was supposedly a planning meeting on how to release information regarding the abrupt transubstantiation of the *Jacob's Ladder* and her crew. In reality, it was a huddled moment of respite over cookies and coffee.

"I want to come away with you," Amanda said, while they were passing cream from hand to hand. "I want to see the solar system."

Cynric's head came up, her eyebrows rising, but if the feeling of his face were anything to go on, it was nothing to Danilaw's expression. "Oh," he said, and settled back.

"This is a chance that will never occur again," she said.

"A chance to live without rightminding, to travel—" Her breath caught. "I can't say no."

"No," he said. He smoothed his right hand over the back of his left. "All this time the dodecapodes have been using the structural quirks of my neurology to try to reach us. It seems ungrateful to go running off—"

"The ones who are leaving are not bound even to the gravity well," Cynric said. "The feeble starlight itself will suffice to feed them, if they spread far enough apart." Cynric cleared her throat. "It's not the solar system they'll claim, but eventually the universe. It might be lonely. It will be strange. Do you really want to be one of them?"

Danilaw's heart leapt up his throat. "I—"

"Do you *want* to?"

"I have Obligations," he said. "Family. Work."

"We always do." Cynric steepled insectile fingers. "You people are all bodhisattvas. You're all such *adults,* with your culture of self-sacrifice and your perfectly myelinated frontal lobes, your beautifully refined senses of consequence. I used to make people like you as servants."

"Head," Amanda said, with a glance at Danilaw as if checking what he thought.

"Angels are servants," said Danilaw, reminding himself that his anger was most likely just ego-defense, and useless. "And so are we."

"Go on. Serve your own self for a while. What I did—it was a lousy thing to do," Cynric admitted. "But once they're made they want to live as much as anything. What are you going to do, unmake them? And if your people are adults, my people are all such *children*—reckless, selfish, egocentric. Waiting for a divine plan to direct us. Maybe it would be good for you and me to trade places for a while. We both might be stretched by it."

Danilaw chuckled. "They're not going to let you run Bad Landing."

"They don't have to," Cynric said. "They just have to let

me talk to the dodecapodes. Do you think they know the divine plan that leads to all this mess?"

"I don't think there's a divine plan," Danilaw said haltingly.

"Then what does any of this matter?"

"It matters to us," Danilaw said. "Isn't that enough?"

"Then go," Cynric said. "Go and explore. Become a thing of light. If you find out you hate it, maybe you can even find a way to come home someday. Not all gates open in only one direction."

Mallory found Tristen and Benedick coiled close, and hurried in on taut-stretched sails, praying to be there in time. But they were not fighting. In fact, as Mallory drew up, it became evident that the conversation was one of mutual comfort, not a prelude to war.

The necromancer drew up and waited. Not too long—Tristen must have noticed, because after a few moments he ended the talk with his brother and came over.

"You lived," he said, brushing fringes.

"After a fashion," Mallory answered. "And as well as anyone. I am still collecting my trees—or whatever it is my trees have been transubstantiated into. I suppose I shall have to herd them now, like a shepherdess with an idle flock. Or let them wither—"

Tristen's mood colored dismissal. He did not believe that Mallory would do any such thing to the orchard of memories so long guarded. And now that they had assumed a more animate form—along with all the other life aboard the *Jacob's Ladder*—the necromancer's task would only grow more interesting.

"You've found your purpose in life," he said. "It's keeping the past alive for the future. A necromancer, maybe—or a guardian of memories? That is not such a small thing."

If Mallory had anything now that could be called eyes,

exactly, they would have been cast down, cold arms folded. "I thought you would kill Benedick."

The color of dismissal deepened. "What good is another death now? It wouldn't bring Sparrow back."

"No," Mallory said. "But I could."

That was a long pause for an energy being. "Excuse me?"

"She's in the library. You have Mirth's pattern. That's enough for a seed that could grow in her old body—or the pattern that was her old body. The pathways are there. I can bring her back."

"Oh," Tristen said. After a time, he said, "It wouldn't be her, exactly."

Mallory said, "Ask Perceval. It would be as much Sparrow, I suspect, as you are Tristen Tiger. Continuity of experience is an illusion, old man."

Mallory felt it when Tristen glanced at Benedick, though there was no visual input to indicate it. The attention shifted, and it was obvious to anyone else so transformed.

A glitter of life-motes flocked past, sparking green and turquoise, chasing each other tumbling through the void. Cynric's parrotlets, transformed. Transformed into something otherwise, as was all the world.

A broad world now, and scattered. Mallory felt confident in its diversity.

Tristen said, "Cynric is not exactly Cynric anymore. And you're probably right. I am not me. I remember what I left behind when I changed, but I can—I cannot feel it. No. To summon Sparrow back from the dead would mean sacrificing Dorcas."

"The terrorist?"

"The freedom fighter. Should I condemn her to death to give birth to a shadow? Let her live, Mallory. Sparrow is dead. It is time I let her die."

Mallory leaned forward, to let their margins overlap.

Whatever they had become, there was a sense of comfort in the touch.

"Some tiger you turned out to be."

"I'm a tiger who does not care to hunt any longer." He turned his back to the world below, his attention to the cold bright stars beyond. Mallory floated beside him, imagining all the forms of farewell.

"Come away with me," Tristen said.

Mallory wished for a painful moment of sense-memory that there were a calming breath to be taken. A thousand ghost voices rang in the necromancer's heart, each one bereft and abandoned, a pattern of loneliness and memories. Everyone loved and lost, and perhaps it took a necromancer to appreciate how truly universal that experience could be.

"Will you pretend you love me?"

"I don't really need to pretend."

Tristen hesitated, then seemed to firm his resolve and spoke on. "It is not the thing I had with Aefre. But it is what I have to offer, and if you want it, it is yours."

Mallory would have smiled, if smiling were an option. "How can I refuse an offer like that? We are all we have. And we are so small, and the night is so large."

—and ye,
What are ye? Galahads?—no, nor Percivales.
—ALFRED, LORD TENNYSON, "The Holy Grail"

acknowledgments

Liz Bourke, who named Fortune for me, as well as the ideological heresies of the modern world. Chance Morrison and Celia Marsh, who convinced me that "Bad Landing" was a better name than "Crash." Anne Groell Keck, the editor who helped it all make sense. Bad Poets galore, who listened to me thrash and moan through the draft. Andrew Phillips, copy editor extraordinaire. Jennifer Jackson, world's best agent. Emma and Sarah and Delia, who held my hand through the worst of the birth pangs. And numerous more—too many to be mentioned.

ABOUT GOLLANCZ

Gollancz is the oldest SF publishing imprint in the world. Since being founded in 1927 Gollancz has continued to publish a focused selection of bestselling and award-winning authors. The front-list includes **Ben Aaronovitch**, **Joe Abercrombie**, **Charlaine Harris**, **Joanne Harris**, **Joe Hill**, **Alastair Reynolds**, **Patrick Rothfuss**, **Nalini Singh** and **Brandon Sanderson**.

As one of the largest Science Fiction and Fantasy imprints in the UK it is no surprise we have one of the most extensive backlists in the world. Find high-quality SF on Gateway written by such authors as **Philip K. Dick**, **Ursula Le Guin**, **Connie Willis**, **Sir Arthur C. Clarke**, **Pat Cadigan**, **Michael Moorcock** and **George R.R. Martin**.

We also have a strand of publishing in translation, which includes French, Polish and Russian authors. Gollancz is home to more award-winning authors than any other imprint, with names including **Aliette de Bodard**, **M. John Harrison**, **Paul McAuley**, **Sarah Pinborough**, **Pierre Pevel**, **Justina Robson** and many more.

The SF Gateway
More than 3,000 classic, rare and previously out-of-print SF novels at your fingertips.
www.sfgateway.com

The Gollancz Blog
Bringing you news from our worlds to yours. Stories, interviews, articles and exclusive extracts just for you!
www.gollancz.co.uk

GOLLANCZ
LONDON